THE GLACIER MURDERS

THE GLACIER MURDERS

Cristian Perfumo
Translated by Fiona Martínez

This is a work of fiction. Names, characters, organizations, places, events, and incidents are either products of the author's imagination or are used fictitiously. Any resemblance to actual persons, living or dead, or actual events is purely coincidental.

Copyright © 2025 by Cristian Perfumo
Cover design by Chevi de Frutos

All rights reserved.

No part of this book may be reproduced, or stored in a retrieval system, or transmitted in any form or by any means, electronic, mechanical, photocopying, recording, or otherwise, without express written permission of the publisher.

ISBN: 978-631-90025-7-7

www.cristianperfumo.com

*To those far from home,
or who have at some time, been so.*

*«Madre roca, padre cielo,
tu llanto descansa al pie de los ventisqueros
y cada estrella se posa en tu cima blanca
alumbrando el camino de los silencios.»*

Hugo Giménez Agüero

PROLOGUE

Of the one hundred and eighty-eight tourists aboard the catamaran, more than half have never seen a glacier. Therefore, once they finally circle the peninsula after forty minutes of sailing among ice floes, the bow is packed like a can of sardines. There are tourists from China, Germany, France, Brazil, Spain, Argentina, and the list goes on. Most are holding their phones up in front of them. Others carry huge cameras with long lenses around their necks. They try in vain to capture the one hundred square kilometers of ice they're sailing toward.

Our tourist, the one we care about, is Italian. He stands on the bow like the others but is one of the few who doesn't take photos.

The loudspeakers, located both inside and outside the ship, amplify the tour guide's voice. She speaks first in Spanish, then in English, then French. Our Italian understands Spanish.

"The Viedma Glacier is the largest in the National Park and the second largest in South America. It's five times the size of Buenos Aires. Although it looks like we're close, we're still about three kilometers away from its front wall."

The guide goes on with her explanation but the passengers aren't listening anymore. How could they, when they're standing in front of that enormous tongue of ice that descends from the black mountains?

An iceberg, larger than any of the others they've sailed past, floats between the ship and the glacier. The captain doesn't seem to want to avoid it. As they get closer, the catamaran motors slow down until they stop, right next to the huge block of ice. The Italian guesses that if he threw a rock hard enough, it would reach it.

"What they say about icebergs is true," the tour guide's voice continues through the speakers. "What we see above the surface is just ten percent of them."

The Italian imagines the size of the ice he cannot see. The visible part is as big as a cathedral and makes the catamaran –three stories tall, with four decks, and room for two hundred people– feel small.

A man and a woman wearing brown vests and carrying professional cameras push through the crowd to either end of the bow, the spots with the best view of the iceberg. They are official photographers for the Glaciers National Park. They take photos of the tourists with the ice in the background which they later sell them. They've spent the past forty minutes explaining that the ice reflects a lot of light, which makes it hard to get good photos with a phone camera. If the person posing looks good, behind them all you can see is a big white blur. If the ice looks good, the person in front of it turns into a black silhouette.

Half the tourists decide to get in line to get their photo taken. The rest keep trying with their phones. Very few actually look at the ice with their eyes instead of through a screen or a camera lens. Our Italian is one of them.

His gaze rests on the drops of water falling from the iceberg, the deep blue color in the cavities, the lines of black sediment that remind him of marble. If he wants to close in on any details, he uses the binoculars hanging from his neck. That iceberg, the size of ten cathedrals – nine of them underwater– is the most beautiful thing he's ever seen. And for someone who grew up eight blocks from the Duomo of Florence, that's quite a statement.

The motors start back up and the catamaran slowly moves away from the iceberg. Some tourists follow it like moths to light, moving from the bow to the stern to capture the last images. Once the iceberg is behind them, many go back inside to warm up. Some order coffee at the bar. Others look at the photos they just took on their phones. The photographers connect their cameras to printers located in the main hall.

"The iceberg we just left behind broke off from the glacier two days ago," the guide says. "In twenty minutes, we'll be right in front of the glacier and if we're lucky, we might be able to see another detachment."

The announcement makes the most excited tourists go back out onto the foredeck to ensure they get the best lookout spots. The Italian is one of them.

A while later, the ship finally stops in front of the face of the Viedma: a cliff made of ice, fifty meters tall and two kilometers wide. If the millions of tons of compact snow pushing toward the lake were an army, that wall would be its cavalry. And if our tourist had to state how small and awed he feels in front of it into words, he wouldn't be able to, not even with the help of the thousand Italian expressions he carried in his DNA.

The ship is now less than two hundred yards from the white and blue wall. The passengers are packed on the deck, silent. He resists the urge to photograph what's in front of him. Images won't do it justice, won't capture the groans deep inside the ice that breaks with such intensity that it sounds like cannons going off.

They float for a long while in the same spot when suddenly the Italian hears a new sound, different from the rest. It's loud and sharp, like one pool ball hitting another. Out of the corner of his eye, he sees movement on the frozen wall. It's a piece of ice that falls from above and crashes into more ice before reaching the water. Compared to the face of the glacier, it's tiny. In reality, it's the size of a car.

The guide speaks for all the passengers to hear.

"Don't stop looking; it's common for a small detachment to come before…"

A deafening roar interrupts her. In front of them, an ice column the size of a twelve-story building comes crashing down. It's so large it appears to fall in slow motion. A collective 'Ohhhh' ripples through the crowd as the lake swallows the ice. The Italian feels adrenaline rush through his body as if he were on a roller coaster. He brings his hands to his head. He can't believe he has the privilege of witnessing such beauty.

A few seconds later, the fallen column emerges, split into two large icebergs and a hundred smaller ones. A wave crashes along the edge of the cliff, making a 'shhh' sound that feels endless.

He looks back at the wall, hoping to see another detachment. Then, he pauses on the piece that's been left uncovered after the break. There's a vertical line in the ice, a reddish-brown color that clashes with the blue hues.

He pulls up his binoculars. The line is shaped like a shooting star pointing upwards. He starts to examine it from the bottom, where the ice meets the water. Down there, the ochre trace is barely noticeable. It intensifies as it rises and at the top, it's almost black. It looks like a huge nail lodged in the ice that's been dripping rust for years.

It's hard to focus binoculars focus on a ship that is constantly vibrating and moving. It takes him a few seconds to get a clear image, and several more to understand what he's looking at.

"*Sangue,*" he whispers in Italian.

He waves his hands, drawing the attention of people around him and points at the ice. He says the word again, this time a bit louder. Some tourists move away from him as if he has the plague. Someone asks what's wrong, but all he can manage to do is point and repeat the word, louder and louder.

His deep voice travels across the foredeck of the catamaran. One of the photographers comes up and asks him to calm down.

"The brown stain. It's blood," he manages to say in Spanish.

The photographer furrows his brow and points the lens of his camera at the ice. Ten seconds later, he makes his way back into the ship through the crowd of tourists.

The Italian ignores the people around him asking questions and musters up the courage to look back through his binoculars. In the dark spot where the line begins, there's a curled-up body. It's wearing a black coat and a grey hat. It looks like tourist clothes to him, but he's not sure. What he *is* sure about is that the person is dead. Because of the old, dark blood that left that body a long time ago, and because there are over ten meters of solid ice on top of it.

It looks like a mosquito trapped in blue amber.

PART I

CHALTÉN

CHAPTER 1

I felt dirty. It was late at night as I walked along the Ramblas in Barcelona, my city. Each step I took was met with a hooker's smile, an offer of cocaine from a man who wouldn't catch my eye, or a hoard of drunken Brits I had to swerve around to avoid being trampled. Through all of it, my hands stayed in my pockets to deter any thieves.

At night, the Ramblas are the nine circles of hell, but that wasn't what made me feel dirty. It was the fact that my wife, Anna, was walking 20 meters ahead of me. Well, we weren't married but we'd been living together for two years. The important thing was that she had been cheating on me for the past two months and that day I was there to confirm it. That was what was making me nauseous.

I never thought we'd fall so low. Her, cheating on me. Me, following her like some sort of criminal.

She'd told me she was going out with Rosario that night, but I knew she was lying. Anna never went out with friends very often. On top of that, her lack of interest in having sex –at least with me– and the fact that two months ago she'd suddenly changed her shower routine from first thing in the morning to right before bed...

I was the opposite of the blind who can't see but wish they could; I saw it, clear as day. However much I didn't want to.

Anna turned the corner to enter the Gothic Quarter down Ferrán Street and walked to Sant Jaume Square. She then turned onto Bisbe, towards the cathedral. As she passed under the famous bridge that joins the *Generalitat* with the *Casa dels Canonges*; I wondered if she remembered what had happened at that spot almost three years ago.

I sure did. We had walked down that same street at dawn, and I had stopped beneath the bridge, using the masonry as an excuse to interrupt our stroll, admiring its intricate shape: a skull with a dagger running through it of which no one knew the origin. She feigned interest in the mysterious carving and kept her gaze on it for a while. When she finally lowered her eyes and they met mine, we kissed for the first time.

If Anna remembered that night like I did, it didn't seem to make a difference, because she walked through the arch without so much as a pause. Right before reaching the Cathedral square, she veered left down a narrow alley that led to Sant Felip Neri Square, one of her favorite places in all of Barcelona.

I personally prefer other spots, further away from the bustle and the tourists, but I admit that this square has its charm. A decadent sort of charm, with its ancient octagonal fountain in the center, and the church façade full of holes. An urban legend says that during the Spanish Civil War people were shot there. The truth is that the holes are shrapnel damage due to multiple bombings. It's also true that before those bombings, Gaudí was heading to that exact same church, when he was killed by a trolley. When you grow up in one of the world's most touristy cities, you learn these kinds of things.

There was a bar across the square, its low lighting and terrace making it a perfect spot for a romantic dinner. A candle illuminated every table and a violinist even played nearby. Anna headed to the terrace and upon seeing that all tables were taken, went inside.

I couldn't follow her any further. The place was too small. I knew this because when we had just started hooking up, Anna had taken me to this exact spot. I decided to wait beneath the stone archway that decorated the front of the shoemaker's union building.

I know you're not supposed to blame cheating on someone outside the relationship, but I always blamed Rosario. If Anna hadn't met her in Zumba class, a young widow, recently arrived from Buenos Aires after losing her perfect husband, I wouldn't be wearing the biggest horns in Barcelona right now.

Let me explain: my wife has always had a soft spot for the helpless. Anna is a big fan of positive discrimination. She's nice to everyone but makes an even bigger effort if they are part of a minority. I once counted how many times she thanked the Chinese shop owner versus the Spanish hardware store clerk. China 4, Spain 1.

So, when Rosario –an immigrant and a widow– told Anna her story, my wife took her under her wing like a mother duck protecting her smallest duckling. She invited her over for dinner several times and introduced her to all our friends. A week before New Year's, she asked me if I minded if Rosario spent New Year's Eve with us. When I agreed, she hopped with joy and announced that her brother Xavi would also be joining, wishfully stating that maybe he and Rosario would hit it off.

And hit it off they did. At two a.m. they disappeared into one of our bedrooms giving a lame excuse. A while later, Rosario declared that she was tired and ready to leave, and Xavi said he'd walk her to the metro. When Anna closed the door behind them, she had a grin, from ear to ear, plastered across her face.

Unfortunately, Xavi and Rosario's fling never went beyond that night. According to Anna, Rosario wasn't ready to get too close to anyone. Apparently, her way of grieving entailed late nights in cocktail bars and nightclubs, as if she were 20.

I haven't felt like going out partying for a long time, but it never crossed my mind to tell my wife she couldn't go, especially if it was to cheer up a grieving friend. That being said, my being a boring homebody is one thing, Anna going out to bang another man is a completely different story.

An hour and a half went by with me standing at the plaza entrance, thinking about all of this. My anxiety made me numb to the last chills of a winter that hadn't completely ended, though it was already early March. I still had no idea how I was going to react when they came out. I weighed my options. The one I liked the most was simply standing in silence in front of Anna, just to see what she would do.

The violinist had stopped playing long before I saw her walk out. And when Rosario came out behind her, I felt like an asshole and a scumbag. My wife hadn't lied. For the first time in weeks, I considered that Anna might not have been cheating on me, that this all sprang out of my own insecurities. That I was fucking paranoid.

I clung to the wall. If she saw me, I was going to die of embarrassment. Thirty-five years old and I was behaving like a child. All I wanted to do was run away.

The square has two exits, so I peered around the wall to see if they were coming towards me or headed in the other direction. They stood in the center of the square by the fountain, saying goodbye for the night. I guessed they would each head off on their own soon.

Rosario said something to Anna, and my wife laughed and gave her a kiss.

Just like Gaudí, a trolley ran into me. Or at least that's what it felt like when I saw their lips meet in that kiss. It was long. With tongue.

A kiss that left me scarred worse than the church façade.

CHAPTER 2

The Hernández-Burrull notary office was located in Ibiza Square, in the Horta neighborhood. If you don't know Barcelona, just a brief walk from my apartment in Sants. Before entering, I took off my sunglasses and spit the mint-flavored gum I'd been chewing into the trashcan. My hangover felt like twenty monkeys were jumping around in my head, swinging from branch to branch, screeching and baring their teeth.

Two nights ago, when I'd discovered Anna with Rosario, I couldn't muster the courage to face her. I'd fled from the square through the narrow streets of the Gothic Quarter until I breathlessly stumbled into a bar and ordered a beer. Then another, and another, until the waiter told me it was closing time. I think I drank about four or five – enough to leave me hammered. I'm more of a protein-shake-and-outdoor-sports kind of guy than the alcohol-and-bars kind.

The epic bender had given me the courage I needed. I got on the metro determined to talk to Anna but changed my mind – or I had a brief moment of lucidity– and got off two stops later. I spent the night at my parents' house; thankfully, they were away on vacation.

The next day, I called the client whose apartment I was painting to tell him I couldn't make it that day. I spent the morning sleeping and the afternoon watching TV. Around four p.m., I turned my phone back on. Twenty-two missed calls from Anna. Call number twenty-three came in five minutes later. We had a heated argument of course, and I said things that less than 24 hours later, I deeply regretted.

I went out a while later to the lure of another bar. Right around the time I'd lost count of my downed beers –three, at least–, I received a phone call from a woman who said she worked for a notary's office. She mentioned something about an inheritance and a will. I told her to get lost and hung up, but she called back and insisted it was important for me to make an appointment. I don't remember much more about the conversation, but fortunately she had texted me the appointment details.

So there I was the next day, with a double hangover and without my mint-flavored gum, standing in Hernández-Burrull notary's fancy offices.

"My name is Julián Cucurell Guelbenzu," I informed the young receptionist, who nodded in acknowledgement as if she were expecting me, and she gestured towards two leather armchairs around a pristine coffee table.

"Have a seat, Mr. Cucurell. The notary will be with you shortly."

It seems that in the notary world, "shortly" means fifty minutes. In the normal world of people who renovate houses for a living, it meant forty euros I wasn't making.

By the time the secretary called me, I was pretty annoyed. To top it off, the air inside the office was stuffy and reeked of cologne. Just what you need when you're hung over.

I was met by a shiny wooden desk the size of the Camp Nou stadium. It was completely barren aside from a laptop, a cardboard folder and a metal vase empty of flowers. Behind it, a small, skinny man stood up. He had sharp cheekbones and deep, dark circles under his eyes which gave him the appearance of an undertaker rather than a notary. He introduced himself as Joan Hernández.

"Good morning, Mr. Cucurell. Take a seat, please. I'm sorry to hear about your uncle."

I was about to tell him there was no need for his pity as, up until the phone call with his secretary, I was unaware my father had a brother. But I chose not to play that card. This guy looked like an absolute vulture, and I presumed it is better to face a vulture that pities you than one that doesn't.

"Apologies for not contacting you sooner, but in these cases we have to wait for confirmation from the police that it was indeed an accident and not a homicide. It's unpleasant, I know, but it's the law."

I nodded silently. Hernández opened the folder and placed the glasses that hung around his neck on the bridge of his nose.

"Fernando Cucurell Zaplana died four months ago after being hit by a car, 200 meters from his residence. This is his death certificate. In 1992, Mr. Cucurell signed a will in this office naming you as his sole beneficiary."

I did the math. I was seven years old in 1992. This supposed uncle of mine knew of my existence, but I never knew of his.

"Mr. Cucurell had an account with the Sabadell Bank with €8102.07 in it. I will provide you with a document to request the change of account ownership to you. That should take at least a couple of weeks. Sign here, please. It's an authorization that allows my fees to be charged to that account, coupled with the inheritance tax deduction."

When I saw the amount, I understood why there's no such thing as a poor notary.

"Additionally, your uncle left you some land in Patagonia."

"Patagonia-Patagonia?"

"Yes. Half an acre in a small town in southern Argentina called El Chaltén," he said, and read from one of the papers, "Located on block seven, lot two, on San Martín Street between Huemul and Los Cóndores Streets."

"I assume that your fees to sell it will also be considerable."

The notary let out a soft chuckle, the way I imagine classy people might laugh at a dirty joke.

"Mr. Cucurell, I'm afraid I can't help you with that. To sell that land you will have to travel there. While you're there, you can honor your uncle's last wish. You aren't legally obligated to do so, but it would be a nice gesture."

He pointed towards the metal vase that stood on the desk, adjusted his glasses, and read out loud.

"I ask Julián to take my ashes to the Laguna de los Tres, one of the most beautiful places on Earth."

No wonder I thought the vase didn't match the rest of the office decor.

"These are Fernando Cucurell's ashes," he said, sliding them towards me solemnly. I noticed that there were paper napkins folded under the vase so that it wouldn't scratch the desk.

My distorted reflection stared back at me from the polished steel surface. Inside were the remains of my father's brother whose existence I had never known about.

"Are you sure there's no way to sell it without traveling?"

"Well, if you know a trustworthy law firm in Argentina, you could sign over power of attorney, and have them sell it and transfer you the money."

"I don't know anyone in Argentina. Never mind a lawyer."

The notary gave me a wry smile that read like a shrug, a 'too bad', and a request to not waste his time.

"I'd have to see if the plane ticket isn't more expensive than what I'd get for the land. Do you have any idea of its value?"

Anna had mentioned that Rosario was from a small town in Argentina, and that the money she'd received from the sale of a plot had barely covered her plane ticket and the first couple of months' rent in Barcelona.

"As you can imagine, I'm not very familiar with the real estate market in Patagonia. However, if I had to make an estimate, I'd say between 300 and 500 thousand euros."

"Damn! Seriously?" I blurted out.

"You haven't heard of El Chaltén, have you?"

"Well, no."

"Look it up."

CHAPTER 3

I spent the afternoon painting the dining room of a Sarrià apartment pastel green. Rich people with bad taste can cause a lot of damage.

When I was done, I thought about heading back to the bar, but as any child of a recovering alcoholic knows, getting drunk three days in a row is a very bad idea.

I made several unanswered calls to my parents who were on a cruise around the Norwegian fiords. They eventually texted back saying they were sailing through an area with poor phone reception and the ship's Wi-Fi was very slow. We agreed to talk at nine p.m., once they'd docked at Bergen.

So, I only had one option: go back to my apartment and Anna, to have one of the most painful conversations of my life.

I got there around seven, with the urn under my arm. I found a note on the dining room table: *I think we should spend some time apart before we talk. I'm going to my parents' house.*

People choose different drugs when dealing with pain. Mine is dopamine. Sorrows become more manageable with exercise. Sixty pull-ups and one hundred push-ups do the trick, every time. I decided to suck it up, change my clothes and get out of the house to do the only thing that might make me feel a little bit better.

I went to the calisthenics park and did my drills with explosive movements. The people around me training at the bars –most of them teenagers who loved to blast their favorite *reggaeton* on powerful speakers connected to their phones– stared at me, a mixture of awe and concern on their faces. I don't easily go unnoticed. I'm bald, 1.9 meters tall, and 88 kilos were of mostly muscle.

The endorphins I got from the workout made me feel a little better, but the second I got back home and read Anna's note again, they abandoned me like rats on a sinking ship.

After my shower, I made a protein shake with some fruit and almonds. I wasn't in the mood for cooking, and had less than half an hour until my call with my parents.

I turned on my laptop and sat down at the dining room table, moving Anna's note and the urn aside. According to Wikipedia, El Chaltén was a town with a population of 2000, founded in 1985, the year I was born. Argentina had created the town out of thin air to end a dispute it had with Chile regarding the area's sovereignty. A sort of 'This is mine, and to make that clear, I'm putting a town here.' And fuck you. The photos included in the article weren't very impressive. Small houses on dry land, and in the background, some snowy mountains. I opened Google Maps and activated satellite view. To the east of the town, there was brown land. To the west, an enormous white mass.

The barely twenty or thirty blocks that made up El Chaltén were nestled between two rivers. It surprised me that the map showed several places to eat and sleep on every single one of those blocks. The town seemed to have more bars, restaurants, and hotels per square meter than Barcelona.

I was halfway through my shake when I discovered that El Chaltén had been founded in the middle of a national park, which made the possibility of the town expanding almost non-existent. The property value the notary had mentioned was starting to make more sense.

I looked through the papers to find the address of the property my supposed uncle had left me. San Martín Street, no number, between Huemul and Los Cóndores Streets. The block was on what looked like the main street. On the left, I could see one of the town's biggest buildings. Google didn't show any tags on it, so I guessed it might be a school or a particularly large house. However, my eyes quickly focused on the other half acre. Desolate. Barren. Unchanged by time. An empty island surrounded by a sea of bar and restaurant signs.

I gulped the last of my shake while I stared at that empty rectangle on the other end of the world.

How much did a plane ticket to Argentina even cost? I found out quickly. Eight hundred euros round trip, not including food or luggage, although a red flashy pop-up announced a one-time-only discount for four hundred euros if I bought the ticket in the next six hours. I had fifteen hundred euros in my bank account, which would soon diminish to three hundred to pay my self-employment fee. It would be best to wait to get my hands on the thousands —minus expenses and taxes of course— the notary had mentioned.

My phone rang, signaling I had an incoming video call. When I answered, the screen showed my mother's ear and my father's double chin.

"Move the phone away from you. I can't see you."

"How about now?"

"Better," I could at least see one of each of their eyes. "How's Norway? Freezing?"

"Not at all. We've been having some spectacular weather. It drizzled a little on a couple of days, but barely a *sirimiri*," my mother answered. She spoke Spanish with a strong Basque accent, and Catalan with a Girona accent. That's what you get when you were born in Barakaldo and raised in Torroella de Montgrí.

"The cruise food?"

"Not bad," my father answered.

My mother shook her head.

"These people eat potatoes all day long!" she complained. "But, if we wanted to eat well, we would've stayed home."

With that statement, one might think that my mother was a fantastic cook. Nothing was further from the truth.

The poor woman had a phobia of knives. Literally. It's called aichmophobia, and she always blamed her culinary limitations on it. We ate well at home, but it was thanks to my father's cooking.

"We met a very nice couple from Sevilla who also live in Barcelona," my mother added. "And we had dinner with the captain last night. You would not believe that man's elegance. A big guy, very poised. Very nice, too."

"You like to think he's nice, he didn't understand a thing we were saying," interrupted my father sorely. "Not a word of Spanish, that guy."

"You, on the other hand, have mastered Norwegian to perfection", I teased.

My father, pixelated and moving at three frames per second, smiled, showing his teeth, as perfect as they were false. He'd lost his real ones in a car accident, driving from Barcelona to Bilbao before I was born.

My mother was also smiling. I could tell they were happy. It was their first trip in a long time. Since their honeymoon in the Canary Islands, they hadn't had many opportunities to travel. Not for lack of money, but for lack of time, which is a prized resource in the life of a successful architect such as my mother.

My dad, on the other hand, had time to spare. After working in construction his entire life, he retired at age 60 due to heart problems. Now, his only relationship with construction was standing in front of building sites, biting his tongue, so as not to yell instructions at the workers.

Only on a few occasions had my father managed to convince my mother that leaving things for later in life was dangerous territory. When he did, they would go on a trip like this one, a cruise around the Nordic countries.

I really didn't feel like bringing up the topic of the dead uncle.

"Hey Dad, I have a question. Do you have a brother?"

He became so still that if it weren't for my mother's movement, I would have guessed their image had frozen.

"What's this about, son?"

"Sorry to ask you about it right now."

"I have a brother, but I haven't spoken to him for many years."

"Do we have to talk about this now?" my mother interjected. "Couldn't you have waited for us to get back?"

"Actually no, Mom, because I got a call from a notary's office notifying me that Fernando Cucurell died four months ago and I'm his only heir."

My father grabbed his head, as bald as mine, and looked away from the phone. I presumed he was looking out of the window of their cabin.

"Relax, sweetheart," my mother said to him.

All three of us stayed silent for a few seconds. My father, completely stiff. My mother, caressing his shoulder. Me, not knowing what to say.

"Where did Fernando die?" my father asked.

"In Barcelona."

That seemed to shock him even more.

"How did he die?"

"He was hit by a car. How long has it been since you last spoke with him, Dad?"

"Since before you were born."

"But he knew I existed. He signed the will to me in 1992 when I was seven."

"He knew because of me," my mother intervened.

My father stared at her, astounded.

"Not too long after you were born, I ran into Fernando on the street. You were in your stroller. I told him he was your uncle."

My father remained silent.

"We didn't speak much. He was with some woman and I was with a friend. I gave him our number, but he never called."

"I didn't even know he lived in Barcelona," said my father, struggling to keep his voice steady.

"Did you think he was in Patagonia?"

"In Patagonia? What are you talking about, Julián?"

"The largest part of the inheritance is a piece of land in a town called El Chaltén in southern Argentina. The deed is from 1988."

My parents looked at each other like I'd just told them I'd adopted a green dog.

"Why didn't you ever tell me about your brother, dad?" I asked, as civilized as I could manage.

"Julián, is now really the time to ask your father something like that?"

"There's no time like the present. If you couldn't find the time to tell me this in thirty-five years, why not now?"

My father wiped away the tears that were welling up in his eyes.

"We'll talk about this once we get back to Barcelona, Julián. Thank you for letting us know. You did the right thing."

Before I could say another word, I saw his index finger move toward the screen, ending the call.

CHAPTER 4

I ended up not talking to my parents. In person, I mean. Although my personal finances weren't in great shape for an expedition to the other end of the world, the red pop-up convinced me. It wasn't the sale price that attracted me but the idea of putting space between Barcelona and myself. That rectangle of land on the southern tip of the planet was the perfect excuse to get away from Anna and having to explain the situation to my parents. When my plane took off from El Prat towards Ezeiza, they still had a day left until their return.

A bonus to breaking up with Anna was not having to get my parents to like her anymore. In our three years together, they had never fully accepted her. Behind their cordiality, I could tell there was a certain coldness toward her. One time, my mother seemed to forget her feminist, progressive thinking –I was the only kid in my class whose parents didn't differentiate between "boy" and "girl" toys– to tell me that it was a law of nature that in a mother's eyes, no woman would ever be good enough for her son. And my father always went along with his wife.

Nearly three days had passed between my departure from Barcelona and my arrival to El Chaltén. After two planes, the last leg of the trip was over land and lasted almost three hours. The bus from Calafate to El Chaltén didn't stop until we arrived at the town terminal. Most of us were tourists, both Argentinian and foreign. Several Spaniards, like me. The person who sat next to me was an Italian, who thankfully didn't speak much.

I felt like a fish out of water. I wasn't a tourist or a local. The only one on board carrying a dead person's ashes in his backpack.

While I waited to pick up my suitcase by one of the bus's huge tires, I studied the map I had received via e-mail from the people at El Relincho, probably the cheapest lodging available in the area. El Relincho was, like my uncle's parcel, on San Martín Street. As I traced the route I would take once I got my luggage, I overheard a conversation between two Spanish women behind me.

"You can't see it," one of them said.

"What a drag," the other answered, "I hope we can tomorrow."

I turned slowly. Two tourists about my age, pointed towards a big house on the side of a mountain that, according to what I had seen on the map, marked the edge of town.

"Maybe you'll get lucky tomorrow, guys," interrupted an Argentine woman who had also just gotten off the bus. She was speaking to the two tourists and me as if we were together. "Some people stay a week and don't get to see it."

"Oh, don't say that! I'd cry if that happened to us," answered one of the women.

"Don't worry. Anyway, it looks like the weather is improving. You have no idea how much it's rained these past weeks."

"Excuse me," I interjected, "What are you talking about?"

"The Fitz Roy", said one of the tourists, pointing back towards the mountain. I noticed her finger wasn't pointing at the house but at the space above it.

"You can't see it when it's cloudy," the woman explained. "It looks like there's nothing but sky behind that house. But on a sunny day, it's spectacular."

From the photos I'd seen, Mount Fitz Roy seemed pretty, but I admit, I hadn't fully understood the women's enthusiasm on that cloudy afternoon.

I grabbed my backpack, waved goodbye, and walked down the main street. The sidewalk on the right was brimming with hotels, restaurants, tourist agencies, and breweries announcing happy hour between five and eight p.m. On the other side of the street, there was a park with a playground made from thick logs, and some municipal-looking buildings. A school, town hall, that kind of thing.

According to my map, two blocks ahead, I would run into the piece of land I had traveled across the world for. Despite my warm jacket, I started to shiver. Some people bite their nails or start to sweat when they're nervous. I, on the other hand, shiver.

I walked in silence, my eyes straight ahead. When I reached the corner of San Martín and Los Cóndores, I encountered the large building that shared the block with my uncle's parcel, according to what I'd seen online. There was a dilapidated sign that read "Hotel", but the wood shutters were closed and the paint was peeling. It had been years since that place had been open to the public.

A man waved at me from the porch. He was probably nearing his fifties, but there was a youthful glimmer in his eyes. I waved back and kept walking.

As I left the abandoned villa behind, a beautiful lawn opened up before me. The rustic log fence that bordered it was in good shape. I guessed the town hall had ensured its upkeep during these years to keep the town looking neat.

The moment I reached the front of the parcel I had inherited, my stomach clenched, as if it had been punched. It wasn't empty like the image Google had shown me. Someone had built four cabins and two wooden sheds. By the fence, a sign read *Aurora Horseback Rides. Cabins for rent by the day.*

I wasn't brave enough to walk in. It was late and I was exhausted. Tomorrow, with a clearer mind, I'd figure out what to do.

Two blocks further, I finally reached El Relincho. The place wasn't very different from the parcel I'd just seen. My parcel, supposedly. I walked through the grass following the wooden signs that pointed toward the reception desk, a modern, metal and concrete building. The inside was like a backpacker hostel you might find anywhere in the world: music, big tables, communal kitchens, tourists in flip flops having pasta with tuna for dinner at seven p.m. or staring into their phone screens, taking advantage of the Wi-Fi.

I was greeted by a guy of about twenty-five who introduced himself as Macario. Odd names they give boys in Argentina. I handed him my passport and he started checking me in on his laptop.

"Julián Cucurell," he said as he looked at the screen. "Here you are. I've got you booked for two weeks, is that correct?"

"Yes."

"Nice, you'll have time to do all the hikes. Normally people who come here don't stay much longer than a week."

I smiled.

"It's good to come here without needing to rush," he went on. "There are hikes that just aren't the same on a cloudy day. It's well worth the wait until the sun comes out to do them."

He scanned my passport and I paid him the second half I owed for the accommodation.

"Follow me, I'll show you to your cabin."

I followed Macario through the grass towards a small wooden house with two rooms, a bathroom and a kitchen-dining room with a fireplace inside.

"Oh, one more thing. The Wi-Fi signal is kind of weak here sometimes," he added. "It depends on the day. If you can't connect, get a little bit closer to the reception area and it should work. Anything else you need, you can find me there."

"Are you from here originally?"

Macario smiled.

"Barely anyone is actually from here. My family came here when I was ten."

"I see. So, you've been here for quite a while then. When I was walking here from the bus terminal I saw a sign for horseback rides. I think it was called Aurora.

What do you think of the people who run it? Would you recommend it?"

Who would have imagined? The guy who'd been scared of horses his entire life asking those questions.

"Yeah, their outings are nice. And Rodolfo and Laura, the couple who run the business, know a lot. They haven't been doing as many horseback rides lately because Rodolfo barely has time for anything. He's been the town mayor for two years. Between that and the new cabins they're building on the lot, he doesn't have time for anything else

Well, that was fucking terrific. The person squatting on my land was none other than the town mayor.

CHAPTER 5

I was woken by the sound of metal scraping against metal. I looked out my window and saw Macario and a girl with a heavy barbecue in front of my cabin, struggling to move it between the two of them. It was basically a 200-liter metal drum placed horizontally on four legs, with a damper on one side.

Macario saw me through the window, waved, and pointed towards the hunk of metal.

"It's called a *chulengo*," he said. "We brought it over in case you feel like grilling some meat while you're here."

I gave him a thumbs-up and headed to the bathroom for a shower. I had another type of grilling in mind.

I mulled over my next steps under the hot water. It was Saturday, so I'd have to wait until Monday to go to the town hall with the deed and the will, but I wasn't just going to sit around idly all weekend.

I left the cabin at eleven a.m. Even though the sky was as cloudy as the day before, the narrow sidewalks were packed with tourists lugging backpacks of all shapes and sizes.

My walk inevitably led me to my uncle's property. I saw a woman about my age by the reception sign brushing a grey horse. I bordered the low fence and walked in, passing the sign that said *Aurora Horseback Rides*.

"Good morning," I said without getting too close to the animal.

"Morning," she answered, looking up to give me one of those smiles that salespeople always have. She had brown eyes and dark hair.

"I wanted to ask about the horseback rides. What they include, prices, all of that."

She gave the horse two pats on the neck and then offered me her hand to shake.

"Of course. I'm Laura. Come on in."

Her name surprised me. Laura, according to Macario, was the mayor's wife. However, she looked far too young to be married to a politician.

We walked into the reception area and she handed me a pamphlet printed in black and white, with prices and descriptions of the various options. I asked several questions about the most expensive one, which she answered patiently. At some point, she mentioned that Aurora was the oldest horseback riding business in El Chaltén.

"Have you lived here very long?"

"No, just a couple of years. But Rodolfo, the company owner, was one of the first townsmen. He came here in the early 90s."

"I heard the town was founded in 1985."

"Nice! A tourist who's done his research."

"Not that much. I just skimmed over some information."

Laura glanced both ways and her tone turned conspiratory.

"People in Chaltén love to say they're part of the first townsmen. The worst are the ones who say that and actually came in the early 2000s. But in Rodolfo's family's case, I think they deserve the title. There wasn't anything here back then. Absolutely nothing."

"It was worth it. I bet a piece of land like this must be worth a fortune."

"That's an understatement. But who'd want to sell? And why? There's a big issue with land here because the town is in a national park and can't expand in any direction. There are people who've been living here for eight, or ten years and can't get their hands on a bit of land to build their own house. Some people even started building on land that wasn't their own."

"So, squatters make it all the way down here."

The woman nodded, apparently not feeling alluded to in the slightest.

"We also offer hikes on the Viedma. Have you ever walked on a glacier?"

"No. Is it dangerous?"

"Not if you go with an expert. Rodolfo's been taking people for decades. It's an unforgettable experience. If you get the chance, don't leave Chaltén without doing it. It's expensive, but a memory that lasts a lifetime is priceless." She was certainly giving me the hard sell.

"Sounds amazing," I said, feeling like I had to say something.

"Can I help you with anything else?"

"No, thank you. Well, actually I was wondering about what you said earlier, about the land here. It's interesting. Is this the parcel that Rodolfo's family received when they moved here?"

"Why do you ask?"

"Because from what I'm told, it belongs to Fernando Cucurell."

The woman looked up from the pile of pamphlets. Any friendliness had disappeared from her face.

"You're not a tourist."

"My name is Julián Cucurell. Fernando Cucurell was my uncle. He died recently and I'm his only heir."

"Why don't you cut the crap and tell me what you want? Why did you waste my time telling you about the horseback rides? Didn't you see I was working?"

"I'm sorry, I didn't mean to bother you."

"Well, it bothers me when people lie."

She pushed down on the desk firmly and stomped out of the reception area. I followed her until we were in front of the horse again.

"I apologize, really."

"Look man, if you have something to talk about with Rodolfo, then come back some other time and discuss it with him," she said and started brushing the animal again.

"I messed up, I'm sorry," I insisted.

Laura sighed and turned towards me. Then, she made a gesture in the air, as if she were wiping off a blackboard.

"You're forgiven," she said with a strained smile. "Now, if you'll forgive me, I need to continue working."

With her free hand, she pointed towards the exit.

CHAPTER 6

At around seven p.m., there was a knock at my cabin door. It was a man in his sixties, handsome, with a full head of white hair. He looked like one of those models for hearing aids or dentures, or in this case, glasses, as he wore some attractive, modern, thin-rimmed ones. He reminded me of Anna's father, one of those men over sixty who still boasted wide shoulders and a flat belly. He had an envelope in his hand.

"I'm Rodolfo Sosa," he introduced himself, "Owner of Aurora Horseback Rides."

"Come in," I said, moving to the side so he could enter.

"No need."

"Listen. I guess you've come because of the conversation I had with your wife. I apologized to her and apologize to you, as well."

The man took a step towards me. For as many pull-ups and push-ups as I could handle, I wasn't sure I'd be able to take him.

"Come, follow me," he said and started walking away from my cabin. "Come on, I don't bite."

For a second, I doubted whether I should follow him but decided I wouldn't get anywhere causing more friction, so I stepped up my pace until I'd caught up with him.

"That Laura isn't my wife," he stated once I was by his side. "My wife's name is also Laura, but the girl you spoke to is a guide who works with us. She helps us with the horses and the hikes."

"Oh."

"She's got an attitude," he added.

"I could see that. In any case, the way I behaved with her was wrong."

Rodolfo Sosa stopped dead in his tracks and tilted his head forward to peer at me over his glasses.

"You're right, it was. Here, we like people who are upfront and speak truthfully."

I didn't know how to respond. The man kept walking until we were at the corner of Aurora Horseback Rides.

"You say this land is yours," he said, waving towards the cabins.

"I have the will where I'm named heir. The deed says it clearly: half an acre on San Martín Street, between Huemul and Los Cóndores. Block seven, lot two."

Sosa shook his head and let out a stifled laugh.

"We're neighbors then. My lot is number one. Lot number two is that one over there."

I looked at where his finger pointed.

"The abandoned hotel?"

"That's Fernando Cucurell's property."

"But the deed says it's an empty lot."

"Looks like they haven't updated it."

I felt utterly embarrassed. When I'd seen the block on satellite view, I simply assumed that my uncle's half-acre was the one that didn't have anything built on it.

"It's falling apart, but it's a beautiful building," he added.

I nodded while I scrutinized the hotel carefully. It was only one story high. The wood on the shutters was gray from lack of care, and several of the stones they'd used to build the exterior walls had fallen off, leaving cement holes that reminded me of the Sant Felip Neri façade. If it hadn't been in such bad shape, that place wouldn't be too far off from the mountain weekend homes my mother designed for her wealthy clients.

"If you're really Cucurell's heir, what's yours is the hotel, not my lot."

"I have the will I can show you if you like."

The man raised his hands in a sign of peace.

"I believe you. You'll show the papers to whoever needs to see them."

"I have to apologize. Between the deed and the pictures I saw on the internet, I just assumed this was his lot. I never meant to insinuate... Shit, what a horrible way to start off, right?"

The man placed one of his big hands on my shoulder.

"Everyone makes mistakes, kid. Don't worry about it. In any case, deeds took a long time to get handed out here, and didn't always reflect what the land was actually like. Most people notarized their land but never updated it."

"Do you know what year the hotel was built in?"

"Oh, before 1990 for sure."

"It looks like it's been abandoned for a long time."

"A really long time. Twenty-five years, at least."

I pointed at the wooden porch in front of the solid wooden door, which was closed.

"There was someone sitting there yesterday," I said.

"Danilo. A local kid."

"No, it was a man, older than me. Probably about fifty."

"That's Danilo. Once you meet him, you'll understand."

Sosa looked at me, uncomfortably, and patted his pockets until he found a set of keys. While he did so, he seemed to remember he still had the envelope in his hand.

"Oh, this must be for you. It was under your door. I picked it up before knocking, so it wouldn't blow away."

"Thank you," I said.

The envelope didn't have any writing on it, front or back. I put it in my pocket so as not to open it in front of him.

"I imagine you have a ton of questions."

"Many. From when it was built to why it closed."

The man gestured to follow him and bordered his lot towards the hotel. However, when we reached the door, he merely looked at it, then turned to walk away from it, crossing the street.

"Where are we going?"

"Just follow me."

We walked through the town until Sosa was intercepted in front of the pharmacy by a woman who wanted to ask him about the extension of the natural gas grid. The politician gestured towards me and I took a few steps back to give them some space.

I opened the envelope while they talked. In it was a piece of paper with a message printed in Comic Sans.

Sell the hotel and go enjoy the money somewhere else. You are not welcome in El Chaltén.

CHAPTER 7

When Sosa managed to free himself from the woman and we resumed our walk, I had the feeling that someone was following me. It was likely my imagination after reading the anonymous note. Even so, I looked behind me several times. The few tourists and locals I saw didn't seem to pay any attention to me whatsoever.

"Is something wrong?" Sosa inquired the third time I looked back.

"No, nothing."

We reached a small building with a sloped roof and dormer windows that protruded from it. It looked like a house from a fairy tale. In the yard, two flags waved: an Argentinian flag and the other, blue, red, and white, which I recognized from my Wikipedia research as the town's flag. A sign over the door read "El Chaltén Town Hall."

Sosa looked both ways as if he were about to break into someone's car. Then, he opened the door with one of the keys from his set.

"Come in, quick. If they see me in here, they'll come ask me for something," he said as he locked the door from the inside. "You have no idea how hard it is to be mayor in a small town. They show up at my house at all hours, for any reason. What I'm doing for you here, opening the town hall for you on a Saturday, is an exception. Don't get used to it."

He was a natural politician. We'd just met and I already owed him a favor I hadn't even asked for.

"Thank you," I said.

We walked past the entry table and down a hallway flanked with offices.

"This is my office," said Sosa, pointing at a closed door with a golden plaque on it that read *Mayor's Office*, "But what I want to show you is somewhere else."

We kept walking to the end of the hallway, then up a wooden staircase that widened into a sort of attic where three desks, overflowing with papers, were pushed against the walls.

"This is the land registry office, where I worked before I became Mayor."

He headed over to a file cabinet, opened one of the drawers, and ran his finger along the folders while he mumbled last names.

"Contreras... Cortés... Cucurell! Here it is," he said, pulling one out.

He opened it and laid the hotel floor map out on one of the desks. Finally, I could put my two years of architecture school, and my being raised by an architect, to use.

"Here you go, you can get to know the Hotel Montgrí better."

"Hotel Montgrí?"

"Yes. That's what it's called."

I smiled. The Montgrí was a small mountain close to where my parents –and presumably my uncle– had grown up. It felt surreal to hear that name on the other side of the world.

The map was hand-drawn. The hotel floor was long and rectangular. The entrance was located on one of the short sides, with a reception area that opened up onto a dining room. Two doors in the dining room led to a large kitchen on one side, and on the other, the main hallway which opened onto eight bedrooms, four on each side.

At the other end of the property, there was a house, probably 100 square meters that appeared small next to the hotel. I guessed that was where Fernando Cucurell had lived. I imagined him alone; if he'd had any family of his own, I wouldn't be his heir.

"You wanted to know the year it was built? Here's a clue. The project was presented by the architect Remigio

Uceta in 1987," said Sosa, pointing to a signature on the paper that came with the map. "It can't have been before that. You'll have to look at the allotment file to see when it opened to the public, but that's not my area. You'll have to come back on Monday for that."

"No problem. In the meantime, could you put me in touch with someone who knew my uncle at that time?"

"Look, to my knowledge, there were twelve houses here in 1987. The books say Chaltén was founded in 1985, that's true, but it didn't really start up until the mid-90s. When I got here, in '92, there were twenty-two houses along with fifty-two people living here. My wife and I were numbers fifty-three and fifty-four. At that time, most of the population was part of the military who'd come for the season and then leave. You should consider that the reason the town was founded was to solve a territorial conflict with Chile."

"Yeah, I read something about that."

"Most of those police officers and military men went back home as soon as they could. Very few of us came here to stay. To give you an idea, our son was the first baby to be born in Chaltén, eight years after it was founded."

"Did you get to see the hotel when it was open?"

"No. When we arrived here it was already closed. It couldn't have been for long, because the building was pretty new."

"And can you think of anyone who might have seen it open and running?"

"I'm thinking. It's tricky. Between the ones who left and the ones who died, there aren't many people left from that time. You've got to think that the people who came here in their forties, are in their seventies now, and people tend to move closer to a hospital at that age. We're 220 kilometers from the nearest one."

"I understand."

"Don't you worry, I'm sure someone will come to mind. In any case, be careful, because this is a small town, and after so many years, people tend to mix reality with rumors. More so if we're talking about a hotel that's been abandoned for so long."

"What rumors exactly?"

"Nonsense. People like to make up stories because it's free."

"I'm interested."

Sosa shrugged. 'Your choice', he seemed to say.

"Until the late 90s, there was only summer tourism here. The winter months were too harsh and the roads were treacherous. The people who worked in the area closed up until late March, they'd leave and come back in October. It's rumored that the guy who built it, which would have been your uncle, closed it after working the first season, said 'See you next year' to everyone, but never came back. Some even say he hung himself in there."

"That can't be, because Fernando Cucurell died four months ago. I have his ashes in my cabin."

"Like I said, just rumors."

"I'd like to go in."

"Do you have the keys?"

"I thought it was an empty lot until a little while ago."

"Right," Sosa laughed. "Then you're going to have to call a locksmith. There aren't any in town, but I know a good one in Calafate. Want me to call him?"

I did the math. If someone was going to have to drive for two hours to open a door for me, it wasn't going to be cheap.

"I can open it," I offered. "The door and the shutters are wooden. I'm sure they'll give with a crowbar."

"Yeah, but that would be such a waste. Have you seen the woodwork? They don't make things like that anymore."

"I just found out I inherited a hotel. Breaking the door isn't a problem for me."

The man gave me a tense smile that I didn't like at all. He fixed his glasses on his nose and rubbed his chin.

"Listen Julián, we live off of tourism here. The hotel is on the main street, where we have the most commercial activity and lots of people walk by. The second someone sees you with a crowbar trying to force the lock, they're going to call the police. Anything that looks like a robbery does the town no good, you see? I'm begging you to make do with the map for a few days until you can enter like a civilized human being. The hotel has been locked shut for decades, I'm sure it can wait a little longer."

"No one has gone in this whole time?"

"No one."

"And the man on the porch?"

"Him either. In a way, we were waiting for you."

"I don't understand."

"Like I said, peace and quiet is our top priority. It's what feeds us and makes us an international tourist destination. Every year, like clockwork, someone pays the property taxes and the municipal authorization for the hotel. Seeing as it's private property, if they choose to keep it closed, the town hall can't get involved."

"Who pays those taxes?"

"We should ask Margarita about that, she's in the finance department. She can also tell you the date of the hotel's authorization to open. Come back on Monday and I'll introduce you."

I nodded. He made a copy of the map and handed it to me.

"Julián, I don't mean to be rude, but I need to get back. I also imagine you must have a lot to take in. If there's anything you need, you know where I live. If you can't find me here, I'm at home."

"Thank you, but I don't want to be yet another person knocking on your door to ask for a favor."

"Your case is different. It's no bother at all, quite the opposite."

I wondered what was driving him to be so accommodating.

"If you're wondering why I'm helping you," he said as if he could read my mind, "It's because I love this town dearly. If that hotel were to come back to life, El Chaltén would be a much more beautiful place. And keep in mind that the nicer it is, the better we all live."

CHAPTER 8

Someone knocked at my cabin door at around eight-thirty a.m., but I'd been awake for two hours. Between the remaining jet lag and yesterday's surprises, it was a wonder I'd been able to sleep at all.

I got out of bed, put on some pants, and opened the door without asking who it was. I found myself facing Rodolfo Sosa's strong figure, once again.

"Did I wake you?"

"Not at all. I was in bed but wide awake."

"Great. I have good news," he said, walking inside, "A locksmith is coming tomorrow from El Calafate to do some work at the gas station, so we can take advantage of the fact that he's here and ask him to open the hotel door for you. You can't take possession until we get confirmation that it belongs to you, but taking a look inside won't hurt, will it?"

"Thank you."

The man tsked as if bothered that I was thanking him.

"What are your plans for today?"

"I don't know, walk around a bit, I guess."

"Well, you're in the national hiking capital. Have you ever walked on a glacier?"

"I haven't had the pleasure."

"Today's your lucky day then. I was going to take a group to the Viedma, but they canceled last night. Would you like to go? It's an unforgettable experience."

It sounded a lot like what Laura, his employee, had told me.

"Sure."

"Amazing. Get your warmest clothes on and let's go."

"Right now?"

"Yes, now. And we need to hurry because even though it's pleasant outside now, the weather can change very quickly here. I'll wait for you at my house while I make some sandwiches. Don't take too long."

I didn't know if I should be suspicious of Sosa's seemingly endless friendliness or admit, to my dismay, that I'd met the only politician in the world that I actually liked.

Twenty minutes later, I arrived at his house. Laura, the employee, was saddling a white mare in the yard. She greeted me with a chin gesture. Rodolfo Sosa walked out of the bigger house, which I guessed was where he lived, with some canvas bags slung across his shoulder. When he saw me, he signaled toward a pickup truck the size of an aircraft carrier. He threw one bag in the back of the truck and placed the other one which was long and skinny, between the seats.

"Is that a rifle?"

"Yeah, a Winchester 1892. In case we're lucky and see a *guanaco*. Do you eat meat?"

"Yes."

"Then you can't leave Patagonia without trying *guanaco*," he announced and started up the truck.

He drove slowly from his house to the town exit, waving through his window like a newly elected president. The tourists smiled shyly and the locals responded with cordial waves or, in some cases, not-so-friendly scowls.

We crossed the Fitz Roy River bridge and drove through fields, moving away from the town and the cloud-covered mountains. Before long, I saw a large mass of water appear to my right. It had bordered the bus in the opposite direction when I'd come from El Calafate two days earlier.

"That's Lake Viedma, one of the biggest in South America. Eighty kilometers long, twenty wide."

"Tiny."

"Everything here is big, the bad and the good. The landscape, the distances, everything. Some tourists tell me that when they come to Patagonia, they feel like someone shrunk them."

A few minutes later, we turned off the pavement onto a dirt road –*ripio*, they called it there– that opened up towards the water. I crossed my fingers that we wouldn't encounter a *guanaco* that would give Sosa the opportunity to use his rifle.

The views were magnificent. I took some photos with my phone and felt like an idiot when my first thought was to send them to Anna.

In the upper corner of the screen, my phone showed there was no reception. I was unreachable, in the middle of nowhere with a suspiciously friendly, armed man. What could possibly go wrong?

After rounding a bend, I saw an inflatable boat on the shore, tied to a small dock. It could hold about 20 people.

"Is anyone else coming?"

"No, just the two of us. We had better be careful, because if anything happens, we're in hot water. Or should I say the freezer?" he chuckled.

"That sounds promising."

"Don't worry kid. I've been doing this for years."

He parked in front of the boat and hid the rifle under the seats.

"Nothing ever happens here, but I'm not about to leave a gun in plain sight."

Sosa loaded the second bag onto the boat and signaled to me to get in. He started up the engine, untied the ropes and we motored away from the shore slowly, avoiding the icebergs that grew bigger as we moved forward.

"We need to be very careful not to crash into the ice," he explained as he pointed at an iceberg bigger than our boat. "If it could sink the Titanic, imagine what it would do to us."

In the name of the entire human species, I thanked the cosmos that that man had decided to go into politics and not psychology.

There was little wind and the lake's surface was calm. I leaned over the side to touch the water.

"It's freezing."

"It never gets above three degrees. There you have the culprit," said Sosa, pointing ahead.

We'd just rounded a peninsula and now the bow of the boat pointed towards a mass of ice that started in the clouds and spread out for kilometers towards us. It ended in a jagged, sharp wall made up of a dozen hues of blue.

"It's breathtaking."

"Have you ever heard of the Viedma glacier?"

"No. Only the Perito Moreno."

"The Perito gets all the attention. It's stunning, there's no denying it, but what makes it so famous is that it's a very democratic glacier. Anyone can drive there and stay all day long, enjoying the view from a wooden bench, drinking *mate*. This one, on the other hand, is like a wild horse. Very few get to see it, and even fewer ride it."

We sailed along the glacier's edge until we reached a dark rocky slope on the opposite shore of the lake and docked at a wooden pier, even more rustic than the one we'd set sail from. Sosa got out first and motioned to follow him.

We walked in silence for over a hundred meters, and then he stopped and pointed at his feet.

"This is where the ice starts."

If he hadn't said so, I'd have thought we were still standing on the rock. Unlike the face of the glacier, where blocks of ice went to die magnificently surrounded by deep blues and sharp cliffs, on the edges, the ice imitated the rock and looked like gray, grimy ice, as if someone had dumped dirt into water before freezing it.

"Powdered rock," explained Sosa. "The glacier pushes against it with so much force that it pulverizes it and stains the ice."

He sat on a rock and pulled two pairs of crampons out from the canvas bag. He put his on and explained the process so I could follow his lead. My first steps wearing them reminded me of the brief –yet unfortunate– period as a teenager when I decided to become a goth and succumbed to the trend of platform shoes.

As we walked forward, the ice beneath our feet became cleaner, whiter, and less smooth. Every muscle from my neck to my big toe was tensed up as I walked like I was stepping on Jell-O. Sosa, of course, was ambling along confidently as if he were strolling around his living room in flip-flops.

After 500 meters uphill, I was panting when a crack, two meters wide, forced us to stop.

"You tired?"

"Not at all," I lied.

"Good, because from here on we need to be really cautious. The ice looks sturdy, but it's actually in constant motion. If we go the wrong way, it can open up in an instant like this crack beneath us. Or close up with us inside."

"Now I see why tourists prefer the Perito Moreno."

"Just follow my lead and you'll have nothing to worry about," answered Sosa, laughing. "Rule number one, don't get too close to any walls taller than you. It's impossible to survive a solid ice detachment."

I nodded silently.

"You look too serious, kid. Stop worrying about it. Look at where you're standing, Julián," he said, waving at the white and blue landscape that sprawled before us. "Don't tell me it isn't incredible. I've been living here for almost thirty years and it never ceases to amaze me."

"I'm sure it doesn't. It's a unique place."

We stood in silence, observing the field of white spires s, high as steeples that got lost in the clouds. The ice appeared still but was continuously creaking, breaking in places we couldn't see. Some sounds were like thunder, others reached us from far away, barely audible over the wind and the sound of running water.

"Is there a river?" I asked.

"There are hundreds of rivers."

Sosa pointed at the crack that had forced us to stop. At the bottom, I could see a small stream of transparent water running through the electric blue ice. The politician started walking along the crack and motioned for me to follow him.

We passed a block of ice taller than a house, and I saw that the stream ran into a cylindrical hole the size of my dining room. I looked down into it and saw that the hole got darker as it became deeper, it looked endless.

"Careful," said Sosa. "Don't get too close. If you fall down there, you won't live to talk about it."

I took a few steps back. We leaned on a round, transparent piece of glacier that looked like one of those sculptures they make at ice hotels. Sosa opened his backpack and took out a hammer.

"I think it's time," he said.

"Time for what?"

Without answering, he smiled and started hammering the ice half a meter from where my gloved hand was. A chunk the size of a watermelon fell and would have crushed my foot if I hadn't moved out of the way just in time. The maneuver made me lose my balance and when I took a step back, I felt nothing but air beneath my crampons.

I slipped down the rock-hard ice, trying in vain to grab onto something to stop my fall.

CHAPTER 9

When I stopped falling, my heart was pounding a mile a minute.

"Are you okay?" I heard Sosa's voice from above.

I could see El Chaltén's mayor's face peering over the blue wall, silhouetted against the gray sky, grinning from ear to ear. I looked down. My feet were partially submerged in the glacier stream. I'd fallen into the crack that ran into the endless hole. A few meters the other way and, in Sosa's own words, I wouldn't have lived to talk about it.

"What happened? Did you get scared?"

Without answering, I grabbed the hand he had extended and climbed up the wall, lodging my crampons into the ice.

"Sorry, kid. I didn't realize you were such a wuss."

"I'm not a wuss. I lost my balance. What were we talking about?"

Sosa put away the hammer and produced two stainless steel cups from his backpack. He put a chunk of ice in each one and poured the contents of a flask into them.

"What I was about to say when you 'lost your balance'," he said, using air quotes, "is that nobody can walk on a glacier and not do this. Do you like whisky?"

"Yes," I said. I actually hated it, but it wasn't as if I could ask him for a mojito instead.

Sosa raised his cup.

"To your visit to El Chaltén, may it be successful."

"To this amazing place."

We drank in silence. The alcohol ran down my throat as smooth as broken glass. At least it would help calm my heart which was still pounding from the fall.

After a couple of sips, Sosa cleared his throat awkwardly.

"Look kid, I prefer you hear this from me and not some other way when you start digging around. We were making arrangements at the town hall to take ownership of the hotel. It's been abandoned for so long, it's a shame. It makes the town ugly, and we live off of tourism. Chaltén is part of a national park so it's impossible to expand in any direction. It would be a great space for a municipal shelter or a cultural center."

Sosa looked me in the eyes and placed his hand on my shoulder once again.

"But forget about all that. Now that you're here, if you are who you say you are, that place belongs to you and we won't put any spokes in your wheel."

I nodded. I didn't really know what to reply, so I took a long sip of whisky.

"What's important is that you do all the paperwork and finish the inheritance process."

"And find out why my uncle abandoned the Montgrí. There has to be someone who remembers the man who built the town's first hotel."

When I said that, Sosa snapped his fingers several times and shook his index finger as if he'd just had an idea.

"I'm an idiot."

"What?"

"The Montgrí wasn't El Chaltén's first hotel. Well, it was the first *hotel*-hotel, but before there was even a town, National Parks had an inn where the information center is now."

I remembered the two-story, stone building we'd passed on our way out of town.

"I don't follow. What does that have to do with my uncle?"

"Juanmi Alonso was one of the inn receptionists. I'm sure when they were full, they'd send guests over to the Montgrí and vice versa. He must have met your uncle, I'm sure of it. He still works for National Parks and lives two blocks from your cabin."

I bit my tongue to not ask Sosa why he hadn't started there.

"I'll go see him."

"You should, although he's not in town right now. I ran into him at the supermarket the day before yesterday. He told me he was buying provisions because he was heading over to fix the Río Blanco bridge; it broke during the storms we had these past weeks. With his seniority, he should be the park director by now, but he's the kind of guy who loves being in the middle of the woods."

"Do you know when he's coming back?"

"No idea. Knowing him, he probably won't be back until they finish repairing the bridge. For tourists that aren't brave enough to cross the river jumping from rock to rock, that bridge is the only way to get to the Laguna de Los Tres, one of the park's most popular hikes. By the way, you can't leave without doing it."

I smiled.

"Well, actually I can't. It was my uncle's last wish that his ashes be scattered there."

"Smart man. It's a beautiful place."

"Is it very far?"

"Nine, ten kilometers. You can get there in four hours."

"Four hours?"

"Maybe five. Depends on how fast you walk. It's difficult, but it's a spectacular hike."

"Ok. Maybe I'll go tomorrow, and while I'm at it I can talk to this man, Juanmi Alonso."

"No! Don't you dare do it tomorrow."

"Why not?"

"Because it's going to be cloudy all day. Going to the Laguna de Los Tres if it's cloudy is like going to a museum blindfolded. Your uncle deserves to be taken there on a sunny day."

I nodded without saying anything, wondering if he was giving me that advice in good faith or if he was trying to control my movements, like a dog barking at its herd of sheep.

"What are you going to do with the hotel?" he asked, pouring more whisky into the cups. "I assume you'll put it up for sale."

"I don't know yet."

"What other choice do you have? Are you going to stay here, half the world away from your home?"

"Honestly, I'd like to spend some time away from Barcelona. Also, I work renovating houses, so I could fix up the hotel myself."

"Not to burst your bubble, but you know it's practically impossible to work in construction here during the winter, right? You can't use cement because it freezes and cracks. It's also hard to get materials. We have a hardware store with the basics, but if you want to do some serious construction you have to bring stuff from Calafate or Río Gallegos. There're even people who order things directly from Buenos Aires. If it snows too much, the roads can get blocked. That's to say... when it gets cold here, it gets really cold."

"I see. Maybe I could spend the winter here, do as much as I can, and finish it in the spring."

"Listen to me, Julián. Do you know how much your property is worth?"

"They told me around three hundred thousand dollars."

Sosa burst into laughter.

"Who told you that?"

"The notary in Barcelona."

"That guy doesn't know what he's talking about."

"It's worth less?"

"More."

I stood up straight, careful to not slip again.

"That makes sense, I guess. The hotel doesn't show up in the deed. The notary meant the price of the land, I suppose."

"Even if it were bare land, it's worth much more than that."

"How much?"

"Whatever you want."

"What?"

"For that land, you can get whatever price you ask for. There isn't, and probably never will be, half an acre for sale in Chaltén. So, if you ask for a million dollars, you'll get it. And if you ask for two million, it might take a bit longer, but you'll eventually find someone with a lot of money who's willing to pay that amount."

In other circumstances, I'd have thought he was pulling my leg, but he spoke so convincingly that it seemed impossible he was making it up.

According to him, I'd become a millionaire overnight.

CHAPTER 10

Sosa's pickup truck bounced along the rocky road that led back to the pavement. I had to admit, he and Laura were right: walking on a glacier was an unforgettable experience.

I imagine most tourists spend their trips back to base, talking about what they'd just seen or looking at the photos they'd taken. I, on the other hand, couldn't think of anything but what Sosa had told me half an hour earlier.

A million? Two? What does one do with that much money all of a sudden? It was like winning multiple lotteries at once.

"Cat got your tongue?" asked Sosa.

"No. I was thinking."

"It's a lot of money, eh?"

"A ton."

"Want my two cents? Get professional advice. What you've got is worth an awful lot, but people know you're not from here and will want to sell quickly to get back home. They're going to want to convince you to lower the price considerably."

"Do you think there will be people interested in buying?"

"Oh, you'll have plenty of people interested. What there isn't much of is people with enough money to pay what it's worth. But there's many a *gringo* that has their eye set on the town. People with deep pockets. You'd have to find yourself one of those."

I spent the rest of the ride back listening to stories of people who'd arrived in Chaltén in the 90s and sold their land twenty years later for enough money to buy four or five properties in Buenos Aires.

We said goodbye at the entrance to El Relincho. I walked to my cabin intent on devouring whatever I had in my fridge, but the moment I saw the envelope with the threatening note on the table, my hunger vanished. It's not that the outing had taken my mind completely off it, but it had at least been a partial distraction.

I sat at the table for almost an hour, the note in front of me. On the one hand, whoever had written it felt very uncomfortable with my visit to El Chaltén. On the other hand, they didn't seem to have any problem with me inheriting the hotel, as long as I sold it and left.

In spite of my exhaustion, I couldn't spend the rest of the day holed up in the cabin without my head exploding from thinking it over too much. I decided to take a walk and breath in some fresh air.

On the porch of the Montgrí, the man I had said hello to upon my arrival was sitting once again. I raised my hand and he did the same, politely. However, the second I stepped on the hotel grounds, he automatically stood up from his chair and strode out from the porch's protection to block my path.

"Good afternoon," I said, as I saw him advance toward me like a steam engine.

He stopped halfway, looked at the ground, and stomped as if he were killing a spider. Then, he continued his march until he was less than a meter away and examined me from head to toe. Even though age was beginning to wrinkle his face and thin his hair, there was something childlike about his gaze.

"Good afternoon," I repeated. "Are you Danilo?"

He didn't react and continued scrutinizing me. I was about to say something else when I noticed his face contorting into a smile that was missing a front tooth. His eyes rested on mine with a peaceful expression.

"You came back!" he exclaimed, pulling me into a hug. "I thought I was never going to see you again."

With that gesture, and the way he spoke, his strength and childish expression made sense. I suddenly understood why Sosa had referred to him as the town's special kid.

Danilo's comment made me wonder, for the first time, if my uncle Fernando and I maybe looked alike. I debated whether or not to tell him he was mistaken.

"Look how well I kept your grass up," he said, pointing at the layer of green that surrounded the hotel and the house on the other edge of the property.

"It's beautiful, yes," I answered. "Did you mow it yourself?"

"Yes," he answered proudly, pounding his chest once with his fist without looking up from the ground. He was looking at the grass as if he were searching for something.

"Thank you very much."

Danilo's answer was merely a grunt and another stomp on the ground. He rubbed his foot into the ground like someone putting out a cigarette.

"Ants," he said. "They're very dangerous."

I squatted down to look at the grass. I managed to find one. It was black, medium-sized, and looked like an ant.

"Do they bite?" I asked, pointing at it.

Danilo's dirty, beaten shoe came down hard, half an inch from my finger.

"Worse than that. Much worse."

I stood back up and decided to change the subject.

"I wanted to thank you for keeping the grass looking so good."

Danilo clicked his tongue and gave me another hug. Once he pulled away, he kept one of his calloused hands on my nape.

"If my friend Fernando asks me to take care of the hotel, I take care of it," he said, looking me in the eyes. He seemed overwhelmed with joy to see me.

"Did you care about Fernando a lot?"

"I still do," he corrected me, patting me on the back. "Do you have candy?"

"No, sorry. I don't," I replied, feeling around in my pockets.

"Fernando used to give me candy," he said, disappointed.

"Danilo, I'm not Fernando."

"You're not... because Fernando gave me candy. People don't give out candy anymore, you know? The other day I got a bunch and wanted to give some to a boy at the park. His mother told him he shouldn't talk to strangers and took him away. The world's an uglier place than before."

Boy was he right. As a kid, I'd also had a generous candy provider. It was a man in a wheelchair we used to call Don Quixote, because of his long moustache and pointy beard. I was maybe seven or eight, and my best friend was Pau Roig, who was like a brother to me at the time, but I never saw or missed him again afterwards. Don Quixote would park his wheelchair by the school gate and watch us play during recess. Then, when the bell was about to ring, he'd throw us a handful of candy that Pau and I would pick up as if it were treasure.

"I also had someone who used to give me candy," I said. "But you can't do that anymore. There's a lot of bad people in the world."

"Fernando was so nice. When we were building the hotel, he'd give me a tooooon of candy," he said, making a broad gesture with his hands.

"You helped Fernando build this hotel?"

Danilo looked at me, a combination of surprise and hurt, like you might look at a friend who just punched you in the gut.

"You don't remember?"

"It's been a long time," I apologized. "Jog my memory. What did you do? Carry the stones? Cut the wood?"

"I scared away the ants."

"That's right," I snapped my fingers. "You scared away the ants."

"The ants eat wood."

As far as I knew, those were termites, but I chose not to contradict him.

"Have you taken a look inside to see if there's any ants?"

My question made him stiffen up.

"You can't go in."

"Why not?"

"Fernando said you can't go in. And I watch over."

"You watch over the hotel so that no one can get in?"

Danilo nodded proudly.

"How long have you been watching over it?"

"Mmmmm. A long time. There wasn't anything here," he said, waving towards the low, fancy constructions across the road, each one of them boasting signs that read *hotel, inn, lodge, bed & breakfast*, and every similar name for a place where you could rent a bed.

"Thank you so much for keeping an eye on it, Danilo. As it's been such a long time, I'm going in, ok?"

"You can't go in!" he insisted, squaring up in front of me.

I raised my hand as a sign of peace. It would be best to come back when he wasn't there.

"Ok. If it's not possible, I won't go in. Whatever you say, Danilo."

Danilo nodded. I said goodbye and held my hand out, which he shook with the strength of a hydraulic press.

On his way back to his spot on the porch, he killed another ant.

CHAPTER 11

The next day, after waiting for the locksmith for three hours, I received a text from Sosa saying that the guy's car had broken down half-way to us and the tow truck was taking him back to El Calafate. He told me not to worry, that the men at the gas station had gotten another guy that was coming in a couple of days. I paced from one end of my small porch to the other with the phone in my hand, trying to think of the most diplomatic way to explain to Sosa that, having flown across the planet, I wasn't going to wait two more days for a man to come and pick the lock in five minutes.

I stopped beside the metal barbecue Macario had brought me. I lifted the top. Sitting on the grease-covered grill, I found a half-used bag of charcoal and a small iron shovel used to move the coals around.

I scanned the area. The two cabins next to mine were closed. The only person in sight, a young tourist leaning against the reception wall, was entranced by her phone. Discreetly, I headed toward the main street with the shovel in my hand.

I crossed paths with only a couple of tourists in the two hundred meters that separated El Relincho from the Montgrí Hotel. At two p.m., most people were still hiking.

I guessed Danilo had taken a lunch break because his chair on the porch was empty. I circled the property trying not to make myself too visible from Sosa's place.

The hotel was a rectangle. One of the shorter sides, opposite the main entrance, was covered by some willows. I jumped over the low fence and sprinted across my own property as if I were a common criminal until I was hidden by the trees.

The back wall was made of solid rock and cement, with a sturdy door and a small window next to it. According to the floor plan, both openings led to the hallway that connected the eight bedrooms. I tried to force the door open with the shovel, but it was so embedded in its frame that I couldn't find a space to lodge the shovel in for leverage.

After several failed attempts, I moved my focus to the window. It was small and high up, almost a skylight. It didn't take long to find a space between the irregular stone wall and the window shutter. I inserted the shovel's iron handle in and pulled. The hinges came loose with a screeching sound that made my teeth hurt. Once the shutter was open, I broke the glass and put my jacket on the frame to avoid cutting myself. I'd always seen people do that in movies.

I'm heavy, big boned, and never found joy in climbing. That's to say it was no mean feat for me to climb up that wall and shimmy through the window. Inside, as if it had been waiting for me, was a small table with a lamp on it that promised to aid my descent. Upside down, with my hands on the table, I edged down until I was hanging from the tops of my feet.

It wasn't elegant or quiet. Once I had freed one foot, the table buckled under my weight and I crashed onto the floor with the grace of a sack of potatoes.

I stood up surrounded by a cloud of dust and walked down the long hallway towards the reception area, passing the closed bedroom doors on each side of me.

As I moved forward, the little light that seeped through the broken window, grew weaker and weaker. The footprints my shoes left on the thick layer of dust confirmed Danilo's words: no one had been in there in a long time.

At the end of the hallway, I crossed the doorway into the large room that doubled as a dining room and reception area. The thin beams of light that filtered through the dried-out shutters gave it an eerie look. I could just make out the reception desk and some leather chairs placed around a coffee table. On top of it sat a teacup and a spoon. Had they not been covered by the same layer of dust as everything else, I would have thought someone had just drunk a cup of tea while sitting in one of the armchairs.

The ceiling bulged and was covered with dark stains. One of the glass windows was shattered. The same dust that covered the shards of glass on the floor was as thick as that which coated the furniture. That window had been broken at the same time the hotel had been abandoned.

It amazes me how human beings can adapt so fluidly the second there's a ton of money involved. A few days back I was remodeling apartments in Barcelona and now there I was, breaking and entering, Mission-Impossible-style, analyzing broken glass like they did on the CSI episodes I watched as a teenager.

A swinging door on one side of the reception led me to the kitchen which was pitch black. With the help of my phone's flashlight, I distinguished stainless steel surfaces, an industrial oven and an enormous fridge.

I retraced my steps back to the hallway that opened onto the bedrooms. There were four doors on each side. The ones on the left had odd numbers, the ones on the right, even.

I opened the first one. The flashlight shone on a queen-sized bed with a maroon comforter on it. Beside it was an empty closet. The next room looked exactly like the first. When I opened the third room, it was also the same, except for the fact that the bed was unmade. Aside from that detail, each bedroom appeared to be as dark, dusty and empty as the one before.

By the time I opened room number seven, I already knew what to expect. However, I was faced with a very different scenario.

On top of the bed lay an old man, staring at the ceiling.

"Hello?" I said.

His only answer was a moan, a sort of whisper I couldn't make out.

I shone the flashlight around the rest of the room. We were alone.

"Hello," I said again, but this time there was no answer.

Without crossing the threshold, I scanned the body from head to toe, following the beam of light. He was lying on the sheets, dressed and with his shoes on. His arms were skinny sticks covered with weathered skin. Even from where I was stood in the dark, I noticed his protruding cheekbones and sunken eyes.

I took a step toward him and he made the sound again. This time it seemed more like a sort of wheeze, as if he were having difficulty breathing.

Once I was beside him and could see his face clearly; his skin was dry and stiff like leather. Where there should have been eyes, there were empty holes.

That wasn't the face of a very old person, it was the face of someone who had been dead for many years.

I recoiled and my back crashed into something. The closet door? Before I could turn around and find out, I heard the moan again and took off running at full speed.

I reached the end of the hallway, desperately climbed up the small table and jumped out the window. I didn't care that I left it open or that anyone might see me running like a maniac. All I cared about was getting out of that place.

I looked back only once. Just for a second, but it was long enough to distinguish a person hiding behind a tree, looking at me.

CHAPTER 12

I spent over two hours in the tiny police department at the town entrance. An officer ten years younger than me took my statement, while his partner went to the hotel to verify that, there was indeed a dead man inside.

"So, you entered the hotel unauthorized."

"I'm the owner."

"But is it in your name?"

"Not yet, but I inherited it."

"So you entered private property that does not belong to you."

"Is that important right now? There's a dead man inside."

"Everything is important, Mr. Cucurell."

When the police officer returned from the hotel, she looked pale. She spoked in a slow voice, glancing between her partner and me.

"There's a body. His clothes have a dark stain on the stomach. It looks like a homicide from years ago."

I didn't recall the stain, although granted, I'd only been beside the body for a total of three nanoseconds.

"Mr. Cucurell," continued the officer, "We're going to call our partners at the forensics unit. Don't go back into the hotel until we authorize it."

"You don't need to worry about that."

I wasn't going back in there even if someone promised me that in room number eight –the only one I hadn't opened– Scarlett Johansson was waiting for me.

"In the meantime, we're going to guard the door to prevent any more curious people from entering."

"I'm the owner of the property, not some curious bystander."

"Sign your statement and you're free to go," her partner told me, handing me the typed version of my report.

I read it, signed it, and rose from my chair.

"Where are you going now?" the female officer enquired.

"To El Relincho. I'm staying there."

"I'll escort you."

"No need, I know the way."

"It's not a problem. I'm headed in the same direction."

The woman directed her colleague to call forensics and we left the police station. I walked with my hands in my pockets, the afternoon air cool on my face.

"I'd estimate the people from forensics will be here in about five hours. Ten, at the most," the officer announced.

"Are they coming from El Calafate?"

"If they have the necessary personnel and equipment, yes. If not, from Gallegos."

"Isn't Río Gallegos 500 kilometers from here?"

"Correct," she replied as if I'd said 'five' and not 'five hundred'.

"I guess you don't find something like this every day in such a quiet town."

"If we confirm that the person was murdered, it would be Chalten's first homicide."

"The first in the town's history?"

"Yes. The biggest issue we have here are drunk tourists. But there are only a few, because the people who come here usually like hiking, climbing, those kinds of healthy lifestyle things."

I was really making a name for myself. Any moment now, they were going to replace the bronze bust in the main square with one of me. When we reached Hotel Montgrí, the woman pointed at the main entrance, now wide open.

"Well, I'm stopping here," she said. "Sorry for the damage, I had to open the door with a crowbar."

"Don't worry about it."

I spent the rest of the afternoon in bed, thinking of that dead man while I searched the internet. For the umpteenth time, I failed to find any reference whatsoever to Hotel Montgrí or Fernando Cucurell online. I couldn't remember the last time I'd had that frustrating feeling that Google simply didn't know the answer to my question. The Montgrí had closed almost thirty years ago, long before we posted and shared our important –or not so important– moments online.

I went back out at quarter to ten that night. Both town supermarkets – 'Don't compare prices, they belong to the same owner,' Macario had told me– closed at ten and I didn't have anything to eat. There was one practically in front of my cabin, but I decided to go to the other one, a bit further away, to have an excuse to walk by the hotel.

A bright light shone through the open door, though no one was in sight. A white van was parked in front, the words *Santa Cruz Police. Forensic Division* printed on its side. The constant purring of the electric generator that illuminated the interior of the Montgrí interrupted the night's silence.

I noticed a figure walking towards the hotel with determined strides. I recognized her when she stopped at the door and the light illuminated her face. It was Laura, Rodolfo Sosa's employee. She looked both ways, ducked under the plastic tape that blocked the entrance, and walked into the Montgrí.

Determined to discover what she was doing there, I too ducked under the police tape and stepped into the reception area. I peered into the hallway where the bedrooms were. It was empty. A bright beam of light poured out of room number seven. I decided that my best option would be to stroll over there with some excuse, but before I was able to move, I heard a man raise his voice and two shadows were cast into the hallway. They were leaving the room. Instinctively, I hid behind the reception desk.

I heard footsteps getting closer.

"How can I make myself any clearer, Laura? You can't be in here and you know it. What the hell do you want?" asked a man whose voice I didn't recognize. I estimated he was less than five meters from where I was hiding.

"What do you think I want?" Sosa's employee replied.

"Laura, this isn't a game. I'm working."

"I can see that. And from what I can tell..."

The voices moved further away, towards the hotel door. I wasn't able to make out the rest of the conversation, but I did catch its end because Laura shouted the last sentences.

"Are you serious? After everything I've done for you? Go to hell, Ricardo. Go straight to hell."

A few seconds later, Ricardo's footsteps made the wooden floorboards creak again. Before he entered the hallway, I was able to distinguish *FORENSICS* written on the back of his vest.

I remained hidden behind the desk for a few more minutes. When I left the hotel, Laura was nowhere to be seen.

I headed towards the supermarket but hadn't managed to walk 50 meters before someone yelled my name from behind.

CHAPTER 13

I turned around to see Rodolfo Sosa walking towards me with a smile that looked fake even in the dim light coming from the lamp posts.

"Julián, how are you?"

"I'm okay. Well, as okay as one can be after something like this," I said, gesturing towards the hotel.

He shook his head and gave me a condescending grin.

"Didn't I tell you not to break in?"

"What are you insinuating? That you knew there was a body in there?"

"No. But if you'd waited for the locksmith and gone in with me, we could have filed the report together, spoken to my contacts in Río Gallegos, and tried to get through this with as little fuss as possible. Keep it contained, if you know what I mean."

"Keep it contained?"

Without losing his smile, the mayor let out a sigh as long as my day had been. He pointed his thumb behind him.

"Tomorrow, journalists from all over the province are going to show up. And with a bit of bad luck, we'll have the national press swarming here in a week. I think I already mentioned that we live on tourism. A tourist murdered in a hotel doesn't help us very much, even if he's been in there for thirty years."

For me, on the other hand, it was terrific news.

"How do you know it was a tourist?"

Sosa closed his eyes and shook his head.

"That's irrelevant."

"What do you mean it's irrelevant?"

"It's confidential information. What matters is that in Chaltén, we follow certain rules. Peace and quiet are what puts food on our table. You can't just barge in and destroy everything like a bull in a china shop."

"Careful with what you say. I have nothing to do with this scandal. One way or another, that hotel was going to get opened and the body was going to be discovered."

"I understand," he said and gave me his classic hand-on-the-shoulder move. It felt heavier than usual this time. "But you have to try to understand. I'm nervous. No one has been in there in years, and now you go in and find this."

"Are you sure no one's been in there in years?"

"Danilo would have noticed and said something. He tells me the story of every ant he kills."

"He guards the hotel a little too closely, don't you think?"

"No, Julián, stop. There's no way he had anything to do with this. The only thing Danilo is capable of killing is ants."

"I'm not accusing him. I just want to know why he's so hell-bent on taking care of the hotel."

"Like I told you, I wasn't in Chaltén when it was built or when it was running. Danilo says Fernando asked him to keep watch for him. People say your uncle cared very much for him, and Danilo reciprocated that care."

"He told me that too."

Sosa huffed as if he were having trouble finding the right words.

"Danilo is different," he finally said. "He has the intellect of an eight-year-old. In a community like ours, you help a person like him."

"Of course."

"What I mean is, even though it's your hotel, you have to understand, that in thirty years no one has ever told Danilo he can't sit on the porch, mow the lawn, or kill the ants. He even painted the fence a couple of times. Last time, I personally got him the varnish through the town hall."

Another favor thrown at me without my asking.

"He spends hours a day on that porch, Julián. The Montgrí Hotel is his life, and if it weren't for him, at some point, someone would have broken in and caused some damage. I know you can't see it, but Danilo did you a favor."

"I understand. But why are you telling me all of this?"

"So that you won't suspect him."

CHAPTER 14

Finding a dead body leaves you little time for paperwork. The visit to the town hall I'd planned for Monday, for example, was moved to Tuesday morning.

The town hall looked very different from how it had on Saturday afternoon, when Sosa had secretly opened up for me. For starters, there were more vehicles in the parking lot. Did people seriously move around in cars in such a small town?

At the reception desk, the secretary interrupted her conversation with a man she was assisting to speak to me.

"Good morning. How can I help you?"

"My name is Julián Cucurell..."

"Ah, yes. You're here to see Margarita?"

Great. By this point, even the town hall receptionist knew the name of the Spaniard who'd inherited the Montgrí Hotel with a dead person inside.

"Rodolfo told me you might stop by today," she added, opening a door beside her desk. "Come on in."

The hallway that had been dark and still three days back, was now brightly illuminated by hospital lighting and flooded with voices coming from the doors on each side. I made out two conversations about soccer and one about food. It seemed that the work ethic of civil servants was the same the world over.

When I walked past Sosa's office, I saw through the crack of the door that he was in a meeting with another man. The girl signaled for me to keep walking until almost the end of the hallway and pointed at an office where I was greeted by a middle-aged woman with dark skin and a perfect smile.

"Margarita, this is Julián Cucurell," said the receptionist.

"Julián! Welcome. I was waiting for you."

She spoke as if she knew me. I smiled and sat down in the chair across the desk from her as the receptionist left and closed the door behind her.

"I think I know why you're here, but why don't you tell me anyway? How can I help you?"

"You see, I'm the new owner of the Montgrí Hotel."

"Oh, we all know that. You're famous around town."

"I'm glad. I've always wanted to know what Antonio Banderas feels like when he walks down the street."

Against all odds, Margarita laughed at my joke.

"I came to see you because Rodolfo Sosa thought you might be able to provide me more information about the hotel."

The woman smiled and picked up one of the dozen folders that sat on her desk.

"I printed out everything I could find in our system for you. I'm sure there's more in the physical archive, but finding something there takes much longer."

There were merely two sheets of paper in the folder.

"Let me explain. This report is called a commercial form. It's a sort of ID with information from every business in town. See? 'Hotel Montgrí. Owner: Fernando Cucurell. Address: San Martín, no number, between Huemul and Los Cóndores. Operation initiation: September 1, 1990. Operation end: does not apply.'"

"What does 'does not apply' mean? The hotel's been abandoned for years."

"Yes, but the system presents it like that because no one ever requested its suspension, nor did it get automatically suspended because of fiscal debt. The other file I printed out for you is the tax payment summary. It starts in 2002 because that's when we implemented the digital system here at the town hall. As you can see, all taxes are up to date. Like clockwork, we get a wire transfer every year."

Her lilac-colored fingernail traced the column on the right, which showed the amount that corresponded to each tax year. The increasing numbers were my first encounter with the rampant inflation everyone talked about in Argentina. Every year, taxes went up twenty or thirty percent compared to the year before.

"Who makes the payments?"

The woman pointed at the page header, where I read *Fernando Cucurell. P.O. box 108. 9405. El Calafate, Santa Cruz. Argentina.*

"The system creates the invoice automatically and we forward it to the owner. In this case, since the option for electronic invoices isn't selected, we mail it."

"Let me see if I'm getting this right. Every year you send an invoice to this address, in my uncle's name, and someone pays the hotel's taxes?"

"Exactly. The last payment, for this year's taxes, was two months ago."

Two months. My uncle had been dead for four.

"I suppose you can't tell me who makes those payments."

"Of course not," she answered, crossing her arms. "That's confidential information."

Before she finished the sentence, she was already smiling and gave me a wink. She then turned the second file towards me, showing me a yellow Post-it with a very long number handwritten on it.

"Thank you."

"For now, that's all I can do to help. If you need more information, as I mentioned, we can look through the physical archive. But it's a labyrinth of boxes that no one comes out of alive."

I thanked Margarita and left her office with the thin folder under my arm. When I walked past Sosa's office again, the door was open. The man he'd been with before had left. The mayor focused on his phone and didn't notice my presence until I was standing at his desk. It felt odd to see him wearing a shirt and tie.

"Julián! I see you're up early. How are you?"

His smile didn't show any trace of the slightly tense conversation we'd had the day before.

"Still a bit anxious from yesterday."

"I can imagine. How'd it go with Margarita?" he asked, pointing at the folder under my arm.

"Good. She gave me some very useful information."

"I'm glad. You know we're here to help with anything you need."

CHAPTER 15

After lunch, with an empty afternoon ahead of me, I decided to follow the motto that kept me centered.

"Sorrows become more manageable with exercise," I said out loud.

Following Macario's recommendation, I went up to the Cóndores lookout. It was a spot that had a view of the entire town, and the point where the two rivers met at the foot of the mountain. I did my push-ups looking at the best view I'd ever had during a workout. If it weren't for the clouds, I would've seen the Fitz Roy too.

Around ten p.m., there was a knock on my cabin door. I opened it thinking it would be Macario, but it was Sosa's employee Laura, the first enemy I'd made in El Chaltén.

"Can I come in?" she said without greeting me.

"I'm about to go to bed."

"That's not a good idea while your fire is still lit. It's dangerous," she said, pointing at the fireplace. "And anyway, I'm here to tell you something important."

Without opening it, she showed me a fabric bag that hung from her shoulder, as if it meant something to me. Her strategy worked because I moved aside to let her in.

"I think we have to leave our conversation from the other day behind us," she said in a practical tone as if she were talking about the weather.

"I think that's a good idea. It would be pointless to continue it," I said, and extended my hand. "My name is Julián Cucurell."

"I know. I'm Laura Badía," she answered, giving it a firm shake. Then, she took off her coat, hung it by the door, and sat down.

"Badía is a Catalan name."

"I also know that. I'm here to ask for a favor."

"Lately, I'm more open to receiving favors than doing them."

She pulled out a ring from her pants pocket and placed it on the table.

"Look. Look closely. Do you recognize it?"

It was a silver-plated signet ring. Judging by its size, probably a man's. It bore the head of a wolf baring its teeth. The level of detail was impressive. The wolf's muzzle had a crease where it retracted its lips behind perfectly detailed teeth, despite the design's minuscule size.

"It rings a bell," I said. "But I don't know where from."

"From the body you found. It wore a ring just like this one."

"No, it can't be from there. As soon as I saw the dead body I ran. I didn't stay around to look at his fingers."

"Sometimes it only takes a fraction of a second for our subconscious to register something."

I shrugged. I knew as much about the subconscious as my mother did about cooking.

"Tomorrow they're going to tell you that the body you found in the hotel has been there for approximately thirty years."

"Thirty years? Shouldn't it be rotten?"

"In ninety-nine percent of cases, yes. But with low temperatures and a dry environment, body tissue can become mummified. Without bacteria to decompose it, it dehydrates slowly."

What was with Sosa's employee? Horses, the subconscious, and mummies. Who was she? Indiana Jones's Argentine sister?

"They're also going to tell you that, aside from cuts on one hand and a cut on the groin, the body had a wound on its abdomen and another in its lumbar area, those are likely the ones that resulted in death. Due to the advanced mummification process, they still don't know if these two wounds are where a bullet entered and exited the body, or if they are two individual wounds from a knife."

"Are you with the police?"

She made a sour face.

"Not anymore. But I was for twelve years."

Her argument with the man from Forensics inside the hotel was beginning to make more sense.

"Let me get this right. You're here to tell me what the police are going to tell me tomorrow."

"No. I'm here to ask you a favor."

"What favor?"

"When the police finish their work, I want to go into the hotel before you touch anything. I need to see where the body was, I need you to tell me what position you found him in and any details you remember."

"I saw that body for less than a minute."

"Something always remains in our memory," she said, pointing at the ring.

"Look," I said, raising my hands in the air. "Why don't you explain exactly who you are and what your connection is with this dead man? Then I'll decide whether or not to help you."

"It's a long story."

"I have time."

Laura Badía pulled a pile of loose papers, held together by a golden clip, from her fabric bag. They were new, fresh off the printer. She turned them towards me, so I could read the only line printed on the first page.

The Glacier Murders.

PART II

THE GLACIER MURDERS

CHAPTER 16

About five meters long, a small, inflatable Zodiac floats in the frozen lake. Next to the catamaran –now devoid of tourists– it looks like a duckling swimming beside its mother.

Our diver is geared up in her drysuit beneath which she wears a thick layer of warm clothes. In her nearly thirty years working for the Argentinian Navy, this will be her fifth dive under ice. She puts her vest on, then her air tank. She connects the hose to the drysuit. She breathes a few times into the regulator to make sure everything is okay.

She makes eye contact with her partner, a diver who, though twenty years her junior, has enough experience to carry out what they are about to do. They both nod. Before jumping into the water, they inspect the surface around the Zodiac to make sure there are no chunks of ice nearby. After all, they're only fifty meters from an iceberg the size of a truck. Ten trucks, if you count the part that's underwater.

She dives backwards. She feels the water on her cheeks, the only exposed part of her body. It's so cold it hurts.

She pops her head above the surface and sees her partner floating a few meters away. They swim toward the iceberg slowly, as if approaching a sleeping beast.

A chunk of ice that breaks off a glacier has an irregular, haphazard shape. As it melts, that shape changes and makes the iceberg rotate. The sudden movement of three thousand tons of ice destroy anything in its path.

They submerge. Visibility is poor. Four meters, at most. Beyond that, the iceberg's rounded edges disappear into the deep blue.

They explore the ice inch by inch, shining their flashlights on it. Two days ago, a group of tourists who were on the same catamaran that now waits for them, discovered a frozen body –Lord knows whose– on one of the faces of the Viedma Glacier. After thirty-two hours under constant surveillance by the Argentinian Navy, the chunk of ice that contained the body broke off into the water. Twenty-four hours later, it was far enough from the glacier edge so that diving near it wasn't a suicide mission.

This is the iceberg our diver is inspecting.

She feels a tug on her sleeve. Her partner has found a reddish stain that gets darker further down. Bad news. The further down they go, the riskier their task becomes.

Fifteen meters in, they find the source of the trace. Just like they had seen in pictures, there's a body in a fetal position, dressed in hiking clothes, frozen inside the iceberg. Our diver can't help but touch its face. It's as hard as any other part of the ice. It is part of the ice.

She looks at her partner who nods and reaches into the bag hanging from his waist, pulling out a pick and a hammer. She does the same and they get to work. Their goal is to remove the body from the iceberg, like a rotten part of an apple.

Sound travels faster through water; our diver hears each blow of the hammer against the pick as if it were inside her head.

After twenty-one minutes underwater, her partner signals her, rubbing his hands on his shoulders. He's cold. She won't last much longer either before she starts shivering. She nods and points her thumb up at the surface. It's time to go up

She nails the end of a rope to the ice and inflates a buoy to the other end. The long, red balloon floats up to the surface. It will signal the divers that relieve them exactly where the body is, as long as the iceberg doesn't move too much and cuts it loose.

When they get back on the catamaran, the support team gives them hot coffee. Our diver wishes she had a flask of brandy on hand.

An hour later, the teammates that relieved them come back up to the surface and it's our diver's turn to dive back down. According to them, there's very little work left.

She and her partner re-enter the icy water. They descend together, following the rope down the iceberg. Once they reach the body, she sees the other team has done flawless work. They removed the ice that surrounded the body everywhere except the left side which is now the only part attached to the iceberg. They won't take long to release it.

With each blow against the pick, fear runs through our diver's body. It's impossible to gauge how delicate the balance that makes the iceberg float in that position is. Breaking off a piece is extremely risky.

Seven minutes later, the body comes loose and floats up to the surface with a large piece of ice frozen to its side, like a rock defying gravity.

The diver's worst nightmare suddenly becomes a reality: the iceberg tries to restore equilibrium and rotates. The ledge they've been working under now traps and pushes them towards the deep, like an enormous shovel moving two tiny pebbles. There's nothing they can do. The ice will do with them what it wills. As it pushes them further down, our diver hears a ringing in her ears. The change in pressure is too abrupt, but broken eardrums are the least of her problems. The main one is that she could die.

The iceberg's rotation stops as suddenly as it started. It's found balance again. Our diver signals at her partner that they need to out of there as fast as possible, but he grabs her arm and points at the cave they just carved out.

A few centimeters beneath the surface of the ice, there is another human face.

There's more than one body in the iceberg.

CHAPTER 17

I skimmed the draft of *The Glacier Murders*. Laura Badía was writing a book. A book with horrific photos that punctuated the monotonous text every once in a while. I flipped to the last page.

"It's gonna take me a while to read 293 pages. I'm usually the kind of person who waits for the movie to come out."

"I'll summarize it. A year and a half ago, two bodies appeared in the Viedma glacier, both wearing this identical ring. They were frozen in the ice, hard as rocks. Guess how long ago they estimate they had died."

"Thirty years ago?"

"Thirty years ago."

"Who were they?"

"No one knows. The police never identified them. They're still at the Río Gallegos morgue."

"Let me get this straight," I said, pressing my finger on the printed pages. "You think the dead man I found in the hotel is connected to the two that showed up frozen in a glacier?"

"Exactly."

"And all this because of a ring?"

"The ring confirms it, but there are other clues. Look," Laura flipped through the pages until she found a photograph that showed pants, shirts, and boots laid out on a table. "These are the clothes that the bodies they found in the ice, were wearing. They're typical tourist clothes from the 90s, high-end international brands. Your body had similar clothes."

My body. I didn't like that one bit.

"Who are you? A CSI script writer?"

"I used to work for the Santa Cruz Police Forensics Department for many years. I left the force and came to live here."

"Right, and now you investigate crimes on your own, as a hobby. Nothing weird about that."

Laura shook her head.

"I worked as a consultant on the glacier bodies case for a while. They never managed to solve it because the police have more urgent problems than two bodies from thirty years ago."

"From what I heard, in a place like this, the police don't have much work."

"But in the rest of the province, they do. Chaltén might look like Switzerland, the same as Calafate, but those are exceptions. The reality in the rest of Santa Cruz, without the constant flow of tourist dollars, is very different."

"Got it. The police didn't pay much attention to it."

"Only as much as was required, but not much more. To me, on the other hand, it became a sort of obsession. I've been writing about this for over a year, though I sometimes think that with the information I have, a book would raise more questions than answers. Or at least, that was the case until now. With what you found, it's a completely different story. Understand?"

"Not really."

"These people disappeared thirty years ago, around 1990. Does that year ring a bell?"

"Well, no."

"Sosa says that when he got here in '92, the hotel was already closed."

"Yes, he told me that."

"Did you already go to the town hall to get the hotel documents?"

"Yes."

"Then I imagine you've seen that the floor plan was presented in 1987."

Damn. The woman had done her research.

"A hotel like that isn't built from one day to the next," she said. "Let's say they took a year to build it. That means it was open, between 1988 and 1991."

"Operations started in 1990," I told her.

"Even shorter. From 1990 to 1991."

Laura raised her chin, a sort of invitation for me to fit the last piece of the puzzle.

"You think my uncle had something to do with these murders."

"He at least knew something. He never mentioned anything about the hotel or Chaltén?"

I shook my head no. I picked up the ring from the table and toyed with it. I even tried it on several fingers. It fit best on my index.

"How did you get this?" I asked.

"When I saw that the interest in the case was waning and had the idea to start writing a book, I got a copy made in alpaca. The originals are silver."

Laura returned to her manuscript and looked for the photo of the victim's rings. They were exactly the same as the one I held, except for the fact that the silver from the original rings had tarnished over time, and Laura's was shiny. In one of the photos, I saw that the rings had an inscription on the inside of the band. I took mine off and there it was.

"*Lupus occidere uiuendo debet*," I read out loud.

"It's Latin. It means 'The wolf must kill in order to live'."

"The wolf must kill in order to live," I repeated.

"What happened to your uncle? How did he die?"

"I don't know. We weren't very close."

"But someone from your family must have told you something."

I didn't answer. I stared at her, determined to demand an explanation of who Fernando Cucurell had been, from my father the next time we spoke.

"So, there's no question that the dead man from the hotel is linked to the two who died frozen in the glacier?" I asked.

"Not frozen."

"You said they were hard as a rock."

"They were frozen, but that wasn't their cause of death. They were murdered."

CHAPTER 18

Laura. Eighteen months earlier.

The last time Laura Badía had been in a morgue was a year ago, during Julio Ortega's autopsy. After everything that happened, she couldn't rejoin the force. Solving the case that the press had called *The Arrow Collector* had cost Laura her job.

Now, the badge that hangs from her neck reads *External Consultant*. She might not be a police officer anymore, but she is still one of the best criminal investigators in Patagonia. That's why they have called her.

The body is still on the autopsy table in the Río Gallegos morgue since being brought in from El Chaltén forty-eight hours ago. At first glance, it looks the same, but Laura knows it's no longer as hard as a frozen chicken. When the navy officials had placed it on the steel table, the body sounded like a marble statue.

"Shall we get started?" asks the medical examiner, the only other person in the morgue apart from herself.

"Yes. Give me a minute to put my gloves on."

"That won't be necessary. I request that you limit yourself to observing."

Laura nods. Damn, she misses working with Doctor Luis Guerra. After helping him with dozens of autopsies, it feels odd to just watch. But she's no longer a police officer, Dr. Vargas isn't Guerra, and Río Gallegos isn't Puerto Deseado.

The doctor speaks in a loud voice so that her words are recorded clearly on the phone she's wearing in her chest pocket.

"The deceased arrived at the morgue in a frozen state. Forty-eight hours later, the autopsy is begun. The body was found attached to an iceberg that detached from the Viedma glacier, fully dressed. It presents with a wound to the abdominal area."

Doctor Vargas undresses the body with incredible dexterity. She never comes close to needing any assistance.

Laura notices the hole in its stomach. She's seen too many holes like that to mistake it for anything else. It's a bullet wound.

"He has goosebumps on his torso and limbs," she observes.

"Correct," the doctor replies. "It's likely that the gunshot didn't kill him immediately and he developed hypothermia before dying."

Doctor Vargas continues with her routine work, examining every inch of the body.

"They must have shot him on the ice," states Laura. "If they'd killed him anywhere else and then thrown him on the glacier, the ice surrounding him wouldn't have been as stained as the photos indicate."

Doctor Vargas peers at her over her glasses, as if looking at some kind of freak. Maybe she's realizing that Laura isn't there to hinder her.

When she finishes with the first body, the doctor asks Laura to help her place it back in the refrigerator and, after cleaning the autopsy table, they take the second body out. This time, the conclusion is different: death from head trauma.

"I agree with you, miss Badía," the medical examiner tells her when she finishes the second autopsy.

"On what?"

"They didn't dump the bodies on the ice, they killed them on the glacier. They don't have many wounds aside from the fatal ones. I'd say they walked on their own to reach the place where they were murdered."

CHAPTER 19

I poured Laura a cup of chamomile tea and went back to skimming through the pages she'd brought me.

"Let's see if I've got this straight," I said. "The bodies of two people, who were shot to death, showed up inside a glacier."

"One had a gunshot wound. The other one's skull was broken."

"Could it have been that one killed the other and then committed suicide?"

"That theory hasn't been discarded, but it seems unlikely. The toxicology reports they wrote after the autopsy revealed that both of them had consumed diazepam, a common sedative, both back then and now. What's interesting is that the drug was found in their blood, but also in both of their stomachs. That indicates they had consumed it not long before they died."

"So maybe someone drugged them and took them there to kill them."

Laura smiled at me, almost patronizingly.

"Anything I say, you've thought of a thousand times, right?"

"Maybe not everything, but I do have a year and a half's head start. In general, when there are multiple homicides, the victims have the same cause of death. If it's a gunshot, they were all shot. If it's a knife wound, they were all stabbed. When you read loads of case studies, it's hard to find a double murder where one victim was killed with a gun, and the other from a blow to the head. It's not impossible, but it would be a statistical anomaly."

"Did you find out anything about the gunshot?"

"A .44 caliber projectile. Probably fired from a Winchester."

The hair on the back of my neck stood up.

"Sosa has a Winchester," I said.

Laura nodded.

"Sosa and half of the hunters in Patagonia. The 1892 Winchester is one of the most common rifles among families that have been in the region for several generations. Back then, you didn't need any permission to own a weapon and every family that lived in the countryside had one. They were necessary to hunt *guanacos* and scare away pumas. As time went by, laws became stricter and people had to declare those weapons, but not everyone did. There are numerous unidentified rifles in Patagonia. And before you ask, Sosa does have a permit."

I nodded, holding back the desire to continue elaborating on theories. Suggesting something about the glacier murders to Laura was like suggesting tips for Messi to score a penalty goal.

"Incredible," I said. "And they stayed there, frozen, for thirty years? I thought only prehistoric cavemen showed up frozen in ice."

Laura shook her head no.

"Do you have sugar?"

I pointed at the sugar bowl on the table.

"I'm going to need more than that."

"Well, you sure like your tea sweet," I said and grabbed the two-pound bag of sugar from the kitchen shelf.

Laura asked for another cup and filled it to the brim with sugar.

"After Antarctica and Greenland, the Patagonian ice field is the third largest frozen mass in the world. Imagine that the sugar in the cup is ice. There's no way for it to escape. It's been there, immobilized, since the last glacial period. But every winter, it snows."

Laura poured a little more sugar into the cup and a thin white thread spilled over the brim.

"That's a glacier. A river of ice that advances forward constantly as it snows up in the mountain."

"But they told me the Viedma glacier is retreating."

"That's a simplification. In reality, it's breaking faster than it grows, which is why the glacier front moves back every year. But if you stick a flag into the ice, you'll see it moves forward every day. The glacier ice can only move forward or melt, but never move backwards. The face of the glacier you can see today, is snow that fell on the mountains when Columbus reached America."

"So how could they have found tourists' bodies from thirty years ago in ice that's five hundred years old?"

"No, no. Five hundred years is how long it takes the snow that falls at the top of the glacier to move down the seventy kilometers to the lake. No one said the bodies started all the way up there. The glacier is like a funnel, it gets smaller as it moves forward. The only way for the same amount of ice to fit through a smaller space is for it to move faster. Close to the glacier front, the Viedma advances about one or two meters per day."

"So, thirty years ago, two tourists went walking on the Viedma, they were killed there and their bodies got stuck in the ice until the glacier spat them out last year."

"That is, at least, the story the glacier tells us."

"What do you mean?"

"That we don't know what we don't know. There might be three more bodies in the Viedma. The weapon, maybe even the murderer, could be there. There might be more clues trapped in the glacier, or they might have broken off before these bodies. The ice moves at its own pace and the chunks break off during the day, at night, with or without an audience. It was practically a miracle that there was a boat full of tourists right in front when that detachment revealed the first body. If it had happened six hours earlier, or later, we never would have found out."

My head was going a mile a minute. Killing three people would have been a good enough reason to abandon a brand new hotel.

"Why weren't the bodies ever identified?" I asked.

"Because what we know for certain, is very little. Two men in their thirties who died sometime between 1987 and 1992."

"Isn't there a register of missing people?"

Laura nodded and sipped on her tea.

"The Federal Police has one, but there are no correlations. If either of them was in the database, it would have identified them. The bodies are extremely well preserved and they were able to perform all types of tests: DNA, hair color, eye color, dental records, scars, fingerprints, etc."

"Can you run fingerprints on someone who's been dead thirty years?"

"If they're as well preserved as the ones from the glacier, you can, and also if they're mummified like yours."

"It's not mine."

"You know what I mean. The rehydration process is quite simple. Maybe we'll be lucky and they can identify this one. As far as the other two go, no one seems to have reported them missing."

"That's odd, isn't it?"

"Extremely. If it were one person, maybe. They could have been someone with no family. But there are two of them, and they aren't related by blood. It's almost impossible that neither of their families reported them as missing. If they were Argentinian, there should at least be a report filed to the Police from back then. And if they were foreigners, Foreign Affairs would have gotten the report through an embassy."

I sat in silence, going over all the information. She poured back the sugar from the cup into the bag.

"That's how far my manuscript goes," she added after a while. "I thought that maybe if there was a new clue, the ice was going to give it to us. I never thought it would come from a Spaniard who inherited the abandoned hotel next door to where I work."

She stood up and placed the bag of sugar back on the kitchen shelf. She took her coat off the hanger. I noticed her gaze settle on the threatening note which I had left on a shelf.

I took two strides forward to grab it, but she beat me to it.

"What's this?" she asked, reading the note. "When did you get it?"

"Three days ago. A few hours after I spoke with you."

"So, before you found the body."

"Yes."

"*Sell the hotel and go enjoy the money somewhere else. You are not welcome in El Chaltén,*" she read out loud. "Why didn't you tell me about it?"

"I barely know you, and you must agree, we didn't exactly get off to the best start. Also, you were the only person who knew who I was and why I was here."

"What time did you get this?"

"Around six or seven in the evening, when Sosa came to see me. He handed it to me himself. He said he'd found it under my door."

Laura closed her eyes and shook her head.

"By the time you got the threat, half the town knew who you were."

"What?"

"That morning when Sosa came back to the house, I told him you'd stopped by. It was Saturday, the day he gets together with his friends for lunch. There are about ten of them. I'm sure he told them about it during their lunch."

"You were there?"

Laura gave me a half smile.

"No, but I know my boss. He's a good guy but discretion isn't his strong suit. He can't keep his mouth shut. In a small town, news as big as the heir of the only abandoned hotel showing up travels at the speed of light. By seven p.m., a lot of people knew who you were."

"Fuck."

"Whoever wrote that doesn't want the truth to come out thirty years later."

"Or the exact opposite," I said.

"What do you mean?"

"I've examined that note for hours. Don't you find it a bit tame? It's like a poker player who shows one of his cards to throw you off. Couldn't they have left me that note precisely to get me to investigate?"

"That seems a bit far-fetched."

"Maybe. In any case, I'm not planning on doing what an anonymous note suggests. I want to know who my uncle was."

Laura frowned at what I had said.

"What are you talking about?"

I doubted whether to tell her or not. I didn't know her at all, but the manuscript she'd brought me had months, if not years of work behind it. At least she wasn't lying about that: she was investigating the glacier crimes.

"I didn't know that my father had a brother until they called me to tell me Fernando had died and I was his heir."

Of course that didn't satisfy Laura; she had a million questions. I told her the little I knew: where, how, and when Fernando Cucurell had died, his last wish about his ashes, and that my father hadn't heard from him for forty years.

"They're going to have to threaten me a bit more strongly to get me to leave without finding out who my uncle was, and most of all, why he abandoned the hotel thirty years ago. In the meantime, I'm going to keep asking. If it helps you with your book, you're welcome to join me."

Laura looked at me for a while sympathetically, as if she were wondering whether or not to tell me what was on her mind.

"What?" I asked.

"I'm going to be upfront because I hate lies."

"I got that the day we met."

"Look Julián, I'm a stubborn person. Too stubborn, sometimes. There's a chance that if I keep investigating the crimes, you won't like the outcome."

"You mean if it turns out my uncle killed those three tourists?".

"Yes."

"He was my uncle, but he wasn't part of my family. Like I said, my father stopped talking to him before I was even born. That's several years before these murders. If we find out that Fernando Cucurell was a monster, I don't care."

Without taking her eyes off the note, Laura sat down again.

"Did they tell you anything about the hotel's history at the Town Hall, aside from when it started operating?"

I nodded and placed the building map and the tax payment summary on the table.

"The woman at the Town Hall, Margarita, gave me this too," I showed her the Post-it stuck on the back of one of the pages. "I guess this is a bank account."

Laura examined the hand-written numbers.

"Yes, it's a CBU. It's a bank account number, the three first numbers determine the bank, and the next four determine the branch."

She took out her phone and transcribed the numbers.

"Zero, eight, six. Banco Santa Cruz. Nine, four, zero, five. The El Calafate branch office."

"The Town Hall sends the invoices to a mailbox in El Calafate," I mentioned. "I need to find out who that account belongs to. Is there a Santa Cruz Bank in El Chaltén?"

"It's the only one we have," Laura laughed. "It's at the town entrance."

"First thing tomorrow, I'm going to go ask. But I doubt they'll give me that information."

"It's open twenty-four hours."

"A bank that's open twenty-four hours?"

"It's not a bank. It's an ATM. The bank itself is in Calafate."

"You have to drive 200 kilometers to talk to someone?"

"220. Not only for the bank, for a hospital, for a notary... For basically everything. Welcome to Chaltén," she said, standing up and opening the door.

"Where are you going?"

"To the bank. Come on."

"Now? 220 kilometers?"

"Of course," she said, smiling.

"We're going to get there at midnight and they won't be open until tomorrow."

"Just follow me and stop asking so many questions."

We crossed the town. When we reached the end of the main avenue, where the small police station guarded the only entrance to El Chaltén and the street became a road, Laura burst out laughing.

"What's wrong with you?"

"You really thought we were going to Calafate?"

"You were lying? Why did you bring me here then?"

She pointed at a small square building resembling a shipping container with windows. The sign above it read *Banco Santa Cruz*. The logo, of course, was the famous Mount Fitz Roy which I had yet to see.

We walked into the small building that looked exactly like the ATMs in Barcelona, except that instead of having the bank office on the other side of the wall, it was two hours away.

"On Mondays, Wednesdays, and Fridays a bank employee from Calafate comes to restock the machines," said Laura as she walked up to one of the two ATMs.

She selected the option for *Cardless cash deposit* on the screen and then *Confirm*. The machine asked her to type in the CBU. After she typed out the numbers from the Post-it, the system displayed a message that Laura read out aloud.

"Verify that the information of the account you wish to deposit is correct. Holder: Estudio González-Ackerman S.R.L. Checking account in pesos."

Laura clicked *Cancel* and started typing into her phone.

"From what I can see, González-Ackerman is a law firm in Calafate."

"And all these years, they've paid the hotel's taxes?"

"Looks that way."

CHAPTER 20

The bus I'd taken in Chaltén at eight a.m. arrived at El Calafate at quarter to eleven. The González-Ackerman firm was in the city center, a fifteen-minute walk from the bus terminal. I decided to walk there and kill time until my eleven-thirty appointment.

Compared to El Chaltén, El Calafate felt more like a city. The main street was a combined landscape of bars, a casino, travel agencies offering visits to different glaciers, banks, souvenir shops, and restaurants displaying whole lambs roasting over fire. The type of tourist was also different. Older and heavier than in Chaltén. I guessed this had to do with making the effort of walking for hours to see something, rather than driving up to it with your car. It seemed that Sosa was right about Perito Moreno being a very democratic glacier.

When it was time, I headed towards González-Ackerman's offic. It was an elegant house made of wooden logs, on a quiet, residential street about two hundred meters from the main avenue.

"Good morning," a man my age greeted me from behind a desk.

"Good morning. I have an appointment at eleven thirty. I'm Julián Cucurell."

"Follow me please, Mr. Cucurell. Mrs. Ackerman is waiting for you."

The secretary walked me down a narrow hallway which ended in a door, he knocked lightly three times and opened it without waiting for an answer.

"Mrs. Ackerman, Mr. Cucurell."

The lawyer stood and walked around the desk to greet me. She was in her late fifties, with dyed blonde hair and skin far too tanned for a person living in such a cold place. She was very thin, with prominent cheekbones and wrinkles around her mouth. She gave off a strong scent –a combination of expensive perfume and cigarettes.

"Thank you, Marcelo," the lawyer said to her employee. She then shook my hand. "Welcome to Patagonia, Mr. Cucurell. Please, take a seat."

"Thank you very much."

I sat in a leather-upholstered chair that cost more than my entire living room.

"According to what Marcelo told me, you're the new owner of the Hotel Montgrí in Chaltén, correct?"

"Yes. I inherited it recently from Fernando Cucurell. I'm his nephew."

"I'm very sorry for your loss."

"Thank you."

"How can we help you?"

"I've been informed that your law firm has been paying the hotel's taxes for years."

"Who told you that?"

"Does it matter?" I said, placing a copy of the will on the table.

The woman took a few seconds to look over the file.

"I need to know who sends you the money to pay those taxes," I said.

The lawyer shook her head and gave me the exact smile I give the NGO volunteers to cut them off before they even start talking.

"Unfortunately, I can't help you with that, Mr. Cucurell."

"What do you mean?"

"That even if this photocopy, with seals that aren't valid in my country, were a true copy of an original will in your possession, I'm still not obligated to provide you with any information."

"But Fernando Cucurell was a client of yours, right? You pay the taxes."

"Your words. I cannot confirm nor deny them."

"This is ridiculous. My uncle is dead and all I want to know is where the money comes from."

The woman shrugged. I had a better chance of getting information from my uncle's ashes than from her.

"Why don't you want to help me?"

"What makes you think that? Wanting is one thing, being able to is another. I cannot reveal confidential information, Mr. Cucurell. Would you like it if your lawyer went around sharing your private information?"

"If I were dead, I wouldn't care."

The lawyer pressed her lips together in a tight smile and I knew she would not open them again. I stood up and left the office, holding back the urge to slam the door behind me.

CHAPTER 21

At seven p.m., Laura and I knocked at the door of the largest house on the property next to the Montgrí Hotel. Rodolfo Sosa opened the door in a button-down shirt, holding a yerba mate drink in his hand.

"The two of you together? This can't be good news," he said, motioning for us to come inside.

The house was both rustic and elegant. The thick log structure that supported the roof was exposed and blended in well with the brick walls. My mother would have approved.

"Do you want something to drink? Mate? Coffee?"

"If you're having mate, I'll drink with you," said Laura.

"Me too," I said, without revealing that I'd never tried the drink that Argentinians seemed so devoted to. They both looked at me oddly but didn't say anything.

We sat down at the kitchen table. You could see a low mountain ridge against a sky full of violet clouds through the window.

"What a great view for washing dishes," I said to break the ice.

"You never get tired of something like that," answered the mayor, handing Laura her mate. "It's different every day. And wait until you see it when it isn't cloudy. Behind that range is the Fitz Roy."

Laura drank her infusion in a few seconds and handed it back before speaking.

"Rodolfo, you can imagine why we're here," she said.

"I don't have to be a genius for that."

"Until now, we hadn't linked the closing of the Hotel Montgrí to the glacier crimes. But now that we've found a body with a ring identical to the ones the other two had, the connection is too clear to ignore."

"I follow you that far, but what do I have to do with this?"

"If we had access to the municipal archives, we might find some clue as to why Fernando Cucurell opened the hotel for only one season. That might help us move forward with the case."

Sosa shook his head as if it weren't the first time he had heard that request.

"Laura, you know very well that those archives are confidential. There are transactions, debts, copies of deeds there... Opening them is like showing someone's medical records except, in this case, it's an entire town's. If the police were to ask with a search warrant, I'd have no choice. But I can't open them for two civilians."

I saw Laura's jaw clench.

"Rodolfo, you know how much interest the police are going to show towards another body from thirty years ago. Zero. Exactly like with the two others."

Sosa opened his mouth to answer, but then looked at me and stopped. He drank his mate before speaking.

"Do you know why I hired you, Laura?"

"Because I'm responsible, I learn fast, and work hard."

"All of that is true, but I only found that out later. For the most part, I hired you to distract you a little and get you to leave those murders alone."

"Are you serious? You can't just sweep everything you don't like under the rug, Rodolfo. It's important to know the truth."

"Are you sure? Even if thirty years have gone by? What do we gain by digging it all up?"

"The truth."

"The truth isn't always a good thing, Laura. Sometimes knowing the truth brings trouble."

"That sounds like military dictatorship propaganda."

"You know what I mean."

"Yeah, yeah. That this town lives off of tourism, and that peace and quiet are our strongest assets. I know it by heart."

An awkward silence flooded the dining room. Sosa gave me a mate. I brought it up to my lips and sucked on the metal straw. *Bombilla*, they call it. The hot liquid burned my tongue and lips.

"Whenever someone tries it for the first time, they get burned. But don't worry, you'll get used to it quickly."

Besides being scalding hot, it tasted disgusting. How could an entire country be hooked on that horrible concoction? Yet another mystery of the Argentinian idiosyncrasy.

Thanks to my struggle with the mate, the tension between Sosa and Laura eased a bit. I took the opportunity to tell them about my trip to El Calafate.

"Yesterday, I traveled two hundred kilometers to speak to the law firm that pays the hotel's taxes and I got nothing from them. The conversation lasted five minutes. The whole day, down the drain."

"You're preaching to the choir," said Laura.

"Welcome to deep Patagonia," said Sosa. "Sometimes you travel for hours, for nothing."

"I don't understand the lawyer's attitude. Even though her firm has been paying the hotel's taxes for years she had no interest in acknowledging me as the heir and refused to tell me anything about my uncle."

"She's not obligated to."

"But she could, right? If she wanted to."

"Of course," interrupted Sosa. "Especially now that your uncle is dead. Unless..."

"Unless what?"

"Do you have *usucapion* in Spain?"

"What's that? A medication?"

"A law. In Argentina, the usucapion law states that if someone can prove that they have paid the taxes on a piece of property for twenty years, they have the right to claim the property as theirs."

"What are you talking about? The town hall sends the invoices in my uncle's name to a mailbox that's also in my uncle's name."

"Yes, but the account the taxes are paid from belongs to the law firm."

Until now, I had thought that my uncle sent the tax money every year to the law firm for them to pay. Now, for the first time, I was wondering if maybe the lawyers had been paying the taxes of their own volition.

"But how do they have access to a mailbox in Fernando Cucurell's name?"

"That's not important. Maybe your uncle signed over power of attorney to them at some point. Or left them a copy to his mailbox key," Laura explained.

I sat motionless with the mate in my hand, trying to process everything.

"Are you teaching it to talk?" asked Sosa.

"What?"

"The mate. Are you going to teach it to talk?"

Laura laughed and put her hand on my knee.

"That means you're taking too long to give it back."

"Oh, sorry," I said and handed the concoction back to the mayor. He looked at it and shook his head.

"You have to drink it all before giving it back."

"This drink is too complicated for me. Next time I'll have coffee."

Laura and Sosa both laughed out loud.

"You think the González-Ackerman law firm has been paying the taxes to keep the Montgrí?"

"Well... I told you I came here in '92 and the hotel was already closed. That means it's been abandoned for at least twenty-seven years."

"Yes, but we'd have to see when they started paying from that account," Laura pointed out.

"According to what Margarita told me at the town hall, at least since 2002, which is when they digitized the system."

"Seventeen years," Laura calculated.

"At the very least," added Sosa.

CHAPTER 22

We left Sosa's house around eight. Before leaving, Laura convinced him to get Margarita to find out how long González-Ackerman had been paying for the hotel taxes, since he wasn't going to give us access to the archives.

When we got to El Relincho where our paths parted, Laura made no motion to say goodbye.

"Can we go to my house?" she said. "I want to show you something."

"Of course."

We walked down an unpaved street to a small house made of wood and cement. Inside, Laura's house wasn't much different from my cabin. The only signs that whoever lived there wasn't a mere tourist, were the paperwork splayed out on the table and a photo on a shelf. It was black and white and showed a woman who looked a bit like Laura pointing a gun at the camera.

"My aunt Susana," she said when she noticed me looking at the photo. "She was a cop too."

"It's a great picture."

"It is."

I saw a wave of nostalgia wash over her face, but only for a second. She turned her back on the shelf and pointed at one of the papers on the table. It was a photocopy of an old Spanish passport, different from mine. A dark, irregular stain made parts of it illegible.

"The body in the hotel had this passport in its pocket. It seems his name was Juan and his first last name was Gómez. The second last name is completely covered by the bloodstain."

"Gerona," I read, pointing at his birthplace. It felt odd to pronounce that word. To me, it was always *Girona*, in Catalan, even though I was speaking Spanish.

"According to the Spanish Ministry of Interior, the only Juan Gómez that has gone missing was last seen in La Coruña in 2015 and was sixteen years old."

"That can't be him."

"Right, because the forensic team estimates that he was about thirty years old in the early 90s, same as the glacier bodies."

I sat in one of the wooden chairs to process the information.

"Our Juan Gómez was born in Girona and showed up murdered in the Montgrí Hotel, whose owner was from the same province," I summarized. "It's very likely that my uncle had something to do with his death. It's too much of a coincidence."

"I told you we were going to dig up things you weren't going to like."

I sighed. I'd traveled to El Chaltén thinking I'd hit the lottery and it turned out the prize was three dead bodies linked to a part of my family I didn't even know. I needed to talk to my father again.

"Why didn't you tell me about the passport at Sosa's house?"

"Someone threatened you and we don't know who."

"You think it was him?"

"No, but you know my boss isn't very discreet. I think from now on we need to tread carefully."

"*We*? You've gotten threats too?"

"Not directly. But I guess the note you got applies to anyone who wants to know the truth about what happened in this town thirty years ago."

"I don't know. I'm still not convinced the threat is serious or if they're manipulating us to investigate further."

"In any case, it's best we lay low."

"In a town like this?" I asked. "How are we supposed to find out anything without sounding alarm bells?"

"For now, going to spread Fernando's ashes at the Laguna de Los Tres."

"I don't understand."

"Fulfilling your uncle's last wish is the perfect excuse to talk to Juanmi Alonso. According to what you told me, he's fixing a bridge, right? We can go tomorrow; I've got the day off."

"Will it be sunny?"

"I don't know, I didn't check the forecast. I'll stop by your cabin at eight. Have a big breakfast, you're going to need it."

CHAPTER 23

I was woken up at seven a.m. by a firefighter pounding on my cabin door so hard I thought it was going to break. Just what I needed, a fire.

"What happened?"

"Good morning. I came by to let you know that we won't be able to take the body away until tomorrow."

I recalled that Laura had mentioned the fire department would be transporting the body to the Río Gallegos morgue.

"Why?"

"The Calafate scientific police want to wait for the team they're sending over from Río Gallegos."

"Okay. Thanks for letting me know. I don't think the dead guy will mind waiting one more day."

The firefighter gave me an awkward smile and walked away.

Still in my underwear, I took a step forward and looked up. It was that time of day when the daylight begins to creep up on one side of the sky while the other is still dark. The sky was clear, not a trace of the clouds that had covered it for the last seven days.

It was unbelievable that so many things had happened in so little time.

I got dressed, made myself a cup of coffee, and headed over to El Relincho's reception area because the Wi-Fi signal was weak that morning. Inside, a group of tourists was in the middle of eating breakfast, so I decided to sit outside, with my back against a wall that would soon be bathed in the sun's first rays.

I started a video call that my father answered after the third ring.

"Where's mom?"

"She's in the kitchen making lunch."

"Mom's cooking? I hope you have the number for pizza delivery nearby."

"Don't be dramatic. Should I tell her to come?"

"No, no. It's okay."

My father's eyes, slightly skewed from looking at me on the screen instead of the camera, blinked twice.

"How's everything in Patagonia?"

"Dad, why didn't you ever tell me you had a brother?"

"I see we're getting right to it."

"If you want, I can ask you about the Barça match."

Even though the image was pixelated and slow, I saw my father take a deep breath.

"Okay then. Let's cut to the chase, son. The reason I never told you about Fernando is because I didn't think there was anything to tell. What sense did it make for you to know you had a family member that I hadn't spoken to since before you were born?"

"Don't you think I had a right to know?"

"What I think is that I did what was best for you."

"Why did you get into a fight?"

"It's an old story, it doesn't matter anymore."

"Tell me."

My father glanced over his shoulder towards the kitchen.

"The usual, son. A woman."

"You fell in love with the same woman?"

"Don't ask me to tell you about this, Julián."

"Mom? You got into a fight over mom?"

"It has nothing to do with your mother. Respect your old man's silence. To me, my brother has been dead for decades and that wound is closed and scarred over. Please, don't stir up that part of my life just out of curiosity."

"Dad, you need to understand, I'm finding out really weird things about your brother. Every answer I get creates three new questions. You're the only thing connecting me to this man I know nothing about. If you don't want me to, I won't ask you about why you fell out, but at least talk to me about him. Tell me what he was like."

Another deep breath and another glance toward the kitchen.

"Fernando was three years older than me. He was also better-looking and smarter. Very proud, he had a really hard time admitting to his mistakes."

"You had that last part in common then."

My father shrugged as if to say, 'Think what you want'.

"He loved adventure. At the school we went to, Santa María de los Desamparados, he spent his entire last year organizing outings with any random justification. Studying plants, geology, whatever. Anything that had to do with exploring fascinated him. He always had an objective: climbing a mountain, crossing some region on his bike, or traveling to faraway countries."

"Or building a hotel on the other side of the world, for example."

"For example," my father laughed.

"Did you know he had moved to Patagonia?"

"No. I already told you we stopped talking before you were born. I think the last time I saw him was in 1983."

"I guess you don't know where he got the money to buy half an acre here and build a hotel, then. And whether he came alone or was married."

My father shrugged.

"Before you stopped talking, was he single?"

"Yes. The last time we spoke, he was single."

"In 1992 he signed a will in my favor in Barcelona. You didn't see him then?"

"No. I never heard from Fernando again. And I thought he hadn't heard from me either, until the day we called you from the cruise, when your mother told us they had run into each other years later in Barcelona."

"Does the name Juan Gómez ring any bells? Maybe a friend or an acquaintance of his from Girona?"

"Honestly no, but with that name I don't know if I'd remember him. Why?"

I contemplated telling my father that Juan Gómez had pulled the prank of waiting for me, dead, inside the hotel. But in the same way he'd kept Fernando's existence from me to protect me, I decided that, for however angry he might be with his brother, finding out that piece of news would only upset him.

"No reason. Someone here in town told me they were friends, but it's been so long that it's hard to know what's true and what's just rumors."

"Ah, rumors and small towns. Tell me about it, I grew up in Torroella."

Half of my mother's face appeared on the screen.

"Hi love, how are you? How's the cold treating you?"

"Good, mom. Very good. We were just talking about Dad's brother."

My mother made a confused face.

"Listen, Julián," my father interrupted. "No matter what they tell you down there, you need to know that your uncle was a good person."

"He couldn't have been that good if you went forty years without speaking to him."

"What does that have to do with anything?"

"A lot. You're one of the nicest people I know."

"Julián," my mom protested.

"Leave him, Consuelo. Listen, Julián. Your uncle was no saint, but neither am I, and you know that very well. I've gone through very tough times. As with you and your mother, I wasn't always good to Fernando."

The 'very tough times' he referred to were his years being an alcoholic. Most of them before he met my mother. And two more when he relapsed when I was a kid.

"There isn't a good brother and a bad brother, okay? There's a relationship that broke. When someone chops down a tree with an axe, it's clear who's responsible, but when the wind blows it over you can't blame anyone. However, the outcome is the same."

With that, my father ended the conversation. I didn't try to delve any deeper, I knew it would be useless. And even though it was barely noon in Spain, my mother announced that the tortilla would be ready soon.

CHAPTER 24

Laura stopped by my cabin a few minutes after I'd finished the call with my parents.

"Ready for some adventure?" she asked.

"Adventure rhymes with torture," I said after washing down my last piece of toast with a gulp of coffee –my second cup of the day–. "I'm not much of a hiker."

"You're gonna love it. And it's a perfect day today."

"Yeah, it's sunny out," I said peering outside with the mug in my hand. "Where's the famous Fitz Roy?"

"You can't see it from this side of town because that mountain range is blocking it," Laura answered, pointing at the same mountains the Spanish tourists had seen the day we arrived. "But in an hour or so, you'll be seeing it in all its glory."

Ten minutes later, we were walking down the main street, away from the hotel and the town exit. The hikers seemed to have multiplied with the sun. When we reached the end of the street, we followed the signs that marked the path to Laguna de Los Tres, El Chaltén's most famous hike.

"You haven't had much luck with the weather lately, have you?" said Laura, looking behind her as if expecting someone.

"With the weather and other things, too."

"Ohh, that's right. Poor thing. The guy everyone feels sorry for. It can't be easy becoming a millionaire overnight."

We entered the forest on a narrow, steep path. Laura looked back again.

"Is something wrong?" I asked her.

"No, nothing," she said and kept walking.

Barely ten minutes had passed when I heard a gunshot. Without stopping, Laura took her phone out of her pocket.

"It's a message from my aunt. She lives in Puerto Deseado and loves to send me pictures of her plants."

"You set a gunshot ringtone for your texts?"

"Yes," she said, unphased.

She then recorded a voice message for her aunt, complimenting her fern and letting her know she wouldn't have phone reception for the rest of the day because she was going on a hike.

"If she had sent me that fifteen minutes later, I wouldn't have gotten it until we got back. Cell reception ends about a kilometer from here."

"That also sounds like torture."

We kept hiking uphill. Every once in a while, we'd move to one side to let an excited tourist pass us. Most greeted us with a smile, a heavy breath, and a foreign accent. As we walked, my lungs begged me to keep quiet. Laura didn't have that issue.

"You like hiking?"

"Of course. Who wouldn't enjoy walking on rocks until they get blisters?"

"Don't be dramatic. You look pretty fit."

"You won't say that in half an hour."

From the face she made, I knew Laura had mistaken my words for false modesty. It had happened to me before. After all, between working in construction and training, my upper body definitely wasn't an insecurity of mine. Even at thirty-five, if the light hit me the right way, you could see my abs. But my legs were a different story. Resistance sports were not my thing. I had the proportions of a flamingo and the lung capacity of a Vatican minister.

After a long trek uphill, we reached a small wooden sign.

Kilometer 1.

"Nine to go," Laura announced.

I did a mental body check. The thousand-meter uphill hike had made the bottom of my feet sore, and my quads were hurting more than I'd ever felt after doing squats. The weight of my backpack felt like I was carrying the ashes of an entire city instead of just one person.

Two kilometers further and my body was drenched in sweat, my tongue was hanging out, and I was parched. Laura, on the other hand, was as fresh as a head of lettuce.

When I was just about to give up and turn back, we reached a sign announcing *Fitz Roy Overlook*. It confused me to see it in the middle of the forest, where the treetops obscured the sky almost completely. Laura pointed to a trail that strayed off the main path, and we emerged onto a sort of natural balcony on the side of the mountain.

It took me less than a second to understand the Spanish tourists insistence on seeing it. The Fitz Roy was a gray, shark-tooth-shaped monster outlined against a blue, cloudless sky.

"Don't tell me it isn't magnificent," Laura said.

"It is."

I sat on a rock without taking my eyes off its vertical walls, totally transfixed. Halfway between the summit and the base was a horizontal line of snow. Further down, at the foot of the mountain, the immense green forest we had been walking through for the past hour.

"It is," I repeated. "It's breathtaking."

Up until then, I was unaware that a view could give you a lump in your throat. I felt a sweet, strange joy, euphoric and peaceful. The closest thing I'd experienced to it was the first time I saw Anna. It might sound corny, but I'd felt we knew each other from another life and were finding each other again in this one. I hoped my story with the mountain would have a happier ending.

"I'm jealous of you," Laura said. "The first time someone does this hike, it's a once-in-a-lifetime experience. And on a day like today, it's a real privilege. This is probably the tenth time I've done it and though they're all beautiful, it never compares to the first. And you still haven't seen the best part."

"The part where I stay in bed for a week recovering?"

"No, the part where... Never mind. I don't want to spoil it for you."

We ate some ham and cheese sandwiches that Laura had bought at the bakery. In between bites, we took photos of the tourists who handed us their phones and posed with the mountains in the background. Some of them offered to return the favor. The first two times we agreed and posed together in that wonderful setting.

It was hard to get back up and resume the hike. After another hour and a half of walking, I saw a tent between the tree trunks.

"The Poincenot campground," Laura announced. "The National Parks people are probably camping there because the Río Blanco bridge is close by."

As we moved forward, more tents appeared. Beside some of them, people sat on logs, eating fruit or heating water on a portable stove. Most of them looked like foreign tourists.

The Poincenot campground was very different from any other I'd seen before. A Spanish campground has, at the very least, a bar and a pool. Some of them have activities for kids and even a nightclub. This one, on the other hand, didn't even have a reception area or separate plots. The entirety of its infrastructure was a sign that read *Welcome to Poincenot* and a tiny wooden cabin the size of a wardrobe with a sign on its door informing it was a dry toilet.

Laura pointed at three green tents. They were bigger and sturdier than the tourists' tents, and also quite a bit worse for wear.

"Good morning. Anyone home?" she asked, clapping her hands in front of the tent zippers.

Silence.

"They must be working on the bridge. Let's go, it's just another kilometer further."

Without even considering the option sitting down to wait for them, Laura took off. When we emerged from the forest, the Fitz Roy greeted us once again. Or rather, its upper half, because another mountain blocked the view of its base.

"Look, see the people hiking up?"

"Where?"

"Over there."

"No, I can't... holy shit, I can see them! They look so tiny!"

They looked like colorful ants. All of them climbing up a path that looked like a gray thread on the side of the mountain from where we were standing.

"That's the hardest part of the hike. The last kilometer uphill before you reach the Laguna de Los Tres. The good news is that the bridge is before that."

The bad news was that sooner rather or later, I'd have to make the trek up to scatter the ashes I was carrying in my backpack.

After crossing a marsh, the path went downhill through a meadow, toward the water.

"That's the Río Blanco. There's the bridge, see it?"

It took me a minute to find it. In my head, I'd pictured a big iron bridge, not a few faded wooden planks camouflaged among the almost white stones of the riverbed. Also, bridges usually cross from one bank to the other. This one, on the other hand, ran in the same direction as the river and was on its side, one of its handrails in the water, the other pointing toward the sky.

"It must have rained a ton for the water to have pulled it up like that," said Laura.

When we got closer, we encountered four men in khaki shirts and pants having a snack on the shore. The river, a milky grey color, was less than three meters wide but with a strong current, forming foamy rapids.

"Good morning. How's it going, guys?" Laura greeted them as we walked down the path.

They recognized her and waved. On reaching them, the oldest of them, a balding man with a stocky build, motioned for us to sit with them on the rocks. That had to be Juanmi Alonso. The other three were too young.

"Want some *mate*?" he asked and stretched over to fill his metal cup with water from the river.

"No, thank you," I replied.

"Spaniard?" one of the others asked.

"Yes."

"Juanmi," said Laura. "This is Julián Cucurell, Fernando Cucurell's nephew, the owner of the Hotel Montgrí."

The man's eyes widened.

"You're Fernando's nephew?"

Without waiting for an answer, he stood up and took two strides toward me until we were face to face. I shook his strong, rough hand.

"I'm Juan Miguel Alonso. I was a close friend of your uncle's. How's the *Gallego*?" Argentinians called all Spaniards Galicians.

I stared at him, not knowing what to say.

"Yeah, yeah, I know you guys aren't *Gallegos*. 'Catalan, dammit' he used to say to me. How is he? Did he come with you?"

"He passed away four months ago."

"What? You don't say, poor guy. What happened?"

"An accident."

Alonso stood in silence. One of the young men stood up and cleared his throat.

"We're going to keep nailing the rails, Juanmi. But you stay and talk, don't worry."

"It's kind of a long story," I said as soon as it was just the three of us.

"Pretty long," Laura interjected.

The man raised his bushy gray brows and let his partners know he'd be waiting for them back at the campground with lunch. Wonderful. More walking.

"Were you going to Laguna de Los Tres?" he enquired, pointing backward as we walked away from the river.

"Yes. My uncle's last wish was that his ashes be scattered there. Now that I think of it, I'm not sure that's allowed. Do you think that would be okay, sir?"

The man, probably around my father's age but with a stride as powerful as a bull's, stopped suddenly and turned to face me.

"You know what isn't okay? You, calling me 'sir'. Call me Juanmi, dammit," he yelled at me, his voice rough.

"Very well, Juanmi then."

"There we go. About the ashes, no problem. It's not allowed but the *gallego* deserves it."

"How did you meet?"

"We came to Chaltén around the same time, when there was barely anyone else here. The only buildings were the twelve alpine houses the government built when it was founded. I came here in January of '87. I think he came a couple of months later."

"What had he come for?"

"Same thing me and most people here came to do. Make a new life. And for the adventure. Chaltén was a well-known place among people who loved nature, especially mountaineers. The tourists came here before the town was established you know what I mean?"

"Not really, to be honest."

The man stopped again and turned.

"This place has been a magnet for adventurers since way before 1985. Look," he said pointing at the two smaller peaks on each side of the Fitz Roy. "That's the Goretta needle, named after the first Italian woman to summit an eight thousand. The other one, the Poincenot, is named after a French alpinist who drowned in the Fitz Roy River in the '50s. So, when the town was founded, who do you think would voluntarily move to a place where there's nothing but mountains? Mountain fanatics. Your uncle was one of them."

Juanmi Alonso resumed his walk.

"Also, he was a great builder. He knew how to really work wood, and as people started moving to the town, he always had work. The Montgrí Hotel was the first tourist lodge in town. Before then, you only had the National Park Inn, which existed before the town was founded."

"What I don't understand," Laura interrupted. "Is that if the Argentinian government founded Chaltén to solve a sovereignty dispute with Chile, isn't it odd that they would give a foreigner half an acre of land?"

"Not odd, impossible. You had to be Argentinian to get land here."

"So how did my uncle get it?"

"He showed his ID."

"What do you mean?"

"That Cucurell the *Gallego,* was Argentinian."

CHAPTER 25

"My uncle was Argentinian?" I asked in bewilderment

"On paper, yeah. In reality, he was more Spanish than paella, but he had dual nationality. His parents emigrated to Buenos Aires before he was born, then returned to Spain not too long after."

My father had never mentioned that my grandparents had moved to Argentina. Could it be that he didn't know? He was younger than my uncle and according to his birth certificate –which I'd seen with my own eyes– he was born in Spain. Or did he know but had never told me, just like the fact that he had a brother?

When we reached the campground, Alonso showed us some logs next to the green tents. I was relieved to sit. He lit a fire and sat across from us with a knife in his hand and several potatoes at his feet.

"What had your uncle been up to all these years?" he asked me while he peeled the first potato.

"Well, I don't know. I didn't even know I had an uncle until I got a phone call about a meeting to let me know I was his heir."

"Every boy's dream. A dead uncle with an inheritance shows up out of the blue. None of the fuss, just the benefits."

I simply smiled. An uncle who was a suspect in a triple murder case, who my father refused to speak about didn't seem like 'none of the fuss'.

"I'd like to find out more about the story of the hotel. Do you know where Fernando got the money to buy the land?"

"During the first years after the town was founded it was pretty easy to get land if you had a touristic project.

Things went downhill later. Political favors, as usual. Once it was clear that Chaltén had potential as an international tourist destination, forget it. I mean I'm sure you know, that even though it's falling to pieces, that hotel is worth millions of dollars."

"So I've heard."

"Your uncle came here at the right time and was full of excitement. He was unstoppable. He was the kind of person that could sell you a fan in Antarctica. He was broke, but no one could beat him when it came to talking. That there was an investor in Spain, that he was creating job openings, that the town would also gain if there were more beds for tourists ... Just by talking, he convinced them to give him the land to build the hotel. On top of that, he was good at everything. He was a one-man show. He could guide a group of tourists in the morning and build a wall for the hotel in the afternoon."

"Did he do that a lot? Guiding tourists?"

"Back then, quite a bit. Although the amount of people that came wasn't what it is today."

"Did he take people to the Viedma glacier?"

Alonso glanced up from a half-peeled potato. He paused for a second, trying to remember.

"I'm pretty sure he didn't go to the Viedma. I can't remember that well, but I think he preferred the forest. He loved it. I taught him about berries and edible roots, you wouldn't believe how fast he learned. In just a couple of years, he was a true expert. Tourists were asking for him, and that was before the internet even existed; he always had work. And in the meantime, he built his hotel."

"I came here thinking I'd inherited an empty piece of land. When I got here, I found a hotel on it."

"Double surprise."

"Triple," Laura intervened. "Inside it was a dead body."

I glared at her.

"When you get back to town, you'll hear all about it," she told Juanmi, although her comment was clearly directed at me.

"A dead body?" Alonso opened his eyes wide. Something about his expression came off as exaggerated.

"Yes, a mummified corpse that had been there for about thirty years," I said.

The man asked all the routine questions. How? When? Why? Laura answered all of them without giving him an ounce more information than what he'd get once he returned to El Chaltén.

"The hotel was open for a very short period, right?" I asked him.

"Extremely short. Just one season. From September of 1990 to March of 1991. You didn't know that?"

"Not the exact dates," I confessed. "Why did my uncle leave and never return?"

"I never knew. In March of '91, I stopped by to say goodbye because I was heading out for a few days to build a wooden platform on the path to the Torre Mountain."

"Weren't you in charge of the inn back then?"

Alonso's expression hardened.

"I was in charge of the inn because I was the youngest and had to do what I was told, but I took every opportunity I got to go out into the countryside. Look at me, I'm over sixty, and I still come here to nail in some wooden planks. With my experience, I could be the director of the Los Glaciares Park and have an office with a view of the Perito Moreno, but I prefer a simple life, outdoors, not behind a desk."

"I'm sorry if my question bothered you."

The man dismissed my apology with a wave. He dumped potatoes, onions, tomato sauce, and a can of mushrooms into a pot he placed on the fire. Afterward, he added some pieces of dried meat, doused everything with some wine, and covered the pot.

"You were saying you went to visit Fernando in 1991," Laura resumed.

"Yes. It was a few days before he was closing and heading back to Spain for the winter. He was excited because he'd only been back once since he'd moved to

Chaltén. I remember it like it was yesterday. We talked at the hotel and had a couple of glasses of wine, I wished him luck on his trip and told him to bring me back a wineskin. He got annoyed, saying that wasn't a thing in Catalunya. We had one of those amazing conversations you have with friends, the kind where you know when it starts but never know when it'll end. We said goodbye once the wine was gone and I left the next day to work on the path. That was the last time I saw him."

The three of us sat in silence. I doodled on the ground with a stick.

"Was he married?" I asked.

"No! He was a bachelor through and through. I don't know if any woman would have put up with him. He was a very particular guy."

"In what way?"

"Well, first of all, he was proud and stubborn. Even when he knew he was wrong, you couldn't get him to change his mind. He would rather bang his head against a wall than agree with you."

"My father said something similar."

"And secondly, if he had something to say, he said it no matter who you were. If he needed to tell you to go to hell, he'd tell you. Mind you, he had a way of saying it without offending you. I don't know how to explain it. He was direct but diplomatic at the same time."

"So, he arrived and left El Chaltén alone?"

"Like he used to say, more alone than the number one."

"Do you remember ever seeing him wearing something like this?" asked Laura, pulling the wolf ring out of her pocket.

Juanmi Alonso picked up the ring with his calloused hand and examined it in the light. Then, he placed it on his ring finger. It fit perfectly.

"No, it doesn't ring a bell. But I like it. Was it Fernando's?"

"No, but the dead guy in the Montgrí Hotel and the two bodies they found in the glacier a year and a half ago, all wore one exactly like it."

"The Viedma glacier bodies?"

Laura nodded and told him a summarized version of what she'd told me. Basically, that the three victims had identical rings and had all died around the same time.

"So, thirty years ago, when the hotel was open, there were three murders in Chaltén."

"We don't know if it happened while the hotel was open," Laura jumped in. "It could have been right after it closed."

Alonso shook his head and got up to stir the stew.

"It seems unbelievable that in such a small, quiet place something like that could have happened and that we just went on with life as usual," he said, waving the wooden spoon in the air.

"My uncle didn't seem to have... gone on with life as usual. Who builds a hotel, opens for just one season, and then closes it for good?"

"I don't know. I wondered many times what might have happened to Fernando, but who would have ever thought –a dead body inside his hotel."

I heard footsteps behind us. Alonso's three partners had returned from the river, drenched in sweat. They sat around the fire next to us and started discussing the bridge.

The stew was amazing. Juanmi told stories of the first European explorers who came to the area while we heartily ate out of metal bowls. Apparently, the mountains surrounding us started to gain worldwide popularity in the '50s. Many of the people who tried to be the first to reach the summits, died trying. And, according to him, even now someone occasionally died.

"How long will it take us to get back?" I asked Laura after I finished the apple I'd had for dessert.

"About two hours. Luckily, it's all downhill."

"Well, if we want to make it back to town while it's still light, we should start heading up to the lagoon, don't you think?"

"You can't leave!" Alonso protested. "Stay the night. Rest today, or if you feel like walking a bit more you can go see the Piedras Blancas glacier, it's beautiful and only a half hour away. Then you can come back, have dinner with us, and sleep here. We have an extra tent and two spare sleeping bags. Tomorrow, you can go up to the lagoon well-rested and scatter Fernando's ashes. It's supposed to be sunny like today."

Laura and I looked at each other.

"If you don't want to share a tent, Julián can come sleep with Carlos and me and we can leave the other one for Laura. It'll be a tight fit with the three of us, but it gets cold at night here, so that's not such a bad thing."

"No need," Laura intervened. "I can sleep with Julián."

"Are you sure?" I asked.

"What's the worst thing that can happen? That you find out I snore? A heads up: I snore."

CHAPTER 26

And man did she snore. She sounded like a chainsaw. It was unbelievable that such a small body could make such noise.

When I woke the next morning, Laura wasn't in the tent. I heard her voice and Alonso's through the tent's fabric. I couldn't make out what they were saying as they were whispering. I guessed it was so as not to wake me.

Getting up and dressed was a challenge. A sharp pain pierced my thighs and calves with every movement. The last time I'd had muscle pain like that was when Anna had convinced me to train with her for a 10K. I never made it past the third training session.

"Poor guy, he still has jetlag," Laura said when I popped my head out of the tent.

She was sitting on a log next to Juanmi Alonso, who had a thermos between his legs and was drinking *mate*.

"I was waiting for you to get up so I could say goodbye, Julián. I have to go work on the bridge today. We're a man down."

"What happened?"

"Rosales went back to town. They sent word on the radio that his son was taken to Calafate with appendicitis."

"Poor kid," I said.

"In three or four days, I'll be back in Chaltén and we can carry on chatting if you'd like. Laura knows where I live."

I still had many questions left. The previous afternoon, he had headed back to the bridge after lunch and Laura and I had walked to the Piedras Blancas glacier very much against my will. We met back up at the campground that night, but with everyone else around, I didn't broach the subject again.

"Thanks. I'll probably bother you with some more questions when you get back."

"It would be my pleasure."

I downed some tea with condensed milk and half a pack of cookies in record time and we set off. While we descended towards the river, Alonso pulled a small plastic bag filled with a gray powder that looked like clay, from his pocket.

"I wrote a letter to your uncle telling him about my life and asking about his. 'Where did you go, *Gallego*?' I asked him as if he were going to read it."

He raised the bag and smiled nostalgically.

"Then I burned it. I'd like you to give it to him," he told me.

I nodded and put it in my pocket.

We said goodbye when we reached the Río Blanco. He joined his partners and Laura and I removed our shoes to cross the river by jumping from one rock to another. I lost my balance on one of them and ended up in water up to my knees. I'd never felt anything so cold in my life. I was sure it hurt less to stick your foot in a piranha-infested river than in that glacial water.

Once we made it across, we started uphill. As we walked up the rocky slope, I started shedding layers of clothes and my conversation with Laura became more stilted. Or rather, my answers did. I was panting and sweating profusely, whereas she went on, unphased.

We stopped to rest under the last tree before the terrain became pure rock.

"Did you look that way?" she said pointing behind me.

When I turned around, I was met with a wide-open landscape. Down by the river, Alonso and his team were barely visible among the gray rocks. Behind them, the forest where we'd slept began, and even further back, a great lake.

"Now we're the ants," Laura said. "This is where the people we saw yesterday were."

"Here? But they weren't even halfway up. Don't tell me..."

"We can go back if you want."

"Absolutely not."

We kept walking, for what seemed an eternity, up a path made of loose stone. Even my hair hurt, and that's saying a lot in my case. Every time I looked up, I saw more and more people stopped by the path, trying to catch their breath.

"It's just up there. I promise," Laura said, panting slightly. I was glad to see she was, in fact, human.

Twenty minutes later, an American couple a few meters ahead of us started repeating 'Oh my God!' like a broken record.

When I peered over the hill, all my exhaustion suddenly disappeared, and if I were American, I also would have yelled 'Oh my God!'. However, it came out a bit more Spanish.

"Hostia."

Against the blue sky, Mount Fitz Roy reigned over a dreamlike landscape. At its feet, a glacier and a trickle of white water that flowed down the rock into a turquoise lagoon.

"The Laguna de Los Tres," Laura announced.

I sat down leaning back against a rock.

"Some say it's called that because of the three glaciers that surround it. Others say it's because of the three French aviators who helped to map out the border with Chile. One of them was Saint-Exupéry, the author of The Little Prince."

Laura's words were just background noise to me. I had no interest whatsoever in where the name came from. All I cared about was what lay in front of my eyes. She seemed to understand, as she stopped talking.

At our feet, several tourists rested on the rocky slope that descended towards the lagoon. Even those who stood in larger groups of seven or eight were silent or barely whispering. There was something very special about that place, a sort of fragile harmony that felt like it could break with just one word spoken too loudly.

I don't know how long I sat still there, staring straight ahead with tears welling up in my eyes. Just like when we'd stopped at the lookout, I felt a unique connection to that mountain.

After a long while, we headed down to the shore. We walked next to the turquoise water, away from the tourists, until a rocky cliff forced us to stop. There, at the foot of Mount Fitz Roy, I pulled out the urn with the ashes of the uncle I'd never met. An uncle who was perhaps a murderer, a victim, or both.

"This letter is from your friend Juanmi," I whispered, pouring the powder from the bag into the urn.

With my back to the wind, I shook the urn in the air. With each movement, a dense white cloud formed and floated in the air, until it disappeared.

The day I die, I thought, I wouldn't mind ending up somewhere like this.

CHAPTER 27

That night, I slept better than I had in years. I collapsed onto my cabin bed, with no strength left in me to think about hotels, dead bodies, or anything else. Two days of hiking does wonders for your sleep.

When I woke, someone had pushed an envelope under my door. It was a letter from the police stating they'd finished their work at the hotel and I could go in again.

A sensible person would have eaten something before starting a day that promised to be long. But if we always made the sensible choice, the world would work more like a Swiss clock and less like Vietnamese traffic.

I brushed my teeth and left the cabin. I fought the urge to turn left towards the hotel but instead walked towards Laura's house. I told myself it was because she'd asked to see it before I touched anything. Actually, the idea of going back in there alone freaked me out a little.

Laura opened the door with a cup of coffee in her hand, looking like she'd been up for a while. When I told her we could go into the hotel, she was ready in less than five minutes.

"Hey, are you sore from yesterday?" I asked her as we walked down the main street.

"No, you?"

"I feel like a train ran over me. One wheel over my legs and the other over my butt. It hurt to sit on the toilet this morning."

"Thanks for that image."

"I've got worse if you want."

"No thanks, I just had breakfast."

When we walked past Sosa's property, two horses sauntered up to the fence. Laura petted them while I kept a safe distance.

The Montgrí hotel was no longer sealed off with police tape. I pushed at the front door and it swung open easily, though the hinges creaked so loudly my teeth hurt. The first thing I did was open all the windows in the reception and dining room. I didn't want to see that place in the dark again.

With natural light, the room wasn't spooky anymore. It felt thrilling, like walking into a place that was frozen in time. I took Laura to room number seven. There, the police had left the shutters open and the autumn morning sun streamed in sideways through the threadbare curtains.

Even after the firefighters and forensics had been through there, the human silhouette cut into the thick layer of dust was still quite visible on the mattress. In the center, the worn fabric had a dark stain.

"It's probably blood," she said.

"Can you know that for sure after so many years?"

"Yes. Well, not completely but because of the wounds, it's very likely."

"If they shot him, the police would have found the bullet in the mattress or the wall, right?"

"Maybe it wasn't a gunshot. Or maybe they did find it. I only know what they choose to tell me."

Laura bent over to examine the mattress closely. Every once in a while, she'd touch the fabric with the tips of her fingers or lower her head to scrutinize it from a different angle.

A whistling sound interrupted the silence. Exactly like the sound I'd heard the day I found the body.

"Did you hear that?"

"What?" Laura answered as she crouched down to inspect the floor.

"That noise. Listen."

It happened again.

"It's the wind blowing through something," she said without lifting her gaze from the wooden floorboards full of police footprints.

I examined the window. Laura was right. My imagination had led me to believe that the whistling sound coming through a crack in the wood was someone moaning. Luckily, I hadn't told anyone about it.

"That's the door to the basement," Laura said as she pointed at a metal ring attached to the wooden floorboards.

"There isn't any mention of a basement in the floorplan. Do you think the police saw it?" I asked.

"Of course. Look, there are footprints in the dust. They saw it and opened it."

Laura pulled on the ring and opened a square trap door. Shining our phone flashlights in front of us, we walked down a wooden ladder that creaked under my weight. It was a tiny room, about two meters square. The floor was made of gray dirt, the brick walls were white with saltpeter. It smelled a bit damp and was empty.

"There's nothing here."

We went back up and she focused on the bed once again.

"If you're bored, you don't have to stay," she told me after a long silence.

"Not at all."

Not at all, at first. After a while, I lost interest in her scarce, repetitive movements. The final blow was when I saw her stand practically frozen in front of the headboard, for almost five minutes.

"Maybe I will go take a look at the other rooms. See you."

She gave me a thumbs-up without looking at me.

I went into each room, opening the windows and coughing from the dust in the curtains. I didn't find anything interesting. Some beds were made, some weren't, old-fashioned bedspreads covered in dust and closets full of empty hangers. I didn't find anything weird in the kitchen or the reception area, besides the broken window I'd seen the first time.

I left the hotel and walked towards the house that had been my uncle's home on the other side of the property. Out of the corner of my eye, I thought I saw movement across the street. At first glance, it seemed there wasn't anyone there, but I had the feeling that something was off. That's when I noticed the two legs by the trunk of a low-hanging tree.

I told myself it was of no consequence. It could be someone who had stopped there to answer a text, for example. I kept walking toward the house, built exactly like the hotel, only smaller.

Once I'd reached a spot where the angle would enable me to see the person across the street, the feet moved so that the tree was still blocking the view. It became clear that they were hiding from me.

I changed direction and walked directly towards the tree. A man wearing a coat with its hood hiding his face, ran out from behind the foliage.

"Hey!" I yelled as I chased him. "Come here!"

The man was fast, but I wasn't going to stop, even if that meant coughing up a lung.

He crossed the main street and turned down a side street, toward the Río de las Vueltas. Slowly, the distance between us decreased. When he was just twenty meters ahead of me, he stopped short and put his hands on his knees. His back shot up and down like a piston.

I slowed my pace, cautiously getting closer. When I was near enough to hear his heavy breathing, he turned towards me and smiled, showing his battered teeth.

"How are you, Fernando?"

It was Danilo.

"Were you spying on me?" I asked him.

"A little bit, yes."

"Why?"

"Candy."

"Danilo, I'm not Fernando. And I don't have candy."

"I know."

"What did you want, then?"

"Candy," he repeated in the most natural tone.

It would have been easy to chalk that answer to Danilo's unique mind. However, something told me I was the one who was missing the point.

"Danilo, can I ask you a question?"

"Of course, my friend."

"Did you know what was inside the hotel?"

"Beds. Tables. Chairs."

"No, I mean the person. There was a dead person inside."

His expression shifted in slow motion. It went from surprise to confusion. Danilo furrowed his brow, then shut his eyes tight and started shaking his head so hard I thought he might hurt himself.

"No, no, no. Not dead. He wasn't dead. He was drunk! Fernando, you said he was drunk! Drunk, you said, Fernando. Not dead. Not dead."

A woman came out from one of the houses beside us.

"Danilo, what's wrong?" she asked.

But Danilo was still shaking his head and screaming. Big tears streamed down his face which he rapidly wiped dry.

"What did you do to him?" the woman asked curtly

"Me? Nothing."

"Nothing? I saw you chasing after him. What did you do to him?"

"Nothing, I promise."

The woman came close and spoke in a low voice, her gaze sharp as knives.

"You're the Spaniard from the hotel, right? You listen to me, kid. We all know each other here, and we look out for one another. Can't you see that Danilo can't fend for himself? Look, I'm gonna spell it out for you: if you come near him again, I'm going to burn down that hotel myself, understand?"

"Ma'am, I didn't do any..."

The woman turned her back on me to hug Danilo. She whispered something in his ear to calm him, and then turned back, glaring at me.

"Come here, Danilo. Come inside so I can give you some candy."

CHAPTER 28

On my way back to the hotel, the weight on my shoulders felt like I was giving an elephant a piggyback ride. Although Danilo's reaction had made it clear that he knew something, I felt like crap for making him cry.

I entered the property, passed by the hotel, and headed to Fernando's house.

The door was easily opened; the doorframe was cracked beside the lock. I looked at it closely and noticed that not all the cracks in the wood looked the same. Some of them were light brown, while others were gray and dry like the rest of the doorframe. The door had been forced open twice. Once, by the police a few days ago. The other, many years ago.

Inside the house, the light pouring in through the window revealed a large dining room with a table, a sofa, and a fireplace built out of the same stone that was used for the outer walls. Here, I thought, my uncle had lived for four years.

I was about to cross the doorway that led to the rest of the house when I noticed something. In contrast to the thick layer of dust on the table, were four perfectly clean circles. The police, I guessed, had removed two glasses and two plates.

In the fridge, I found jars of jam that had turned black, a bottle of milk that was completely dry, and vegetables that had turned to ash.

I took my time exploring each of the three rooms. The floor was full of footprints; however, the police didn't seem to have paid much attention to the house itself. There were open drawers that had been dusted off here and there, and marks on the floor indicating they'd moved a piece of furniture, but aside from that, everything seemed intact.

In the largest bedroom, I found a queen-sized bed, unmade. On the nightstand, a pipe and a lighter, and in the closet, clothes belonging to a man and a woman. Another one of the rooms had two single beds, also unmade. On the floor lay a small wooden train and a blonde doll, with a dress that had once been pink.

I was about to bend down to pick up the toys, when I heard a scream and I felt something stick into my ribs. I let out a howl and spun around out of pure reflex. Laura was laughing her ass off.

"You almost shit your pants!" she said once she caught her breath. "Sorry, I wanted to scare you, but not that much. I feel bad now."

She burst out laughing again. She couldn't control it, she clearly enjoyed having almost given me a heart attack.

"Did you find anything interesting?" she asked me.

"Danilo was spying on us."

"You just noticed?"

"You knew?"

"Of course. The day we went to the Laguna de Los Tres, he followed us all the way through town until we reached the path."

"And you think that's normal?"

"Danilo has been guarding the hotel for almost his entire life, it's understandable that he'd want to know who you are."

"When I told him there was a dead body inside, he had a sort of panic attack. He started yelling, saying he wasn't dead, that he was just drunk. What do you think he meant?"

"No idea."

"It doesn't sound odd to you?"

"Yes and no. His mind works in a way that the rest of us have a hard time understanding. And that reaction is pretty common in him. Sometimes he yells the same sentence twenty times at an ant."

Without giving me chance to answer, Laura started examining the house as meticulously as she had the hotel. Before she entered her trance and I lost her once again, I pointed at the clothes in the closets and the toys on the floor.

"Juanmi Alonso said my uncle had always been a bachelor, but a family was living here."

Laura nodded.

"A family that left with their beds unmade and food in the fridge."

CHAPTER 29

As I'd imagined, the morning dragged on. By the time Laura had finished examining the house and the hotel, it was past lunchtime. We only just made it to a pizza place that turned away a couple of tourists right after giving us a table, telling them that the kitchen was closed.

"The perks of being a local," she had said as we sat down.

I made it back to my cabin around four p.m. I lay down for a nap, but as my head touched the pillow, my mind was filled by a thousand questions. I thought about Fernando Cucurell while I played with the wolf ring Laura had given me. Who abandons their house and their business? Why leave a dead man in a room, when there's a basement to hide him in right there? If there was a logical answer to all of this, I definitely wasn't finding it. The silver wolf seemed to laugh at me from my finger.

Accepting the fact that I wasn't going to fall asleep, I turned on the computer. The Wi-Fi signal was good that afternoon. I video called Anna's brother Xavi, perhaps the only person who could help me. He answered on the second ring.

"Julián, dude. Are you in Patagonia?"

"I see news travels fast."

Between Xavi's square face and dreadlocks, I couldn't see an inch of what was behind him. Knowing him, he could be anywhere. Xavi worked in IT and had one of those dream jobs. Even though he had a house in Barcelona, he spent most of the year elsewhere. He spent his summers scuba diving off the Costa Brava, and his winters skiing in the Pyrenees. In his free time, he opened his computer and worked.

"Where are you?"

"In my apartment. I just came back from Anna's place."

"Where exactly is Anna's place?"

"She rented an apartment in El Born. I'm helping her move."

I somehow squelched the urge to comment out of dignity. Even though, during the horrible conversation with Anna after I'd seen her with Rosario it was I who said the relationship was over I felt it was too soon for her to have already found a new place. I wondered if she had moved on her own or in with her little Argentinian widow.

"To think we celebrated New Year's together just four months ago, man. What a bummer what happened with you and my sister."

"What happened to us? I'd say the bummer is what she did to me."

"I'm not going to go there, Julián. When a couple breaks up there's never just one guilty party."

"Doesn't it make you mad at all?"

"Me? Why?"

"Oh, nothing. It's completely normal that your sister is hooking up with the girl you slept with a year ago."

Xavi smiled as if he'd seen the question coming.

"Rosario and I didn't sleep together on New Year's, Julián. We talked for a while alone, and we left your place together, but nothing happened. In any case, if we want to stay friends, I think we should leave my sister and her life out of this, don't you think?"

"Yeah," I agreed. "In fact, I'm calling to ask you for a favor that has nothing to do with her."

"Anything, man."

"I need to find out everything I can about my father's brother. Write down 'Fernando Cucurell Zaplana'."

Xavi burst out laughing and shook his head. His dreadlocks danced like Lenny Kravitz's in a 90s music video.

"Do you think I work for the CIA?"

"You're a hacker, aren't you?"

"I'm a cybersecurity consultant."

"Isn't that similar?"

"As similar as a vet and a lion tamer. They both work with animals."

"You can't help me then?"

"I can try. Ask around, see what public information there is..."

"Anything helps."

"Have you asked your father about his brother yet?"

"Yeah, but they haven't spoken since before I was born. He made it very clear that he prefers not to talk about it."

"Maybe he's got his reasons."

"What do you mean?"

"According to Anna, you're there to collect an inheritance from an uncle you never met, right?"

"Yes."

"Then you won't be missing him. He died and left you everything. Enjoy it. Why stir up the past?"

I sighed. Partly because Xavi's words were practically the same as the threatening note I'd received the week before. And partly, because if I didn't tell him the truth, my former brother-in-law would never understand. So, I did.

"A body? You found a body inside the hotel?"

"Exactly. Mummified. He was killed about thirty years ago. Around the same time, my uncle abandoned the hotel—he was there one day and gone the next, vanished into thin air."

"Do you think your uncle killed him and took off?"

"I don't know."

Xavi ran his hands through his hair, bunching up his dreadlocks with one hand and then letting them fall behind his shoulders.

"Holy shit, man. Four months ago, you were celebrating the new year with me, and now you're the owner of a hotel on the other side of the world with a dead guy inside."

"Life is full of surprises."

"Lately, yours is kicking your ass."

"Thanks, Xavi. If I'm ever about to kill myself, I'll give you a call," I told him, and raised my middle finger in front of the camera to give him a full screen 'fuck you'.

"What am I seeing? You've been in the mountains for less than a month and you're already a hippie. Rings and all. When are you getting your dreads?"

I realized I was still wearing the replica of the ring.

"This? No, it isn't mine. Do you think I'd wear something like this? It's ugly as shit! Look," I said, moving it close to the camera.

"Let's see. Move it a bit closer."

I moved my finger so that the wolf's head was in full view. Xavi furrowed his brow and looked like he was solving a hard sudoku.

"What are you doing with a Brotherhood of the Wolves ring?"

"What?"

"Where did you get it?"

"No. You first. Do you know this ring?"

Xavi gestured for me to wait and went off-screen. I sat for a few seconds looking at his empty chair. When he returned, he showed me a ring identical to the one Laura had given me.

"How the fuck do you have that?" I asked him.

"Every member of the Brotherhood of the Wolves had one."

"The Brotherhood of the Wolves? What are you talking about?"

"A secret society of students of Santa María de los Desamparados. Like a student club."

Santa María de los Desamparados was the only school in Torroella de Montgrí, the town where my parents and uncle grew up. It was also the town where I was born, although my mother's job had led us to Barcelona when I was still a baby.

Xavi and Anna were also from Torroella. I met them the summer we went there to clean up my grandparent's house before selling it.

"Xavi, it's extremely important that you tell me everything you know," I said, rubbing my temples.

"The Brotherhood of the Wolves was a sort of club that you could only join by invitation. In my family it was tradition. My grandfather was a member, then my father, then me. It dies with me, I tell you, because I'm not planning on having kids."

"What do you mean 'a sort of club'?"

"Something like that. We had meetings that were kind of cult-like, kind of masonic."

"I need you to be more specific."

"Have you ever heard of fraternities and sororities in the US?"

"No."

"Man, where do you live? Inside a yogurt cup? Those university clubs with Greek letters for names: *pi, delta, gamma.*"

"Oh yeah, it rings a bell from some movie."

"Well, there you go. These are societies that go back many years, with very solemn origins, but that today have lost all meaning. Members get together to get drunk and haze new members. The Brotherhood of the Wolves was something very similar in my time. We'd do a ritual every once in a while, but they were just excuses to drink, smoke tobacco, and talk about girls."

"Rituals?"

"Well, if you say it like that it sounds ominous. We'd play with a Ouija board, draw tarot cards, things like that. But those were all secondary. Like groups of old guys that get together to play cards. The cards aren't what's important, you know? What matters is being together, talking about stuff, and mostly feeling like you're a part of something. Looking at it from my age now, it was just kid's stuff."

"Well, it's pretty elaborate for kid's stuff, don't you think? Silver rings with a wolf's head..."

"Silver? No way, man. This ring is brass."

Xavi put his ring back up to the camera and I noticed the metal was golden.

"Do you know what the inscription means?"

"What inscription?"

"On the inside. *'Lupus occidere uiuendo debet'*."

Xavi shook his head no and showed me the inner face, completely smooth.

"I don't know what you're talking about."

Maybe Xavi's ring was cheaper because he was born over two decades after the victims. Everything got cheaper and of poorer quality as time went by.

"Have you ever seen your dad's or your grandfather's?"

"My dad's is exactly like this one, brass and no inscription. My grandfather didn't have one because it's a symbol that didn't exist in his day. They incorporated it later on. Your turn: why do you have one? Didn't you grow up in Barcelona?"

"I did."

"But the only people who have these rings are the members of a brotherhood, and the brotherhood belongs to a school that's in Torroella, not Barcelona."

I took a deep breath, deciding what to tell him and what not. I took the easy route. In three minutes, I'd spilled everything.

"I can't believe it," my ex-brother-in-law answered when I finished. "Three members of the brotherhood, dead?"

"Yes. Two in the glacier, one in the hotel. What are the odds of me running into three murders on the other side of the world linked to the school my uncle went to?"

"Zero."

"Well, that's where I'm at."

"Give me a couple of days to see what I can find out about Fernando Cucurell. But don't get your hopes up."

"Thanks, man. It would also help if you could get me any info you can on that brotherhood, especially twenty-five years before you were a member."

"I'll ask my dad and see what he knows."

"You're the best, Xavi. If you were a girl, I'd kiss you."

"You sure? Look how it went with my sister."

CHAPTER 30

At around six p.m., I headed to Aurora Horseback Rides and found Laura brushing a brown mare. She told me to wait for her to finish, and that after a few minutes she'd have the rest of the day off.

I watched her as she worked. With each brush swipe, she'd pat and whisper things to the horse. I didn't know her well, but I couldn't picture her treating a person with the same care she showed the animals.

"If you'd like I can take you riding one day," she said to me once she was done.

"Maybe," I answered, slightly nervous.

"Are you scared of horses?"

"A little. I know it's silly if I try to rationalize it, but that doesn't make me less scared of them."

"Phobias aren't rational. I have the same thing with dogs."

I'd never thought of my issue with horses as a phobia. I wondered what the correct word to describe it was. There had to be one because even the weirdest fears –like my mom's fear of knives– had a name.

Laura brushed off her clothes and we strolled out into the street, away from Sosa's house and the Montgrí Hotel, with no clear destination.

"Catalans," I told her as we walked past a hotel that called itself a 'lodge' just to charge higher prices. "The dead people in the glacier were also Catalans, just like Juan Gómez, the mummy. Specifically, from Torroella de Montgrí."

Laura looked up the town on her phone.

"Do you know the place?"

"Yes. I was born there, but my parents moved to Barcelona when I was a baby. I've only been back a couple of times since."

"If the bodies really do belong to people from that town, it's likely they knew Fernando Cucurell because they were around his age."

"And they went to the same school," I added. "My father told me about the outings Fernando organized when he was a student."

"Are you one hundred percent sure the victims were from Torroella?"

I explained what "my friend" Xavi had told me about the ring and the Brotherhood of the Wolves. When Laura asked me if I trusted him, I had no choice but to reveal the nature of our relationship. I also told her, with perhaps more detail than necessary, that his sister had cheated on me, with a fellow countrywoman of hers, just a few weeks back.

"That's got to hurt," she said.

"Nothing shows up online about this brotherhood," I replied, changing the subject. "According to Xavi, it was a harmless students' club."

Now Laura was walking with her brow furrowed, squeezing her lower lip between her fingers. I could almost hear the cogs churning inside her head.

"What are you thinking?"

"About Fernando's relationship with the victims. About what your brother-in-law said, that there's no question that they knew each other."

"Ex. Ex-brother-in-law. And not even that, because Anna and I weren't married."

"Sorry. Your ex-fake-brother-in-law then," she said, laughing.

We walked in silence for a bit. Every once in a while, I'd kick at the pebbles that covered the unpaved street. We reached the town plaza, a park with low trees and an Argentine flag waving on a flagpole in its center.

"Two tourists can't walk on that glacier alone," I said. "They had to have gone with a guide. Then there are two alternatives: either the guide killed them, or someone who followed them from town did."

"Both are possibilities, but there might be others. What we know for sure is that the two bodies had large amounts of diazepam in their system, so they were likely drowsy when they were killed. If they didn't consume it knowingly, someone they trusted could have mixed it into something they consumed."

"The guide, for example," I said. "Sosa gave me some whisky with glacier ice when we went, and I drank it, no questions asked."

"It's a possibility."

"According to Juanmi Alonso, my uncle was also a guide when he wasn't working at the hotel."

Laura nodded.

"If it was the guide," I added, "it had to have been premeditated. What kind of a guide takes sedatives and a rifle on a walk?"

"I think we're getting too caught up with what fits and forgetting about what doesn't. For example, why did your uncle disappear? Why did he leave a body in the hotel? He knew that sooner or later someone would find it. If you consider, it's almost a miracle that Danilo guarded the place so well for thirty years. Is all very confusing ... we don't know which is the first link in the chain."

"What do you mean?"

"No one kills three people in two different places at random."

"Much less if they know each other."

"We need to talk to someone who was part of that brotherhood during the years your uncle was in school."

The most obvious option would have been Anna's father because, according to Xavi, being a member of the brotherhood was a family tradition. But I really didn't feel like talking to my ex-father-in-law. Between never having gotten along too well with him and my recent breakup with his daughter, I decided I'd only play that card as a last resource.

"I'll ask Xavi if he knows any older members."

Laura nodded.

"There's something else," I said. "His ring is made of brass and doesn't have the inscription in it. I've been on the computer all afternoon trying to find another meaning to *'Lupus occidere uiuendo debet'*, but I can't find anything beyond the literal translation."

"I've been researching for a year and a half and haven't found anything either."

CHAPTER 31

The next day, Sosa came to my cabin at two o'clock and handed me the key to the municipal archive. He told me he'd had a hard time making the decision, but something about me made him feel he could trust me. It surprised me that he didn't give it to Laura directly, but I didn't ask. He said goodbye, announcing he'd be out of town for a few days, but to call him if I needed anything.

An hour later, Laura and I were rummaging through a room full of file cabinets and folders full to bursting. I remembered what Margarita, the town hall worker, had told me: 'Finding something in there takes a long time'. It sure did. Most of the paperwork wasn't in any logical or chronological order. For example, in one folder I found a restaurant bill from 1995 and a house floorplan from 1992.

We had no luck finding anything referring to the Montgrí Hotel in that cemetery of files. I headed back to the cabin exhausted and empty-handed. At nine p.m., I drifted off as I read the news on my phone while lying in bed. My sweet slumber was interrupted by my phone vibrating on my chest.

"Hey, Julián, can you talk?"

On the screen, my ex-brother-in-law's dreadlocks moved to the rhythm of his voice.

"Yeah, of course. Go ahead."

"You owe me twenty euros."

"You can deduct that from all the beers I bought you in the last three years."

"Done. You owe me seventeen euros."

"You have a shitty memory when it's convenient, you bastard."

"Listen. I have a friend: Merche. She works at the Treasury. Fernando Cucurell Zaplana stopped paying his taxes in Spain in 1987 and started paying them again in 1991. Since then, he's filed his tax returns on time until last year."

"That adds up to what they've told me here: my uncle moved to Chaltén in 1987 and disappeared in 1991."

"According to Merche, since he came back to Spain, he's always kept the same address: Pere Pau Street 32, apartment, floor 1, door 2, in Barcelona. That's in Horta. On the ground floor of that same address, he had a restaurant with a partner, Lorenza Millán Rodríguez. The place is called *El Asador de Anguita*."

I scribbled down the information while I digested it. My unknown uncle, who had left me a hotel with a dead person inside it, had lived in my city for the past thirty years. But also, why hadn't the notary mentioned anything about the restaurant when he read me his assets?

"Thank you so much, Xavi. This is very useful."

"There's more. I also have a friend in the National Police. It cost me to get him to talk, but he finally confirmed that your uncle had no criminal record."

"Bribes have gotten cheap in Spain, haven't they? Were the twenty euros for the Treasury or for the police?"

"The twenty euros are for a subscription to the archive of *La Vanguardia*. I just emailed you an article I think you'll be interested in."

"About my uncle?"

"Not exactly. Read it and see."

"Why won't you just tell me?"

"Because you're going to read it anyway. Why should I waste my spit?"

"You have motor oil, not saliva. You're a robot with no feelings."

Xavi laughed and swung his dreadlocks behind his shoulders, his signature tic. I said goodbye, fighting the urge to ask about Anna.

His email contained a La Vanguardia article from July 14, 1985. True to eighties sensationalism, its title read: *From Innocent Student Club to Macabre Cult.*

Yesterday, the National Police carried out three raids in the town of Torroella de Montgrí –located in the Baix Empordà region– as part of the investigation into an alleged rape. Two months ago, Meritxell Puigbaró, 22, reported having been kidnapped and raped in Torroella by a group of hooded men. According to the young woman's testimony, the attackers all wore a ring shaped like a wolf's head, which belongs to a secret society called 'The Brotherhood of the Wolves'.

The sources this newspaper has consulted with, confirm that said brotherhood is an association that belongs to the Santa María de los Desamparados School, in Torroella de Montgrí. Despite its suggestive name, many ex-members have tried to clean the the club's good name. The club has existed for nearly half a century.

"Back in my day, we wolves were a group of kids, who'd get together to have fun, without hurting anybody. The worst thing we did was stick some gum onto a classmate's chair," states Artur Casbas, ex-mayor of Torroella de Montgrí and member of the club between 1956 and 1959.

If those innocent wolves Casbas mentions ever existed, they are far from the rabid beings Meritxell Puigbaró describes. The young woman, who was aided by emergency services after the attack and is still undergoing psychological treatment, has offered to give us her version of the facts, and pleads, that measures be taken "to stop this from ever happening again to another woman."

"I was coming home from work. I always walk through an empty lot to avoid taking a much longer route. Torroella is a quiet town, I never thought something like this could happen to me." As the young woman shares her story, her voice cracks, and she stops several times to regain her composure. She says that on the night of May 17, a group of

men surrounded her in the empty lot and forced her into a van.

"They say some people don't remember these kinds of traumatic moments. I wasn't that lucky. I can't stop picturing them, hearing their voices, even smelling them," says Puigbaró with tears in her eyes. "They took me to some sort of industrial building, threw me on a mattress on the floor and raped me. There were four of them. I couldn't see their faces because they were covered, but I know who they are. I recognized their voices. They all wore that ring with the wolf head."

The ring Puigbaró refers to is, in fact, the symbol that identifies the Brotherhood of the Wolves. In her story, the woman has no qualms about sharing the names of her four attackers. They are four men, native to Torroella de Montgrí, about twenty-seven years of age. This newspaper has chosen not to include their names until the case is solved.

With regards to the ring, ex-members of the institution tell us that all members of the brotherhood receive one when they join. When they finish their studies at Santa María de los Desamparados, they must leave the society but are allowed to retain the ring as a keepsake. "There was an oath we made on our last day, where we swore to take care of the ring but to never wear it again. It was a kind of rite that dated back to the origins of the brotherhood when it was a more formal and serious association," Artur Casbas clarifies.

It is now up to the justice system to investigate Meritxell Puigbaró's rape and find those responsible. Despite numerous calls, the school of Santa María de los Desamparados has not replied to our requests for an interview for this article.

What is the true nature of the Brotherhood of the Wolves? Is it a macabre secret society or merely a harmless teenage club?

CHAPTER 32

"Sometimes the dead aren't as good as we think," Laura said after reading the article. She'd showed up at my cabin just after I called her to tell her what Xavi had found.

"Until now, I'd assumed the victims of the glacier crimes were, in fact, victims."

"They are, Julián. They're murder victims, despite the kind of people they might have been."

Laura was doing something on her phone while she spoke to me. Nothing annoys me more than people who chose to look at a screen instead of the person standing in front of them.

"We need to find out if my uncle was a member of the wolves," I said, not completely sure if she was registering anything I was saying. "I can call Santa María de los Desamparados."

"It's as good a place as any to start."

"Also, the article states that the members had to abandon the brotherhood once they finished high school, but it also says that the attackers were twenty-seven. If we could contact that woman... Would you mind looking at me when I'm speaking to you?"

Laura smiled and showed me her phone.

"Meritxell Puigbaró has her own website," she said, "she's an English and German translator."

"You really should have a job investigating crimes. You're good."

"Not as good as your jokes. Want me to contact Puigbaró and you contact the school?"

"Task division. I like it. Look at us, working like a real team."

"We also need to find out everything we can about the wolves."

"Leave that to me."

Laura opened the cabin curtain to look outside. It was nine at night and the day's last light had just disappeared. After a moment of silence, she went back to her phone and showed me a photo.

"Ricardo, the chief of Calafate forensics, sent me this a couple of hours ago."

"Last time you saw him he didn't seem to like you too much."

"How do you know that?"

"I was walking past the hotel and heard you arguing," I improvised, omitting the fact that I'd been hiding behind the bar.

"That's water under the bridge. I was wrong, and I apologized to him. We worked together on the glacier crimes for several months and get along well. He's a good guy."

In the photo, I recognized the main bedroom from my uncle's house at the other end of the hotel property.

"Look at the floor."

Instead of the mess of footprints I'd seen there, the dust showed a single pair of footprints that even I could interpret. Someone had walked up to the bedside table and then turned around to leave.

"Forensics took that photo when they entered the house," said Laura, "before any police officer set foot in the room."

"That means someone was in there not long before them."

"With a clear objective. They knew what they were looking for and where to find it. Do you remember what was in the nightstand drawer when we went?"

"A pipe and a lighter. Apart from that, it was empty."

"Do you know anyone who keeps so few things next to their bed?" asked Laura.

"No."

"The owner of the footprints broke into the house, went straight to the nightstand, and took something. Why do you think they'd do such a thing?"

"Because it incriminated them."

"That's exactly what I think."

CHAPTER 33

The next day at noon, I called Santa María de los Desamparados to request information about the Brotherhood of the Wolves. The secretary told me she had no idea what I was talking about. I asked to speak to the headmaster, who, according to the school website, was Professor Castells, but the woman kindly told me that he was away at a conference and wouldn't be back until the following week. I fabricated a story about wanting to interview him and she assured me that as soon as Castells returned, she'd relay my message. Her tone made me doubt she was actually going to.

I hung up and called my father. On the screen, half of the great Miguel Cucurell's face popped up.

"Julián, how are you?"

"I'm good, dad. If I could actually see you, I'd be even better."

"I don't understand these things," he answered, moving the phone away from his face. As usual, he was sitting on the couch in front of the TV.

"Dad, do you remember if your brother Fernando had a ring like this one?"

I put the replica Laura had given me up to the camera. My father squinted as if that would improve the video call's low resolution.

"I don't know if you can see it clearly. It has a wolf head."

"Yes, now I can see perfectly. It doesn't ring a bell, why do you ask?"

"It seems that in Santa María de los Desamparados there was a secret society of students called the Brotherhood of the Wolves, and this was their symbol."

"My brother in the Brotherhood of the Wolves? Impossible."

"You knew about them?"

"Of course. Everyone did. They were some rich kids who would meet up in secret to raid their parent's expensive whisky cabinets. They smoked, talked about women, as if they knew anything, and exchanged porn magazines. My brother wouldn't have hung out with them if they paid him to."

"But are you one hundred percent sure he wasn't a member?"

"No. I am also not sure that man made it to the moon, but if I had to bet on it... Fernando was a very open person, with few secrets. He preferred life outdoors and flirting with girls from Inmaculada Concepción than meeting in secret to smoke, drink, and drool over photos of tits."

"How do you know what went on in those meetings?"

"Well, they would tell you about it, to brag and get you to want to join. The more members, the better. Each one of them paid hefty dues, and they used that money to hire a woman of the night once a month."

"A hooker?"

"More like what you'd call a stripper nowadays."

"For a secret society, it doesn't seem very secret."

"It wasn't, at all. It was a gang of big-mouthed losers."

"Did your brother ever talk to you about the brotherhood?"

"Not that I recall, no. Why is this so important?"

"It's a long story, dad."

"I don't have anything better to do."

"Let's see, where do I start...? Did you know your brother was born in Argentina?"

"Yes. My parents moved to Buenos Aires in the mid-50s. My father set up a business with a partner who ended up scamming him. They came back to Catalunya two years later, poorer than they'd left and with Fernando still a baby. Your grandparents didn't talk about that very much. It took me years to find out what I'm telling you."

"Thanks to the fact that Fernando had Argentinian nationality, he was able to get the land where he built the hotel, which only opened for one season and then remained closed for thirty years. The next person to enter was me, and I found a mummified body, likely to be from around the time Fernando left. He was wearing a ring just like this one, which turns out belongs to the Brotherhood of the Wolves. I'm sure you agree it can't be a coincidence that the dead person went to the same school as Fernando."

My father wiped his brow, processing what I'd just told him. I was thankful not to have mentioned the two other bodies found in the glacier. His heart was weak and he'd already given us more than one scare.

"Son, I don't know what to say. My brother and I never had a close relationship, but I have a lot of trouble believing he was a murderer. We had some serious clashes, but he was a good man."

"I think it might be useful if you told me why you stopped talking."

"Again, with that? I told you it was over a woman."

"That's the same as not telling me anything. I know so little about him that any bit of information is valuable. A fight that distanced him from his brother speaks volumes about him and could help me get an idea of what he was like."

"It also speaks volumes about me. You realize how unfair it would be for me to give you my side of the story now that he isn't around to defend himself?"

That's how ironclad my father's values were. Miguel Cucurell was part of a dying breed.

"Whatever, Dad. Don't sweat it. What matters is that Fernando had some sort of connection to the Brotherhood of the Wolves. Are you still in touch with any of your classmates from Santa María de los Desamparados?"

"A couple of years ago I was added to a WhatsApp group of students from my time. Every once in a while, someone sends a funny video or makes some comment about politics. If that's being in touch, then sure."

"Could you ask if your brother was somehow connected to the brotherhood?"

"If it helps you, of course. Although I don't think they'll know something I don't, seeing that I lived with him."

I didn't think so either, but it was worth a try.

"Thanks, Dad."

"Of course. Hey, just wondering. What are your plans? What are you going to do with the hotel?"

"I haven't decided yet. I could sell it as is, but I kind of like the idea of restoring it."

"So, you're planning on staying in Argentina for a while?"

"I don't know."

I was being honest. I had no idea what to do. My rational side said I should sell and get out as soon as possible. But there was a force that drew me in like a magnet, begging me to stay and search for the truth.

CHAPTER 34

Two days went by with no news. My father hadn't been able to discover anything and Laura was very busy with a group of Chinese tourists that had booked horseback rides for three days straight. I used the time to clean up the hotel.

I'd just lit the dining room fireplace when my phone rang. It was a video call from Xavi.

"How's everything going in the middle of nowhere? Any more bodies show up in the last three days?"

"You're hilarious. You should've been a comedian."

"My ex-brother-in-law pays me much better to be a P.I. I found something that might be useful."

"Well, what are you waiting for?"

"Josep Codina. Thirty-one years old. Murdered in Torroella de Montgrí, stabbed four times. Guess which school he went to."

"Santa María de los Desamparados."

Xavi's pixeled face moved up and down.

"He was killed in 1989. He lived in Barcelona but had gone back to the town on vacation."

"A few years before the glacier crimes," I whispered, more to myself than to Xavi.

"I found an article about the murder in *La Veu de Torroella*. I've just emailed it to you."

La Veu de Torroella, as its original name hinted, was Torroella de Montgrí's newspaper.

"Thanks. Why do you think it's connected to the deaths here?"

"Maybe it has nothing to do with them. But remember that Torroella isn't Baltimore. The homicide squad is like Halley's Comet, it passes once every 76 years. If there's a dead man, about the same age as the ones killed in Chaltén, it happened around the same time, and they all went to school together, there might be a connection.

I thanked him and hung up to read the article. It was from August 27th, 1989. It didn't have much more than what Xavi had already told me. It said that Josep Codina had been stabbed in the town center, and the officer in charge of the investigation, one Gregorio Alcántara, made the typical statements that don't really say much. "For the time being, there are no suspects. We cannot reveal any more information." After that, the journalist who had written the article went into a detailed description of how the man's death had caused a commotion, in the otherwise peaceful community.

As I wondered if this was related to what had happened in El Chaltén, I toyed with the brotherhood ring, which I had been carrying with me lately. The metal reflected the orange flames in the fireplace, giving the wolf's bare teeth a more menacing look.

I couldn't sit around and wait for Xavi to call me back, or for Laura to find something. I needed to make a move, and I could only think of one.

I put on my coat and headed towards the point where the rivers met. I unenthusiastically waved back at tourists and locals as I walked. I passed the police station, where there were now two different officers than the ones who had taken my statement the day I found Juan Gómez, dried out like a raisin. I left town, crossed the Fitz Roy River bridge, and walked on the side of the only road that connected me to the rest of the world.

A two-story, wooden building appeared a few hundred meters ahead. The old National Parks inn –the only accommodation older than the Montgrí Hotel – was now a tourist information center.

Inside, the walls were covered in posters about native flora and fauna, the park history, and hiking routes. Several park rangers, wearing khaki uniforms, handed out brochures to tourists and answered questions in different languages.

"Hola, hello," one of them greeted me. He was barely twenty and still had acne on his cheeks.

"Good afternoon. I'm looking for Juan Miguel Alonso. Do you know if he's back from fixing the Río Blanco bridge?"

The youth looked surprised. He probably wasn't used to someone with a foreign accent asking about one of the rangers instead of the hikes.

"Give me a minute," he replied and ducked under the piece of red rope blocking the access to the first floor.

Less than a minute later, Juanmi Alonso came down the stairs.

"Julián. What a surprise. How are you?"

"Good. Can I ask you a few questions?"

"Of course, let's go outside."

We sat on a wooden bench in the garden. The Fitz Roy was visible in front of us, though a small cloud covered its tip.

"It looks like a volcano," I said.

"Yes. In fact, lots of people like to say that Chaltén means 'smoking mountain', but that isn't true. In the Tehuelche language, 'Chaltén' means something awfully vulgar. Sometimes I think it's appropriate that a town born out of a conflict carries that conflict in its name."

I nodded in silence. Perhaps at another time, I would have been interested in what Alonso was saying. I might have even asked him what the vulgar word was.

"But you didn't come here to talk about that," he said, beating me to the point.

"Not quite. I'm here to ask you who Fernando lived with at the house by the hotel."

"No one. Didn't I tell you he was a bachelor?"

"Yes, but I found clothes inside that belonged to both a man and a woman. And toys. A family was living there."

Juanmi smiled and shook his head.

"No, your uncle lived alone. Back then, it was common practice to host people in your house. The coalman, for example, would come twice a month from the Río Turbio mines and stay at someone's house. Remember in those days, there were few houses in the town besides the twelve original ones the government built. Your uncle always lent out the hotel, and if there wasn't any room left, he'd open his own home to host merchants, travelers, and even new townspeople who came here with a government job and a promise of a house that hadn't been built yet."

"But there were empty rooms in the hotel. I found several perfectly made beds. And you told me that the last time you saw him was at the end of the season, and he was about to leave for Spain. Why would he host a family in his house if the hotel was available?"

"I have no idea, Julián. But I can assure you that your uncle was single and didn't live with anyone else. I don't know what happened the last few days before he left because I was out of town, as I mentioned."

"The day we spoke at the campground you mentioned that a few years before he went missing, Fernando had gone back to Spain on vacation. Do you remember what year that was?"

"Yes, 1989. Impossible to forget, because Argentina was in the midst of a presidential election and to piss me off, your uncle kept saying that, even though he was going to be in Spain, he'd go to the consulate to vote for Menem."

"Do you remember what month that was?"

"April, one month before the election. He came back in November."

I nodded without saying anything. My uncle was in Spain when Josep Codina was murdered in Torroella de Montgrí.

CHAPTER 35

If Chaltén wasn't the town with the most beer breweries per square foot in the world, it was definitely in the top five. After a long day of hiking in the mountains, everyone felt like they deserved a cold pint of craft beer.

Tap Tap was one of the biggest. Built out of wood and corrugated metal, it had an old-timey look that was impossible for a town as old as I was. Inside, I was greeted by rock, in English, playing on the speakers and the tempting smell of French fries. A big copper pipe that crossed the ceiling led me toward a dozen chrome taps commandeered by two bearded hipsters. There were few people at the bar, but the tables –sizeable ones made to share with strangers– were full of young people speaking in several different languages.

I chose a porter from the list written in chalk on one of the walls. Beard One charged me for it and passed the order to Beard Two. Before he was done pouring it, I felt a hand on my shoulder.

"Laura! I just ordered. You're making me look bad!"

"Don't be dramatic. Mauricio, a porter please."

Beard Two nodded and placed another glass under the tap.

"Did you understand the article I sent you?" I asked, opening up said article from La Veu de Torroella on my phone.

"Codina, an ex-student from Santa María de los Desamparados, was stabbed in Torroella de Montgrí. He was thirty-one years old, studied medicine at the University of Barcelona, and was finishing his residency in plastic surgery at the Hospital del Mar. The town of

Torroella was shocked because it had been years since their last violent crime."

"You understand Catalan?"

"I don't, but my phone's translator does."

Beard Two placed the beers on two felt coasters and pushed them toward us.

"Bet you don't know what ring Codina was wearing when he was killed," she said to me.

"You're kidding me."

"Not kidding. A friend who works for the Federal Police collaborated on a case for Interpol. I've been nagging him for months to ask someone there to use their database to look up other crimes where the victim had a wolf's head ring. As soon as I got the article you sent me, I called him again and finally got a result."

"Is Interpol's database that detailed?"

"It is since the advent of the internet. Even so, there isn't much information about cases from thirty years ago. We were lucky, Codina's case is digitalized."

"Are you sure it's the same ring?"

Laura took a sip of beer and tilted her head to the side as if offended by my comment. To answer my question, she placed her phone on the bar.

"This photo is from Josep Codina's autopsy," it was funny to hear her say 'Shosep' in her Argentinian accent.

The image showed three pale fingers on a steel surface. On one of them was a ring identical to the one I carried in my pocket like some kind of cursed amulet.

"If we add this to the fact that, according to Alonso, your uncle was in Spain when they killed Codina..."

"It's impossible that all this is a coincidence."

"Exactly. And we aren't going to find the answers we need in Chaltén."

"What are you suggesting?"

Laura looked me in the eyes.

"We need to go to Spain."

"We? Wait a minute. I want to know the truth because this has to do with my family, but why do you care about this case so much?"

"When you were a teenager, did you ever like a girl that didn't give you the time of day?"

"Only ninety-nine percent of the time."

"What was the advice your most popular friend gave you? The one who acted like he knew everything. There's always one of those."

"I don't know. Generally, people said you shouldn't pay attention to them. Ignore them. The less attention you gave them, the more they wanted you."

"Same as they say here. That stuff about women liking being ignored is sexist bullshit."

"And what does that have to do with..."

"It's sexist bullshit but it's also true. Though it has nothing to do with gender. Everyone hates being ignored. Men, women, whomever. The harder something is to get, the more we want it. Whether it's a person, money, social standing, or the answer to a question."

"I'm guessing that in your case, the question is what happened with the glacier crimes."

"Julián, up until two years ago, I worked solving crimes. I love it and I'm very good at it. When those bodies showed up, I wasn't part of the police force anymore, and I was forced to watch from the sidelines. I was asked to join in a few times as a consultant, but I wasn't allowed to fully work on the case. I've been investigating on my own for a year and a half. Do you know why? Because not even the horseback rides around this amazing place prevent me from thinking about the bureaucratic nightmare I'm stuck in and how long it'll take for me to get my job back. The only thing that's keeping me from going insane is focusing on this, which has been my obsession since way before you showed up and the third body was found."

"You never told me why you stopped being a cop."

Laura took a long sip of beer.

"There was a case where I didn't follow protocol. Instead of doing what the law states, I did what seemed fair and right to me. That was my mistake and I paid for it with my job."

"What did you do exactly?"

"It's a long story," she huffed. "You can look up 'The Arrow Collector' online; that's the name the press gave the case. I don't regret what I did, but my superiors didn't see it the way I did. They removed me from my job and a disciplinary case was opened against me. I went to San Martín de los Andes to wait for it to get sorted out, it's a beautiful place where I'd always wanted to live. The judge told me it would take six months, but it's been two years, and the case hasn't progressed at all."

"San Martín de los Andes is pretty far from here, isn't it?"

"Six hundred kilometers."

"How did you end up in El Chaltén?"

"Six months after I'd moved to San Martín, they called me in to consult on a homicide in El Calafate."

"I thought you were suspended."

"Yes, but that doesn't mean I can't be hired as a consultant for specific jobs. That's the good thing about having contacts. When I finished the investigation, they offered me a job teaching a crime forensics workshop for police officers, and I accepted. I rented a tiny apartment in Calafate but didn't last two months, because the Viedma glacier bodies showed up and I came here."

"They called you as a consultant again?"

"Yeah, and I got so absorbed in the case that once they didn't need me anymore, I decided to stay. That's when I started working for Rodolfo. Some time went by and I could see that the case had stalled, so I started writing the book. It started as a dissertation about frozen bodies and ended up turning into the chronicle of the crimes you read."

We each took a pull on our beers.

"See now why we both need to go to Spain? You have to go to find out who your uncle was, I have to go to close this chapter."

"Where are you going to get the money for the trip?"

"I have some savings and a house in Puerto Deseado I rent out. Plus, I still get paid my salary from the police department."

"You get paid without working? I want your life."

"I assure you, you don't want my life."

There was something about her I still didn't get. While I contemplated what to say to her, I ordered another round.

"I agree that if we're going to find answers, it'll be there and not here, but I don't know if I can leave before I sell the hotel."

"The hotel's been here for thirty years. It'll be here for a couple more months. In any case, the cold months are almost here. Construction is complicated in winter."

"Yeah, Sosa told me."

"See? We need to go to Spain. Let's go find some answers, *tío*," said Laura, raising her pint in the air. For some reason, when Argentinians try to fake a Spanish accent, they always sound like a combination of Antonio Banderas and a Basque boulder-lifting champion.

I smiled and clinked my pint against hers.

"Let's go find some answers, *tía*."

PART III

DON QUIXOTE

CHAPTER 36

Many years earlier.

The boy takes out the scissors he had hidden in his underwear. He's in the bathroom with the door locked behind him. He has chosen the sharpest scissors in the house, the ones his mother uses to cut fabric.

Princess. You're a little princess, a mocking voice whispers in his head.

He brings his face close to the mirror and looks at his skin, as smooth as a porcelain doll's. He's already sixteen and there isn't even a shadow of a beard on his cheeks. Not even after a week of rubbing chicken feces on himself, as his friend Manel told him to do.

He stares at his upturned nose and almond-shaped brown eyes. His eyelashes are so dark it looks like he's wearing mascara. Once, when they were leaving the movie theater, his neighbor Marta asked him if he was wearing makeup.

He takes his shirt off and steps back to look at his naked torso. Manel's other piece of advice doesn't seem to be working either. After a month of eating like a pig each time he sits at the table, his arms and shoulders are still as thin as a scarecrow's.

He knows that no diet or magic cream will make time move faster, but he can't wait. He's even lost hope that he'll have his friend Joan Cases's luck, had a growth spurt and whose voice changed all in one summer. There are days he thinks he might never become a man.

He needs a miracle and wishes for it with all his strength. That's why he stares at himself in the mirror every day as if that might make his Adam's apple bigger, his body hair fuller, or his shoulders broader.

Little princess. That voice again.

He steps close to the mirror again and gazes at his hair. His short, smooth curls amplify the movement of his head. His mother always cuts his hair right at the limit that's permitted at Santa María de los Desamparados. She says it's too beautiful to be cut any shorter.

He agrees with her on that. He likes his hair. That's why, when he raises the scissors to his forehead and cuts the first curl flush with his scalp, he feels angry. Very angry.

Little princess.

CHAPTER 37

Laura

Sitting by the oval-shaped window, Laura watched the flight attendants push the food cart at a snail's pace while they handed out dinner trays. "Chicken or pasta?", they asked with a Spanish accent. *Whatever you prefer, just give me something because I'm starving*, she answered in her head and went back to counting the aisles remaining until they reached her. She hadn't anticipated that the trip would make her so nervous she'd forget to eat before leaving for the airport.

It was her first time abroad and she'd read that Spain required her to show a return flight, a hotel reservation, and ninety euros per day for the extent of her trip. Out of those three requirements, she only met the first.

She'd spent the first hour of the flight worrying what she'd say if they asked her anything at Customs but reached the same conclusion as she had the previous days: sometimes, not even the best answer can save you. She'd learned that from years of conducting interrogations.

She'd only managed to calm down by resorting to the lowest form of relaxation: turning on the little screen in front of her and choosing a rom-com. Now that the movie was over and the cheesy love story had loosened the knot in her stomach, her body begged for food.

"Would you like pasta or chicken?"

"Chicken," she said quickly.

"Pasta for me," said Julián.

He was sitting to her left and had spent almost the entire flight writing in a notebook. She'd spied without him noticing a few times, but far from deciphering his writing, all she'd been able to conclude was that even a doctor could give Julián penmanship lessons.

Finally, the flight attendant placed a tray on her table. The smell of roasted chicken and potatoes was heavenly. She cut a piece with her plastic knife and fork. The lack of space between herself and the table forced her to keep her hands close to her chest.

"I look like a T-rex," she said.

"Eating on a plane is always so comfortable," answered Julián as he put away the notebook in the seat pocket in front of him.

The first bite tasted sublime to her. Plane food's bad reputation must have come from people who weren't very hungry. Like Julián, who didn't seem to have any intention of eating his pasta.

"Are you nervous?" she asked him.

"Nervous, scared, anxious. Everything at once. Three weeks ago, I was flying in the opposite direction to sell a piece of land that was going to solve my money issues. Now I'm coming back without having sold the land, with a million-dollar hotel to my name, and three murder victims connected to an uncle I never met."

"Were you writing about that?"

"Something like that. I was writing a summary of the things we don't know," he said right before trying his first bite of pasta.

"Oh, then you're going to need another notebook."

"I know. There are so many unanswered questions."

Julián crossed his fork and knife over his practically untouched plate and opened the notebook back up.

"What's my uncle guilty of and what is he a victim of? Why did he leave a body behind? What did he do during the next thirty years? What does the inscription inside the ring mean? Why are those lawyers paying the taxes? There are too many questions. I don't know where to start."

She understood Julián. If she, a professional, sometimes got overwhelmed with questions, it made sense he'd feel paralyzed by them.

"All I can say is that solving a tough case is like eating an elephant."

She cut another piece of chicken and raised it to her mouth. Partially, to add some theatrics to her explanation, and partially out of hunger. Julián made the same confused face she'd made years back, when Superintendent Lamuedra had said that phrase to her.

"There's only one way to do it: one bite at a time. There aren't any shortcuts. Your list of questions is extensive and it's good that you wrote it, but don't try to answer all of them at once because you'll go crazy. The first step is to find out anything we can about the Brotherhood of the Wolves. For example, if your uncle was a member or not."

"My father says he wasn't, but I'm not so sure. Hey, could you ask your friend at Interpol about our dead guy from the hotel? I know that Juan Gómez is a common name, but I'm sure that with a passport number..."

"I don't have a friend at Interpol. I have a friend at the Argentine National Police who once worked with someone from Interpol. I already asked him a big favor and had to push for months to get him to do it. That door's closed. In general, police officers aren't very open to sharing information with someone who's been removed from their position, no matter how well they get along."

"No harm in trying."

"Too late," she lied to stop Julián from insisting. "I already did. No luck."

"It would also be good to talk to someone involved in Josep Codina's murder investigation in Torroella de Montgrí. A police officer, someone from the forensics team... if we're lucky maybe even a judge. The article in *La Veu de Torroella* mentioned someone named Gregorio Alcántara as the person responsible for the investigation. We could try to get in touch with him."

She stifled a smile. She found it adorable when Julián suggested something she'd already done two days back.

"That's taken care of as well," she said. "Alcántara accepted my friendship request on Facebook today. Can I eat your pasta?"

CHAPTER 38

Laura

As the plane descended, Laura gazed out the window at the sea, which then turned into a shoreline covered in pine trees and buildings. When they landed, she heard the pilot's voice welcoming them to El Prat airport in Barcelona. Local time: seven fifteen a.m., thirteen degrees Celsius.

"We escaped the cold," Julián said to her.

She nodded and looked back at the tarmac. The knot in her stomach was back from just thinking about going through Customs.

Fifteen minutes later, she handed her passport to a police officer her age. She recognized the annoyance in the way the woman scanned her document inside the tiny glass cubicle. No one decided to become a police officer to work in a fish tank.

Without asking any questions, the woman stamped her passport and slid it back to her through the opening in the glass, then looked at the next person in line. Laura muttered a 'thank you' and walked toward Julián, who had gone through the line for European citizens.

"Welcome to Spain."

"This part looks a lot like Ezeiza," she answered, pointing at the airport signs.

They followed the arrows and screens until they reached the conveyor belt where they waited for their luggage.

"Are you sure you're ok with me staying at your place?" she asked again.

"My answer is the same as the four times you asked me on the plane," he replied. "I have three bedrooms and now live alone."

She picked up on the hint of sadness in Julián's last remark.

Once they got their luggage, they headed toward the airport's main hall, where dozens of people waited for family members, friends, and loved ones. Some held signs or flowers. Others hugged recently arrived travelers.

"The metro station is that way," Julián said to her.

Laura followed him, pulling her luggage behind her. Once they'd made it through the crowd, she heard a voice behind them.

"Julián, honey! There you are."

She watched Julián turn around and furrow his brow as a tall, skinny woman walked toward them. Her brisk pace made her short blonde hair swing like a hyperactive poodle's tail.

"Mom? What are you doing here?"

"We came to pick you up," said the bald, slightly overweight man walking behind the woman.

"Laura, meet my parents. Consuelo and Miguel."

She noticed that Julián's parents scanning her with an intensity comparable to the x-ray machine her luggage had just gone through.

"Nice to meet you," said the woman. "I didn't know my son was traveling with company."

"Very good company, I'd say," added the father.

"Nice to meet you," was all she managed to say. She smiled too, for good measure.

"This way. The car's in the parking lot," the father said pointing in the direction opposite to where they'd been walking. "Laura, let me carry your bag."

"No need."

"I insist, you must be tired."

"Miguel, dear. Leave the poor girl alone," Julián's mother interjected and then turned towards Laura. "My husband's a good guy but can be a little old-fashioned sometimes."

"I thought I said I didn't need you to come pick me up. In any case, shouldn't you be at work?" Julián asked his mother.

"They canceled the visit to the site I had scheduled for this morning. The construction manager is sick."

"My mother's an architect," Julián explained.

"One of the best in Barcelona," added his father, looking at his wife with a tenderness Laura had rarely seen in a couple that age.

"Don't exaggerate. I'm an architect and I'm good at what I do, that's it."

They got into an elevator the size of a bedroom and descended into the parking lot.

"Our car is at the end of this row," Julián's father announced.

The car was a BMW X5. The only thing it had in common with Laura's Corsa, was the fact that it had four wheels. Julián's mother sat in the driver's seat, his father next to her, and the two of them in the back. The upholstery smelled brand new.

They left the maze of columns and ramps and drove out onto a four-lane highway without a single pothole in sight.

"Is it your first time in Barcelona?" Consuelo asked her.

"It's my first time out of Argentina."

"Well, you've come to a wonderful city. Look, Barcelona is everything that lies between that mountain and the sea, which you can't see right now."

"What mountain?" she asked. All she could see were tall buildings.

"That one," Julián said, pointing to a hill in the distance with an antenna on top. "The mountains here aren't like in Patagonia. If the Tibidabo were in Chaltén, it wouldn't even have a name."

"I don't mean to be rude, but..." said Miguel, turning to look at his son.

"You want to know what Laura's doing here."

"It sounds rude if you put it like that."

Laura dismissed the comment with a wave of her hand.

"As you know," she said, "inside the hotel that Julián inherited there was a body that had been there for about thirty years. It was wearing a ring that happened to be the insignia of the Brotherhood of the Wolves. What your son might not have told you, is that a year and a half ago, two bodies were found frozen inside a glacier. Those two people were murdered around the same time and wore the same ring. I'd been investigating the glacier crimes long before Julián arrived in Chaltén."

"That's horrible," said Consuelo as she sped down the underground segment of the highway.

"Are you a police officer?" Miguel asked.

"Yes," she simplified.

"When were you planning on telling us all of this?" Consuelo chastised her son.

"I didn't want to do it over the phone. I preferred to tell you in person. Dad, your brother didn't leave Chaltén out of boredom. As I told you, I think Fernando either belonged to the Brotherhood of the Wolves or had some sort of issue with them. Also, a few years before these murderers, a man who was also wearing the ring was stabbed to death in Toroella."

"I remember that," Julián's mother butted in. "Wasn't that in Pere Rigau Square?"

"Yes, in 1989. The same year Fernando came to Spain on vacation."

"Let me get this straight," Miguel Cucurell said. "You think my brother killed four people?"

"That's what we're trying to find out," Laura intervened.

"That's absurd."

"It might be," she admitted. "But whatever the truth is, we had to come find it. That's why we're here."

Julián's father exhaled, nodding slowly. Laura knew that look. It was the face of someone trying to process too much information at once.

"The problem is that we don't know anything about Fernando Cucurell," Julián said.

Miguel turned around in his seat. Laura noticed him glance at her abashedly before glaring at his son. It was obvious that Julián's father didn't want to get into family business in front of a stranger.

They drove on in silence until Consuelo left the tunnel and the BMW emerged in the heart of the city.

"Look, that's the Camp Nou stadium," Julián's father commented as he pointed at the cylindrical concrete building to their right. "This is where your fellow countryman Messi plays. Do you like soccer?"

"Not much."

"No? I thought that as an Argentinian..."

"My father's a huge Barça fan. He doesn't miss a match."

Laura thought she should make a comment about soccer or Messi but couldn't think of anything to say. Her last conversation about the subject was two years back in the Puerto Deseado casino, with a moneylender she was investigating. Things hadn't ended very well.

Julián's house was less than 500 meters from the stadium, on a narrow street with trees on both sides that formed an arch overhead.

"Do you want to grab something to eat at our place?" Consuelo asked them. "I can make a *tortilla*."

"When it comes to cooking, my mom's a great architect."

"Oh, Julián."

"Let me finish, Mom. I was going to say that your *tortillas* are the exception and yours are awesome."

"It's the only thing I learned to cook. I'm sorry son, for getting distracted with minor things like going to college and designing houses."

"She's also a hard-core feminist."

"That makes two of us," said Laura, and exchanged a smile with Consuelo through the rear-view mirror. "Thanks for the invite, but I'm exhausted. Could we maybe take a rain check?"

"Of course! You're welcome whenever."

They said goodbye on the street and Julián opened the door of a narrow building. They walked up three flights of a staircase so old, the steps were rounded from use.

His apartment was minimalist and tastefully decorated. On top of the mantle that connected the kitchen to the dining room, Laura saw some envelopes that appeared to be bills.

"Come, let me show you your bedroom."

Julián led her to a small bedroom. There was a desk and a computer against one wall, and a single bed against the other.

"As a friend likes to say, it's small but uncomfortable."

"Compared to the pension I lived in when I was studying in Buenos Aires, this is a suite."

CHAPTER 39

Julián

I collapsed onto the sofa the second Laura went to take a shower. The trip had been exhausting. On my phone, there was a notification from Sabadell Bank. It announced that according to the acceptance of inheritance presented by the Hernández Burrull notary office, I was officially the new owner of Fernando Cucurell's account with them. To gain access to the login information, I needed to get in touch with them.

Surprisingly, it wasn't as cumbersome as I'd expected: I called, downloaded an app on my phone, filmed an identification video holding my ID up to the camera, and accepted a whopping ninety-euro commission. Once all those steps were complete, I had access to the account.

I discovered that when you inherit a bank account, you not only get the funds left over after several vultures take their share, but also get access to the account history. With a simple click, I could see all of Fernando's bank transactions from the past two years.

There are few things that tell you more about a person than how they spend their money.

I quickly found out that every November, my uncle wired money to the González-Ackerman firm in Argentina under the title 'Montgrí Hotel Taxes'. The last one, according to my calculations, was made a few days before his death.

The lawyer's hostility was just her being professional. The woman had simply done her job in maintaining her client's privacy. The only thing she was guilty of was paying the taxes three months after receiving the money, which I guessed was a way of taking advantage of the country's high inflation to make some extra profit.

Additionally, my uncle's income consisted of a seven-hundred-euro pension and a monthly payment of 500 euros from El Asador de Aguita, the restaurant he'd owned for almost thirty years in Horta. Twelve hundred euros in total, three or four hundred of which were withdrawn every month from an ATM, and the rest went toward supermarket purchases, movie theater tickets, and other sundry expenses paid in plastic. In short, my uncle, who owned a million-dollar piece of property in one of Patagonia's most touristic towns, barely made ends meet every month.

The sound of a key in the lock made me jump. Before I could react, the door was wide open.

"Julián. What are you doing here?"

It was Anna.

"Weren't you in Patagonia?" she added.

"Yeah. I'm back. What are you doing here?"

"I can't find my passport. I think I left it inside a drawer here."

"You're leaving the country?"

Anna raised her head and looked at me with those magnetic dark eyes that still captivated me. She gave me a bitter smile, almost as if it pained her.

"Yes. To Argentina."

"With Rosario?"

She nodded.

"It'll be good for me to have some time to think. I don't know what I want to do with my life."

"Clearly."

"Juli, I'm not going to ask you to forgive me, but please don't attack me."

Right at that moment, the bathroom door opened and Laura came out, freshly showered, her hair wrapped in a towel, wearing shorts and a tight T-shirt. Anna looked at her and raised an eyebrow.

"It's not what you think."

"You don't need to give me an explanation. As if."

"Laura is a friend...colleague... it's hard to explain. She's helping me sort out some loose ends from the inheritance ordeal."

"Hi, how are you? Nice to meet you," Laura said and gave Anna a single kiss on the cheek, Argentinian style.

Anna went in for a second kiss on the other cheek, but Laura had already stepped back.

"Oh, sorry, I forgot you guys give two kisses here. In Argentina, we only give one."

It would have been the ideal moment to explain to her that, thanks to Rosario, Anna knew quite well how people kissed in Argentina. But I managed to keep my mouth shut.

"Well, I don't want to interrupt," said Anna. "Can I go into the bedroom to see if I can find the passport?"

"All yours," I said, bowing slightly.

Perhaps for the last time, Anna entered what had been our bedroom for the past two years.

"That relationship ended like shit, didn't it?" asked Laura.

"What?"

"The atmosphere between you guys is so dense I could cut it with a knife."

"It's not that bad. We can talk to each other, which is more than most people can say."

"Depending on what you're saying, sometimes silence is better."

"Don't you want to go put on some more clothes and dry your hair? You don't want to catch cold."

CHAPTER 40

Julián

El Asador de Anguita was three hundred meters from the notary office where I'd gotten the news of Fernando Cucurell's existence and his death, simultaneously. It was clearly a high-end restaurant with low lighting, jazz playing in the background, and a twenty-three-euro lunch special. At the tables outside, an older couple quickly ate their dessert, and a group of suit-clad office workers sipped their coffee. It was almost four p.m. when Laura and I walked through the door.

Inside, the sound of silverware clinking and the coffee machine filled the air. It was a traditional, elegant place, but not pretentious. Lots of wood on the walls, and a perfectly shined floor. A waiter, so thin his white shirt looked like it was still on a hanger, greeted us without interrupting his task of placing empty cups on the bar.

"Good afternoon. Table for two?"

"No, we're actually here to see Lorenza," I said.

"I guess you don't know her."

"No."

"Thought so," he said, pointing at a woman in her seventies, dressed in bright red, who was organizing coins at the cash register.

"Lorenza Millán?" I asked her.

"Yes, that's me," she said as she closed the register.

"My name is Julián Cucurell."

She froze at the mention of my last name.

"I'm Fernando's nephew. From what I gather, you were his business partner for a long time."

"Nearly thirty years."

Lorenza Millán walked around the bar and gave Laura and me two kisses each. She gave the waiter some instructions and asked us to follow her.

We walked into a large dining room full of oil paintings of rural landscapes on the walls, and tables with black tablecloths. Only one table still had people seated at it, two elegant men, with pomaded hair drinking coffee. We sat at the table furthest from them.

"Have you eaten?"

"Yes, thank you," I replied.

"How can I help you?"

"You see, ma'am, I don't know anything about my uncle. I just recently found out he existed."

"Oh, you're off to a horrible start calling me 'ma'am'. If you don't call me Lorenza, I won't say one more word."

I couldn't help but laugh. Her words reminded me of Juanmi Alonso. Certain people take formality worse than an insult.

"Lorenza, then. I was saying I don't know anything about my uncle."

"He was an amazing person."

"How did you meet?"

"Phew," she made a gesture with her hand similar to someone indicating a long road. "An old boyfriend of mine introduced us. It was back in late '91. We hit it off immediately because both Fernando and I were interested in gastronomy. We wanted to open something up in the center of the city, but at that moment Barcelona was preparing for the Olympics and rental prices were insane. So, we expanded our search until we found this place. We turned it into what it is today, little by little, putting almost thirty years of work into it. Without your uncle's drive, this place would have never been anything more than a neighborhood bar. Up until two years ago, Fernando was a steam engine."

"What happened two years ago?"

"His wife Rita passed away."

"He was married? Did he have children?"

"No, and no. But they'd been living together for twenty years. He called her his companion. I always loved that word. They met at this very table," she said, tapping on the tablecloth twice. "She worked close by and often came to eat here. A lovely woman, poor Rita. She got sick five years ago. When she passed, Fernando told me he didn't have the strength left to carry on and wanted to retire."

"How old was he?"

"Seventy-one. He could have retired much earlier, but he was one of those people who live to work. Like me."

Lorenza Millán paused and looked me in the eye.

"Listen, you don't know how much I insisted to pay him his half of the restaurant. I swear, I didn't want him to leave it to me. After he left, I transferred some money to him every month because I knew he had a very low pension."

"Lorenza, that's not what I'm here for."

"I still want you to know that I wanted to buy it from him."

"Understood. But the only thing I came here for is to learn about my uncle. For example, how did he die? At the notary's office, they just told me he was run over by a car."

The woman gulped and looked around her.

"It was my fault."

"Fernando's death?" asked Laura, who hadn't said a word up until that moment.

"Yes. I was the only person he had left in the world. If I hadn't been so wrapped up in the business and paid more attention to what really mattered, I could have convinced him to stay at the restaurant. And if he'd stayed here, he would have been here with me that day instead of doing who-knows-what on the other side of the city."

Behind her glasses, her eyes welled up with tears. Laura slid her hand across the table and placed it on Lorenza's.

"I know it's hard, but we need to ask you some questions," she told her. "Did he ever talk about Argentina?"

"Of course, he loved tango. Sometimes he played Gardel here in the restaurant. And even though he was about as Spanish as you can be, he always used to tell people he was born in Buenos Aires."

"Did he ever mention anything about traveling to Argentina as an adult?"

The woman shook her head.

"How old was he when you met him?" asked Laura.

"Early forties."

"And he never told you about what he did before meeting you?"

"No. He was very outgoing when he wanted to be. Everything else, he hid, using that unique grace of his. He was very clever."

"I've been told he was also very proud and had a hard time admitting to his mistakes."

Lorenza Millán furrowed her brow.

"Your uncle, proud? Not at all. He had no problem apologizing when he made mistakes. I always admired that about him."

Her answer surprised me. Either my father and Juanmi Alonso had a very different perception from Lorenza's, or Fernando's personality had changed radically.

"Does the Montgrí Hotel ring any bells?" I asked her.

"I guess it must be a hotel in Torroella de Montgrí, Fernando's hometown."

Laura and I looked at each other.

"Did he ever talk to you about Patagonia?"

The woman stood.

"Not exactly, no. Come with me."

We followed her down a hallway that led to the bathrooms and the kitchen. Halfway down the hallway, an archway opened onto another dining room, much smaller than the one we'd been in. A sort of private room for large groups.

"Look," she said pointing at one of the walls.

Instead of the rural images of Castilla-La Mancha that decorated the other walls of the restaurant, this one had a photo of a mountain shaped like a shark's tooth...

"The Fitz Roy," I said.

"That's in Patagonia, isn't it?"

"Yes."

"Well, your uncle brought it the day we opened the restaurant. We had a big argument because I didn't understand what that photo had to do with a Manchego grill, but he insisted we hang it up. I finally gave in because I didn't want to start off on the wrong foot over a photograph."

I nodded in silence. That photo of the sharp mountain was the thin line that connected the two Fernandos: the old man who owned a restaurant, and the young entrepreneur who'd built a hotel halfway across the world.

I looked at the image, wondering who Fernando Cucurell had been. Was he like me, as Danilo had insinuated? Was my father's alcoholism part of the reason they stopped talking before I was born? I thought about the many things a family can hide about its past. When I was just a kid, four people connected to the uncle my father had decided not to tell me about, died. An uncle who apparently everyone loved and considered to be a wonderful person.

"Did he like hiking?" I asked, pointing at the photo.

Lorenza Millán looked at me as if she didn't understand my question.

"You really don't know anything, do you?"

"No."

"Come."

The woman headed back to the bar, circled the cash register, and pointed at a small picture frame that was practically hidden between the bottles. Despite the distance, I recognized Lorenza Millán, about ten years younger. She was smiling next to a man in a wheelchair.

"Your uncle had a car accident not long before meeting me. He was left hemiplegic."

Lorenza handed me the photo so I could take a closer look. It was the first photo of Fernando Cucurell Zaplana I'd ever seen. I never imagined him in a wheelchair. He had a pointy mustache and a beard, as gray as the thin hair on his head. He looked familiar, even though he didn't look like my father. I had the feeling I'd seen that face before. But where?

The answer hit me like a punch in the gut. Pau Roig and me in the school playground. A man in a wheelchair, throwing us candy from the other side of the fence. His hair was darker and fuller, but he had the same style of mustache and beard. We called him Don Quixote. That same smile he used to look at us with. Or rather, the same smile he used to look at *me* with. I always suspected he was smiling at me and not Pau. Now, thirty years later, that theory was confirmed.

The hair on my arms stood up. Don Quixote was my uncle Fernando. Danilo in Chaltén, and me in Barcelona, we'd both gotten candy from the same person.

CHAPTER 41

Julián

"You can keep it," Lorenza said, pointing at the photograph still in my hands. "I've got another copy at home."

"Thank you."

The few times I'd remembered Don Quixote during my adult life, it had been to wonder if that person in the wheelchair who threw us candy, without our teachers noticing, was a pervert. For some reason, I always arrived at the conclusion that he wasn't, that he was just a poor old man who felt lonely.

"Did he ever mention me?" I asked her.

"At some point, he mentioned he had a brother and a nephew. But he didn't have a good relationship with his brother."

"Do you know why they fought?"

The woman cleared her throat and flattened an invisible wrinkle in her dress.

"No. And even if I did, shouldn't you talk to your father about that?"

"That's the problem, Lorenza. My father has completely shut me out on this topic."

"Maybe you should respect that."

"I'm trying, but it's hard."

"Look, I don't want you to leave here thinking I'm keeping a huge secret or that I have the answers you're looking for. I know very little about your uncle's family life. Your father showed up here once and things didn't end well. They had a very big argument. I never asked Fernando about it, and he never said anything either."

"My father was in this restaurant? When?"

"It must have been in '95 or '96."

I did the math. In 1995, I was ten years old and my mother was struggling to raise me without having to quit her job at her firm. My father lived at home, but he was different back then. Many nights he wouldn't eat with us, and many mornings, he'd wake up on the couch. Years later, I discovered he'd relapsed at time after twelve years sober –from the time he met my mother, to when I was nine. When I grew up, my mother admitted she'd been close to filing for divorce, but my father managed to redirect his life just in time.

"Was my father drunk?"

"Like a sailor."

I remembered that period of my childhood well. Alcohol had turned him into a different person. My mother had kicked him out of the house, and for two years I saw him sporadically. I also remembered the joy I'd felt the day he told me he was coming back. By the time I turned eleven, my parents smiled beside me while I made my birthday wishes and toasted me with sparkling water.

Later, I found out that my mother hadn't let him back in the house, until she was sure he'd been sober for months. Thanks to his strict discipline and the help of AA, my father hasn't touched a drop of alcohol since.

"Do you remember anything they said to each other?"

The woman looked at me with distrust.

"Please. It's very important."

She shook her head no.

"It's not right for me to get into it."

"Lorenza, I don't think there's anything you can tell me about my father that will surprise me. When you grow up with an alcoholic parent, you learn the hard way that there's no such thing as rock bottom, that things can always get a little bit worse."

Lorenza emptied her lungs with a long sigh.

"I only heard one thing your father yelled at Fernando."

"Do you remember?"

"Like it was yesterday."
"What did he say?"
"You're one of the murderers."

CHAPTER 42

Many years earlier.

The young boy walks up the four stone steps and enters Santa María de los Desamparados. The damp air in the gloomy entrance chills his freshly buzzed head. He sticks out his chest and opens his arms a bit to make his back look wider. He walks confidently, swaying slightly from side to side, a movement he has practiced a thousand times in front of the mirror. He was inspired by the Westerns his father liked so much. There's always a scene where an outsider arrives in town and challenges the sheriff. He isn't an outsider and doesn't want to challenge anyone. He just wants to be left alone.

At the end of the entrance hall, the cloister opens before him. Santa María de los Desamparados is a seminary that used to be a convent. Even the old building has conflicts with its sexual identity.

The hallway that leads to his classroom is on the opposite corner of the cloister. But *they* are also in that same corner, just like every morning.

There's no avoiding them. It doesn't make a difference if he walks diagonally across the cloister or if he walks in an L shape, following the veranda. Whatever he does, once he makes it to the other end he'll have to walk by them.

He straightens his back a bit and makes sure to add a little more confidence to his walk. He decides to take the shorter, diagonal route. He takes a deep breath and raises his chin. He counts them. There are four of them. When they see him, they smile like they always do, that wolf-like smile of theirs. The boy wonders if they practice it in their 'secret' meetings.

"Look guys, the little princess cut her hair," says Pep Codina.

"Is she trying to turn into a prince?" another responds.

The four of them laugh. 'Little princess'. That's the nickname those idiots gave him. If he could, he'd beat them up. But there are four of them, they're bigger than him, and to top it off, they belong to the town's most powerful families.

Pep Codina, the pack leader, hops off the ledge he's sitting on and steps in front of him. A camera hangs from his neck, most likely the latest gift from his rich parents. The boy notices his hands getting sweaty but keeps his gaze straight and his shoulders back.

Codina is standing in the middle of the opening that connects the cloister to the hallway. Whatever he does, if the wolves don't want him to make it to class, he won't. In a brief moment of courage, he walks forward until he's about half a meter away from their leader.

"Why? You looked good with curls," asks Codina, reaching forward to touch his head.

The boy steps back.

"Are you scared of me? Or are you scared that if I touch you, you might like it?"

The other three laugh mockingly.

"Why don't you leave him alone, for fuck's sake?" says a voice from behind them.

It's Manel, his only friend. Perhaps the only reason why Santa María de los Desamparados isn't a complete hellhole. As usual, he's carrying a pile of books under his arm.

"Sooner or later, the prince always shows up," Codina says, still looking at the boy, and flashes a smile of white, crooked teeth.

"Oh, fuck off," Manel retorts, and uses his free hand to push the wolf with so much force that he falls to the ground.

The other three jump off the ledge and puff out their chests, but don't go near Manel. No one's crazy enough to do that.

Manel is the town blacksmith's oldest son. Before he learned how to read or ride a bike, he was already hammering hot steel on an anvil. Now, at sixteen, he's built like an armoire, with arms as thick as tree trunks. He weighs almost twice as much as the boy, even though they're the same age. Next to Manel, an unstoppable steam engine, he feels like a toy train.

"Come on," Manel says to him.

He follows him. They walk through the pack of wolves like a mother rhinoceros and her offspring walking through a group of hyenas that lick their lips, but are too afraid to attack.

"Someday you're going to have to stand up to them, man," Manel complains once they've left them behind. "They aren't going to leave you alone unless they respect you."

"It's easy for people to respect you when your body's the size of a dresser."

"Well, I've told you already, stop by the forge a couple of hours every day and you'll see how those muscles grow."

Just like every time Manel makes him that offer, the boy considers it. But there's a problem. Muscles don't grow from one day to the next. He needs a solution *now*. Every day at Santa María de los Desamparados is a nightmare.

"No need," he says as they walk down the hallway toward their classroom. "In two months, the year's over and those assholes graduate."

"I see it the other way around," his friend replies. "You only have two months left to make them respect you. If not now, when? They might be graduating, but Torroella's a small town. They might end up being your bosses, your clients, your neighbors, who knows? Life takes many turns."As they walk into class, Manel's last sentence is stuck in the boy's head.

Life takes many turns, he repeats to himself, like a mantra.

CHAPTER 43

Julián

We took the metro back home from the restaurant. When we reached Badal station, I asked Laura to head over to my apartment and wait for me there. The next step was one I had to take on my own.

I walked up the Brasil Rambla toward Les Corts, my parents' neighborhood. I found my father alone at home, as I had presumed.

"How are you, Dad?"

"I'm good. Just waiting for your mother to come back from work. We're going to the movies tonight."

He made coffee and brought out some chocolates while he told me about the film they were going to see. As soon as we were both sitting on the sofa, I cut to the chase.

"I'm here to ask you a question Dad, that I need a truthful answer to."

"I don't know why I suspect it has something to do with my brother."

"What year did you stop talking to each other?"

"Well, a few years before you were born. It must have been 1982 or 1983."

"How many times did you see him after that?"

"Never again."

"So, you haven't spoken to him since the early '80s."

I took a sip of my coffee as if it were liquid courage.

"Does a restaurant called El Asador de Anguita ring a bell?"

He turned the corners of his mouth downward and shrugged.

"Well, they sure know you there."

His expression hardened and his face paled, looking like it had turned to marble. Avoiding my eyes, he wiped his hand over his shaved head.

"Son..."

"Dad," I interrupted. "If you're going to say something, it better not be another lie."

"Oh, don't be dramatic. I'm not a compulsive liar."

"You aren't? You kept the existence of an uncle from me and said you hadn't seen him since before I was born. However, in 1995 you showed up at his restaurant and made such a scene that they still remember you."

"You know very well that wasn't my best year."

When I saw his hands shaking, I knew I had to tread lightly. A recovered alcoholic is fragile, just like a person with heart issues. He was both.

"Are you ok?"

"Yeah. Don't worry."

He looked at me and smiled. His expression was that of a beaten man. Filled with regret.

"Why did you go to the Asador de Anguita in 1995?"

"Because I hadn't seen my brother in years. And because I was drunk."

"Why did you want to see him?"

"I missed him."

I could feel the blood boiling inside my veins. I needed to get out of there to avoid hurting him more, but I couldn't. I needed answers.

"So, you go see your brother because you miss him and end up yelling 'You're one of the murderers' at him?"

My father's eyes opened wide like saucers.

"Lorenza Millán, Fernando's partner heard you. Twenty-five years later and she still hasn't forgotten."

My father shook his head as if I didn't understand.

"I want you to tell me who your brother killed. I want you to tell me what you know, Dad. If you said 'one of the murderers', that means there were others."

"How old are you, four? I want, I want, I want, why, why, why. You want, yeah. What about what I want?"

"What do you want, Dad?"

"For you to leave your uncle's memory alone."

"What memory? What's a dead man's memory? He's gone. He isn't here anymore. And in any case, you weren't speaking to him anymore. Fernando Cucurell and the three men he apparently killed in Chaltén don't matter. What matters is who's left. Those people who died might have children, parents, siblings, who've been waiting to know the truth for thirty years."

My father nodded, placed both his hands on his knees, and stood up.

"Your mother will be here any minute and we're going to be late for the movies," he said, opening the apartment door.

"Really, Dad? You're kicking me out?"

"Come back anytime, son, but stop asking the same question. You have no right to demand that I open a door I shut many years ago."

I nodded and showed him my open hands like a fighter surrendering before the fight has even begun. I said goodbye with a defeated hug. He could sell his honor, his values, and all that shit to someone else. I needed my father to help me, and all he was giving me was silence.

CHAPTER 44

Julián

I was fuming when I got back home.

"How'd it go?" Laura asked me.

"Like shit. He's shut tighter than a clam. He says he isn't going to open a door he closed years ago."

"He isn't obligated to tell you, Julián."

"He's my father. He should be on my side."

"Maybe he is. He thinks it'll do you no good to find out the truth."

My phone rang. It was an unknown number calling.

"Hello?" I answered.

"Mr. Cucurell, I'm calling from Santa María de los Desamparados. I'm headmaster Castells's secretary. We spoke a few days ago, remember?"

"Yes, of course."

"The headmaster has returned from his trip and has said he's open to an interview. We'd have to keep the time difference in mind to coordinate a phone call at a time that's convenient for both of you."

"I'm no longer in Argentina. In fact, I can stop by the school if the headmaster agrees. It's always best to speak in person."

Laura gave me a thumbs-up. We weren't going to miss the opportunity of seeing the place where everything started.

"Of course. The headmaster has some time tomorrow at ten, if not it would have to be next week..."

"I'll be there tomorrow."

When I hung up, Laura was looking at me with a half-smile.

"See? There are other people we can talk to besides your dad. I also had two good developments while you were gone."

"Oh yeah?"

"Yes. Gregorio Alcántara replied to the message I sent him on Facebook this morning. He agreed to talk to us. And Meritxell Puigbaró, the woman who was raped by the wolves, just replied to my email saying she'll call me soon to arrange a meeting."

Speaking of phone calls, mine started ringing. I thought it was the secretary again, but it was my mother.

"You just couldn't let it be, could you? You couldn't respect your father's decision?"

"You too, mom?"

There was silence on the other end of the line. When she spoke again, her voice cracked.

"He's at the clinic with Doctor Torres."

"What?"

"He had an anxiety attack. His heart rate went up to 130."

I felt a crushing weight on my shoulders. A spike like that in his heart rate put him in considerable danger.

"I'm heading to the clinic right now."

"No. Doctor Torres says he'll be able to come home in a couple of hours."

I sighed. Doctor Torres was our family's doctor since long before he became the owner of one of the most reputable clinics in uptown Barcelona. In my family, Eligio Torres's word was sacred.

"I'll see you at your place, then."

She took a second longer than was normal before answering.

"It's best that you wait, Julián. He needs to rest."

"What are you talking about, Mom? I need to see him. This happened because of me."

"Doctor Torres has made it very clear that he needs to rest and stay away from any source of stress."

I closed my eyes, trying to make sense of her words. When I spoke, the lump in my throat made my voice tremble.

"Whenever he's ready, I'd like to visit him. He deserves an apology."

"Once he feels better, I'll let you know and you can come over."

After a quick goodbye, my mother hung up. I stood there with the phone in my hand, swallowing my anger toward myself. I hated that I'd upset my father so much, but what I hated even more, was that I was so selfish that I was still mad at him for lying to me.

CHAPTER 45

Laura

Laura gazed out the window at the alternating rows of apple trees and green fields that they drove past on the side of the road. They'd left Barcelona an hour and a half ago, right after dawn.

During breakfast, she was relieved to see that Julián was slightly more relaxed than the night before. When she'd gone to bed, he was still very upset about his father.

However, the calm didn't last long. Julián's car wouldn't start and he had to go over to his parents' house to ask his mother if he could use the BMW. He'd returned half an hour later, annoyed because Consuelo had waited for him at the front door and hadn't let him go up to see his father.

Luckily, the hour and a half long trip had gone by quickly. Despite Julián's attempts to rant about his parents, she'd been able to maneuver the topic towards what they were going to say to Santa María de los Desamparados's headmaster. Twelve years working among police officers and criminals had taught her how to veer any conversation in any direction at will.

"That's the Montgrí," Julián said to her, pointing through the windshield at a mountain with a castle at the top. "Torroella is the town you can see at the foot of it."

After crossing a bridge that went over a river, Julián parked the car in a supermarket parking lot.

"Let's walk the rest of the way. The school is in the town center and it'll be impossible to park there."

When she thought of the 'town center', Laura had imagined a bustling neighborhood full of people and cars.

However, as they ventured further into the town, the houses got older and the streets narrower.

The high school Fernando Cucurell had attended was in the main square, which that morning also accommodated a vegetable market, several bar tables, locals doing their morning shopping, and many tourists, most of them French. Julián rang a modern doorbell that contrasted against the ancient stone building front. They were greeted by a doorman dressed in a navy blue smock.

Though Julián spoke to him Catalan, she was able to make out what he was saying.

"Bon dia. Tenim una reunió amb el profesor Castells." *Good morning. We have a meeting with Professor Castells.*

The doorman nodded in a cordial manner and asked them to follow him. Past the entrance hall, a large inner garden with centenary olive trees and wrought iron benches opened up before them. It looked more like a cathedral cloister than a school courtyard.

"It used to be a convent," Julián explained. "I read it online."

She thought about how much her aunt Susana would enjoy those hundred-year-old stones. Though she'd ultimately chosen her police uniform over a nun habit, her aunt had maintained a religious devotion and an unparalleled fascination with churches, cathedrals, in fact any kind of Catholic building. When Laura told her she was going to Barcelona, the first thing she told her was to send lots of pictures of the Sagrada Familia.

The doorman led them to a large office where a short, slender man wearing a black suit and white shirt stood up from his desk to greet them.

"Mr. Cucurell?" he asked Julián.

Julián nodded and shook his hand.

"This is Laura Badía, my girlfriend," he said, sticking to their plan.

"Take a seat," Castells told them, flattening his tie which was fastened with a golden brooch shaped into a crucifix. Her aunt would have fallen in love at first sight.

"Thank you for making time in your busy schedule for us," said Julián.

"It's my pleasure. Please, tell me how I can help you. My secretary informs me that you are journalists."

Julián looked at her for help.

"Researchers," she clarified.

"Who do you research for?"

"We're independent researchers. We'd like to write a book about the Brotherhood of the Wolves."

"Really? Why are you interested in a group of teenagers from the distant past?"

"The brotherhood doesn't exist anymore?"

"These days, what young person wants to do something secretly? Teenagers today live their life to post it on social media."

While Castells spoke, she scrutinized each one of his gestures. It was a professional flaw of hers. A useless tic. Why did it matter that the professor's expression seemed genuine? Appearances had fooled her more than once.

"Even if it no longer exists, the Brotherhood of the Wolves did belong to this school, correct?" asked Julián.

Castells sat straighter in his chair and averted his eyes toward the window which looked onto a back garden, much brighter than the cloister, full of olive trees and other fruit trees Laura couldn't recognize.

"Can you explain why you wish to know that?"

Laura placed her hand on Julián's and smiled at the professor.

"It's a bit complicated," she said. "Julián's uncle went to this school and was a part of the Brotherhood. A few years back, he started writing a book about the history of the Wolves and I'm helping him, just trying to be the best niece-in-law I can be."

She capped her last words by giving Julián a kiss on the cheek.

"She's just so sweet," he added. "And an excellent writer, too."

"Oh Juli, you're going to make me blush. Don't listen to him, professor. He's just saying that because he loves me. I write, but I'm an amateur."

"And wouldn't it be appropriate for your uncle to come in person if he's the alumnus?"

"That's the problem," Laura answered quickly. "Fernando isn't doing well. He was diagnosed with dementia a few months ago."

"I'm very sorry to hear that."

"He's turning 75 soon, and for a while now he hasn't stopped talking about his time at this school and his brotherhood friends. In his words, those were the best years of his life."

Castells gave her a wide smile.

"This school is known to leave its mark on everyone who passes through it."

"We know," Laura said.

"How can we help?"

"Telling us about the Brotherhood of the Wolves. We'd like to include some stories in the book to surprise Fernando."

"Well, I know very little. Barely anything, I'd say. I didn't actually attend this school. I've only heard rumors."

"Do you know anyone who might be able to help us?"

Castells took a few seconds to think.

"There's an alum, an older man, who comes every once in a while, to give lectures here. It might be useful to talk to him. He's a writer, like you Miss Badía."

Laura dismissed his last sentence with a gesture as if she were utterly embarrassed.

"Could you put us in touch with him?"

The headmaster took out his phone and recorded a voice message in front of them.

"Hi Jaume, I'm here with an alum's nephew and his girlfriend, they require some information regarding the Brotherhood of the Wolves. Can I send them your contact details?"

Castells left his phone on the desk.

"This man resides in Barcelona, so you wouldn't have to make the trip back to Torroella again. As soon as he answers, I'll let you know. My secretary has your number."

Castells' phone made a soft ping.

"No need," the headmaster corrected himself, "he's answered already. Jaume Serra is quicker with technology than a teenager. He says yes, no problem."

"Jaume Serra? The famous writer?" Julián asked.

Laura looked at him, confused, but Julián told her with a gesture that he would explain later.

"Of course. Several illustrious figures have come from this school. Is there anything else I can help you with?"

"Yes. It would be very useful to see a list of my uncle's classmates."

"We'd love to interview some of them for the book," she added.

"That should be in the school yearbooks," Castells answered, standing up. "Follow me."

They followed him through the cloister. From the floors above them, Laura recognized the universal tone of voice teachers speak to their students in, despite not understanding a word of Catalan. They entered a large, silent hall. The floor-to-ceiling wooden bookshelves full of old books gave it an almost sacred look.

"This is the school library," Castells announced as he walked between the rows of books.

Behind a desk, a tall, broad man with a gray beard was swiping a barcode reader across a stack of books. She'd only seen stone walls like those in movies where people rode horses, fought with swords, and held torches. It was difficult for her to comprehend that on this side of the ocean, those buildings weren't part of a movie set.

"We're here to see the yearbooks, Mr. Castañeda," said the headmaster announced.

The librarian nodded and guided them through the labyrinth of books.

"Here they are," he said, pointing at a row of thick, leather bound books with golden lettering on the spines. The first was from 1990, the latest was from 2018.

"Where are the older ones?" Castells asked. "They're interested in ones from the '60s and '70s."

"They started making the yearbooks in 1990, professor."

"There wasn't a student list before then?"

"The class records. But they weren't printed with pictures, like these."

"Could we see those records?" asked Laura.

"They're in the basement archive."

Castells shook his head and sucked air through his teeth.

"I've only ventured down there once. I wouldn't know where to start looking. Could you maybe help them, Mr. Castañeda?"

"Of course, I'll handle it."

"Amazing. In that case, I'll leave you all to it. Traveling for a conference is lovely, but when you return there's always a backlog of work to get through. I'm leaving you in good hands."

"Thank you so much for your time," Laura told the headmaster, who waved goodbye with a friendly expression.

When we could no longer hear Castell's footsteps, the librarian returned to his desk and went back to scanning books.

"What are you interested in exactly?" he asked without looking at them.

"My uncle's list of classmates. He was a student roughly between 1968 and 1973. Fernando Cucurell Zaplana."

Laura thought she saw the librarian's face harden ever so slightly.

"This week won't be possible, I have too much work. Come back next Friday."

"A week from now?"

"Eight days," the librarian corrected him with a smile. "Today's Thursday."

"Is there no way it could be sooner?"

"Impossible. That basement is a maze," he said pointing at the old wooden door covered in thick ironwork behind his desk.

If that door had been in Argentina, it would have been in a museum, Laura thought. At Santa María de los Desamparados, however, they used it to stick up signs with library rules.

"I have to organize it a bit if we want to find anything."

Laura tried to reason with the librarian, but neither she nor Julián were able to sway him. Five minutes later, they were walking out the door.

"At least we got the contact information for that former brotherhood member."

"You really don't know who Jaume Serra is?"

"No."

"He's one of Spain's most prolific writers. He writes mostly for teens."

She shrugged back.

"What did you think of Castells?"

"I think he wants to help. The other guy's the weird one. I thought he seemed surprised to hear your uncle's name. Also, do you really think that in the twenty-first century, a librarian has so much work that he needs us to come back in a week?"

"Eight days," Julián said, imitating the man's deep voice in such an amusing way that she burst out laughing.

They walked down the town's narrow streets for a while, skirting around the French tourists and women carrying shopping bags. During those moments, Laura allowed herself to look around and smile like any other tourist would, briefly putting aside the four deaths that had led her there. But the mirage evaporated quickly.

At the end of a winding street, they stumbled upon a small square with a big tree in the center. Julián stopped by an old sign made out of glazed tiles with the silhouette of a gaucho riding a horse painted on them. Beneath it, Laura read 'Fertilize with Chilean nitrate'.

"On this corner," Julián said, pointing at the sign promoting fertilizer, "Josep Codina was murdered."

CHAPTER 46

Julián

We walked into my apartment three hours after saying goodbye to headmaster Castells. I stopped to check my mailbox and Laura sprinted up the stairs with even more energy than she'd had on the hike up to Laguna de los Tres.

"I'll meet you upstairs. I need to go to the bathroom," she said.

Between pizza shop and real estate agent flyers, a blank envelope stood out like a sore thumb. Firstly, because no one hand wrote letters anymore. Secondly, because my name was written in capitals, in handwriting that looked like a five-year-old's.

I opened it as I walked up the stairs. Inside, I found a recent photo of my parents posing in front of a paella at a restaurant. It was a photo my mother had posted on her Facebook profile a few months back, for their wedding anniversary.

Inside the envelope, there was also a folded piece of paper. It was a note printed in Comic Sans, the same ridiculous font they'd used for the threat I got in El Chaltén.

Lovely, aren't they? Very vulnerable, too. She could be a victim of a violent robbery any Tuesday or Thursday on her way home from yoga. He could get served a poorly cooked plate of food on Monday when he meets his former colleagues for lunch. But that isn't going to happen, right Julián? Because you're going to be good and stop sticking your nose into things that aren't your business. I told you in

El Chaltén and I'll say it once more: sell the Montgrí Hotel and enjoy the money, but leave the past alone.

I felt my head get lighter and had to lean against the wall to stop myself from collapsing down the stairs. Once I'd read those lines for the third time, I heard Laura's voice from above.

"Julián? Are you coming? I can't find the keys you gave me."

"Yes. Coming."

When I made it to my floor, Laura was waiting, pointing at an imaginary watch on her wrist.

"Good thing you didn't decide to be a firefighter."

The smile disappeared from her face the second she saw the envelope.

"What's that?"

"Nothing."

She grabbed the envelope from my hands.

"Those are your parents," she said and read the note.

"Yes."

When we entered the apartment, Laura collapsed onto the sofa with a long sigh. She put her hands together and rested her mouth on her thumbs. Her brown eyes, locked on the blank TV screen; she didn't blink.

"Weren't you going to the bathroom?"

"I don't need to anymore," she said pointing at the note that I was reading once again. "Clearly someone's uncomfortable with us poking around. This person must have a lot at stake if the truth about the murders comes out. We're close."

"'We're close?' Laura, did you not read what it says? They're threatening my parents. This game is getting out of hand."

"This isn't a game to me."

"I'm sorry. I didn't mean that. But I'm scared for my parents."

"What do you want to do? Should we drop everything? Should I pack my bags and go back to Argentina?"

"I don't know, Laura but I don't like this at all."

Laura shot up off the sofa and dashed into the bathroom. When she came back out, she headed straight for the door.

"Where are you going?"

"I need some air, and you need to think about what you want to do."

I would've liked for her to slam the door behind her, or yell at me, so I could have a reason to get mad at her. That would have distracted me from what really mattered. But Laura was not only nice and closed the door softly, she was also right. I needed to think.

The note's last words kept ringing in my head long after Laura had left me on my own.

Leave the past alone.

CHAPTER 47

Laura

She'd given Julián a whole day to think about whether he wanted to continue or not. She needed a break herself, and she'd used it to explore Barcelona a bit. And think.

Now, twenty-four hours later, she was standing next to him, in front of a ten-story building with an extensive garden surrounding its entrance. In the center of the garden, several turtles basked in the sun around a marble fountain.

According to Julián, you could split Barcelona in half, with everything north of Diagonal Avenue on one side and everything south of it on the other. The writer Jaume Serra's house was way up in the northern half.

Laura turned toward Julián, who was watching the turtles.

"Are you sure you want to keep going with this?" she asked him.

"Yeah, I'm sure," Julián answered. "Let's go."

Inside the lobby, a doorman wearing a suit and tie told them which way to go. An elevator with a polished wood interior took them up to the third floor. There were two apartments per floor. Before they could knock, one of the doors opened, turning on silent hinges.

Laura recognized the writer from photos she'd seen online. He was a tall man, with good posture and thick white hair. He carried his 73 years –according to Wikipedia– well.

Serra greeted her with a firm handshake which he repeated with Julián.

"Come in, please. Welcome."

The morning sunlight streamed in through the dining room windows. If she compared it to Julián's apartment, Laura could see the two Barcelonas clearly.

"Do you want some tea? Coffee? A beer?"

"Coffee," said Julián.

"Me too, please," she added.

"Very well. Follow me and you can help me with the coffee machine. I can't stand coffee, drugs, vegetables, or lies."

Laura looked at Julián and could tell they were thinking the same thing: *I hope we didn't come and visit a complete lunatic.*

They returned to the dining room with their coffee and a glass of water for the writer. Serra plopped on a sofa, crossed his legs, and pointed at another one across from him. His movements seemed like a teenager's, rather than a man in his seventies.

"So, you want me to tell you about the Brotherhood of the Wolves."

"Yes," said Laura.

"May I ask why? And don't say it's because your uncle has dementia, I make a living making up stories."

Julián started to stammer, but Laura interrupted him.

"Four ex-members were murdered between 1989 and 1991," she said.

Far from looking surprised, Serra replied as if she'd asked him for the time.

"From what I know, the only one murdered was Pep Codina. The other three disappeared in the Pyrenees."

"In the Pyrenees?" asked Laura. Repeating the speaker's last words was usually a good way to keep them talking. Luckily, it worked.

"Well, actually the last time they were seen was in the Pre-Pyrenees. Close to Cadí, have you been there?"

Laura saw Julián nod. The only thing she knew about the Pyrenees was that they were mountains.

"If you think about it, that group had a tragic story. One of them stabbed, the other three missing not long after."

"How long?" Laura asked.

"Let's see... let me do the math. Pep Copina was killed around 1990."

"1989," she corrected. "On August 27th."

The writer's keen gaze rested on hers.

"I see you're familiar with the facts. In that case, let's not trust my memory. Let's resort to the written word," said the author as he got up from the sofa and motioned for them to wait.

The man disappeared down a hallway full of books and came back a few minutes later with a brown folder with the words *Lost in the Cadí* written on the cover.

"The title's a mess, but it's a working title. I'd never publish something with such an obvious title."

"You're writing a book about these deaths?" Laura asked.

"Not deaths. Disappearances," Serra replied, pointing at the folder. "Open it up, it won't bite you."

Inside, Laura found a couple dozen pages with indecipherable notes and a newspaper article.

"My novels are usually born from an image that I take from reality," Serra explained. "Some people call it the seed of a story, I prefer to think of it as a grain of sand in an oyster."

In other circumstances, Laura would have explained that pearls don't come from grains of sand in oysters but rather from a parasite, but she decided to not be a snob.

"These pages," said the writer as he laid his hand on the manuscript, "are the summary of a story I'll write someday. Pure fiction. On the other hand, this newspaper article from 1991 is the small piece of reality. That initial grain of sand. When I read this article, it stuck in my head. Can you imagine the suffering of a mother who doesn't know what happened to her child? Go ahead, read it if you want."

Laura scooched closer to Julián so he could read as well.

AUTHORITIES END THE SEARCH FOR THREE MEN MISSING IN THE PYRENEES

After twenty-one days with no findings, the Generalitat de Catalunya firefighting service has ended the search for Gerard Martí, Mario Santiago, and Arnau Junqué, who went missing on April 5th in the Cadí-Moixeró Natural Park.

The three men, all 33 years old, were native to Torroella de Montgrí and lived in Barcelona. They left their homes with the goal of hiking some of the most iconic paths on the Catalan mountain. "They had planned to hike up the Pedraforca, in the Cadí natural park, and then hike over to the Aigüestortes National Park path over fifteen days," explains Gerard Martí's wife Arlet Magano while she holds little Biel in her arms, the couple's three-year-old son.

Martí, Santiago, and Junqué were last seen in Bagá, the town where most mountaineers who visit the Cadí-Moixeró National Park begin their hikes. According to testimonies from park employees, the men went to the information office on the afternoon of April 5th to ask about the conditions for hiking the Pedraforca trail, which are still wintry at that time of year.

Twenty days after their departure (five after their expected return), their families alerted the authorities. The Generalitat firefighters and the National Police have worked together during the past three weeks with the help of search dogs, but to no avail.

According to Daniel Ruiz, the fire department inspector in charge of the operation, one of the greatest difficulties is the extensive territory to be covered, since the missing persons did not provide precise information about their itinerary.

The phone line that has been open for seventeen days has received hundreds of calls from people who report seeing the men in different areas. "These are people who want to help, good Samaritans no doubt," explains Ruiz. "However, the number of calls, the lack of details, and the vast geographic area they've supposedly been spotted in, makes it very difficult to extract useful information."

On the other hand, the families of the missing men ask authorities to continue the search effort. "Don't abandon our sons," Arnau Junqué's mother, Montserrat Abella, demanded tearfully yesterday of a group of journalists, who stood at the front door of her house in Torroella de Montgrí.

CHAPTER 48

Laura

When Laura finished reading the article, she looked at the date on the upper corner of the page. May 1991. The year fit within the estimated time frame of death of the three dead found in Patagonia, who were also estimated to be between 30 and 35 years old.

However, none of the three men missing in the Pyrenees was called Juan Gómez. There was a possibility that the body in the Montgrí Hotel had a fake passport on him, but in Laura's experience, that was something that only happened in spy movies, not in real life.

"From what we've investigated," she told the author, "other bodies were found wearing the Brotherhood of the Wolves ring, just like the one Josep Codina was wearing the night he was murdered."

"Where?"

"We can't give you any details. This is an open investigation."

"Are you a police officer?"

"Not in Spain, no. I'm a tourist trying to understand. Do you know the ring I'm referring to?"

The man went back down the hallway. When he returned, he had a ring in the shape of a wolf's head in his hand.

"I suppose you're referring to this."

Laura studied it closely. The wolf head with the open mouth was identical to the one the Chaltén bodies had. However, Serra's ring was golden and didn't have any inscription on it. Just like the one Julián had seen on his ex-brother-in-law Xavi's ring.

"What can you tell us about this ring?"

"They are a creation of mine. Before I went to school there, the Wolves didn't have anything to identify them. I had the idea of asking my uncle, who was a jeweler, to carve the mold in wax and have it made in brass."

"I think it would be best if we started at the beginning," Laura suggested. "What exactly was the Brotherhood?"

Jaume Serra sat back down on the couch, with his legs crossed. As he spoke, he played with the ring putting it on and taking it off his ring finger.

"It was –or is, I don't know– a student club within the Santa María de los Desamparados school. It was founded in the 1940s. A sort of secret society inside the school."

"Secret how, exactly?" Julián asked.

Serra smiled. "There were no masonic rituals or anything of that nature if that's what you're imagining. It was, so to speak, a group of young boys which few people knew of, and even less were invited to join."

"From what we heard, it was open to anyone willing to pay. In fact, we were told they wanted new members because they hired strippers for their meetings with the dues."

"At least when I was in school it wasn't like that. We didn't bring women to the meetings, much less pay dues. Most of the members were among the poorest students in school. Some of them would save up for months to buy the ring which, as you can see, is a piece of junk."

"Do you know of any members who had their rings made in silver instead of brass?"

"That would have been ridiculous. One of our values was equality."

"The one on Pep Codina's body was silver."

"I don't know what to tell you. I can only speak from my experience."

"These people went to Santa María de los Desamparados between 1970 and 1975. If my numbers are correct, that's about five or ten years after you. Do you think the brotherhood could have changed so much in that time? Silver rings, steep dues, little secrecy, women of the night…"

"There are countries that go from protectionism to neoliberalism and back again in ten years. If that can happen in a government, imagine a student club."

Laura nodded, wondering if Serra had just described Argentina's politics intentionally or by coincidence.

"Only boys were admitted?" she asked.

"Yes, because Santa María was a boys' school. They only made it co-ed a few years ago."

"What was the purpose of the brotherhood?" Julián intervened.

"What purpose does a seventeen-year-old boy have? Back then, it didn't even make sense for us to conceal a drink or smoke, because it wasn't frowned upon. We'd play pranks, like writing a love letter to our typing professor and signing it as the custodian. But the purpose itself was belonging. Being a part of something. Being able to wear this ring, which was only allowed during meetings. That was the purpose."

"Where were meetings held?"

"Usually at one of the members' houses, or in one of the many empty classrooms in Santa María. There weren't very many of us wolves, only ten or twelve, so anywhere worked for us."

"Did you keep going to meetings after you graduated?"

"It wasn't allowed. If you weren't part of Santa María de los Desamparados, you couldn't be a wolf. You were allowed to keep the ring as a keepsake, but one of the rules was that you had to leave the brotherhood."

The writer ended his sentence by spinning the ring on the small wooden table at his feet.

"Aside from being silver, Pep Codina's ring had a phrase written in Latin on the inner face of the ring. *Lupus occidere uiuendo debet.*"

"A wolf must kill in order to survive," Serra translated.

"You know the phrase?"

"Not at all. But I studied Latin for many years. They were very insistent about that in Santa María."

"Do you have any idea why that phrase was engraved on Pep Codina and the other victim's rings?" Julián asked.

"Don't you think it's time you tell me what's going on?"

"I promise you that as soon as we're able to share more information, you'll be the first to know," Laura stepped in. "Everything you've told us is very useful. Was there a rulebook? Something in writing?"

The writer huffed but answered anyway.

"'On the reproductive habits of the Iberian wolf', by Narciso Ballabriga."

"Excuse me?"

"There was a book in Santa María that was called that. It was a copy of a doctoral thesis written by an alum. As you can imagine, no one ever read it, so on page 66, I stuck the manifesto of the Brotherhood of the Wolves. Before I wrote it down, it was just some hand-written pieces of paper that went from person to person. It was hard for me to get hold of them because the brotherhood hadn't been active for four years when we rekindled it."

"How did you find out about that manifesto?"

"A cousin of mine had been a member some years back. It was a secret society, but not that secret. At the end of the day, we were just some kids who thought we had something others didn't. And allow me to insist on this, our purpose was completely innocent."

Innocent or not, Laura thought, there were four murders linked to that society.

"Do you remember the name of any younger members who remained in the brotherhood after you graduated?"

"There were none left."

"No one?"

"No. We restarted the society in 1962, when we were in our first year. Out of arrogance, we made the mistake of not allowing any younger students join as the years went by. By the time we left Santa María, the wolves were left as deserted as we'd found them."

"Evidently someone decided to revive them in the years that followed."

There was a long silence. As the seconds ticked by, Laura noticed Julián looking at her nervously, almost begging her to say something. She merely settled into the couch.

"I can confirm that the brotherhood was active a few years later," the writer said after a while. "Someone I know, Adrán Caplonch. Maybe that last name sounds familiar to you, Julián."

"The cockles?"

"Exactly. His family owns Caplonch Canned Foods."

"Every self-respecting Catalan has had a vermouth with Caplonch cockles," Julián explained to Laura.

"Adrián is several years younger than me, he mentioned once that he was part of the brotherhood. If you'd like, I can send him your phone number and ask him to contact you. He might be able to help you a bit more, though I imagine he'll be busy as elections are coming up."

"Elections?" Julián asked.

"Yes. This year, Adrián Caplonch is running for vice president of the Barcelona Football Club."

CHAPTER 49

Many years earlier.

"Here, for you."

Manel's enormous hand holds a paper bag. When he takes it, the boy finds it heavy. They're in one of Santa María de los Desamparados's empty classrooms, surrounded by dusty desks, boxes full of maps, and cleaning products.

The boy guesses that there's a new book inside the bag. Despite his rough appearance, Manel is an avid reader who devours any piece of literature he can get his hands on. And he's been gifting the boy books for months, to lift his spirits.

Judging by the weight of it, this one must be at least four hundred pages long, he estimates. He opens the bag wondering how to tell Manel that he hasn't read any of the previous three books he gave him. However, inside he finds a package that's too narrow and long to be a book.

"Open it carefully."

The boy rips the paper and discovers the round end of a knife. He grabs it, unsheathing the blade from the package. The bluish-gray iron blade is huge. Everything in Manel's world is huge.

Aside from its size, the knife has a shape the boy has never seen before. The straight lines give it a look and feel of a saber from the future. It's shaped like one of those bullet trains recently launched in Japan. Its spine runs parallel up until the last third, then descends diagonally to form a point that the boy doesn't dare touch.

"It's beautiful. I've never seen a knife like this."

"I'm glad you like it. I made the handle using wood from an olive tree behind my house. I saw it a long time ago in one of my dad's magazines. It's a Viking seax. They used it to fight, hunt, cook. Everything. In the magazine, it said that a Viking and his seax were inseparable."

"I don't hunt, fight, or cook."

"You'll become a Viking eventually," Manel says and growls, baring his teeth like a gorilla. "And when you finally grow some hair, look what you'll be able to do."

Manel takes the knife and brushes the blade across his own forearm. A small pile of hair collects on the edge, leaving a clear patch on his skin.

"It's very sharp. Careful," he tells him before handing it back.

The boy looks at Manel. Behind that strong, coarse façade, there was an amazing person. The person he enjoys being with the most. Sometimes, it feels so good to be with him it makes him uncomfortable. It was one thing to have feminine features, being a fag was a different story.

"This knife is fucking amazing, man. I don't know how to thank you. It must have taken you ages to make."

"Several days. But you don't have to thank me. It's my pleasure, I made it thinking about you."

The boy blushes. His heart beats a mile a minute. Not out of embarrassment, but out of fear. He's terrified of what might happen.

Before he can say another word, Manel takes a step toward him and kisses him on the lips.

The boy closes his eyes and surrenders to the kiss. Manel's poorly shaven mustache feels prickly against his lips. His strong, calloused hands make him uncomfortable. At that moment, he realizes he doesn't like boys. Or at least not that one.

After a few seconds, they both step back, like two magnets repelling each other.

"Gross, dude," Manel says, laughing. "Sorry, I needed to make sure. Sometimes I think…"

"I was thinking the same thing," the boy interrupts.
"Please don't tell me you liked it."
"What if I did? Is there something wrong with that?"
"No, of course not. Well, I don't know. But being a fag seems much harder than not being one."
"I didn't like it."
"Swear?"
"I swear."

The boy's telling the truth. Man, is he telling the truth. He feels an enormous weight lift off his chest.

But the relief doesn't last long as he hears a noise at the door, and when he looks over, he sees Pep Codina. A canine smile plastered across his face, his brand new camera in his hands.

CHAPTER 50
Laura

"Here we are," said Laura, ringing the doorbell of an old stone building. They were at the address Meritxell Puigbaró –the woman who'd been raped by four members of the Brotherhood of the Wolves– had given her over the phone.

"Now do you understand what I told you about the two Barcelonas?"

She certainly did. After seeing Jaume Serra's neighborhood, she didn't need to check the map to know that now they were on the other side of the Diagonal.

They'd gotten off the subway five minutes back at the Drassanes station, and Julián had guided her down a maze of narrow streets, the smell of spices wafting from the shops and the smell of piss from every corner. The streets were so old, Julián explained, that they hadn't been mapped out by architects, but by mules searching for the shortest path. They walked past women wearing hijabs, blond boys in flip-flops speaking English, and bearded men wearing djellabas down to their feet.

With Julián right behind her, Laura walked up three flights of stairs, trying not to touch the concrete handrail that was blackened by hundreds of hands.

Meritxell Puigbaró was waiting for them at the door. Judging by the *La Vanguardia* article, Laura estimated she was about fifty-six. She looked younger, even without makeup and her gray hair tied back. She wore round glasses on her small nose, which made her look like a rodent.

"Come in."

The two Barcelonas weren't only visible on the street. Jaume Serra's spacious and luminous house was a stark contrast compared to the damp, dark shoebox Meritxell Puigbaró lived in. Laura counted four steps from the door to the sofa the woman motioned for them to sit on. The white paint and the minimalist design of the furniture minimized the minute gloominess of the kitchen-dining room with great dignity.

"Do you want something to drink? I have beer or some soda."

"Water for me," Julián said.

"A beer," Laura requested.

While Meritxell Puigbaró went to fetch the drinks, Laura looked at the photos on a shelf above the TV. They were images of her at different times in her life. At thirty, at forty, at fifty. Always alone. Always wearing glasses and her hair up. Letting it down and putting on some makeup would have been enough to make her a very attractive woman, but the photos gave her the notion that Puigbaró swam against the tide: while most people tried to enhance their beauty, she seemed to want to contain it.

"You said over the phone that you wanted to talk about the wolves," she said, handing them their drinks.

"Yes," Julián answered. "We read the article in *La Vanguardia* from when…"

"When they raped me. You can say it. I'm not allergic to the word."

Seeing her partner's tactlessness, Laura decided to take over the conversation.

"I work for the police in Argentina. I'm investigating some crimes that might be related to the wolves. As I'm sure you know, everyone we ask insists that it was just an innocent boys' club."

"They're telling the truth."

Laura definitely wasn't expecting that.

"What I mean," Puigbaró clarified, "is that for the majority of the eighty years the brotherhood has existed, it was just that."

"So, the ones who attacked you were the exception rather than the rule," Julián suggested.

"Something like that. Let's see... I'll start at the beginning. As you know, I was raped in an empty lot in Torroella in 1985. Some rape victims overcome the trauma. I guess they don't try to understand why, they let time heal their wounds and they get on with life however they can. But others, like me, can't stop scratching at that wound, and it becomes chronic. We wonder what we did wrong, and most of all, why. Why me? Where does that kind of evil come from?"

The woman took a long sip of beer and looked Laura in the eyes.

"It's hard to explain. Nearly impossible. It's like when someone bites their hangnails and when they see blood, they still keep doing it. It's a vicious, self-destructive circle. In my case, when I realized there wouldn't be justice, that no one would go to jail for what had been done to me, I decided to investigate. To find out who those wolves really were."

"It can't have been easy," Laura ventured.

"No, it wasn't, but thirty-five years is enough time to achieve almost anything if you put your mind to it."

"In the article we read, you said you knew they were members of the brotherhood because they were wearing the ring. Do you remember if it was silver or golden?"

"Silver, definitely. In time, I learned that that was odd because members of the brotherhood wore gold-colored rings made of brass."

Puigbaró smiled with resignation.

"Not that it's done me any good, but I think I'm one of the few people who knows the most about the Brotherhood of the Wolves."

"Whatever you can tell us..."

"It was formally founded in Santa María de los Desamparados in 1941, but its origins go back twenty years before that, here in Barcelona. A high-society group that called themselves 'The LOUD Club'."

"Loud? As in a loud noise?"

"Yes, but it's not English. For a long time, I thought it meant 'wolf' in some foreign language. It sounds like 'lobo' in Spanish, and the Catalan version: 'llop'. But then I realized it was an acronym."

"*Lupus occidere uiuendo debet*," Laura recited.

"Exactly. Some say Gaudí was one of the founding members, but from what I've been able to find out, that's just a rumor. What is true is that there are newspaper articles from back then that talk about murders and rapes perpetrated by a club of men who signed as LOUD. On certain occasions, instead of the acronym, they'd write the whole sentence."

Puigbaró took another long sip of beer and when she set the bottle back on her thigh, Laura noticed it was almost empty.

"Over time, the members of the club started showing up dead, until it was clear that someone was eliminating them one by one. I guess it was someone who took matters into their own hands, something I myself dreamt of doing many times. In a way, they were successful because their identity was never revealed and the club dissolved."

"Did you manage to find out who it was?"

"No. And it doesn't matter anymore, because they'd be dead now, or over a hundred years old. What I did find out was that there was a manifesto written in 1921 by the club founders. That book apparently showed up in Santa María de los Desamparados in 1941. Some people say one of the members fled to Torroella, escaping the vigilante, and worked at the school as a professor. It's possible he recruited students to reactivate the society. Those details are unclear to me, but by the '50s, some people openly spoke about being members of the Brotherhood of the Wolves but said that the activities they were involved in were merely innocent pranks. One of them was my father, the only person I trust completely."

"Do you know if there were others like you?"

"I haven't been able to find one single incidence of rape or a crime linked to the brotherhood from before or after what happened to me. I think that, as I said before, for the most part the brotherhood was a group of harmless students. Until at some point, they returned to the original LOUD club values, radicalized, and attacked me."

Meritxell Puigbaró seemed to have the same theory Jaume Serra did. Organizations go through different stages throughout their history.

"In the article in *La Vanguardia*, you also say you know who the four hooded men who attacked you were."

"Josep Codina, Gerard Martí, Mario Santiago, and Arnau Junqué. I recognized their voices."

Laura could feel Julián's eyes on her. The names corresponded to the man stabbed in Torroella and the three who disappeared in the Pyrenees.

"Did you report them?"

"Of course. I gave their full names. But things work differently in a small town. It all depends on who you know, and mostly who has the power. The four men who raped me belonged to the wealthiest families in Torroella. They hired the best lawyers. The judge ended up determining that there wasn't enough proof to confirm they had been the attackers. Once they were acquitted, no one ever spoke about the case again. Another thing small towns are great at is sweeping things under the rug."

Laura knew exactly what the woman was talking about. Puerto Deseado and many other towns in Patagonia were full of pacts of silence.

"Society is very unfair sometimes. Some people accused me of making it all up to get money from the families. One of the things that hurts the most is people not believing you, asking you questions trying to catch you in a lie, thinking no one actually raped you. They don't treat you like what you are: a victim. Instead, you're asked to explain, justify, and provide proof. It's all backwards. I guess that in their minds, they don't want to believe that an atrocity like that happened; they prefer to think it's all just a figment of a crazy woman's imagination. I couldn't stand it anymore so I came to live in Barcelona. I'd go back to Torroella often to see my mother and continue my investigation, but I felt like I was asphyxiating there, like I'd become allergic to my hometown's air."

Meritxell Puibgaró told her story with a deep, genuine sadness, but without ever losing her calm or shedding a tear. She spoke like a parent who lost a child long ago and could finally mention them without crying.

"I don't know if this helps you at all."

"A lot," Laura said. "All this research you've done, is it written down anywhere?"

The woman stretched over and pulled out a box from under the TV stand.

"Here are the newspaper articles, notes, everything I could find out about the Brotherhood of the Wolves is in here. Even my father's brotherhood diary is in there."

"Brotherhood diary?"

Puigbaró smiled and rummaged around the box until she pulled out a brown notebook.

"That's what he called it. He wrote down what happened in the meetings. Nothing that could help you solve a murder, I can assure you. The juiciest thing in here is a story about the time he drank the whisky they stole from the priest's sacristy."

"Are you sure?"

"Yes. I've tortured myself with this stuff for years and it hasn't done me much good. I hope it will for you."

"Thank you."

It was time to go and leave the woman alone, Laura thought. If they had any questions after going through the documents, they could call or pay her another visit.

"I believe you," she told her. "And we're working to make the truth come out."

"Thank you," the woman replied, her chin trembling slightly. "But I've known the truth for a long time."

They said goodbye and walked down the stairs. They walked out of Meritxell Puigbaró's calm apartment into the chaos of her eclectic neighborhood. Less than fifty meters from Meritxell's door, Laura heard a gunshot. She handed Julián the box and pulled out her phone to read the message she'd just received.

"It's Adrián Caplonch's secretary. Her boss has agreed to talk to us. She asks if we can meet at his house tomorrow at three p.m."

"Of course, where does he live?"

"Las Aguas Road, number 79."

Julián looked confused.

"Las Aguas Road? Are you sure?"

"It says so here. Why?"

"Because no one lives on Las Aguas Road."

CHAPTER 51

Laura

At three p.m. the next day, Laura understood Julián's confusion regarding Adrián Caplonch's address. In order to get to Las Aguas Road, they had to take a metro, a train, and then a cable car that went up the mountain Consuelo had pointed out on their way from the airport.

The cable car –a single, inclining car– had only one stop between the departure and arrival stations. It only stopped there if a passenger requested it by pressing a button that was hidden next to the doors. That stop was called Las Aguas Road.

They were the only people to get off when the cable car stopped, suspended above the mountain by an iron cable as thick as Laura's arm. The station was merely a sign and a bench in the middle of the woods. They were greeted by air that was fresher than the city's.

"Which is Las Aguas Road?"

"This is it," Julián answered, pointing at the dirt road in front of the station.

Laura let a group of bikers pass and then crossed the dirt road. Through the clearing that the cable car tracks opened in the forest, she could see the city. She recognized the towers of the Sagrada Familia surrounded by cranes, Montjuic Castle and the two skyscrapers in the Olympic Village. Framed by the sparkling blue Mediterranean, Barcelona seemed to surrender at her feet.

"From up here, it looks like a perfect city," Julián said.

She nodded in silence. She didn't want to answer yet. She wanted to savor that unique view a few seconds longer.

"According to the map, number 79 is that way," Julián spoke again, pointing in the direction the bikers had gone.

Laura started walking. To her right, the dense, dry forest creeped up the mountain. To her left, the gaps in the canopy of trees gave her a glimpse of the city.

"To me, Las Aguas Road sounds like a place where people come to work out," Julián said. "I didn't know anyone lived here."

"I don't see any houses."

"That's what the GPS says," he answered, pointing ahead.

After rounding a bend, a treeless slope gave them a new panoramic view of Barcelona.

"According to this, the house is less than half a kilometer from here," said Julián.

Laura followed without looking at him. She couldn't peel her eyes away from the view to her left. A few minutes later, after another bend, they stumbled upon a house that looked straight out of a fairy tale. Bright green and red tiles formed a pattern that reminded Laura of the back of an exotic lizard. On one side, a tall tower with windows on each side looked like a steeple. The building was like a halfway point between a modernist mansion and a church.

They stopped in front of a massive rust-colored gate that prevented mere mortals from seeing into the estate. Under a wrought-iron number 79 there was a modern doorbell with a camera. Laura pressed the button and the gate opened with a buzz.

"This guy stole the gardener from a golf club," Julián said, as the gate opened onto a lawn of grass so perfect Laura thought it was artificial at first.

Out of the main entrance, protected by a tiled veranda, a thin man in his sixties walked out, his body strong and his skin tan. He was wearing a light blue shirt, cream-colored pants and dock shoes.

"Miss Badía, Mr. Cucurell, I'm Adrián Caplonch. Welcome. This way, please."

Caplonch walked into the house, circled a marble staircase and led them to a kitchen-dining room area that was bigger than any house Laura had ever lived in. It was straight out of an architecture and design magazine: an island, a rustic wood table, and a window looking onto an infinity pool behind which was a view of the city and the sea.

She never would have thought there was so much money in canned goods.

"Something has cropped up and I don't have much time, so I'll have to skip the pleasantries and ask that you get to the point. You told me over the phone that you're writing a book about the history of my beloved school."

"Something like that," Laura replied. "Were you a member of the Brotherhood of the Wolves?"

The question surprised Caplonch.

"Yes, for two years. Why?"

"Does the name Pep Codina sound familiar?"

"Of course. He was a classmate of mine at Santa María de los Desamparados."

"He was also a member of the brotherhood?"

"Yes."

"I suppose you also know he was murdered and that his body was found wearing the wolf ring."

Caplonch's perfect smile was still there, but now there was tension in his jaw and a certain coldness in his eyes.

"What is this?" the businessman asked.

"That's what we're trying to find out."

"Who are you? The police? Did you lie to me?"

"We aren't with the police exactly, and we might have lied a little. But as you can imagine, we needed to have a face-to-face meeting with you because this is such a delicate matter."

"Leave my house, immediately."

"Mr. Caplonch."

"Am I going to have to call the police?"

"No need. We'll be on our way," Julián said. "But think about it: if you have nothing to hide, it might be convenient for you to speak to us. We're going to publish our investigation. Do you understand what I'm saying?"

Laura wanted to kill him.

"Are you threatening me?" Caplonch asked.

"No, not at all," she intervened. "What my partner means is that when you haven't done anything wrong, the most natural reaction is to talk. On the other hand, if you choose silence, it allows anyone to talk about you, make up theories."

Caplonch waved at his surroundings.

"Do you think you get to live in a house like this when you're afraid of what others say about you?"

"Of course not," Laura said. "But why don't you listen to our questions before you kick us out?"

Caplonch looked at the gold watch on his wrist and huffed.

"You have two minutes. What do you want to know?"

"If Codina, and the other members of the Brotherhood of the Wolves, kept having meetings after they finished high school."

"Yes. They weren't supposed to, but they had developed a strong bond. They weren't going to cut that off just because of a rule that said you had to leave the brotherhood once you graduated."

"You speak as if you weren't a part of the group."

"Because by that time I wasn't anymore. After a year in the brotherhood, I realized I didn't have as much in common with them as I'd thought."

"What do you mean?"

"They were really into esoteric stuff. You know, rituals and that shit. I preferred the more mundane parts of it," he said pointing at a cabinet full of liquor.

"Why do you think they had such a strong bond?"

Caplonch gave her a suspicious look.

"At the time they believed they were actually brothers. Even I believed it for a while. That what we shared made us family."

"What did you share?"

"That's the thing. It wasn't anything special. We'd get drunk, talk about girls, pulled an innocent prank on a classmate that wasn't part of the brotherhood. We disguised the meetings with a veil of esotericism. You know, we'd light some candles, play Ouija... and based on that, we forged a friendship."

"How do you know they kept up the brotherhood after they finished Santa María de los Desamparados?"

"Because many years later, I ran into them at a bar in Torroella. When I went over to say hi, I noticed they were all wearing the ring. The four of them were visibly uncomfortable."

"Codina, Junqué, Santiago, and Martí?"

"Exactly."

"Do you remember what color the ring was?"

"Silver. The members of the highest circle had the right to wear a silver ring."

The comment surprised her. Not only had Jaume Serra said that all wolves held the same rank, but she'd gone through all the documents in Meritxell Puigbaró's box the night before and hadn't found any mention of a hierarchy in the brotherhood.

"There were different levels? Like in the Masons?"

Caplonch let out a mocking laugh.

"There were two levels. On one level were the four of them. On the other, the rest of us. They made up the inner circle. I know that because an uncle of mine had been a member of the brotherhood before me and he told me that all members held the same rank."

"Do you know if it was possible to access that circle, like when masons go up a level?"

"No, I don't know. Now please, if you'll excuse me," said the businessman as he gestured toward the door.

"Of course," said Laura. "One last question. How many years after you graduated from Santa María did you run into them at the bar?"

"Ten or fifteen. I can't remember exactly it was a long time ago."

Caplonch opened the door and showed them the way out.

"Do you remember what time of year it was?" Laura asked before saying goodbye.

"End of August. The streets were decorated with signs for the town's big festival. They all lived in Barcelona and told me they'd come back to town for the festival. Now please, I do have to go."

"Thank you for your time. If we have any questions, can we get back in touch?"

The businessman hesitated.

"You can ask my secretary for a meeting, although I have some very busy weeks ahead."

They said goodbye and walked toward the cable car station.

"What are you thinking?" Julián asked her once they were far enough from the house.

"That Caplonch said he ran into the wolves in late August, about ten or fifteen years after graduating from Santa María. Pep Codina was killed while wearing the ring, on August 29th, fourteen years after he graduated."

"Do you think he would have given us so many details if he had anything to do with Codina's death?"

"Probably not."

"Then what? He either told us the truth or he lied. There aren't any other options."

Laura nodded, not because she agreed but because she didn't want to start randomly guessing. But she knew there was a third option aside from the truth and a lie: a half-truth.

CHAPTER 52

Laura

Laura fanned her face with her hand, trying in vain to cool off. It had been hot since dawn and where they'd waited in the subway felt like an oven. To top it off, the train they'd gotten on had no air conditioning.

"This is our stop: Sagrada Familia," announced Julián, who was standing in front of her, holding on to a ceiling grab rail.

Half of the people who got off with them were tourists. Laura followed Julián through a maze of tunnels until they walked up some stairs and emerged into a park full of trees.

"Is the Sagrada Familia very far from here?"

Julián smiled, took two steps toward a stone wall and patted it.

"Not at all."

Laura turned around and looked up. The metro station was facing the park, so she hadn't realized they were standing practically at the foot of one of the huge cone-shaped towers decorated with stone animals and plants, that appeared on almost every postcard of Barcelona. She crossed the street to get a better look and see the steeple from another angle. The biker who almost ran over her gave her a friendly 'fucking tourists', but all she could focus on was the building in front of her. Now she understood why it was one of the city's symbols.

Gaudí's church was unlike any other she'd seen before. For starters, there were barely any straight lines. The columns looked like tree trunks, or bones, and the tops of the towers were bouquets of flowers and grapes. The walls were covered in people, animals, and plants created by true masonry artists. The façade had so much detail that even standing right in front of it, it was overwhelming to take in.

They walked among tourists, multilingual guides, and street vendors. A few times, Julián had to pull on her arm to prevent her from bumping into others walking with their eyes to the sky just like her.

"How long until they finish it?" she asked, pointing at the cranes.

"The official answer is 2026, which will mark a century since Gaudí's death. But us locals who've seen these cranes for decades have a hard time believing they're ever going to actually finish it. There are running jokes about it."

Laura grabbed onto Julián's arm so she didn't have to worry about where she was walking. She could have stopped for hours at each wall, and still wouldn't have had enough time to take in all the details. Every once in a while, she'd peer over at her chaperone and see that he too was staring up at the cathedral. It felt as though Gaudí had made it his mission for no one to be able to walk past his masterpiece without admiring it, not even those who'd been looking at it their whole lives.

After making a full circle around the block, during which she took dozens of photos for her aunt Susana, they walked away from the church. The streets returned to that Sunday morning feeling, with people walking their dogs, closed storefronts, and no tourists flooding the souvenir shops.

They walked into a bar called Panxot, which looked like it had been frozen in time for the past fifty years. Laura recognized the balding man sitting at one of the tables in the back, from the photos she'd seen on Facebook.

"Mr. Alcántara, thank you so much for agreeing to meet with us."

"It's a pleasure to help a colleague."

"Well, I'm actually not part of the police force anymore. I investigate on my own now."

"Once a cop, always a cop."

Laura smiled and nodded in silence. It was the exact same phrase Superintendent Lamuedra had told her in Puerto Deseado three years back.

Gregorio Alcántara pointed at a thick folder that lay on the table.

"I brought you a copy of the Codina case file."

"Thank you," she said as she flipped through the folder's content. "How about you tell us about what isn't in here?"

"I guess you mean my own impressions?"

"Exactly."

"A homicide in a wealthy town in one of Spain's most affluent regions. Low crime rate. The victim was a young man, no criminal record. From a good family. His wallet was missing, but I never really believed that robbery was the motive."

"Why?" Julián asked.

Alcántara leaned back in his chair and exhaled through his nose. Before speaking, he took a swig from an almost empty bottle of non-alcoholic beer.

"It had been five years since there had been a homicide in Torroella, and six more passed until the next one. A murder to steal a wallet is extremely unusual. Too big a risk for not much of a reward. We also found twenty thousand pesetas in one of Codina's pant pockets."

She had no idea if that was a lot of money or not.

"That's about 120 euros," Alcántara translated. "If we consider inflation, that's about 250 euros today. Can you imagine a thief killing someone for money and not going through all their pockets?"

"Then what do you think the real motive was?"

"I don't know. At first, we thought it might be drug related. Back then, heroin was wreaking havoc in Spain. But the toxicology report turned out cleaner than my mother's kitchen. They didn't find any trace of narcotics in the tests they ran on his hair either. His hair was thirteen centimeters long. In other words, he hadn't had so much as an Altoid in the past year."

Laura noticed Julián looking confused by Alcántaras's explanation.

"Hair grows about a centimeter per month," she clarified.

"The theory that makes most sense is that it was payback," the cop concluded, "but I was never able to find a reason. You have to have done something really bad to end up like that."

Laura thought of Meritxell Puigbaró.

"What can you tell us about the ring?"

"A wolf's head with its jaws open was the symbol of a secret society of Santa María de los Desamparados students. A group of teenage boys who got together to drink. I never gave it too much mind. In the end, the crime occurred fourteen years after Codina had finished school."

Laura and Julián exchanged a look.

"Does the name Fernando Cucurell sound familiar?"

"No. Is that the body you said might be connected to Codina's?"

"It's a bit more complicated than that," Laura explained. "As you know, Codina died fourteen years after finishing his studies at Santa María de los Desamparados. Approximately two years later, three men of about the same age were killed in El Chaltén, a town in Patagonia, Argentina. The three bodies were wearing the wolf ring on their fingers."

Alcántara's eyes widened.

"Also, one of those three bodies appeared in a hotel called Montgrí, owned by a man native to Torroella who all but disappeared after 1991, which is around the time these three people died. That's Fernando Cucurell."

"My uncle, by the way."

"Wow."

"During your investigation, did you talk to anyone who was a member of the Brotherhood of the Wolves at the same time as Codina?" asked Laura.

"Yes. You can find the transcripts in the folder. But none of them were called Cucurell," Alcántara stated as he flipped pages in the case file. "Here they are. Gerard Martí, Arnau Junqué, and Mario Santiago."

Laura made an effort to not look at Julián and spoke calmly.

"The three men who disappeared in the Pyrenees," she said.

"I see you're well informed. Do you think there's some sort of connection between the bodies in Patagonia and these missing people?"

"Only one of the three bodies in Patagonia had an ID on it. Juan Gómez," she said and placed the passport photocopy on the table. "The second last name is illegible. Since it's such a common name, we haven't been able to find anything about him online."

"Let me see what I can do," Alcántara said and stood up, leaving the bar with the photocopy in his hand.

Through the window, Laura saw him make a phone call.

"Why do you think he's so willing to help us?" Julián asked.

"Because he needs a bone."

She knew the expression on Alcántara's face when he talked about the case all too well. His eyes had shone and his body had visibly tensed up, like a bored dog happy to be thrown a bone after a long time.

Of all retired police officers, murder investigators were the ones who suffered the most from retirement. Their life suddenly became redundant. Yesterday, your big question was, who is the shooter. Today, you were wondering what TV channel to watch.

Laura hadn't made it to retirement, but she knew that feeling of emptiness. She'd also lost interest in everything.

The glacier crimes had been the bone that had reignited the fire in her.

Alcántara returned to the table.

"The passport number belongs to Jacinta Velázquez Mellado, born in Seville in 1943. An ex-colleague just confirmed it."

"The body had a fake passport on it?"

"Seems so."

Laura clenched her teeth to hide how angry she was to have found out this way. Her ex-colleagues in Santa Cruz Police had probably known for days. After all, it only took a phone call from the superintendent to the Spanish embassy to find out what Alcántara had just told them.

She took a deep breath, trying to leave those thoughts aside.

"Now, the possibility that the three members of the Brotherhood of the Wolves who disappeared in the Pyrenees are the Chaltén victims, seems more feasible," she said. "Do you think you could get us the Martí, Junqué, and Santiago files? I'd like to compare their fingerprints."

"They're in here," Alcántara informed her and opened the case file at the end of it. "Back then, my division used to keep the fingerprints of every person we interrogated. I think it'd be illegal nowadays. Anyway, I don't know how much they'll help. Between the quality of the photocopies and the state the bodies must have been in, I'm guessing it'll be hard to tell if they're the same people."

"You'd be surprised," Laura answered as she quickly scrolled through her phone's photo gallery. "The glacier bodies were so well preserved that we were able to get fingerprints that were almost as clear as a living person's. Look, here's a few of them."

She showed Alcántara the photos she herself had taken at the Río Gallegos morgue a year and a half earlier when she'd worked as a consultant, guiding the medical examiner who took those fingerprints, step by step. As she swiped through the fingerprint photos, Laura compared them to the ones in Alcántaras's file.

"The whorls on the pads of their fingers match," she concluded. "The two glacier bodies are Gerard Martí and Mario Santiago. Most likely, the one in Hotel Montgrí is Arnau Junqué. Once they rehydrate the body, it won't be hard to confirm that."

"Those men never went missing in Catalunya," Alcántara summarized.

"No. They told their families they were going to the Pyrenees to justify their absence for several days. Once they were declared missing, the search only took place within the country. Spanish police never looked for them abroad."

"There was no reason for us to do that," Alcantara explained.

"If those three men left Spain under false names, it's because they didn't want anyone to know where they were going. In fact, they cared so much about having an alibi that they went to the park and asked about hiking trails at the information office. Afterward, instead of going into the woods, they left the country to go to Patagonia with fake passports."

"Do you have any theories?" asked the retired policeman.

"In winter of 1989, summer here in Europe, Fernando Cucurell comes back to Spain and spends two months here. During those two months, Pep Codina is stabbed to death in Torroella de Montgrí's center. Two years later, the three wolves travel to Argentina with fake passports."

"They traveled to kill Fernando Cucurell."

"The wolf must kill in order to live," said Julián, repeating the phrase engraved in the rings.

"But something went wrong because they ended up dead," Alcántara guessed. "Maybe Cucurell found out and set a trap for them."

"If the guys went to avenge their friend, why would two of them go on a hike in the middle of a glacier?"

They sat in silence for a while. Alcántara rocked the empty non-alcoholic beer bottle between his hands.

"We have to notify the authorities about this."

At that moment, Gregorio Alcántara's phone rang. The man looked at the screen and apologized.

"It's my daughter. I have to pick up," he said and left the bar to talk outside.

Laura sat motionless, staring at the files of the three men on the table.

"Two days ago, someone already knew that the Chaltén victims were the missing men from Cadí," said Julián. "If not, they wouldn't have threatened me. Whoever that person is, they know exactly what we're doing."

Before Laura could answer, Alcántara walked back into the bar.

"My apologies. She hadn't called me in several days and I was worried," he said, pointing at his phone.

Laura waved his apology away.

"I was saying that we have an obligation to report this as soon as possible," Alcántara said. "If what you're saying is true and the fingerprints belong to these people, we'd be giving closure to three families who've been waiting for thirty years."

Laura nodded silently. Next to her, Julián was quiet as well. No matter what they said, the retired policeman had made the decision to notify the authorities. The cat was out of the bag and there was no putting it back in. The case would go from an amateur investigation to a diplomatic affaire and she'd no longer be a part of it.

Maybe it was better this way, Laura thought. Maybe it was time to go back to doing what the law stated and not what she thought was right.

CHAPTER 53

Many years back.

After the kiss with Manel, the boy puts all his effort into avoiding the wolves. First, he misses several days of school due to an alleged stomachache. When his parents force him to go back, he makes sure he gets there early and waits for class to start, hidden near his classroom. He doesn't want to run into them, and much less have to resort to Manel's protection. He counts the days until school is out and he can spend the entire summer without setting foot in Santa María de los Desamparados.

One afternoon, professor Calvet asks him to help decorate the courtyard for the end-of-year show. He doesn't want to in the slightest, but at Santa María, saying no to a professor's request isn't an option.

After a few hours hanging streamers together, Calvet announces that he has to leave. He asks the boy, or rather demands, that he finish what's left on his own.

An hour later, the boy has completed his task. He goes back to the classroom to grab his books and coat but doesn't make it past the door. On the floor, right in front of the door, he finds a photograph. It's taken from far away, but it clearly shows him and Manel kissing.

"Assholes," he mutters, looking around him.

The hallway is empty. He notices there's another photo just like the one he's holding a few meters away. He picks it up, then sees another further ahead. The wolves have plastered the image all over school.

The more copies he picks up, the further he wanders from the classroom. He knows it's a trap, but he doesn't have any other choice. If he can't find a way to destroy all the copies, he and Manel will be expelled from Santa María de los Desamparados.

The fifth photo is in front of the library door. As he kneels down to pick it up, a foot rams into his ribs. He wants to scream, but the kick has knocked the wind out of him. Someone drags him into the library by his feet. He manages to let out one single cry. Before he can muster a second, a blow to his head knocks him out.

In a semiconscious state, he feels several hands pick him up and carry him somewhere. The tall bookshelves make way to damp stone walls and frigid air. They throw him on the ground like a sack of potatoes.

When he opens his eyes, he's surrounded by men wearing black ski masks covering their entire face except their eyes. He knows they're the wolves but something doesn't add up. There aren't four of them, there are five.

He can hear sobbing coming from somewhere nearby but can't tell from where.

"Your prince won't come save you here," one of them says.

He recognizes that voice. It's Pep Codina. He's sure that three of the remaining four are Arnau Junqué, Gerard Martí, and Mario Santiago, his henchmen. He has no clue who the last one could be.

"Why don't you leave me alone?"

"It's too late for that," Codina replies and motions to the other four. Three of them quickly bind each of the boy's limbs to chains fixed to iron shelves full of books.

"Leave the boy alone!" the fifth wolf yells as he stands, frozen, watching them.

The other four turn toward him and laugh. Pep Codina puts his hand on the dissenter.

"Calm down. If you aren't ready for the test, there's always next time."

"Leave him alone! You're crazy," the hooded boy answers and makes a run for the stairs.

He doesn't make it very far before they catch him.

The boy watches the wolves tie up one of their own, just like they did to him.

"Don't you want to join the inner circle? Don't you want to stop wearing that piece of junk and become a real wolf?" Codina says to him, showing him the ring on his finger.

He then signals to one of his minions, who lifts up the bottom of the fifth guy's mask and shoves a rag in his mouth. The boy can't see his face but he knows exactly who it is. He recognizes his voice.

Once the fifth wolf is gagged, they tie him up in a corner of the basement. That's when the boy sees that there's someone else in the room. He's also tied up and wearing a mask. His head droops down, his gaze locked on the floor. That's where the sobbing he heard is coming from.

Codina walks toward the two of them and grabs them by the jaw to force them to look up.

"If you stop looking, you're gonna end up like him."

After saying that, he walks toward the boy who has never been so afraid as he was at that moment. He has to squeeze his legs together to stop from pissing himself.

"Sorry Cucurell," Codina says. "There are also weak wolves. Where were we? Ah yes, that it turns out you're a faggot."

"No," the boy answers.

"No?" Codina waves a copy of the photo in the air. "Then what's this?"

"That...was a mistake" he stutters. "I wanted to try, but I didn't like it."

"You wanted to try... there's nothing wrong with that. At the end of the day, everyone has the right to try... don't they?"

The boy doesn't know what to reply. Codina grabs his jaw, just like he did with the other two wolves. He feels a sharp pain run from his ears all across his skull.

"Yes or no, Cucurell?"

They boy nods. Pep Codina lets go of him and turns toward his friends.

"See? He said it himself. We all have the right to try," he says, unzipping his pants. "So let's try."

PART IV

LUPUS OCCIDERE UIUENDO DEBET

CHAPTER 54

Laura

"We have to go back to Santa María de los Desamparados," Laura said as soon as they arrived at Julián's apartment following their meeting with Gregorio Alcántara.

"What for? The case is solved. My uncle killed those three men in Chaltén. There's no other possible explanation."

"First of all, there's always another possible explanation. Second, if your uncle killed those three people, he must have had his reasons. We have to go back to where everything started. We don't know if Fernando shared a classroom with the wolves, for example. Also, if we find the brotherhood manifesto Jaume Serra mentioned we might understand..."

"This isn't our responsibility anymore. Alcántara's probably informed the authorities, just as he said he would."

"And what do you think is going to happen? That diplomats from both countries are going to reach an agreement and the Spanish and Argentinian police are going to allocate resources to solve a thirty-year-old case together? That only happens in movies."

"I don't care what happens. I have enough answers," Julián said, opening a drawer in his dining room cabinet and taking out the note that accompanied the photo. "Someone's following us and asking more questions in Torroella is dangerous."

"Who said we were going to ask questions?"

"You did."

"No, I said we have to go back."

It took a while to convince him, but at six p.m., Julián was parking Consuelo's BMW in the supermarket parking lot at the entrance of Torroella de Montgrí.

During the drive there, Laura had looked behind them several times. It was impossible to be certain no one was following them on a busy highway, but when they turned onto a side road, she felt confident that no one was trailing them.

"There's more people than the last time we came," she observed as they walked down Torroella's winding streets.

"It's Sunday. These towns are packed on weekends, even in winter. We're very close to the Costa Brava, one of Spain's top tourist spots."

They passed the square where Pep Codina was killed. When they made it to Santa María de los Desamparados, Laura sat down on a stone bench in front of the school. On the building's front steps, a group of teenagers was practicing a dance routine in front of a phone on a tripod.

"There's too many people," Julián said.

"To walk in the front door, yes. But as you can see, it's locked anyway."

Laura beckoned him to follow her and left the plaza. After turning two corners, she saw one of the small houses that ran along the back of the school property. On the other side of a tall fence, she recognized the garden that headmaster Castells's office looked onto. Next to the olive trees, there was a gravel parking lot with space for three cars. It was empty.

She looked both ways. After ensuring they were the only people around, she climbed the fence and swung down into the garden.

"What are you doing?"

"Come on. Stop talking and follow me."

Julián huffed and pulled himself up the iron bars. Right when he was at the top, with one leg hanging on each side, Laura heard voices. It was two women who were chatting as they walked down the street. Julián jumped down headfirst and fell next to her.

"Did they see you?"

"I don't think so. I'm ok, thanks for asking."

Julián started getting up but Laura stopped him with a slap. The fence sat on a stone wall about a meter high. If they stayed on the ground, they wouldn't be seen.

She held her breath. If the women had seen Julián, they might call the police. She heard them slow their step as they passed close to them. She didn't understand what they were saying as they spoke Catalan, but they didn't sound alarmed. They were chatting and laughing like two friendly neighbors.

After a few minutes, the voices trailed off. When Laura could no longer hear them, she poked her head through the iron bars. There was no one else around. She motioned to Julián to follow her and crossed the garden until she was under a veranda that a small grapevine was starting to cover.

The door was locked. They'd have to break a window to get in. She chose a classroom that wasn't visible from the street thanks to the cover provided by a large olive tree. She leaned onto Julián and prepared to kick the glass in.

"Wait," he told her.

"What?"

"It'll be six o'clock in one minute."

Sixty seconds later, Laura heard the first bell toll come from the town church. Julián kicked right as the third toll rang, covering the sound of glass breaking.

"You're smarter than you look," she told him as she stuck her hand through the shards of glass to unlock the window.

Everything was quiet in the medieval cloister. The sounds of the town didn't penetrate the thick stone walls of the old convent. Although the afternoon sun shone brightly on half the cloister, the place seemed gloomy to

Laura. The leaves on the trees were still. The fountain was off.

Without wasting any time, she headed toward the library.

"Let's look for the book Jaume Serra mentioned first. Then we'll go down to the basement."

"Where should we start?" Julián asked, waving at the thousands of books illuminated by the multicolored light streaming in from the images of saints and crucifixions in the stained-glass windows.

According to Laura's limited knowledge of libraries, books were classified according to theme and then within each theme, alphabetically by the author's last name. Since she had no idea what that place's classification system was like, they'd have to explore the bookshelves one by one.

"Let's split up, that way we can move faster," she suggested.

Laura headed over to one of the side walls and told Julián to start on the opposite end of the library. She walked down a hallway full of books that looked like they belonged in an antique shop. Her eyes skimmed over the authors' last names and the small signs stuck on the edge of the shelves. Soon enough, she found one with the letter B on it. She ran her finger across all the books, from Pere Babot to Cipriano Buxadé, but didn't find any by Narciso Ballabriga.

"Laura!" she heard Julián call from the other end of the library.

She ran over and found Julián standing with a book in his hand.

"'On the Reproductive Habits of the Iberian Wolf', by Narciso Ballabriga."

Julián's fingers flipped through the pages until they reached number 66. Jaume Serra had told them he'd stuck the Brotherhood of the Wolves manifesto there.

The page was ripped in half. Someone had torn a piece several centimeters wide off the top. On the part that remained, they'd drawn a big red arrow pointing right. Below that, in the same red ink, a hand-written phrase: *Lupus occidere uiuendo debet*.

"What the fuck is this?"

"Someone tore out Jaume Serra's manifesto," she concluded.

"Why?"

"Maybe because they didn't agree with it and wanted to change the rules."

"What about the arrow?" Julián asked as he flipped through the rest of the pages in the direction the arrow was pointing. "There's just more stuff about Iberian wolf biology in here. There's nothing in the direction the arrow's pointing."

Julián's words gave her an idea.

"Where did you find the book?

Julián pointed at an empty space on the bottom drawer, just a few inches from the gray stone floor. Laura knelt. With Ballabriga's book open, the arrow on page 66 pointed to the right. However, with the book on the shelf, just like Julián had found it, the arrow pointed toward the back of the thick bookshelf. She examined the empty space where 'On the Reproductive Habits of the Iberian Wolf' had been and discovered another, much older book, behind it. Though the golden letters on its spine were illegible, she could make out a filigree shaped like a wolf's face at the bottom.

She pulled out the hidden book. The only inscription on the cover was the title, in golden letters.

"*Lupus occidere uiuendo debet*," she read out loud. "Now we know where the inscription on the rings came from."

CHAPTER 55

Laura

Despite the title in Latin, the book was written in Spanish. Within the pompous leather covers decorated with golden lettering, Laura found typewritten pages with no publishing details. The only piece of information aside from the title was that it was written in 1921. It didn't even mention the author's name.

A quick skim revealed 126 pages of dense text split into two parts. She read the preface out loud, which was titled 'Manifesto'.

Man today is like a dog. A weak, softened version of the wolf it once was. However, we must not forget that yesteryear's wolf instincts are often present even in the most docile dogs. The wolf obeys no one. The wolf explores, fornicates, kills when it wants, without asking permission from any master. Man's basic nature is the same. But the centuries of society, of noblemen and commoners, landlords and peasants, bosses and workers, have turned us docile, weak, and faint-hearted like dogs. If a dog kills another, their masters argue, apologize, and even go as far as putting down an animal that followed its instincts for a moment. In the same way, if a man kills another, its master –meaning modern society–, he is convicted to life in prison or to death. On the contrary, if a wolf kills another in the forest, the world does not bat an eye. The time has come for us to break the chains that force us to renounce our instinct. The time has come to explore, fornicate, and kill when we wish to. The time has come to eliminate the dog and make way for the wolf.

"This is the original wolf manifesto Meritxell Puigbaró told us about," Laura concluded.

"It doesn't really match the innocent belief everyone has about the brotherhood."

"Everyone but her. Once we read the whole thing we might find an answer. Didn't I tell you it was important that we come here? Now let's go rummage around in Mr. 'eight days" archive."

Laura tucked the book into her backpack and circled the librarian's desk. She carefully opened the old wooden door and walked down the granite steps into the dark. At the bottom, she found an open iron gate framed by damp stones, which made it look like a dungeon.

She felt around for a light switch. A dim, yellow lightbulb illuminated the wide basement, with a ceiling so low, the thick wooden beams almost grazed the top of her head. Julián, who was taller than her, had to walk hunched over.

Apparently, the Santa María de los Desamparados archive shared a space with the school's old junk and obsolete textbooks.

"The librarian wasn't lying. This place is a mess," Laura observed.

She walked among metal file cabinets of varying sizes that took up most of the basement. Many of them didn't have any labels on their drawers. She tried opening a few at random and found that more than half were locked.

"Let's start with the ones that are open. When did your uncle come to school here?"

"He was born in 1956, so he should have started first year of high school in 1968. Back then there were only six grades in elementary school."

The first drawer Laura looked through was full of teaching programs from the 1940s. If she'd wanted to know how they taught math during World War II, this was the place to look. The next four drawers were as irrelevant as the first, and judging by Julián's huffing, he wasn't having much luck either.

The sixth drawer revealed something more encouraging. It was filled with hundreds of cardboard binders, ordered by year from 1921 to 1971. She went through them until she found the one for 1968. However, inside there were merely a few sheets with class schedules for each grade.

"This is going to take forever," she told Julián. "And once we start with the locked drawers it'll be even worse…"

She was interrupted by a loud crash behind her. The sound startled her so much that she dropped the folder she was holding.

She heard footsteps running away from her.

"What was that?" Julián asked.

Laura ran toward the stairs but the gate now blocked the way out. The noise they had heard was the gate banging shut. When she looked up the stairs, she saw a pair of feet running up and a second later, the wooden door that led to the library was closed. She didn't have time to make out if the shoes belonged to a man or a woman.

She grabbed onto the bars and tried to move them, but it was like pulling on a statue's arm.

"Hey! Open up!" she yelled.

The only answer was the echo of her own voice against the stone walls. A second later, the basement went completely dark.

"They've locked us in," she told Julián, panting. She took her phone out of her pocket but there was a little red x in the top corner. "There's no phone signal."

"Yeah, same here."

The gate had a blind lock, with no handle on either side. You could only open it with a key. They tried opening it in every way possible, from sticking a wire into the lock to slamming a file cabinet into the bars, but it didn't budge.

With every try, Laura was sure someone would come down to make them shut up or threaten them. But no one opened the wooden door. They'd simply locked them in.

"If something happens to my parents, I'll never forgive myself," Julián said, his voice hoarse from yelling.

"Thinking like that won't help."

"If they locked us up it's because they know we're still investigating this, Laura. It said so clearly in the note. If something happens to them it's my fault."

She walked up to him and stroked the nape of his neck with a tenderness she usually reserved only for the horses.

"Don't worry. Everything is going to be okay," she told him, and he lay his head on her shoulder.

As the hours passed, the thin line of light under the door at the top of the stairs disappeared. From time to time, they'd yell and try to open the gate. They drifted in and out of sleep against their will and urinated into an old flowerpot when they couldn't hold it anymore.

To make time go by faster, they went back to looking for the class list in the labyrinth of file cabinets several times, but their nerves and the fact that half of them were locked, made it hard to find anything useful before their phone flashlights were completely depleted.

By the time they finally heard noises again, daylight was creeping back. It was eight a.m.

"Help! Open up, please," Julián yelled. "We're in the basement."

"Who's there?"

Laura recognized the librarian's deep voice. He was speaking to them from the other side of the wooden door, without opening it.

"Mr. Castañeda? It's Julián Cucurell and Laura Badía. We visited the school a few days ago. Remember us?"

Silence.

"Someone locked us in the basement," she added.

The wooden door opened slowly. Laura saw the librarian's tall figure silhouetted against the multicolored light filtering through the stained-glass windows.

"We've been here since yesterday afternoon. Please, open up," she said.

"Since yesterday afternoon? Liars! The school is closed on Sundays."

"We broke in. I swear we had a good reason to. We broke one of the classroom windows. Go and check if you want."

"The only place I plan to go is the police."

"No, Mr. Castañeda. Please, don't leave us in here. We're going crazy."

The man's figure disappeared from the doorway and the sound of his quick footsteps echoing across the massive library grew gradually fainter.

The next half an hour felt longer to Laura than the entire night they'd just spent. When she heard footsteps again it was more than one pair. Then, she heard voices murmuring and the wooden door swung open.

"You're going to have to explain what's going on here," headmaster Castells's voice echoed down the stone staircase.

"Professor!" said Julián. "Please, let us out of here."

"I won't open that door until the police arrives."

Laura's mind was going a mile a minute. They had to get out of there soon, however they could.

Think, Laura, she instructed herself.

She opened a drawer where she'd seen bookstore supplies. She grabbed a red pen and rammed it into a wall. Then, she placed the decapitated pen on her groin until a red stain the size of a tennis ball formed on her pants.

"It's an emergency," she yelled. "I'm bleeding. I think I'm having a miscarriage. I don't want to lose my baby, please, professor."

"Laura needs help, professor," Julián joined in. "Think of the baby!"

She heard the sound of shoes against stone steps getting louder. Castells came down slowly, like someone approaching a lion, until he reached the foot of the staircase.

"Thank you, professor. God bless you," said Laura, both hands on her belly.

The headmaster looked down at the dark stain on Laura's groin. He hastily took a key out from his pocket and struggled with the lock but couldn't open it.

"We might have damaged it when we were trying to break it open," Julián explained.

Castells exhaled loudly.

"Allow me, professor," said the librarian.

It took him five minutes to open the door. The second they were free, Julián took off, running up the stairs.

"Wait, Julián. Where are you going?"

He didn't answer and didn't stop. Castells yelled and the librarian stood in front of Laura to ask her if she was okay, but also to block her access to the stairs. Despite the man's size, she managed to push him aside and took off running after Julián.

The last thing she heard, as she leaped up the steps two at a time, was Castell's voice saying the word 'police'.

CHAPTER 56

Julián

"Bastards," I said when I reached my parents' BMW.

All four tires were flat. Each one had a slit in it, a couple of centimeters wide.

I opened the car door and plugged my phone in. As soon as I turned it on, I knew things were even worse than I'd imagined.

"Shit," I said.

"What?" Laura asked.

"Twenty-two missed calls from my mother."

I dialed her number. The line rang once, twice, three times.

"Come on, come on, come *on*," I muttered.

The seconds felt like hours until her answering machine picked up.

"If something's happened to them, it's my fucking fault."

"Calm down, Julián."

Those words were the most absurd I'd ever heard. How was I supposed to calm down? I called again and suffered through every ring. This time, my mother picked up at the sixth.

"Julián, where were you?"

"Mom, are you guys okay?"

She answered with the stiff voice she only used when her mind was elsewhere.

"This morning your father offered to take me to work in his car, since you have mine. A few blocks from home he realized his brakes weren't working. There wasn't anything we could do and we crashed into a tree to avoid running over a woman."

"But are you okay?"

"No! We aren't okay! We're scared, Julián. The mechanic told us someone cut our brakes on purpose."

"I'm sorry, mom."

"Honey, it's not your fault..."

"Yes, it is."

"What do you mean?"

I would have loved to tell her anything but the truth, but I couldn't. I told her about the threats I'd gotten, both in Chaltén and in Barcelona.

"And you kept going after that? It wasn't enough that your father ended up in the hospital after you hammered him with questions?"

"I didn't know... really, I didn't believe they were serious, mom."

"Well, you can start believing it."

A few seconds after I hung up, my phone started making more pings than a slot machine. My mother was sending me pictures of the accident from every angle.

My dad's car, wrapped around a tree. Its bumpers and hood completely destroyed. Airbags deployed. Liquid dripping from the motor.

"Someone is clearly trying to send a message," Laura said to me.

"A message? Laura, they cut their brakes. They could've died."

"But something doesn't add up. If your parents had died, how would that guarantee we'd stop looking? It could've gone in the exact opposite direction. Sometimes pain..."

"Laura, I don't want to talk about this anymore. It's over. I'm not going to put my family in danger again."

"A little late for that, don't you think?"

"No. I'd say just in time. My parents are alive."

"What do we do now? Stop investigating and never find out why three people showed up dead 15 thousand kilometers away from home?"

I wanted to chalk up her total lack of empathy to the events we'd just gone through. Laura was probably as anxious as I was, or more. It was time to drop the conversation, to not 'pick up the gauntlet'. But I couldn't help myself.

"They weren't saints, so I don't really feel sorry for them," I said. "And don't give me that bullshit about everyone deserving justice, because all you care about is finishing your little book. You don't care about anything else."

"My little book? You know what? Do me a favor and go to hell. You, the hotel, your uncle, all of you."

"Wait, we're exhausted," I said. "We shouldn't be arguing right now."

She answered by walking away from the car with a strident step.

"Laura, let's finish the conversation like adults, shall we?"

"I don't think there's anything to talk about," she said without turning. Some bystanders turned to look at us.

"Laura, come on."

I spent the next ten minutes following her down the streets of Torroella, trying to get her to speak to me. Once we'd passed the same corner three times, she finally stopped and glared at me.

"Where the fuck is the train station in this town?"

CHAPTER 57

Laura

The moment the train started moving, Laura leaned her head against her seat. They were departing Flaçà station, headed to Barcelona. An hour ago, the tow truck driver had come to pick up the BMW and had been kind enough to drop them off at the station.

Since they'd sat down, Julián had been looking out the window, his back to her. They were sitting just a few inches apart, but they were kilometers away.

Laura pulled the book she found in the library out of her backpack. She saw Julián straighten up in his seat and peer over at her.

"You don't mind me reading this, do you?" she asked him.

"Do whatever you want."

It took her less than an hour to read the sixty pages that made up the first part of *Lupus occidere uiuendo debet*. They were all a rehash of the first paragraph, arguing that man's true nature was to do whatever he pleased, whenever he pleased. The anonymous author seemed to have one goal: encouraging the reader to act without considering the consequences. According to the bible of this strange religion, humans were the only beings that constantly weighed the consequences of their actions. Our superiority granted by our rationality, the book argued, was actually a prison for our instincts.

Laura found a grain of logic to this reasoning. It was true that humans lived in a numbed state. Even more so in the hundred years that had passed since the book had been written. A famous tango once said that the twentieth century was chaotic, problematic, and feverish, but the twenty-first century felt ten times worse. The problem was that, taken literally, the manifesto gave men the green light to rape a woman, for example. Or beat their neighbor to death.

The book was proselytist crap full of cheap propaganda. And Laura, like any Latin American with any knowledge of history, knew that cheap propaganda worked.

When she reached the end of the first part, she re-read the final paragraph several times.

Thus, today a new man is born. A man who will not be afraid to take life by the reins. A man who is no longer domesticated like a dog, but instead wild, like a wolf. And for all men willing to live a sincere life to have a place to find other members of their species, today in the city of Barcelona, the L.O.U.D Club is founded.

The second part of the book described the club's rules. It detailed who could be a member –men of age–, and the protocol to become a member, which included killing a dog. There was no mention of Santa María de los Desamparados or the rings. She closed the book with a fire burning inside her. That shit had destroyed more than one person's life.

"This doesn't sound like what Jaume Serra told us at all," she told Julián.

He nodded in silence, as if he didn't care. His phone rang and Laura saw him decline a call from Anna, his ex.

"It sounds more like what Meritxell Puigbaró told us," she went on. "The Brotherhood of the Wolves wasn't born as a student club but as a group of adult men in Barcelona. Over time, it moved to Santa María de los Desamparados and went through different stages. The brotherhood Serra described and the one that responds to this monstrosity don't seem to have much in common."

Julián looked at her for a second, but quickly returned to the playlist on his phone. He is shut tighter than a clam, she thought.

"Not even the ring is the same," she insisted. "It didn't have the Latin inscription, which turns out is the title of this piece of shit."

She saw Julián huff. Good sign. He was getting annoyed, but at least he was going to talk to her.

"Laura, Serra was very clear: any group evolves over time. And as far as this book goes, there's literature that doesn't find its most fundamentalist readers until centuries after it's written. The Spanish Inquisition was founded fifteen centuries after Christ was born. Al-Qaeda is younger than we are."

Laura snapped her fingers and pointed at Julián as if he'd revealed something useful. It was a technique to keep him interested.

"I get it now," she said. "This book proves that the Brotherhood of the Wolves was founded by a group of fanatics. It mellowed into the innocent group Jaume Serra and many others spoke of until the book reached Codina and company, who decided to take it literally. They resignified the brotherhood. The book gave them the legitimacy to commit atrocities without guilt. The question is: why did they all end up murdered?"

Julián shrugged, but Laura knew that this time his lack of interest was more feigned than real. She continued.

"Why would someone kill four guys who belong to a sort of cult, where respect for others doesn't exist?"

"To stop them from hurting people," Julián answered, declining another call from Anna.

"Exactly. What precisely did your father say when you asked him if his brother had been a member of the wolves?"

"Laura, seriously, drop it. Please."

Now Julián stared at his knees. His open eyes didn't blink. Laura had seen that expression in many witnesses.

It was the face they made when they finally realized something that had always been right under their noses.

She was unsure what Julián would do next. If she asked, he'd tell her to stop and that he didn't want to stir up the past anymore. But maybe, just maybe, she'd just planted the seed that would lead them to the truth.

CHAPTER 58

Laura

She walked alongside Julián from the Sants metro station to his house. Once they were there, he said he was going to see his parents. She made up something about going to explore Barcelona. Their longest interaction was when they spoke about how much they both needed a shower.

After half an hour in the bathroom, Laura left the apartment and walked in the direction she presumed the center to be. Aided by a guidebook she bought and some friendly locals, it took her less than an hour to make it to Catalunya Square.

She spent the day wandering down the streets on each side of the Ramblas. On one side, the neighborhood was El Raval and on the other was the Gothic Quarter. Ten minutes after closing the guidebook she'd forgotten which side was which. She crossed the Ramblas twice, discovering old churches, ancient storefronts, and museums in buildings that deserved to be in museums themselves. After crossing a narrow alley overflowing with bars and tattoo parlors, she walked through an archway into a port full of sailboats and luxury yachts, sparkling under the late afternoon sun.

She was walking along the pier when her phone rang.

"Laura? It's Gregorio Alcántara. I have something that might interest you."

"Shall we meet?"

"No need. I can tell you over the phone."

"I'm all ears. I guess you're going to tell me you notified your former colleagues in the police about the Chaltén murders."

"Yes, I have. By now, I'd imagine diplomatic agreements between our countries are underway. That's not why I called you, though. I'm calling to tell you there weren't four wolves, but six."

"What do you mean?"

"Aside from the victims, there were two other people that were part of the brotherhood between 1970 and 1975."

"How do you know?"

"I met my wife on one of my trips to Torroella during the investigation. We've been married for thirty years, so I've made many friends from there. Asking around among people of Codina and company's age, I found a man who was about to enter the brotherhood but didn't pass the first trial."

"There were trials to become a wolf?" Laura asked, feigning surprise.

"Like in all secret societies, I suppose. In this case, it entailed the killing of a dog."

The same thing she'd read in *Lupus occidere uiuendo debet.*

"This person couldn't bring himself to do it," the former policeman went on, "but says there were two others with him that did and entered the brotherhood."

"Did he give you any names?"

"Adrián Caplonch, one of Torroella's most successful businessmen. He's in…"

"The canned food business. I know him," Laura interrupted. "And the other one?"

"He didn't tell me his name. Says he doesn't remember."

"Do you believe him?"

"Not really, no. You don't forget those kinds of things, especially in a small town."

Laura, who grew up in Puerto Deseado, agreed.

"Miss Badía. One more thing…"

"Yes."

"Be careful. Remember that if you go missing on the other side of the world, it can take a long time for anyone to find you."

In another tone of voice, Alcántara's words would have sounded like a threat, but the retired policeman had pronounced them as a piece of advice. An old fox helping a younger one.

"Thank you," she replied and looked around her, searching for a metro station through the sea of yachts and restaurants.

CHAPTER 59

Julián

After our train ride back from Torroella, I said goodbye to Laura before jumping in the shower. I'd considered going straight to my parents' house from the train station, but if I showed up covered in dirt after the worst night of my life, they'd hound me with questions.

Laura told me she'd take the afternoon to explore Barcelona, but I suspected that she made that up. I think she was the kind of person who finds a bone and then doesn't let go no matter what. We didn't discuss how much longer she could stay at my place or when she'd go back to El Chaltén. It wasn't the time for that.

When I left the house, the neighborhood was bustling. Traffic, buses, and lots of people on the sidewalks, out doing their morning shopping. At the first corner, I ran into her.

"Anna."

When she saw me, she gave me a kiss on each cheek.

"Julián. I was headed to your house. I called you several times."

It was so weird to hear her say 'your house'.

"I couldn't talk, sorry. I was going to call you as soon as... Wait, weren't you going to Argentina?"

"I canceled my trip. Can we go upstairs?" she asked, pointing at my building.

"Is something wrong?"

"It's important. For you, and for me."

We walked back the way I'd come and headed up to the apartment we'd shared up until a month and a half ago. In that brief period, it had turned into the man cave of a guy living with a sort of friend or colleague from the other side of the world, who isn't particularly tidy either. It's unbelievable how quickly chaos takes over if you don't keep it at bay.

"Go for it."

"There's so much I need to say. First, I want to apologize."

"Anna..."

"Listen to me. A real apology. I want to ask you to please forgive me."

I took a deep breath, trying to find the strength to choose my words wisely and not hurt her out of spite.

"Look, what you did flattened me, but everything heals with time. I'm still holding a grudge, but less than I was a month ago. I'm sure at some point I'll be able to forgive you completely."

She looked at me, trying to decide if she believed me or not.

"We might even end up being friends," I added. "It'll be hard, but we can try. Maybe, with time, I can even see you with Rosario and not feel angry."

"You won't see me with Rosario again. We broke up."

I'd never felt like yelling at someone as much as I did at that moment. But I didn't have to. Everything I could have thrown in her face, was summed up into one sentence she delivered with surprising calm.

"I ruined our relationship for an affair that didn't even last three months."

I wanted to shout that she had done just that. Blame her for everything. But I wouldn't have said anything she didn't already know. As a British friend of mine used to say, there's no point beating a dead horse.

"That's the thing about affairs," I said. "You never know how long they're going to last."

"Didn't yours in Patagonia last either?"

"There's nothing between Laura and me."

"I don't mean that. I mean your trip and what you discovered there."

"Oh, yeah, there's a heck of a story behind that. It feels like one that won't last too long though. I'm going to put the hotel up for sale."

Anna nodded.

"Juli, there's something else I want to tell you."

"What?"

Please don't tell me you're pregnant, I thought.

"My brother told me you asked him for help while you were in Patagonia. He told me three bodies were found with the Brotherhood of the Wolves ring."

"You know about the brotherhood too?"

She pulled a notebook from her leather bag. It was old, with cardboard covers and yellowed pages. She opened it on a dog-eared page and read aloud.

"The patient thinks he'll never be able to forgive himself. He says that what they did that night to Cucurell will haunt him for the rest of his life. He blames himself for not stopping them. He claims he frequently has trouble sleeping. During these episodes of insomnia, he remembers what happened and says he hears a voice in his head that tries to comfort him by telling him he couldn't do anything because his hands and feet were bound. He blames himself for not speaking up afterwards. It has been thirty-six years since what the patient refers to as 'that atrocity'. He says the guilt is worse now than ever, but that it is also when he has the most to lose. In his words: 'Power and money are double-edged swords. The higher up you are in society, the more you have to lose. And the less freedom you have.'"

Anna looked up at me. Her eyes were filled with tears and she was gazing at me the way she did whenever she was about to apologize for something.

CHAPTER 60

Laura

The old streetlamps, covered in dust and dead bugs, projected a yellowish halo of light on Las Aguas Street. Every so often, a bright light would appear from around a bend and seconds later, a pumped cyclist would zoom past Laura at full speed.

She shoved her hands into her pockets and quickened her pace. She hadn't dressed warmly enough. Up there, the temperature was several degrees lower than in the city that buzzed at her feet. The darkness gave Caplonch's house an even more majestic look. Surrounded by the dark outline of the forest and illuminated from below with bright floodlights, the house stood out like a monument.

She had to ring the doorbell several times before she got an answer.

"Yes?"

"Mr. Caplonch, it's Laura Badía. I came to visit you a few days ago. I need to speak with you."

"Now?"

"Sorry for showing up unannounced. I tried calling but couldn't get through."

It would have been more accurate to say 'I called, but you gave your secretary instructions to ignore me', but luckily Laura had the occasional brief burst of diplomacy.

"I'm busy."

"Mr. Caplonch. I know you were a member of the Brotherhood of the Wolves alongside Josep Codina, Arnau Junqué, Gerard Martí, and Mario Santiago. All of them were murdered."

"Only Codina. The other three got lost in the Pyrenees."

"That's what they wanted you to believe. But they weren't in the Pyrenees, they were in Patagonia. And they ended up dead as well."

Laura heard static, and fifteen seconds later the front gate opened with a buzz.

Caplonch was waiting for her at the door just like the first time, but he looked different. His clothes were just as expensive, but he lacked the confident demeanor of their last visit.

They moved to the kitchen. Behind the illuminated pool, the city twinkled like an orange galaxy.

"Look, Mr. Caplonch. I'm going to be straight with you. The truth is going to come out, it's up to you how you're going to look once it does."

Caplonch stared at her, his glare as sharp as knives.

"If you tell me what you know, I'll use it to solve an old mystery and help Julián understand more about his family. If not, the police will find out what I know and they'll be the ones asking the questions."

The businessman exhaled, his chest deflating like a balloon.

"Fine," he said. "They made me kill a dog to get into the brotherhood. I hated doing it, I swear."

"I don't work for animal rights."

"I'd never felt so terrible in my life. But they had a way of talking, of convincing you..."

Caplonch rose from his chair and got a bottle of whisky out of a cabinet. He poured two generous glasses and handed one to Laura.

"I thought the dog was the trial by fire, but it was just the first test."

"The first of how many?"

"They didn't tell you that. The first of many. Then came other things that I'm not proud of either but which were less harmful. In fact, I had the feeling that as I moved forward, they became easier."

"Until?"

"Until the day of Cucurell's rape."

Laura took a big gulp of her drink, trying to maintain her composure.

"I had no idea what was going to happen. They told me to wait in the basement of the Santa María de los Desamparados library. It was almost nighttime and the school was practically empty."

"Students were allowed in the building after the school closed?"

"Not in theory. But these boys were the children of the town's most powerful families. They did whatever they wanted."

Laura couldn't stop herself from looking up at the tall ceilings of the mansion Caplonch lived in.

"Make no mistake. I earned all of this with my own sweat. The company I inherited from my father was nothing more than a regional cannery that could barely make ends meet."

Other people start much further down, she thought, but merely nodded.

"They told me it was the last test. The one that would give me access to the inner circle. To the true Brotherhood of the Wolves. Then they brought in Cucurell. He was half out of it from a blow on the head. They had tied him to some heavy bookshelves and waited for him to wake up. While Pep Codina talked to him, Arnau Junqué came up to me and told me what was going to happen. After they'd raped him, they wanted me to do the same."

"Judging by how you're telling this, I'm guessing you didn't do it."

"Of course not! I yelled at them to leave the boy alone, but they laughed at me and told me to calm down, that I'd be able to do it. When I tried to leave, they tied me up like him."

Caplonch's eyes were red and brimming with tears.

"Then they raped him, one by one. And they forced me to watch. I thought they were going to do the same to me, but when the four of them finished they untied me and told me it was my turn. I tried to run away but Junqué pulled me over to Cucurell who was in shock; he wasn't even crying. I'll never forget the image of that boy, naked and tied up. I still remember his uneven breath and his blank stare."

Caplonch paused and finished his whisky in one gulp.

"When they finally realized I wouldn't and couldn't do what they asked, they kicked me out of there and threatened to do the same to me if I ever said anything."

"I guess you never reported what you saw, did you?"

Caplonch shook his head.

"The more time goes by, the more you become an accomplice of the secret you're keeping. I eventually got married and thought I'd never be able to reveal this because my wife would be horrified that I hadn't said anything at the time."

"So why are you telling me this now?"

"Because of you."

"Excuse me?"

"Your first visit made me think about that night and realize that I don't want to take that secret to my grave. Thanks to you I mustered up the courage to talk to my wife. Now that she knows, I don't have anything to lose."

Caplonch showed his empty hands, as if saying 'that's all'.

"That night, in the basement, there were six wolves," she said.

"Who told you that?"

Caplonch's question confirmed that she was on the right track. Actually, Laura had no idea how many people werethere that night, but Alcántara had said that back then there were six members in the brotherhood.

"It doesn't matter. Was there or wasn't there a sixth wolf in the basement?"

"Yes, but he was so scared they didn't even try to get him close to Cucurell."

"And that person never said anything either."

"If I didn't, he definitely didn't. We're talking about someone much more vulnerable than I."

"More vulnerable back then or now?"

"Both. Back then, because he was just a kid. Now, because a scandal like that can ruin a politician's career for good."

"Could you be more specific?"

"The sixth person in the room was Quim Riera. Ex-mayor of Torroella de Montgrí and candidate for the Catalan Parliament."

Laura paused at that last name. Riera. It sounded familiar.

"How did they choose their victim? Why Fernando Cucurell?"

Caplonch looked her in the eyes. After a few seconds, he pointed to a chair.

"I think you'll want to sit down to hear what I have to tell you."

CHAPTER 61

Julián, a few hours earlier.

Anna dried her tears with the back of her hand and pointed to the old notebook she'd just showed me.

"They're a therapist's notes," she told me. "The patient is my father."

It felt as though someone had pulled the floor out from under me. Did Anna's father have something to do with what happened to my uncle?

Even after dating his daughter for three years, I knew little about Quim Riera. Our longest conversations were always about exercise and nutrition. Even though he was the same age as my father, Quim looked ten years younger. Like Sosa, he was one of the few sixty-somethings who could afford to worship their body.

Another thing Riera and Sosa had in common was politics. Anna's father –handsome, charming, and a widower– hadn't had much difficulty winning the election for mayor of Torroella de Montgrí. His time in office had ended two years earlier, and now he was preparing to run for the Catalan parliament.

Like any good politician, he was always pleasant even though it was clear he didn't completely accept me. Now, perhaps, I understood why. My last name and my family reminded him of his worst nightmares.

"Remember what he said when we suggested he come to dinner and meet your parents?" Anna asked me.

"'We'll meet when you get married.' Like I'd forget that."

I'd taken it for an old-fashioned comment, an initial reluctance that would soften over time. However, after three years and despite our insistence, we never managed to convince Quim Riera to meet my parents.

"They didn't show much enthusiasm either," Anna said.

It was true. Even though my parents didn't meddle in our relationship because I wouldn't let them, they never fully accepted Anna either. Whenever they could, they'd shine a light on her defects. Of course, I didn't understand why. To me, Anna was perfect.

"Our fathers lied to us, Juli. Remember when we realized they were around the same age and had gone to the same school? We asked them if they knew each other and they both said the same thing."

"I've seen him around."

Anna pointed at the book.

"This proves that wasn't true. My father knows about something really bad that happened to your uncle."

Anna's words lifted the veil inside my head. If my father had always been against my relationship with Anna, it was because he knew something as well.

"I need to go talk to my father," I said, standing up.

Anna got up at the same time and we stood facing each other, our bodies almost touching. I hugged her like I hadn't in months. I couldn't contain the tears that fell on her shoulder. While I squeezed her close to my chest, I knew I'd be able to forgive her. Not get back together with her, but I wouldn't resent her forever. I gave her a soft, salty kiss on the cheek.

"Thank you for these three amazing years. I wish you every happiness. And whenever you need me, I'll be there for you."

Anna nodded, dried her own tears, and hugged me back.

"I love you, Juli."

"Me too," I told her.

We stayed there in silence, our bodies joined in an embrace, for I don't know how long. It was the embrace of two friends who knew they wouldn't see each other for a long time.

CHAPTER 62

Julián

I showed up at my parents' unannounced and found there was no one there. Had it been any other Monday, I would have guessed my father was having lunch with his former co-workers and that my mother was working. But they'd just been attacked.

I sat on the sofa and waited. As soon as they got home, I'd ask my father what the wolves had done to his brother. I'd decided to listen to the threats and stop investigating, but that didn't mean I wasn't going to ask him to tell me what he knew.

As the minutes went by and I rehearsed how I'd broach the subject, I became more and more convinced that my father would clam up at the first uncomfortable question. Perhaps that was why I decided to get up and go to his bedroom.

I felt dirty again, like the day I followed Anna to Sant Felip Neri Square and discovered she was cheating on me. It's horrible to spy on a loved one and invade their privacy, but sometimes you're left with no other choice.

I went straight to his side of the bed and opened his nightstand drawer. I shuffled through pills, papers, reading glasses, and a penis ring. The only useful thing I found there was the certainty that I'd never be ready for the image of my parents using sex toys.

I moved on to the closet, opening boxes on the floor under my mother's dresses. I rummaged through their memories like an intruder, although many of those memories were mine as well. I found old pictures, some postcards I'd sent them when I started traveling, and even the plane ticket from their honeymoon in the Canary Islands. However, I didn't find a single reference to Fernando Cucurell. It was as if my father's brother had never existed.

I was about to give up when I found an old black-and-white photo that gave me hope. I recognized the woman with her hair up in a bun, wearing a black mourning dress and a serious expression. It was my grandma Montserrat. On each side of her was a young boy. One must have been nine or ten, and the other, about six or seven. The younger one was my father. The older boy, taller, with a wide smile across his face, had to be Fernando. I turned the photo over but there was no inscription.

Once I was done with the closet, I recalled my parents had recently changed their bed for one with storage underneath. I pulled on the handles beneath the mattress and the bedframe lifted like the trunk of a car. It was packed like a can of sardines. Everything was perfectly organized. Labeled boxes, winter blankets, two foldable chairs, and several black plastic bags.

I started with the boxes, but all I could find were my mother's old floor plans. Then I moved to the bags which were full of clothes. When I moved the last one, I recognized a dark wooden box from my childhood that my father used to store the cigarettes he bought at the tobacco shop in front of the Cathedral. It had disappeared years ago when he stopped smoking.

There wasn't tobacco inside. Instead, there was a small, manila folder with two sealed envelopes inside. They were letters that my father had sent to Fernando Cucurell, to the apartment he rented above his restaurant. Both had been returned. The postmark on the first one read 05/13/1997. The second one, exactly one year later.

I heard a key in the lock of the front door. Just my fucking luck. Thankfully, I'd left my key on the inside of the lock. I scrambled to leave the bed just like I'd found it, put the folder with the envelopes in my backpack, and opened the door.

"Hello, son. What are you doing here?" my father greeted me, giving me a kiss on the cheek. He was carrying a grocery bag.

"I came to see how you were after the accident."

"Alive, which is no mean feat."

"Mom?"

"She's on her way, she stopped at the pharmacy. Do you want some coffee?"

"No need. I don't think I can stay long."

"I just got here and you said you came to see me. Give me a second, I need to use the bathroom. I'll be right back."

I sat on the sofa, feeling even dirtier now. Not only had I gone through his things, now I'd also lied to his face.

After a while, I heard the toilet flush and my father's footsteps head back toward the bedrooms. He came back into the dining room five minutes later.

As soon as I saw him, I felt as though a block of the Viedma glacier had fallen on me. In his hands he held the empty box of cigars.

"So, you've come to see how we're doing have you?"

"What are you talking about?"

"If you want to lie to me and invade my privacy, that's your problem. But I'm not going to let you treat me like an idiot."

Checkmate. The only way to get out of there without losing my dignity was by trying to get him to see where I was coming from.

"You have to understand, Dad. I needed answers."

"You're the one who won't understand. It's best that you don't get those fucking answers. Give me back what you took, please."

"Dad, there are several murders linked to your brother, someone I know absolutely nothing about besides your three generic comments."

"Give me the envelopes, Julián."

"I know they did something really bad to him. You know it too. He took revenge and killed the four wolves, didn't he?"

"The envelopes."

He stood in the frame of the door, blocking my way out. His puffed-up chest and crossed arms sent a clear message: 'You're not leaving through here'.

I snorted in resignation. I'd lied, gone through his things, and for what? I took the folder out of the backpack, showed it to him, and threw it on the table like a criminal throws his weapon when the police have him surrounded.

As soon as my father took two steps toward the folder, I sprinted out of the apartment. I was lucky that the elevator was still on our floor. By the time it started going down, I saw my father run onto landing through the elevator window with his fist in the air.

I looked in my backpack. The two envelopes were still in there. The folder I'd thrown was empty.

CHAPTER 63

Julián

If following Anna down the Ramblas or rummaging through my father's things had made me feel grubby, opening the first of those two envelopes felt like swimming in a septic tank. I felt physically ill. But my curiosity was stronger, and at no point did it cross my mind, that if my father had gone to such lengths to hide something, there might have been a good reason for it.

I was so nervous that it took me almost a minute to decide which envelope to start with. Finally, I chose the one with the older postmark. May 1997. I was twelve, and my father had been sober for over a year. It had been two years since the argument between him and Fernando, that Lorenza Millán had told me about.

Inside the envelope, I found a single handwritten page, with my father's tall, slanted script.

Dear brother,

It's taken me two years to muster up the courage to write to you. Today, your birthday has given me the push I needed to do it.

I know there's no forgiving the way I treated you the last time we saw each other, but I'd like to apologize anyway. Even though you haven't gone through it yourself, you know how hard the fight against alcohol is. Two years ago, when I showed up at your restaurant and said those atrocities, I was about to lose that fight for good. I was at my lowest, and that's why I gave you the lowest blows.

I want to know how you're doing, Fernando. And what happened to you that put you in a wheelchair? How and when did you come back to Barcelona? What happened to your beloved Montgrí Hotel? You have no idea how guilty I feel.

We're well. Julián is growing strong and healthy. I'm sure he'd love to see you again.

The doors to my home are always open for you, you know that. I hope one day you'll walk through them.

I love you, even though I've never told you. I love you very much, brother.

Happy birthday,
Miguel

CHAPTER 64

Many years earlier.

The boy isn't sixteen anymore. He's thirty now. Half a lifetime has passed since that night in the library basement. A few weeks after raping him four times, the wolves finished high school. The following year, they were all in Barcelona, studying at the best universities.

He has stayed in town, working in construction and hasn't fantasized about his revenge for a long time. He's resigned himself to living with a chronic wound, like someone who gets used to an ulcer.

Luckily, six years ago he met her, the closest thing to a magic ointment. The woman before him, drinking coffee at a bar, makes all his pains disappear.

The boy, who is a man now, is drinking a cup of coffee the bar's only waiter –a young man listening to his Walkman at full blast– has just brought him. The coffee mug is at his lips when he hears a voice that makes his hair stand on end. A voice he'll remember his whole life. A voice that will always exhale fetid breath on the nape of his neck as he struggles to free himself of the ropes.

He turns slightly and looks at the four men who've just entered the bar. It's them. They laugh, smoke, choose a table to sit down at and snap their fingers at the waiter, who probably won't hear them because he's in the kitchen with his headphones on.

"Are you ok?" his wife asks him.

"Yes, of course," he answers and reaches over to stroke the head of their three-year-old son.

"Can you get the check while I go to the bathroom?"

"No," he says, calculating the route she'll have to take, the same way he'd done with his own route a thousand times in Santa María de los Desamparados's cloister.

"You don't want to get the check?"

"Yes, of course. But the bathroom here's dirty. Who knows what you might catch."

"Do you think women sit down on public toilets?"

Before he can say another word, his wife smiles at him sweetly, blows the little one a kiss and heads toward the back of the bar. She walks like she always does, swinging her hips, which look wide and firm under her tight dress.

As soon as his wife walks by the wolves' table, he feels a fire burning inside his stomach. Pep Codina, who is apparently still their leader, devours her with his eyes and then, with a half-smile, makes a comment that makes the other three laugh. She glares at them and walks into the bathroom.

The wolves look over at him to see who that stunning woman is with. He looks down, pretending to concentrate on the chocolate stain on his son's shirt.

He tries to calm down. They aren't going to recognize him. He isn't the skinny, almost girlish-looking teenager they once knew. He's a man now, with wide shoulders from years of hard work, and short hair because it's started growing in patches like a badly sown field.

He makes faces at his son, who laughs and says words that are missing half of their consonants.

He has never told anyone about that night. Not even his friend Manel. Or rather, especially not his friend Manel. If he'd found out, he'd have beaten them up so badly he would have been expelled from school and gotten a lifetime of trouble with four of Torroella's most important families.

Seeing what transpired for Manel in the end, he's glad he never told him. His friend preferred books over his father's anvil and went to study in Girona as soon as he could save up some money. Years later, he came back to town and got his dream job. A job he wouldn't have been able to get if he'd been expelled from Santa María.

"What's wrong with you, you idiots?"

The person yelling is his wife. She came out of the bathroom and is now standing with her hands on her hips in front of the wolves' table.

"Is there something you want to say? Say it to my face. Haven't you never seen a pair of tits?"

"Not like those," Pep Codina answers, looking at her chest lasciviously. The other three follow suit.

"And you aren't fucking going to. I bet you couldn't even fuck a blow-up doll."

"You want to find out?"

"Go fuck yourself."

Without losing his smile, Pep Codina turns toward him.

"You aren't going to say anything?" he yells from one end of the bar to the other. Luckily, the place is empty. The waiter is still in the kitchen.

He feels paralyzed. He couldn't talk if he wanted to.

"I don't need my husband to defend me, you asshole," she intervenes. "But why bother explaining that to you? You have the IQ of a frog in heat."

Codina ignores the woman's comments as if they were arrows bouncing off a giant's skin. He yells at him again.

"Of course you aren't going to say anything, Cucurell. If you couldn't defend yourself back then, no wonder you can't defend your bitch."

The boy, who is a man now, leaves money for his bill on the table and walks toward the door with his son in his arms.

"Are you sure it's yours?" Codina yells. "Faggots don't usually have kids."

"*Adéu*, little princess," Junqué adds.

"Go fuck yourself," his wife yells, who takes the 'little princess' as if it were directed at her. Better that way, he thinks.

When they leave the bar, he hands her the child and tells her to go home, that he'll catch up in a few minutes.

His wife says no, but he doesn't give her time to stop him and goes back inside. He pulls up a chair and sits at the wolves' table. He feels a tingle ripple across his body, as though someone had put a hundred spiders down his shirt.

The first thing he looks at is their hands. They're all wearing the rings they wore that night. Then, for the first time in his life, he looks up, fearless, and stares each one of them in the eyes. He calculates his chances of breaking a bottle against the table and killing the four of them there and then. None. That's for brave people in movies, not real-life softies like him. He knows that no matter what he tries, they'd break him easily. Like they did once already.

"What do you want, little princess? Want to have a drink with us and then head to the library basement? It's only five minutes from here."

The boy, who is a man now, doesn't say a word. He gets up and leaves the bar. Someone once said there are only heroes and rats. He, certainly, is no hero.

CHAPTER 65

Many years earlier.

After they leave the bar, he walks the half block to their house slowly.

"Where did you know those assholes from?" she asks him.

She's sitting on the living room floor. Between her legs, the boy plays with a wooden truck and a doll, his two favorite toys.

"From school," he answers and walks toward the bedroom.

He rummages through the closet until he finds the long, heavy object wrapped in a rag tucked away in the back. He hides it under his jacket and heads to the door.

"Where are you going?" his wife asks.

"Where go?" the boy repeats.

"To take a walk. I need to think."

"What were they saying about you not defending yourself?"

"The truth."

He leaves his house and walks quickly, feeling the weight in his jacket's inner pocket. Once he reaches the bar, he sees through the window that they're still there. He won't have to wait long; the waiter is bringing them their check.

A few minutes later, they depart. He walks behind them through the town streets until they reach the main square. Once there, one of them parts ways with the other three. It's none other than Pep Codina.

He follows Codina down the narrow streets flanked by medieval buildings. He tries to determine the best place to run toward him and beat him to a pulp. When they pass a dark alley, he knows it's his moment. He quickens his pace, but Codina turns a corner and walks into another bar.

He waits outside for an hour. He smokes, and paces under the arches of a nearby building, but mostly he relives that night fourteen years ago a thousand times. At times, he pauses his suffering to think of Meritxell Puigbaró's. Ten years after the wolves raped him, they did the same to that twenty-two-year-old girl. Though she was braver than him and reported them, it didn't do much. The judges absolved them. It probably helped that those scumbags' families brought in Barcelona's best lawyers.

The wait grows long. He unrolls the rag and looks at the knife Manel gave him. It's the only trace that's left of a friendship that began to drift apart the day they kissed, and finally broke during the years Manel was studying in Girona. Nowadays, they're just two acquaintances who exchange the same three sentences whenever they cross paths in a local shop. They have nothing in common anymore, except perhaps, the loyalty you owe an old friend.

He hasn't used the knife much over the years. Once in a while at a barbeque, or to slice a Christmas ham. Time has covered the leaf with a gray patina that barely reflects the light coming from the bar. The blade, however, remains intact.

He finally sees Codina leave. It's dawn and the cobblestones are shiny with dew. In a dark corner of Pere Rigau Plaza, he decides to approach him.

"Why don't you lay your hands on me now, you son of a bitch?" he says without yelling, but making sure Pep can hear.

"You? What do you want, little princess?"

He takes out the knife and walks toward the wolf, holding it close to his thigh, the tip facing down. Even in the dark, he can see Codina's face tense up in panic.

While he waited for him to leave the bar, he practiced what he was going to do a hundred times. He would put the knife up to his chest and tell him, while Pep cried in fear, that if he ever came near his wife again, he was going to cut his throat. If he was lucky, he might make him piss his pants.

"Wait, I can explain. I didn't want to," the wolf says, looking from side to side.

"You didn't want to? Then why did you do it?"

"The others. They pressured me. They threatened me."

"Congratulations," the boy says as he tightens his grip on the knife. "You must be the first person ever to get a boner under pressure."

"I swear, I didn't want to."

"You were the one who led that herd of assholes. They always did what you said, and from what I can see that hasn't changed."

The memories rush into the boy's head with the force of a high-speed train. The damp smell, the dirty basement floor, the tightness of the ropes on his wrists, the cold oil they poured between his buttocks. And the pain. So much pain.

There was one of them who didn't want to, that was true, but it wasn't the man standing in front of him.

"You really didn't want to?" he asks.

"No, I swear."

"Well neither do I," he says, and sinks the knife into his stomach, up to the handle.

The wolf doesn't yell or move. He opens his eyes and merely lets out a grunt, like someone trying to move a heavy piece of furniture. The boy, who is a man now, plunges the knife into his stomach two more times.

By the time Codina hits the ground, he knows he just ruined his and his family's life. Before the wolf's heart has stopped beating, he knows he's made the biggest mistake a man can make. He has acted without thinking.

He looks around. The square is empty. He kneels next to the body, which is no longer breathing, grabs the wallet so it looks like a robbery, and takes off running. The wolf's sticky, warm blood is wet on his hands and on the rag, that is wrapped around the knife once again. His own blood beats through his temples, booming like the sound of a giant's footsteps.

CHAPTER 66

Julián

I finished reading the first letter feeling sad but curious. What did my father mean when he said that I'd love to see him again?

I opened the second envelope which, according to the big stamp across it, had never reached its destination either. Inside was another letter, even shorter than the previous one:

Dear brother,
A year ago, the postal service returned the letter I sent you. I know it's not because the address is wrong but because you don't want to hear from me. I understand and respect your decision.
I'm writing back, for the last time if that's your wish, to send you this photo. I hope you keep it. Hopefully, it'll help you remember that despite everything, we were happy.
Happy birthday.
I love you.
Miguel

The letter came with a polaroid, I could tell it was from the '80s because of the distinct reds that only the cameras from back then could capture. In the background was Mount Fitz Roy. In the foreground, five people smiling on a rock ledge that looked familiar. I searched in my phone gallery and found the photo the tourists had taken of Laura and me at the viewpoint on our way to Laguna de los Tres. It was the same place.

The tallest man in the picture was Juanmi Alonso. Wearing his unmistakable khaki uniform, he was pointing at the mountain with one hand. Next to him stood my uncle, a beret on his head, and no sign of the mustache or the wheelchair he had when I nicknamed him Don Quixote. The other three people were a family. A man and a woman were hugging; they held a boy of about four between them. The man was wearing sunglasses and his hair was thinning. The woman, tall and elegant, had a cascade of curls that fell around her shoulders.

I finally understood Danilo's 'you came back'.

Now everything I'd felt when I saw Mount Fitz Roy made sense, that feeling that the mountain and I knew each other from another life.

I looked at the young couple and the boy. The clothes and their bodies had changed, but their smiles and eyes hadn't. Those people were my parents. And the boy they were holding in front of Mount Fitz Roy was me.

The mountain and I didn't know each other from another life. We knew each other from this one.

PART V

THE MONTGRÍ HOTEL

CHAPTER 67

Julián

The doorbell snapped me out of the trance I'd been in for nearly an hour, rereading the letters and staring at the photograph. It wasn't the electric buzz from the intercom on the street, but the 'ding-dong' of someone at the door of my apartment.

I looked through the peephole and saw my father's face, distorted by the glass.

"I know you're in there, Julián. Your key's in the lock."

As soon as I opened the door, he marched in like a bull. However, the second he saw the open envelopes on the table, he collapsed into a chair as if he'd just been unplugged.

"I think there's no turning back now, Dad," I said with all the calm I could muster. "It's best if you tell me everything. I won't judge you, I promise, but I know too much. If you don't tell me what happened, whatever I imagine might be much worse than the truth."

"That's not possible."

"Please, Dad. Trust me."

He sighed deeply, like a child does after crying for a long time and nodded ever so slightly.

"I don't even know where to start."

"At the beginning."

"That's the problem. What is the beginning?"

"The fight with your brother."

"That's the end."

"Why didn't you ever tell me I had an uncle?"

"Because I wanted you to be happy, son. As long as you didn't know about Fernando, you'd be safe from all the shit we went through."

I looked him in the eyes without saying anything. The corners of his mouth pulled up into a bitter smile and he emptied his lungs with another sigh.

"As you know, your uncle and I grew up in a lower-middle-class family. Our mother was a housewife and our father worked in construction. They migrated to Argentina, but things went worse there than they did here. They had Fernando in Buenos Aires and came back when my mother was pregnant with me. Can I have some water?"

I poured him a glass. He drank it with his gaze locked on the coffee table as if the memories he was sharing were etched on it.

"During grade school, my parents realized I was a good student. A teacher told them he knew the headmaster of Santa María de los Desamparados and that he might be able to get me a scholarship. I started there at twelve. I was one of the few students that didn't come from money. The school was very exclusive, full of rich kids who didn't have anything in common with me."

"You didn't manage to make any friends?"

"Yes, Manel Castañeda, the cook's son. He gave me the knife."

"What knife?"

My father took a deep breath, like someone about to jump into a deep pool.

"Besides being poor, I was unlucky enough that I had very feminine features during puberty. A thin nose, curly hair, eyes that looked like I was wearing makeup. When I was a teenager, people quite often mistook me for a girl. I suffered all sorts of harassment while I was at Santa María de los Desamparados. They call it bullying now. Why do you think I make crude jokes or sexist comments sometimes? It's a sort of tic from back then. It's a way of saying to myself 'Of course you're man enough, Miguel. Don't you doubt it'."

"Mom says you were really handsome when you were young."

"Oh, yeah. So handsome they called me 'Little princess'."

He spat out each syllable of the words with disgust.

CHAPTER 68

Many years earlier.

The knife in his jacket pocket weighs a ton. When he made it home, his wife was waiting for him on the sofa. She signals for him to speak quietly and points toward their little boy's bedroom.

"Where did you go, Miguel?" she manages to whisper before her gaze settles on the red stain on his hand.

"I'm sorry," is all he manages to say.

He's sure that if he tells the truth, his relationship with Consuelo will be over. But he can't imagine adding another secret to his life. Not with her. So he speaks. He tells her about the horror that unfolded after that meaningless kiss with Manel. He confesses that after what happened that afternoon to her, he couldn't help but follow them. And as the hours went by, the rage in him had grown so much it had completely clouded his judgement.

"I swear I only took the knife to scare him."

"Did you kill him?"

He nods. She paces from one side of the dining room to the other.

"If what you're telling me is the truth, you did what was right."

"I swear."

She comes up to him, looks him in the eyes for a few seconds, and hugs him. For a second, there is no space in Miguel's mind for the past or the murder he just committed. All he can think of is that this might be his last hug with his wife before he's sent to jail. He may never feel her warmth against his chest or see his son grow up.

But he also knows that even though the current is pulling him away, he won't stop rowing as long as he has strength to row.

"Consuelo, we need to go."

"Where?"

"Anywhere. We need to run. They're going to want revenge, I know them," he says, looking at his blood-covered hand. "What have I done? My God, what have I done? I've ruined your life and Julián's."

"Wait, calm down."

"I can't calm down. Seeing me behind bars won't be enough for them. They're going to hit where it hurts most. Our son is in danger, get it? So are you."

Before he can say another word, the front door opens. He takes a step forward, putting his body between the entrance and his wife. He takes the knife out of his jacket and points it forward. The blade trembles.

A tall, sturdy figure appears in the doorway. It's his brother Fernando. He's visiting from Argentina and is staying with them for a few days. Or rather, he was staying, because he is supposed to be sleeping at a friend's house in Barcelona tonight.

"Fernando, what are you doing here?"

But his brother doesn't answer. He stares at the knife, still covered in blood. Miguel drops it to the ground as if it had suddenly turned into a snake.

"What happened? Whose blood is that?"

He doesn't know what to answer. He can't.

"Miguel, honey. I think it's best you tell your brother everything."

His wife is right. There's no hiding what's in plain sight. And tomorrow, once the news of the murder comes out, even less so. He collapses onto the sofa as if a thousand bricks had fallen onto his shoulders.

"I've killed a man," he whispers.

He guesses that his older brother, who has always thought he had the right to tell him what to do, is going to yell at him. But Fernando simply nods, as if confirming he understood that first piece of information and inviting him to go on.

For the second time in half an hour, Miguel tells the story. He includes some details he forgot to tell Consuelo. Both she and his brother listen in silence. The only interruptions are his own sobs.

"As soon as they find the body, they're going to start an investigation," Fernando says as if Miguel didn't know that yet. "Codina's friends will mention the altercation in the bar and soon you'll have the police asking questions."

Miguel takes a second to digest the fact that his life is about to fall apart, again. And it'll be, once again, the wolves' fault. Or maybe it's all his own fault, for not standing up to them when he was a teenager and for not knowing how to control his anger fourteen years later. He thinks about how important it is that justice is served on time. If he –or anyone– had reported his rape, would things have ended like this?

"There's no way out," he says. "I'm going to jail. What matters is that Consuelo and Julián are safe."

"What?" she asks.

He breaths in and looks at her, choosing his words carefully.

"These people live by their own rules. Two eyes for an eye. Two teeth for a tooth. They aren't going to get revenge only on me, understand?"

He knows she does.

"Wait," Fernando intervenes. "Consuelo, you told me you got offered a job in Barcelona, didn't you? Take it."

"You think they aren't going to find her in Barcelona?" Miguel asks.

"Call and say you're taking the job. And tomorrow, the three of you disappear. But you're not going to Barcelona."

"Where then?"

"To El Chaltén, with me."

"That's insane," Consuelo says.

Fernando points at the room she uses as her office.

"You designed my hotel, didn't you? Well, now you're going to help me build it."

Miguel considers his brother's words. The plan Consuelo has been working on for days to adapt to Fernando's requests, is still open on the drawing table in the office. Two years ago, when he moved to El Chaltén, he asked her for the plans for a hotel she'd built in the Pyrenees. He said he wanted something similar for his project in Patagonia. Now that Fernando has come back on vacation before construction started, he's asked her to make some changes.

"When the hotel is finished, you might be able to return," Fernando says. "Or not, who knows. But now you have to leave, to protect Julián."

"Protec Ulián?"

Miguel looks toward the bedrooms. His son is standing in the doorway, sporting his dinosaur pajamas.

"Come, let's go to bed, Juli," Consuelo hastily says, and picks him up to take him back to his room.

Before they leave, Miguel sees his son's gaze linger on his blood-stained hand.

CHAPTER 69

Many years earlier.

Seven candles dimly illuminate the old country house. Despite the fact that their weak flames are incapable of heating the night's brisk air, Arnau Junqué's face is burning. He doesn't have a fever. He's been sitting there for an hour, completely still in front of the altar, smoldering with rage.

He hears footsteps behind him but doesn't turn. He recognizes Mario and Gerard's voices, who enter the room with their usual greeting.

"Lupus occidere uiuendo debet."

"Lupus occidere uiuendo debet," Arnau repeats back.

Without taking his eyes off the altar, he caresses his ring. Only three real wolves remain, ones with silver rings with inscriptions inside. The others, the hundreds of members who've passed through the brotherhood throughout the decades, aren't more than boys who want to drink and drool over girls, decorating their hands with brass pieces of junk. Not them. They've been the first in a long time to discover the true meaning of being a wolf. And now, Pep Codina, one of the real ones, is dead.

He hears his friends take off their coats and sit beside him, ready to begin a very different meeting to the ones they hold each month in that abandoned house. Today's meeting is as secret as usual –not even Gerard and Mario's wives know about them–, but a thousand times more important.

They called the meeting five hours ago, at the cemetery gate, right after the undertaker shoveled the last bits of dirt on Pep Codina's coffin.

He tears his gaze from the altar and onto his brothers.

"Miguel Cucurell is going to pay for this. No one harms a wolf and avoids the wrath of the pack," he says as he clenches his fist and looks at his ring. "What did you say to the police?"

"What we agreed on. That we had something to drink at the bar and then we said goodbye. Nothing out of the ordinary."

"Any mention of the argument with Cucurell?"

"None," they say in unison.

Arnau Junqué smiles.

"Good. We're going to deal with this our own way."

"What are we going to do?"

He sees the other two look at him, waiting for an answer. Now that Pep is gone, the pack needs a new leader. A wolf doesn't ascend through a vote or a consensus. A wolf bites.

"The only thing we can do. Kill Miguel Cucurell and his entire family."

"How do we do that without getting caught?"

"I'll find a way. The first step is to let some time pass. Revenge is a dish best served cold."

CHAPTER 70

Many years earlier.

Fernando Cucurell has never been so happy to pay his taxes. He walks down the unpaved streets with a folder full of receipts under his arm and a smile across his face. Today marks the end of the six-month grace period granted to him by El Chalten's town hall as an incentive for his business. Tomorrow makes six months since the Montgrí Hotel had its first guest. And almost two years since Miguel, Consuelo, and Julián flew across the world to come live with him.

In a way, his brother has been lucky. The police didn't show up the day after Pep Codina's murder. Or the day after that. Or ever. No one seemed to link him to the victim. Instead of ending up in jail, Miguel lives with his family in a paradise at the end of the world.

Every once in a while, the memory of what happened casts a shadow over his face and Fernando fears that he might fall into the pit of alcoholism he'd been in a few years before meeting Consuelo. But for now, his brother manages to stay strong.

Both he and his sister-in-law have turned out to be great housemates and colleagues. And little Julián is adorable. The four of them share the house Fernando built on the other end of his half-acre of land.

During the year it took to build the Montgrí, Consuelo supervised the construction which was carried out mainly by Miguel and Fernando. Once in a while, a local builder lent a hand and would bring his son Danilo along to play with Julián. Despite the age difference, Julián and Danilo got along great.

Since the business opened its doors, the family has been adapting to their new roles as hotel managers. His sister-in-law is struggling the most. She helps at the front desk and in the kitchen while she waits for a new project to come up. It won't be easy because even though El Chaltén is a town with much potential, it has less than fifty permanent residents. An architect has as many job offers there as a coat salesman in the desert.

Little Julián, who is now five years old, is one of the four students in the town's kindergarten. It shares a building with the elementary school, the town library, and a health center that's managed by a single nurse. In the afternoons, he runs around the hotel's yard and the next-door lot, which is empty, like most of the town. His friend Danilo often joins him.

From a commercial standpoint, Fernando can't complain. Chaltén's popularity as a tourist destination is growing at an incredible rate. Every year there are more visitors, both foreign and Argentinian, who drive 500 kilometers down a battered road from Río Gallegos to visit what some have begun to call the national hiking capital. Besides lodging, the Montgrí Hotel also offers excursions to the mountains. Without a doubt, the star outing is the hike on the Viedma glacier, one of the largest in the world.

Fernando Cucurell smiles as he contemplates all of this on his walk back to the hotel. His dream has come true, and in the process, he has helped prevent his brother's family from falling to pieces. He's happy.

Suddenly, he sees something that makes him freeze. The folder he carries under his arm falls to the ground and the Patagonian wind blows away the receipts of the first taxes he has so happily paid. Thirty meters from where he stands is the town's only restaurant, and out of its door walk the last three people he would have wanted to see in El Chaltén.

The first one he recognizes is Mario Santiago. His hair is shorter, but he looks just like the last time he saw him, back when they were teenagers. Then he recognizes the other two. It's them. His brother Miguel's worst nightmares have come true. These three lunatics crossed the world to avenge their cult brother's death.

He runs to the hotel as fast as his legs can move him. He finds Miguel at the front desk.

"Where are Consuelo and Julián?"

"Outside, playing."

He runs outside. They're playing with a ball in the empty lot next door.

"Consuelo, come into the hotel right now."

"Will you tell us what's happening?" asks Miguel, who's followed him outside.

"Listen to me. You need to go. Now. They're here."

"Who?" Consuelo asks.

Fernando knows he doesn't need to explain who. He walks toward the reception, motioning them to follow.

"Where will we go?" Miguel asks.

"Anywhere, but far away. For now, get into the house and don't leave under any circumstances. Do you hear me? Don't leave for any reason."

Fernando looks at the couple and their young son walk down the hallway and leave the hotel through the back door. Once they're out of sight, he places a small triangle-shaped sign on the desk that reads 'I'll be back shortly' and heads toward the door.

"Fernando," he hears his brother's voice behind him.

"What are you doing here? Didn't you hear what I said? You need to hide right now."

Miguel shakes his head no.

"We're not going anywhere."

"They're here. What do you think they came for?"

"You and I know that very well."

Fernando huffs and looks at the clock in the hotel reception. His heart is racing.

"Listen to me," he says.

"No, *you* listen to me."

Miguel explains his plan in a calm, clear voice. Judging by how precise the details are, he knows his brother's been mulling it over for a long time. Once he's done, Fernando is silent, considering what he's just heard.

"No," he says. "I can't do what you're asking of me."

"Why not?"

"Look, Miguel, what those motherfuckers did to you is horrible. But you can't go killing people for revenge."

"It's not revenge, it's survival."

"If you want to survive, you and your family need to leave and go somewhere safe."

"Somewhere safe? If we aren't safe in a lost town at the end of the world, where do you think we will be?"

Fernando looks into his brother's eyes. He thought he'd find anger in them, but there's only a plea.

"I'm begging you, Fernando. Help me, just once more."

CHAPTER 71

Many years earlier.

Fernando Cucurell leaves the Montgrí Hotel and quickens his stride toward the restaurant where he saw the wolves. He finds them walking in the direction of the town exit.

"Gerard!" he yells as he runs toward them.

Gerard Martí turns around. Fernando knows he's recognized him because his eyes are full of suspicion.

"Gerard, man, what are you doing here?" he says as soon as he catches up. "Mario? Arnau? Fuck, it's good to see you guys."

He smiles as he speaks. He pulls each of them into a tight hug. Then he gives them each a handshake and notices the three of them are wearing the wolf ring.

"What... what a coincidence," Gerard Martí stammers.

"I'll say. What a coincidence and what a great surprise. When did you arrive? How long are you staying? Tell me everything."

"Well, we just got here a few hours ago," Martí says. "We're killing time until they prepare our rooms at the inn so we can check in."

"What are you talking about? I'm the owner of El Chaltén's best hotel. Well, it's also the only one. You're all invited to stay with me."

The three of them shake their heads.

"We'd love to, but we've already paid there," Arnau Junqué is quick to answer.

"That's not a problem," waving away the comment. "Juanmi, the manager of the inn, is a dear friend of mine. I'll talk to him; he can give you back your money and you can come settle in to the hotel. And don't you dare try to pay me. As long as you're in El Chaltén you're my guests. It's not every day I get visitors from my hometown."

He smiles again and pats each of them on the back, trying to conceal the trembling of his legs.

"This makes me so happy, man. Really, what a nice surprise," he repeats. "Let's go talk to Juanmi."

Without giving them a chance to answer, Fernando walks toward the town exit. During their walk, the three wolves try to stop him with all sorts of excuses, but he manages to brush all of them off gracefully. When they reach the inn, they find Juanmi sanding down a wooden board by the inn entrance.

"Juanmi, you aren't going to believe this," he says pointing at the wolves. "They're from my town! I'd like to invite them to stay at the hotel, could you give them back their money?"

"If it's the *gallego* Cucurell asking, absolutely."

"Thanks, Juanmi."

"Are you okay? This is the first time I've called you *gallego* that you don't try to explain the difference between Galicia and Catalunya to me."

"I'm just so excited," he explains, waving at his fellow Spaniards.

"I didn't know you had feelings," Juanmi says with a smile, and turns toward the wolves. "Come with me and I'll reimburse you."

Fernando waits outside for fifteen minutes until the wolves come out carrying their luggage. He thanks Juanmi and motions for the three to follow him. When they're fifty meters from the inn, he pats his pockets and shakes his head.

"My lighter. It must have fallen out of my pocket when I was waiting for you. I'll be back in a second."

Without giving them time to answer, he takes off running toward the inn.

"What names did they register under?" he asks Juanmi, who's gone back to sanding the board.

"They're your friends and you don't know their names?"

"Come on, go look and tell me."

"No need to look. Juan Gómez, Pablo García, and Carlos Ruiz."

"Did you ask them for IDs?"

"Passports, all three of them."

"They had passports with those names?"

"Of course. What did you expect them to say? John, Paul, and Ringo?"

"Thanks. Now give me a lighter."

"What?"

"I need a lighter."

"What's up with you today? You're being really weird. You know I don't smoke."

"Neither do I. Just get me one."

Juanmi shakes his head and walks into the inn. He comes back holding a small red lighter that Fernando rips from his hand.

"Don't tell anyone about this. I'll explain later," he says before running off.

As he leaves the circle of trees that surrounds the inn, he sighs with relief when he sees the three men waiting right where he left them. He'd feared they'd disappear as soon as they had a chance, but he had to make sure their trip to El Chaltén wasn't a huge coincidence.

It wasn't. No one uses fake passports to go on vacation.

"Sorry, guys. Like they say here, the only reason I don't lose my head is because it's attached to my body," he apologizes and shows them the lighter. He points forward and they keep walking. "How long has it been? Fifteen years? Twenty? This is crazy. What are the odds that we'd run into each other at the other end of the world?"

He gets short, ambiguous sentences for an answer. Not without a struggle, Fernando manages to keep up the conversation during the 500 meters between the inn and the hotel.

"This is the Montgrí Hotel," he finally announces when they arrive. "I named it that to honor our land."

Tense smiles.

The four of them walk into the reception area. Fernando circles around the front desk, puts away the sign announcing his absence and places his elbows on the wooden surface, looking at the wolves.

"Usually, this is when I'd ask guests for their passports. But no need with you guys. In fact, I'm not even going to register you guys in the books. One thing is inviting you to stay here, paying taxes for it is a different story," he says with a wink.

He turns toward the keys hanging on the wall. All of them are there, because it's late in the season and the hotel is empty. He takes down three of them and asks the men follow him. After showing them their rooms, he invites them to have some wine with him in the reception area. They decline, but Fernando insists until they accept.

"My brother's also here. He moved here with his family a while back, did you know?" he asks as he pours the glasses.

In an almost choreographed gesture, the three wolves shrug and arch their mouths downward, as if they're just now finding out that Fernando has a brother.

"They're not in town right now," he clarifies. "They have a little boy, Julián. They had to take him to the pediatrician in Río Gallegos. They'll be back in two days. You remember my brother Miguel, don't you?"

"We saw him around in Santa María de los Desamparados," Gerard Martí says. "But he's a year younger than us and we never really got to know him. At least I didn't."

"Me neither," Mario Santiago says.

"Me either," Arnau Junqué adds.

"Oh, he's a great guy, I'm sure you'll like him. By the way, what are your plans in Chaltén?"

"Same as everyone, I guess. Walking around in the mountains."

Fernando holds his hands in the air to stop them from saying anything else.

"I'm going to take you on the most amazing hike of your lives."

"You don't need to do that, Fernando," Martí tells him. "Staying in this hotel is already an abuse of your hospitality."

"I won't hear a word. I'm happy to do this. I bet you've never walked on a glacier, have you?"

The three wolves shake their heads no.

"It's a once-in-a-lifetime experience, so that's that. We leave tomorrow at seven."

CHAPTER 72

Many years earlier.

Fernando Cucurell walks up an ice hill. His sunglasses and the woolen hat pulled down to his eyebrows disguise his nervousness. His heart is about to beat out of his chest. Fifteen minutes ago, they moored the boat and now Gerard Martí and Mario Santiago are following him across the glacier. The closest human being is about 20 kilometers away. With one exception.

Only two wolves have come on the hike. Arnau Junqué woke up with a high fever and joint pain. No doubt a flu, according to his self-diagnosis. He had to cancel.

After walking on that glacier a hundred times, this is the first time the landscape hasn't left him in awe. He doesn't focus on the range of blues, doesn't imagine that the groans coming from the ice are the sounds of a wounded beast, as he likes to tell the tourists. He barely even feels the cold on his face as he walks on that ice cube ten times the size of Barcelona. Today, all his attention is placed on the two sets of feet that make the ice crunch behind his own. If something goes wrong, he only has a hammer to defend himself with.

He wonders if the magic spell has been broken for good. If after today, each time he walks on the Viedma his back will tense up as it does now, and if he'll think of humanity's worst facet.

He guides the wolves through walls of solid ice that form deep cracks. Mario Santiago asks if they can take a minute to rest.

"Yes, of course," he answers. "We're very close to my favorite spot."

As soon as he utters the words, he holds his breath. A glacier is a river made of ice, and as he always tells tourists, you can never swim in the same river twice. It's impossible to have a favorite spot because the glacier changes every day. But the wolves don't pick up on his mistake.

They take ten minutes to make it to the small waterfall Fernando chose a few hours back when he brought Miguel. The stream of water that emerges from one of the walls, falls into a blue hole about a meter in diameter that swallows the water with a never-ending roar. The place is absolutely beautiful, but that's not why they chose it. They chose it because it's shaped like an amphitheater, surrounded by ice walls as tall as houses. Whatever happens in there, only the condors will see.

He pulls out a bottle of whisky from his backpack along with three glasses. In keeping with his usual ritual when he brings people to the Viedma, he pours the drinks and chills them with ice that he breaks off from the glacier with a small hammer.

"To reconnecting," he says as he offers each of the wolves a glass.

"To reconnecting," they repeat.

They clink the glasses together. He takes the whisky up to his lips but before the liquid touches his lips he pretends to slip on the ice and lets the glass drop from his hand. It shatters at his feet, sending shards flying everywhere. Some slide several meters across the ice and fall into the blue hole.

"Want some of mine?" Mario Santiago offers.

"No need. I've done this a thousand times. You guys enjoy."

The wolves drink.

"It isn't the best whisky I've ever had, but it definitely comes with the best view," Gerard Martí says. "This place is amazing."

Fernando nods while he thinks about how to proceed. According to the plan, now is when he should give his brother the signal –a mariachi cry, with the excuse of showing them how his voice echoes on the ice– for him to leave his hiding place and carry out his part. But the fact that Arnau Junqué stayed behind complicates things. He needs to warn Miguel. It's one thing to wipe the three wolves off the map out there in the middle of nowhere, but doing it to two of them, and then going back into town for the third, is a different story.

"Wait here a second. I need to pee," he excuses himself.

He circles the large ice column where he left Miguel three hours ago wrapped in a heavy coat. His brother isn't there anymore. He knows he's in the right place because he sees hundreds of crampon marks on the ice. Looking at them closely, he thinks he can guess the reason behind Miguel's absence.

There's a fracture in the ice. It isn't a crack yet, just a thin line, like when a windshield cracks. A line in the blue marble. He's been on the glacier enough times to know it isn't dangerous, but his brother hasn't. Maybe he got scared and looked for a new hiding spot.

Too many deviations from the original plan for this to end well, he thinks, as he walks back to where he left the wolves. The diazepam and the whisky are working; they're already slurring their words.

"Want to hear how sound echoes on the ice?" he asks them.

Martí and Santiago nod groggily. Fernando cups his hands to the sides of his mouth but doesn't manage to cry out before his brother jumps out from behind another ice column with the Winchester in his hand.

"Hello, motherfuckers," he says. "Were you looking for me?"

He points the gun at Mario Santiago and pulls down the lever just like Fernando taught him the first time they went guanaco hunting. Now the rifle's ready to shoot. One of the wolves shakes his head and blinks as if there's something in his eyes.

"What was in that drink?"

"You've got about five minutes until you fall asleep," Miguel answers. "And trust me, no one wakes up from a nap on the glacier."

"What do you want?"

"Peace, but you aren't going to give me that, are you? It wasn't enough to fuck up my life, now you want to kill me to avenge a piece of shit."

Mario Santiago tries to tackle him, but he moves in slow motion. Miguel has no trouble dodging him.

"Pep was our brother and you stabbed him in Torroella."

"The same Pep that raped me in 1975?"

"We were just kids," Santiago says.

"I was even more of a kid. And you destroyed my life."

Without saying another word, Miguel pulls the trigger, and a boom echoes off the thousand ice walls around them. Mario Santiago falls to the ground, and beneath him, a red stain grows like grenadine in a cocktail glass.

Fernando hears another boom, louder than the first one. It's the unmistakable sound of ice breaking. The bullet that went through Santiago opened a vertical crack as wide as a fist in the wall behind him. Fernando estimates it's over six meters tall. If that piece of ice breaks off, they're all dead.

The crack distracts him for a fraction of a second. His brother must have also lowered his guard because Gerard Martí jumps on Miguel with a move surprisingly swift for someone as heavily drugged as he is.

The wolf's tackle makes him drop the rifle. The two of them roll across the ice, delivering blows. Fernando runs to grab the weapon, but it's fallen down a crack that wasn't there a second ago. The ice is quite literally breaking open under their feet.

He weighs his options. If he stays where he is, he'll die any second. But he can't leave his brother, who Gerard Martí is now strangling with both hands.

He lunges at the wolf and squeezes his neck just like he's squeezing his brother's. But Martí has several seconds of advantage over him and Miguel's eyes are already rolling backwards as he starts to lose consciousness. If Fernando doesn't change his strategy, his brother will be the first to die.

He releases the wolf and frantically looks around. The hammer's too far away. The closest thing is a chunk of ice the size of a shopping bag near his foot. He struggles to lift it above his head. Smashing it to pieces on Gerard Martí's skull, however, is much easier. Gravity helps.

The wolf falls to the ground, unconscious. A thread of blood flows from his scalp.

"Are you ok?" he asks Miguel.

His brother coughs and wipes the tears from his eyes.

"Yes," he says hoarsely.

Fernando looks at Martí, lying still on the ice. Has he killed a man? Maybe not. Maybe he's still alive.

Before he can find out, the glacier groans again. The crack on the wall is now as wide as a person. It's the first time he feels the ice move beneath his feet. As he looks up, he's sure it'll be the last.

Fernando has lived in Chaltén long enough to know that no one can predict which is the next block of ice to fall off a glacier. The ones that look like they're hanging from a thread can take days to break off, and the most solid-looking walls tend to slough off without warning. However, the block that's in front of them leaves no room for doubt. It's moving, almost in slow motion, before his eyes. They are going to be crushed.

He grabs Miguel by the arm and runs in the direction they came from. He hears a roar behind him but doesn't look back. He runs faster, pulling his brother behind him. He feels something hit his heel. It's one of the thousand pieces of ice that are now flying across the ground like hockey pucks. At any second, the ice they're running on could open up, sink, or turn in any direction. They have a better chance of escaping from a whale's stomach than from that frozen crater.

They run up the same way they came, at a speed that only someone who's running for his life can reach. Fernando doesn't look back until they make it to the surface and are out of danger. He then realizes that the waterfall where they were wrestling thirty seconds ago, no longer exists. It's buried beneath an ice avalanche the size of a truck. And with it, the two wolves.

CHAPTER 73

Julián

I'd made a mistake when I told my father, that if he didn't tell me the truth, whatever I imagined could be worse. My mind could not have made up something worse than what he'd just confessed. Up until that day, I thought the darkest part of his past was his alcoholism. Now I understood that it was just a consequence of his real horror.

"I've spent thirty years wondering what other option I had. With them, it was kill or be killed. Those were the rules they lived by."

I swallowed. I guessed that my father had also spent thirty years worrying how I'd react if I ever found out what happened. If I said the wrong thing, I could break him for good.

"I would have done the same thing, Dad."

It was as if that phrase had pulled a trigger in him. He buried his face in his hands and started crying like I'd never seen him cry before. He wept so hard that his entire body shook. It was a sadness that he had contained for three decades.

I sat next to him and stroked his back. At times, it seemed as though he'd controlled the sadness and tried to speak, but then started sobbing again. He muttered words I couldn't comprehend but whose meaning I could guess.

"You did the right thing, Dad," I repeated several times. At times he nodded, at times he shook his head.

After endless minutes, the shaking in his body started to subside and he managed to dry the tears from his face.

When he was finally able to raise his head and look at me, he touched his own shoulder.

"I didn't want you to find out that this back carries the weight of four deaths, Julián. I killed two people with my bare hands. And I might as well have killed the other two."

With the first two, my father was referring to Pep Codina in Torroella and Mario Santiago at the glacier. Gerard Martí's death on the ice was my uncle's doing, according to what he'd told me.

He took a deep breath and continued his story. He revealed what happened to the fourth wolf. The one I'd found thirty years later in the Montgrí Hotel.

CHAPTER 74

Many years earlier.

In room number seven, Arnau Junqué wakes up for the fourth time that morning. The rays of sunlight that stream in through the shutters are almost vertical now. The watch on his wrist tells him it's half past noon.

He isn't drenched in sweat like the previous three times he has awoken. Now, a deep chill runs through his body, sending shivers down his spine. Even so, he feels much stronger than he did at seven when Fernando Cucurell knocked on his door to take them to the glacier.

On the other side of that door, there's silence now. The only thing he hears is the sound of the soft wind buzzing against the windows. And his stomach. He hasn't eaten anything in over twelve hours, and no matter how high his fever might be, that's far too long for him.

When he gets up from the bed, his joints hurt. Between that and the fever, his diagnosis is clear. Like his father – one of Torroella de Montgrí's most renowned doctors– liked to say, he's got *the flu of a thousand demons.*

He puts on warm clothes and leaves the room. The dining room and reception are both empty. He rings the brass bell on the counter, but to no avail. He even peers into the kitchen, but everything in there is quiet, clean and orderly. He's alone in the hotel.

He lights a fire in the dining room fireplace and sits in a chair to wait. Although he knows Fernando Cucurell is hiking on the glacier with Mario and Gerard, he presumes he's left someone else in charge. Someone who will show up at some point to make him some food.

Forty minutes later, the logs are now embers and his stomach has gone from asking for food to demanding it. He considers searching for something to eat in the kitchen, but he doesn't want to risk being caught doing something he shouldn't. In his position, the less attention he draws to himself, the better.

He returns to his room and puts on all the warm clothes he has, including a scarf and a woolen hat. Partially because of the cold, but also because he'd prefer that no one recognize him. He's not going to make the mistake of letting people see him like they did the day before. That mistake has caused too many problems already.

He walks out into the warm sunlight. There are barely a dozen houses spread across the deserted blocks. He walks toward the town entrance. The bus that they took from Calafate the day before, dropped them at the building that functions as the town's only restaurant, grocery store, and service station.

He walks into the restaurant and picks a table in the back, next to a window that looks onto the street. Thirty seconds later, the same woman who waited on them yesterday comes up to the table.

"Good afternoon. Are you having lunch?"

"Yes."

"We've got stew and potatoes."

"Good."

"Water or wine?"

"Wine."

The woman nods and goes back into the kitchen. Arnau Junqué looks out the window at the still, empty town. He has to admit that Miguel Cucurell chose the ideal place to hide. And yet, he managed to find him. He smiles. All that's left is to wait for Cucurell to come back with his family, so that they can finally make him pay for Pep's death.

The stew could be better, but his hunger will take anything he gives it. After eating just a few bites, he sees a gangly teenager walk in with a dumb smile on his face.

When he walks, his head wobbles like those plastic dogs people put on their dashboards.

Of the twelve tables in the restaurant, the boy chooses the one closest to him. Arnau swears to himself. He's had to take the scarf off to eat, and he doesn't like the idea of people seeing him up close.

The woman comes out with another plate of stew and places it in front of the boy.

"Danilo, let the man eat in peace. Okay?"

"Yes, Clara," the boy says. He then looks at Arnau Junqué and gives him a mischievous smile.

When he sees the smile, he relaxes a bit. The boy is retarded.

"Clara doesn't like me bothering the customers," the boy whispers once the woman has left them alone.

Arnau nods and keeps eating.

"Does it bother you if I talk to you?"

He looks out the window without answering.

"Where are you staying? At the Parks inn or at the Montgrí Hotel?"

"..."

"I hope it's at the hotel. Fernando is a good friend of mine. So is Miguel. So is Consuelo. So is Julián. I helped them build the hotel. I killed the ants."

When he hears that, Junqué turns toward the boy.

"I'm also a friend of Miguel's," he says. "I'm really looking forward to seeing him."

"He'll be back soon, I'm sure. He left early this morning."

"This morning?"

"Yes."

The boy points his chin toward the street as he chews.

"I live across the street from his house," he says once he swallows. "I saw him leave with Fernando this morning. It was around five."

"Are you sure?"

"Absolutely."

If what the boy says is true, Miguel wasn't out of town like his brother said. Where did the two of them go at five a.m. if Fernando was back at seven to take Gerard and Mario to the glacier?

Fernando Cucurell lied to them. He and his faggot brother set them up and they bought their lies like idiots. At this point, his friends might be dead. He looks at the ring on his finger. He might be the only wolf standing.

"I'm also friends with Consuelo," he says. "Do you know where I can find her?"

The boy arches his eyebrows as if it were the stupidest question in the world.

"At her house, next to the hotel."

"Do you know if she's in town? Fernando told me they were planning on going to Río Gallegos for a few days."

The boy shrugs.

"She was here yesterday at noon."

He nods, wipes his mouth with a napkin and stands up.

"Aren't you going to finish your stew?" Danilo asks him.

"I'm not hungry anymore."

"Can I have it?"

"All yours," he says and empties the glass of wine.

"Don't drink too fast, you'll get drunk."

Without bothering to answer, he leaves some money on the table and rushes out of the restaurant.

As he walks toward the Montgrí Hotel, he considers his chances of helping his friends. None. He has no idea how to get to the glacier, much less what he'd do once he got there.

The hotel reception is still empty. He looks behind the front desk, trying to find something that'll give him a clue. He looks through the guestbook and confirms that Fernando hasn't registered his name or his friends'. He finds a letter opener between the papers, but it isn't very sharp and is far too small. He throws it on the desk, annoyed, and goes into the kitchen. He grabs the biggest knife he sees. That'll do.

He walks out of the hotel and heads toward the other end of the lot. Once he's close to the house, he slows his pace and moves forward cautiously. He puts his ear to the front door and hears a child crying. He smiles. He lifts his hand to knock, but changes his mind and decides to step back and kick the door open instead.

The lock opens and the door breaks in. The child's crying stops. It's replaced by a woman's scream.

She's sitting at the table in front of two plates of food and cups of juice. She hugs a small boy wearing blue flannel pajamas. He recognizes her. It's the same woman who stood up to them two years ago in Torroella, a couple of hours before her husband killed Pep Codina.

"Hello again," he says and shows her the knife.

The woman glares at him with that mixture of fear and hatred that victims always have before they feel the first blow. The boy, on the other hand, looks at him calmly.

"If you come any closer, I'll kill you," she says, picking up the boy with one arm and wielding a fork with her free hand.

Junqué smiles and takes another step forward.

"Give me the kid and nothing will happen to you."

"Son of a bitch."

He smiles again and nods. That's exactly the reaction he was expecting. She'll defend her pup to the death if necessary. Like a mother wolf.

"What do you want?" she asks without letting go of the boy. Her eyes flicker defiantly. Her ample bosom rises up and down to the rhythm of her agitated breath.

The woman's arrogance doesn't intimidate him. On the contrary, it turns him on. For a second, Arnau Junqué forgets about the fever and his friends. His body can only think of one thing: penetrating her.

"I'll make a deal with you. Lock the kid in his room and come here," he says, grabbing his crotch with his hand, feeling himself getting hard.

She stares at him, petrified.

"Want to save your kid? I'm offering you the way to do it."

She seems to understand, because she nods. That disappoints him a bit. The bitch looked like she'd put up more of a fight. His bulge gets a bit softer.

"Ok, I'll be right back," she says and takes a step toward the door that seems to lead to the rest of the house.

What follows happens in a flash. In one swift movement, the woman grabs something from the table and throws it in his face. It's liquid, cold, and burns his eyes like acid. It takes him a moment to recognize the smell. Orange juice.

"Come here, you bitch," he says and lunges toward her blindly.

The woman manages to dodge him and runs out of the house with the child in her arms, yelling for help. Arnau Junqué wipes his face on his sleeve and runs after her. It doesn't take him long to catch her. Before she makes it to the gate, he grabs her, and with a smile, he puts the knife to her neck.

CHAPTER 75

Many years earlier.

Consuelo Guelbenzu Ochotorena has never been so afraid in her life. The man holding a knife to her throat and leading her to the hotel is over two meters tall and has arms the size of her thighs. She knows that to save her own life and Julián's, who she's holding against her chest, she needs to get rid of this man. But she doesn't know how.

They walk into the reception. Without letting go of her, the man locks the door behind them. She takes advantage of his momentary distraction and grabs the letter opener that's lying on the front desk and stuffs it in her pocket. He drags her across the room as he draws all the curtains, one by one.

When they reach the last window, Consuelo sees Fernando's truck down the street, moving toward the hotel. She doesn't know if that's good or bad news. In two minutes, her husband and brother-in-law will come into the hotel. If the man still has the knife to her throat by that point, he'll be able to manipulate them at will.

She needs to act fast.

"Why don't you just tell me what you want already?" she asks.

"What I want to do is one thing. What matters is what I have to do. Your husband killed someone very close to me. Closer than a brother."

"Then sort things out with him. Let us go."

Arnau Junqué lets out a laugh. Consuelo looks around her, looking for a way out. The room she designed herself doesn't give her any answers. Even if she didn't have little

Julián stuck to her chest like a limpet, she wouldn't know what to do.

The doorknob turns. On the other side of the door, Fernando or Miguel are trying to come in. Her attacker notices too, and his surprise makes him briefly move the knife away from her throat. She knows this is her chance. She stabs the letter opener into his groin and bites his wrist. The man groans and his hand opens, dropping the knife to the ground.

She moves backwards with Julián in her arms and hears the sound of breaking glass. Her husband and brother-in-law smash in through the window and lunge at the wolf. But the man has already pulled out the letter opener and grabbed a poker from the fireplace, which he slams into the side of Fernando's head.

From a corner of the dining room, Consuelo sees her brother-in-law fall to the floor unconscious, like a puppet whose strings have suddenly been cut. They no longer have a two-to-one advantage. Miguel won't be able to beat that monster, who is double his size, on his own. She knows she has to help him, but can't put Julián in danger.

She hurtles down the hallway toward the hotel's back door. She wants to get out and scream for help. But before she gets there, she realizes that if she loses those precious seconds, her husband might not survive.

She stops in front of the last room and opens the door.

"Mommy's going to leave you here for a little while, but she'll be right back to get you. Ok, honey?"

Julián shakes his head and starts crying, grabbing onto Consuelo's leg. She pulls him off, locks the door from the inside, and closes it behind her. She sees the doorknob turn frantically, but Julián can't get out.

By the time she makes it back to the dining room, Arnau Junqué has her husband pinned to the floor. Miguel spits out blood and teeth after each punch. Consuelo knows her only option is to pick up the knife and sink it into the man's back with all her strength. But there are two problems. The first is that fear is preventing her legs from moving. The second is that the knife is all the way across the dining room. To reach it, she needs to pass dangerously close to Junqué.

Miguel takes another punch and one more tooth rolls across the wooden floor. If she doesn't act soon, her husband is going to die.

She manages to move. She slips behind Junqué, who miraculously doesn't notice her, and picks up the knife. Her hand shakes as she wields it.

She takes a step but a voice makes her freeze.

"Mommy."

Julián is standing in the doorway that connects the dining room with the hallway to the bedrooms. It's only taken him a few seconds to open the door lock.

Her son runs toward her.

"Julián, no!"

Her scream alerts Arnau Junqué. When Julián passes next to him, the wolf moves away from Miguel and intercepts the child. Her son kicks and screams, calling for her.

"Let him go," she screams, her throat tearing.

Junqué smiles and takes a step toward Consuelo, using one of his arms to hold Julián.

Another sound of broken glass. Her husband has gotten up and smashed a bottle against the table. He brandishes it by the neck.

"Let my son go, you piece of shit."

Arnau Junqué turns toward Miguel and says something she can't make out. She doesn't care. The only thing she can think of is that the wolf has his back to her. She leaps at him and plunges the blade into his back.

Julián falls to the floor and runs to his father. Junqué turns around and grabs her by the neck, making it impossible to breathe. Without loosening his grip, he tries to grab her hand which is still holding the knife. She waves it around in the air, cutting his hand several times until she manages to stab him in the belly.

The pressure on her neck eases and the man falls at her feet. He doesn't speak or look at her anymore. All his energy is going toward trying to stop the bleeding coming from the wounds on his body.

She runs toward Miguel and hugs him, pressing Julián between the two of them so that he can't see the man bleeding to death a few meters away. They need to get out. She has to get her son out of that violence-infested room. But once again, her legs don't respond. She can't leave until she's sure that piece of shit is dead. Miguel hands Julián to her and kneels beside Fernando, who's just regaining consciousness.

When her brother-in-law finally comes to, the first thing he asks is:

"Are you all ok?"

Consuelo nods and looks around. There's blood everywhere and Arnau Junqué lies lifeless. It's over.

Or so it seems, until a voice breaks the silence.

"What happened?"

Juanmi Alonso is the person asking. He's looking into the hotel, his body halfway through the window Fernando and Miguel broke. Behind him is Danilo. When they see Consuelo covered in blood and Junqué lying surrounded by a red puddle, they both freeze.

"Is he dead?" Danilo asks.

Fernando rushes over to where they're standing and pushes them away from the window. Consuelo, holding Julián, looks at her husband. His gaze is lost in the blood that's spreading across the floor of the hotel they built with their own hands.

We're done for, Consuelo thinks. They'll put her in jail, take her away from Julián and Miguel in a country that isn't her own. She picks up her son and dashes down the hallway toward the back door. She runs through the grass, looking around her in every direction, and finally locks herself in the house her family has shared with Fernando for the past year and a half, while they still thought they could be happy.

CHAPTER 76

Many years earlier.

Still dazed from the blow to his head, Fernando briefly explains what's going on to his friend Juanmi. He repeats over and over that it was self-defense. That those men had come to kill his brother.

"That man was a monster. I swear it on our friendship, Juanmi. I need you to help me keep this secret, please. And confuse Danilo so that if he says anything, people won't believe him."

Young Danilo is sitting several meters away from them on the wooden fence that surrounds the hotel. He looks at the ground between his feet. Hopefully, he's looking for ants and not remembering what he has just seen, Fernando thinks to himself.

When Danilo came to ask if the man was dead, Fernando told him no, that he'd tripped because he was drunk, and when he fell, he got a nosebleed. It's a ridiculous explanation, but it's the first thing that came to mind. Luckily, the boy's unique mind seems to accept it, because he replies that he'd seen Junqué drinking a lot of wine.

"We don't know anything about it, Fernando," Juanmi says to him, looking him straight in the eyes. "If anyone asks, we didn't see a thing."

"Swear it."

"I swear."

Fernando hugs his friend and thanks him. He asks him to take Danilo away and distract him and to try and figure out if he's worried about what he saw or if he actually bought the lie.

When he turns to go back to the hotel, all the shutters are already closed. When he tries the front door, it's locked from the inside. He has to knock several times before Miguel opens up.

Arnau Junqué's body is still there, surrounded by a shiny crimson puddle that has grown even larger. His brother paces from one side of the room to the other, eyes on the ground like a caged animal.

Fernando thinks about his future. Or rather, the future he no longer has. He regrets agreeing to help his brother. He knew it was a bad idea from the second Arnau Junqué decided not to go to the glacier. They should've aborted the mission, but Miguel fired the rifle before he could tell him about the change of plans.

"Why did you move away from the spot on the glacier?"

"There was a crack in the ice. Why does that matter?" Miguel answers without looking at him, still pacing.

"If you'd stayed where I told you, I could have warned you that Junqué had stayed behind," he says and points at the body.

"What difference does that make now, Fernando?"

"We could have found another way to trap all three of them at once, far away from town, like we'd planned."

"Do you really think we would have had another opportunity? Don't be naive. And calm down, I need to think."

"How do you expect me to calm down? Your wife just killed someone in my hotel! There are two witnesses."

Raising his voice causes a sharp pain to shoot through his head, starting on the side he took the blow. He shuts his eyes and grits his teeth as the strongest wave of pain subsides. When he opens his eyes again, Miguel stops pacing and looks up at him.

"Consuelo was defending Julián. She didn't know Danilo and Juanmi would show up. Anyone would have done the same. If you had kids, you'd understand."

Deep down, Fernando knows his brother's right, but the anger and the pain in his head cloud his mind. The only thing he can see through the rage is the Montgrí Hotel, his lifelong dream, slipping through his fingers like sand.

"Well, I don't have kids."

"That's a shame, because it would do you good to care about something other than your hotel."

"What did you say?"

"The truth, Fernando. You're thinking about yourself right now. You think I ruined your life and you're incapable of seeing that you're not the only one who's in it up to his neck."

He takes a deep breath, trying to contain himself. But self-control has never been his forte.

"So, I'm selfish now?" he says without raising his voice to stop the pain from increasing. "I open the door to my house and give you and your family a place to start over, and it turns out I'm selfish. If it weren't for me, you'd be rotting in jail."

"And look where that got us."

"You're an idiot. And your wife is an even bigger idiot," he feels the pain in his head intensify. He feels as though his head is about to explode. "Damn the fucking day I told you to come."

"Do you think we liked having to hide like rats? Do you think we enjoyed having to uproot our lives and move to the other end of the planet?"

"You shouldn't have stabbed someone, then."

"Those motherfuckers put me through hell sixteen years ago!"

Fernando looks his brother in the eyes. If he could think, he'd shut up. But he can't. The pain and his jangled nerves have gotten the better of him and force him to dig even deeper.

"Are you ever going to take some responsibility?" he says.

"Responsibility? What are you talking about?"

"You let them walk all over you, Miguel."

"How can you say that to me, you jerk?"

"If you hadn't been such a pussy and defended yourself back then, none of this would've happened."

He doesn't have time to block Miguel's punch. A new kind of pain –different, sharper, but less dangerous– spreads up his nose to the crown of his head. He grabs his face with both hands and tastes blood in his mouth.

"What part of 'there were four of them and I couldn't move a finger' don't you understand? Do you think I liked being tied up by my hands and feet while they took turns on me? Do you know how I felt?"

"And you think you're the only person in the world who's had a rough time and that gives you the right to ruin my life? Now you're going to leave with your family, escaping just like you did last time. But I'm going to stay here, and sooner or later someone will find out about these men's deaths, even if Juanmi and Danilo keep their mouths shut. Then, when it's me who's rotting in jail instead of you, I'm going to remember you and hate you. I'm going to hate you more than I do right now."

"You have no fucking idea what you're talking about," Miguel counters, and walks away toward the hallway and the hotel's back door.

CHAPTER 77

Julián

"How can it be that I don't remember anything about this?"

"You were five."

"But some people have very vivid memories from when they were much younger than that."

My father nodded as if he'd expected that question.

"How old were you when you started losing your hair?"

"Twenty-eight, what does baldness have to do with my memory?"

"Nothing. But some start losing it at forty, and some lucky men never do. Some people are tall, some are short. If you go to the beach, you'll see cellulite and smooth butts, light skin and darker skin, hairy backs, scars."

My father paused and put his index finger to his temple.

"Up here, we're just as different, but it's harder to understand because we can't see it. Some people have memories from when they were three, others don't have clear images from before they were seven."

"How did you and mom know I wouldn't remember?"

"We didn't. We started noticing as time went by. You started speaking less and less about El Chaltén and your uncle Fernando. We spoke to a therapist and he said it was normal for kids that age to forget some memories to make space for new ones. You had a few sessions with him and his diagnosis was encouraging: you didn't show any signs of trauma."

What my father was telling me, in his own words, was that I was lucky to not remember. And he was right.

According to my memory, the worst thing about my childhood was having a drunk father for a few years.

"Now do you understand why I never spoke about your uncle? My brother Fernando is one end of a ball of yarn I never wanted you to unravel, Julián. I kept my secret from you so you wouldn't know what happened. Not for my honor, not because I was ashamed, but because I wanted that pain and anger to die with me and not pass on to you."

He looked me in the eyes and offered me a weak smile, full of fake teeth that up until that moment I'd thought replaced the ones he'd lost in an accident driving from Barcelona to Bilbao.

"Do you think Fernando left me the hotel because he wanted me to know the truth?"

"It's likely. After all, he knew what you were going to find inside."

"Why would he want me to find out something like that?"

"To help us."

"Who?"

"Me, you, and your mother."

"What do you mean?"

"Ever since Fernando found out what the wolves did to me, he chalked up all my problems to that. My drinking, the ups and downs your mother and I had, losing a job... To him, my biggest problem was having kept what happened to me a secret. He thought that if I let the truth come to light, I'd be free and happier."

"How do you know what he thought if you didn't speak to each other?"

"Up until we left El Chaltén, he told me every chance he got. And he repeated it the only time I saw him after that."

"When you went to his restaurant in 1995."

"Yes. Fernando was a completely different person. He was in a wheelchair and managing the restaurant. He looked happy. I'd spent a few days sitting at the door of the place, trying to muster up the courage to go talk to him. I didn't know what to say. I wasn't at my best back then, you know that. Half the time I was too drunk to think clearly, the other half, the hangover and the withdrawal symptoms drove me crazy.

"Did you ever discover what happened to him after we left El Chaltén up until you went to see him?"

"Over the years, I've gathered bits and pieces of the story."

CHAPTER 78

Many years earlier.

Fernando Cucurell has lost all notion of time. He's sitting at one of the chairs in the reception area, the tip of his shoe ten centimeters from the pool of blood that surrounds Arnau Junqué's body. He can't tell if he's been there fifteen minutes or an hour.

Probably an hour. Maybe more. It's been a good while since he heard his brother's car leaving down the town's main street.

His headache has finally subsided and now he's wondering why he said those awful things to Miguel. How could his brother hold any blame for what happened to him? But Fernando Cucurell isn't one to admit a mistake easily, he is the kind who prefers to carry the consequences of his actions indefinitely.

In any case, what matters now is surviving. Erasing any trace of the three wolves having been in his hotel. He doesn't have to worry about the glacier bodies, it'll take years for them to emerge from the ice, if they ever do. But the one in front of him is another matter.

If Juanmi and Danilo hadn't seen it, it would be easier. Actually, if Danilo hadn't seen it. That boy is too pure-hearted to lie. The only way to stop him from speaking is to make him believe that what he saw was unimportant. Fernando will find a way to make sure that was the case.

The next step is getting rid of Arnau Junqué's body.

He exhales and stands up. He grabs Junqué by the ankles and pulls. Moving him requires all his strength. If he hadn't spent these last years building a hotel, his muscles wouldn't have been able to move that body at all.

It takes him twenty minutes to drag him to the foot of the bed in the only room that has a basement. At first, the kitchen was going to be bigger and have an underground wine cellar, but they made some changes to the construction and the basement ended up beneath room number seven. Fernando never used it for anything.

He pulls on the metal ring on the floor and a square trapdoor opens, revealing a staircase that disappears into the dark. What he's about to do is irreversible. If he pushes the body down, there's no way he's ever getting it out. He allows himself a few minutes to catch his breath and think.

The basement isn't in the hotel floor plan. The only people who know it exists are Miguel, Consuelo, and himself. It has a dirt floor so he could bury Junqué down there. Over time, he could even bring dirt from outside and fill the basement up completely to make it disappear.

He pushes the body down, which falls like a sack of potatoes. He closes the trap door. There's a wide trail of blood on the floor, as if someone had marked the route from the reception to the bedroom with red paint. It takes him half an hour to remove the stain with a mop, water, and a lot of disinfectant.

He sits back down on the sofa. Where there was a body, blood, and several of his brother's teeth just a while ago, now there's merely a damp trail that smells strongly of ammonia. He could use a glass of whisky to calm his nerves, but he needs to be as lucid as possible for the next few hours. He decides to make a cup of strong black tea instead.

He drinks the hot liquid and wonders how long it'll be before the police knock on the door of the hotel. Hours? Days? Months? Fernando Cucurell knows he's buying time by making the body disappear, but he's not dumb enough to believe that three murders can stay hidden forever. Those people have families who, sooner or later, will start looking for them.

He leaves the tea half drunk and goes from one room to the next, grabbing the wolves' luggage. He thinks about his brother, Consuelo, and especially poor Julián. Will he ever see him again? Now that the adrenaline is leaving his body, he's overcome with a feeling of dread. Not for being involved in the murders of those three monsters –Darwin would be proud–, but because of the atrocities he said to his brother with the sole purpose of hurting him. He put his hotel first, pushing aside something that had marked Miguel his entire life.

He stands up and makes sure all the shutters are closed. He walks outside, locks up the hotel and his house, and leaves, prepared to do something he has never done before: apologize.

CHAPTER 79

Many years earlier.

Fernando gets in the truck and accelerates so hard the wheels skid. The green numbers on the dashboard clock mark 8:14 p.m. It's been at least two hours since his brother left with Consuelo and Julián, probably to Río Gallegos. It'll be hard to catch up with them, but he's going to try.

He only slows down when he crosses the bridge over the Fitz Roy. It's the third time that day he's left El Chaltén down route 23. The first was to take Miguel to the glacier. The second, to take the wolves to him.

There's a scant half hour of daylight left. Both he and Miguel will reach Río Gallegos after dark. Or maybe, if Fernando manages to get them to forgive him, they'll all come back to Chaltén together.

Once he's driven thirty kilometers from town, he takes an old side road that veers off to the right, away from the main road. From that moment on, every second he takes on the detour puts him further away from his brother, but he can't risk going any further with the cargo in his truck.

He drives 700 meters down to the shore of Lake Viedma. The same shore –though several kilometers closer to Chaltén– where he boarded a boat twice that morning to go to the glacier.

He drags the three suitcases, one by one, to a small rock ledge on the edge of the water. It's barely one and a half meters high, but it's good enough for what he needs. The lake has mostly flat shores, and it gets deeper toward the middle. However, here, where he has brought Miguel and his family on a summer afternoon, has a small cliff that's the perfect place to jump off of without breaking any bones. The water is over three meters deep there.

Of course, he isn't going to jump on this occasion. He opens up the suitcases and fills them with as many rocks as he can, mixed amongst the wolves' clothing. One by one, he closes them up and throws them into the water. He waits until the foam in the water disappears and checks that none are floating. He breathes three times and then runs back to the truck. He's lost thirteen minutes.

He gets back on the main road and drives for an hour through the monotonous landscape. Once night has fallen, he sees two shiny red circles in the distance. It's the first vehicle he's seen since he left Chaltén.

He accelerates, but his excitement is short lived. Two bright white lights appear under the red circles. Fernando thought they were the backlights of a car, but they top the cabin off a truck about a couple of kilometers away.

He flashes his lights, a customary practice on Patagonian roads, but the truck doesn't respond. He slows down and tries again. Nothing. Flashing lights isn't just a greeting, it's also a way to make sure that whoever's driving toward you isn't asleep. It's common for thousand-kilometer drives to take their toll on tired drivers.

When they're two hundred meters from each other, Fernando realizes that the truck is driving in the wrong lane. He flashes his lights again and honks. The truck swerves suddenly and Fernando understands, in a fraction of a second, that the driver has woken up and is trying to switch lanes to avoid crashing into him.

Everything happens in a blink. The impact sounds like a bomb going off. Fernando grabs onto the steering wheel with all his strength, then hurtles through the windshield and lands on his back on the frozen gravel.

CHAPTER 80

Many years earlier.

The room he wakes up in has white walls and smells of disinfectant.

"Good morning," a nurse wearing a blue uniform greets him.

"Where am I?"

"At the Río Gallegos hospital. You had an accident. You crashed into a truck a hundred kilometers from Chaltén. Do you remember?"

"What time is it?" he asks, trying to sit up in bed, but his body doesn't respond.

"Eleven a.m."

"Of what day?"

"Tuesday."

"Shit."

"What's wrong?"

"Shit!" he repeats and punches the mattress.

"Calm down. I'm going to get the doctor," the nurse says, and leaves the room.

He curses again. Miguel and his family probably left for Buenos Aires over a day ago. He thinks about screaming, yanking the IV out of his arm and running out, but he doesn't have the strength to fight off the sweet sleepiness that overpowers him.

A warm hand on his shoulder wakes him.

"Fernando Cucurell? I'm Doctor Muñoz."

The doctor, a middle-aged woman, has a perfect white smile. The nurse that went to get her watches from a few steps back.

"Do you remember what happened?"

"A truck. He crossed into my lane. Where's the driver?"

From the look she gives him, he knows it's bad news.

"He passed away."

Fernando closes his eyes and clenches his teeth.

"Mr. Cucurell, I know it's difficult but right now it's important that we talk about you. How are you feeling?"

"From the waist up, everything hurts."

"And from the waist down?"

He sees the doctor place her hand on his shin.

"Do you feel this?" she asks, squeezing his legs with her fingers.

"No."

"What about this?" she asks again, moving to the other leg.

"No."

The doctor nods.

"What happened to me?"

"Mr. Cucurell, you were found at ten meters from your vehicle. You were likely ejected from your car due to the impact. You have three fractures in your spine. Your spinal cord has probably suffered damage as well."

"Will I be able to walk again?"

"It's too soon to know."

"What do you think?" he asks, as two teardrops roll down his cheeks.

"What I think doesn't matter, what I know does. I know that willpower and hard work play a key role in recovery. So don't throw in the towel before you've even started."

Fernando Cucurell laughs bitterly. The doctor turns around and tells the nurse to leave them alone.

"Your ID says you live in Chaltén."

"Correct. I own a hotel there."

"It also says you were born in Buenos Aires, but I see you have a Spanish accent."

"I was raised in Spain. What does that have to do with anything?"

"Where in Spain?"

"Barcelona," he answers, trying to simplify the answer.

"Lovely city. I was lucky enough to visit it once. I went on an exchange program to Valencia while I was in med school."

"Doctor, I don't know if I'll be able to walk again. I'm not really in the mood to talk about tourism."

"Neither am I."

"Well then?"

"As you know, Mr. Cucurell, Patagonia is a wonderful place to live, but it's a very hard place to be sick in. There are few hospitals, not many specialists, and not much medical equipment. If you want to improve your chances of walking again, Chaltén isn't the best place for you to be. Do you want my advice?"

"Of course."

"Go back to Barcelona."

CHAPTER 81

Many years earlier.

Fernando Cucurell has gotten used to moving around Barcelona in a wheelchair. After three-dozen tests and rehab exercises, multiple doctors come to a unanimous conclusion: he'll never walk again.

He returned from El Chaltén six months ago. Or rather, from Río Gallegos. When he was released from the hospital, it didn't make sense to go back to the hotel. Without the ability to walk he wouldn't have even been able to pack his belongings on his own. He could've asked Juanmi for help, but he'd already placed too big a burden on his shoulders.

He simply called him from the airport to let him know he wouldn't be back for a while. Juanmi's only question was how he might help. 'Take care of the hotel and don't let anyone in', he answered. Juanmi told him that Danilo was already on top of that because he said that Fernando himself had asked him to.

He smiled when he heard that. In a way, Danilo was telling the truth. Two years back, Fernando had gone to El Calafate with Miguel and his family, and he'd asked Danilo to watch the hotel. When he returned, he brought him some candy, and the boy was so happy that he promised him, that he would be the one to guard the Montgrí Hotel whenever he was gone.

He thinks about that conversation he had with Juanmi nearly six months ago, almost daily. It wasn't only a goodbye to his friend, but rather an ending to his story in Patagonia. An hour after hanging up the phone, he boarded a plane and left everything behind.

Now that the doctor's appointments are fewer and farther apart, he has to find something to do with his time so as to not go crazy. He's considering opening up a restaurant, taking advantage of the fact that Barcelona is preparing to host the Olympics. An old childhood friend has introduced him to his girlfriend, who'd been considering a similar venture for a while. Her name is Lorenza and she's a very smart woman. She also has two working legs.

The morning is pleasant. Fifteen minutes ago, a taxi dropped him at the Camp Nou ticket booth where he bought three tickets to Sunday's match. He wants to invite Lorenza and her boyfriend, to celebrate their signing of the rental contract for the spot in Horta where they're going to set up their business.

With the tickets in his pocket, he rolls down the narrow streets of the Les Corts neighborhood. After six months, he can handle longer outings without his shoulders cramping up.

He stops on the sidewalk and is waiting for the light to change when he sees them. Across the street, Consuelo and little Julián are holding hands, waiting to cross in his direction. He tries to roll backward in the chair, but right then the light turns green. All he manages to do is pull his hat down as low as possible. Between that and the beard he's grown, they won't recognize him.

He could look down, but his curiosity gets the best of him. Consuelo and Julián, who's wearing a small yellow backpack, pass a meter away from him without stopping or making any comment. She doesn't even look at him. Being in a wheelchair is the closest you can get to becoming Medusa: no one wants to make eye contact for fear of turning to stone.

Julián, on the other hand, does look at him. Their faces are at the same height. Fernando smiles at him and the little boy smiles back but doesn't seem to recognize him.

After they've passed him, he swivels the chair around in their direction. He waits for his nephew to pull on his mother's hand, turn around and point at him, but none of that happens. The little boy doesn't know he's just crossed paths with his uncle.

He wants to call to them. Hug them. Finish the apology he set out to give them seven months ago. But he's also afraid that they'll see him in his condition and feel sorry for him. And even more afraid that they'll find out that the accident happened while he was trying to reach them.

He follows them at a safe distance. A few blocks down, his sister-in-law squats down, kisses Julián on the cheek, and watches him walk into school. Once she's alone, she doesn't turn around. Instead, she keeps walking in the same direction. He sighs with relief. He won't have to cross paths with her again.

The school playground looks onto a park. He stops his wheelchair by a bench and waits. An hour later, the bell rings, and the playground fills with children. It doesn't take him long to find Julián, he runs more than most of the others.

His nephew stops very close to the fence to talk to another boy. Fernando cautiously moves closer. Will he recognize him this time? Does he even want him to?

The boy looks at him and, once again, doesn't recognize him. Fernando searches his pockets and finds some candies. He throws them through the fence and the boys lunge for the sweets. Once they calm down, he sees Julián has managed to grab one.

He says goodbye with a wave, releases the brake, and leaves. He promises himself he'll be back soon with a lot more candy.

CHAPTER 82

Julián

My father's eyes were full of tears again.
"Fernando lost everything because of me. His hotel, his legs, everything."
"What are you talking about, dad? It wasn't your fault."
"No? Whose was it then?"
"No one's. Life. I don't know. As much as we might want to, we can't control everything that happens to us."
I felt like a hypocrite. I was one to talk, the guy who still felt like he was partially to blame for what Anna had done.
"Now you know the truth. My worst nightmare has come to life."
"Well, the only difference it makes is that now I understand you a bit more. Aside from that, I love you exactly as much as I did yesterday. What bothers me most about you, is that you vote conservative and that you gave me the bald gene."
Laughing together felt like a rest. I would have loved to pause time at that moment when we did the best thing one can do with one's tragedies: laugh about them. But soon enough, a silence between us announced it was time to continue.
"You never spoke to him again after that time you went to see him at the restaurant?"
"No."
"Why didn't you ever make up?"
"Partly out of pride, partly out of guilt, and partly because we tend to think life is very long and we'll always have time to solve the big problems."

I didn't know if I should keep asking about that. I had so many questions, but I wanted to ask the less painful ones first. As I considered how to proceed, the doorbell rang. I was as grateful as an exhausted boxer.

"That must be your mother. I told her to come quickly."

I opened the door and my mother walked in with a strained smile, looking around like a military officer conducting an inspection. When she saw the open letters and my father sitting with his shoulders slumped forward, she let out a few Basque swear words.

"Son…" she said, tilting her head forward like she used to when I was a little boy and she'd tell me she couldn't pick me up from school that day because of work.

"He knows everything, Consuelo. And it's okay."

"Well, I don't see anything wrong with it," I intervened, trying to conceal my shock. "You told me and I'm processing it. I understand you both, I really do."

"Forgive us," my father said. "I always thought that by hiding the truth from you, you'd be able to live a better life. I already ruined my brother's life, I didn't want to do the same to you. That's why we tried to get you to stop, by sending the note and the photo."

"You sent the threat?"

"Yes," my father admitted, his head bowed.

"But I got one in El Chaltén, too. And it was printed out in the same font."

"That was us, too. Well, technically it was Juanmi Alonso, but because I asked him to."

"Alonso was fixing a bridge in the middle of the woods when I got it."

"Not exactly."

"What do you mean? I walked four hours to go see him."

"Yes, but before you went to him, he came to you."

"I don't understand."

"The day after you arrived at El Chaltén, Alonso found out that the heir to the Montgrí Hotel was in town over the National Parks radio. You know how fast rumors spread there."

I recalled that when we'd been at the Laguna de los Tres, one of the workers had been notified about his son's appendicitis over the radio. I didn't know they used it to spread gossip as well.

"When he found out you'd traveled to El Chaltén, he went back to town and called me. We hadn't spoken in thirty years."

"What did he say?"

"He asked if I needed help. I told him I did, and we wrote the note together."

"Wait. He offered to help, no questions asked?"

"By not reporting Arnau Junqué's murder, Juanmi became an accomplice in his murder. He didn't want the secret to come out either."

"But he gave me a clue when he said Fernando had traveled to Spain in 1989, right around the time Josep Codina had died."

"I told him to tell you that. I guessed your police friend wouldn't have any difficulty finding out about that trip. I also asked him to break into the house by the hotel and take all the papers Fernando kept in his nightstand."

"Among them was the floorplan your uncle used as the template to design the Montgrí, with my signature on it," my mother jumped in. "And probably other documents that would've made it obvious that we'd lived in El Chaltén."

I recalled the footsteps the forensic police had found in the house.

"We wanted you to lead a peaceful life and for us to take this horrible story to our graves," my father added.

"No one can live in peace with anonymous threats and a past they can't understand."

"We didn't know how to get you to drop it, Julián. At first, we thought the threats would be enough. That when you smelled danger, you'd decide to get rid of the hotel. But you cared too much about finding out the truth about your family, so we made up the story about my anxiety attack."

"Yes, but that didn't stop you either," my mother added, in a scolding tone.

"The slashed tires and the crash was also you?"

They both nodded in silence.

"Wait. Something doesn't add up. If you crashed in Barcelona, who followed us to Santa María de los Desamparados to lock us in the basement and slit all four tires of our car?"

The doorbell rang again. Just what we needed, more people.

CHAPTER 83

Julián

It was Laura. I hadn't seen her since we'd returned to my apartment to shower after the train ride.

"I just met with Caplonch. I've got news," she said, walking in like a whirlwind. "I know you don't want to know about any of this but it's important. It's about your father and Anna's."

The words rushed out of her mouth like a train with no brakes, a second before she realized we weren't alone.

My father buried his head in his hands again. My mother looked at me with her typical nonchalant face, which was anything but nonchalant.

"What about Anna's father?" I asked.

Laura didn't say a word. Suddenly, you could hear a pin drop in my dining room.

"Whatever it is, you can say it in front of my parents."

"What do you know? Or rather, what do you think you know, Laura?" my mother asked.

Laura told us that Caplonch had explained what the wolves had done to my father. She spoke with tact, though in a situation like ours, the choice of words didn't make much difference. Her account made it clear that she'd reconstructed the story my father had just told me, in a more general –but surprisingly accurate manner.

"Caplonch told me that Anna's father was also in the basement that night."

My father nodded.

"It's true. He was there and they forced him to watch. Like a rite of passage. They told him he had to earn the silver ring. One of the sounds I recall most from that night are his sobs. His eyes were shut tight, but once in a while one of the others would go up to him and tell him to open them, or he'd end up like me."

"Did you talk to him after what happened?"

"Only once, a few weeks later. He asked me if I wanted to report what they'd done. I said no."

"Why not?"

My father's mouth curled up into a bitter smile.

"Back then... What am I saying? The same thing happens now. There are thousands of rape victims that keep quiet about what's happened to them. Out of shame, out of fear. Why do you think those reports of priests abusing children come out twenty, thirty, or forty years after the fact? Because for most people, speaking up is a last resort. They try everything before that. Burying it deep in their memory, ignoring it, understanding why it happened to them, even feeling guilty. 'I must have done something to deserve what they did to me'. That's how disturbed the human mind can be at times."

"Did Anna's father respect your decision to not say anything?" I asked.

"Yes, and I hated him for it. Deep down, I was screaming for someone to speak up about what happened. I didn't have the courage to do it myself. I needed his help but he couldn't see it. I don't blame him anymore, we were sixteen."

Now I understood my parents' reluctance to meet their future in-law. And vice versa.

"We were never able to stop seeing that girl as his daughter," my mother added. "We did what we could to not interfere in your relationship, but we couldn't welcome her into the family with open arms."

"Well, you won't have that problem anymore."

"Don't be so sure of that. Couples make up sometimes."

"We won't. Anna likes chicks. She's a lesbian."

"In any case, she's bisexual. And putting labels like that on people is very old-fashioned, Julián."

I would've expected that comment from my mother, but it came from my father's mouth.

"What do you want me to do? Gift her a rainbow flag?"

"For you to separate things. She cheated on you and that's a serious matter, but the fact that it was with a woman doesn't make it worse."

His response unsettled me. First of all, because in my family, the roles had always been open-minded-mother, cave-man-father. And secondly, it bugged me that he was right. It was a kick in the balls that the third party in our relationship was named Rosario and not Carlos, José, or Raúl.

I decided to do what one does when their mistakes are pointed out: change the subject.

"Did you ever speak with Anna's father again?"

"Not until two days ago, no."

"Two days ago?"

My father took his phone out of his pocket.

"Your mother's car has a tracking system in case it's stolen. As soon as I saw that you were going back to Torroella on the GPS, I called Quim Riera."

"I suppose it wasn't a coincidence that my car wouldn't start that morning, and I had to ask mom for hers."

Besides having a key to my garage and my car, my father also knew much more than I did about mechanics.

"No," my mother confessed, "but it was the only way..."

"Never mind that," my father interrupted. "What matters is that I called Anna's father. In the end, he has more at stake than I do if all this comes out. Something like this can destroy a politician's career."

"Did he lock us in the basement?"

"No. He followed you until you jumped the fence and then called me to let me know. I then called an old friend."

"Who locked us in?" Laura asked.

"Manel."

"The one who gave you the knife?"

"Yes."

"I don't understand. What was he doing there? How did he get into the school?"

"Through the door, with his own set of keys. He's the librarian."

"Manel is Mr. Castañeda?"

"Correct. I asked him to go to the school and surprise you there, but when he realized you were in the basement, he took advantage of the opportunity to give you a scare and locked you in."

"Now I understand his reluctance when we asked him for information," Laura commented.

Laura's words got me thinking. Something wasn't adding up.

"Wait," I said. "If you never told Manel what they did to you, why didn't he help us the first time we went to Santa María?"

"Because of your last name. He told you to come back in a week to give himself time to call me. He did, that same night. He told me you'd shown up asking for information about those years. I had no choice but to tell him the truth and ask him to help prevent you from finding out."

I stopped for a second to process what he'd just told me. My father had revealed his biggest secret to someone he hadn't spoken to in years so that I wouldn't find out. I didn't know if I should hug him or strangle him.

"Scaring you, and making you believe you were putting us in danger, was the only way we thought we could get you to drop all this. I would've done almost anything to keep you from finding out the truth."

"Well, now I know."

"Now you know, yes. And I hope one day you'll understand me. I didn't want to hurt you too. It was already enough to have ruined my brother's dream and fucked up your mother's life twice."

"Don't say that, honey," my mother comforted him.

"It's the truth, Consuelo. There's blood on your hands because of me. And how did I pay you back? Making you spend four horrible years when the only thing I did was drink wine."

"That was years after the fact. Relapsing into an addiction can happen to anyone."

"An addiction that wouldn't have existed in the first place if I hadn't let those assholes walk all over me!"

I took my father's hands between mine. For the first time, I felt like I was holding the hands of someone old and tired, instead of the strong, calloused hands of someone who'd dedicated their life to work.

"Listen to me, Dad. You aren't responsible for what happened to you. Neither are you, Mom. You understand? You are the victims here. The people responsible are all dead."

The four of us sat in silence, each of us lost in our own thoughts. It didn't last long. My mother, in that sense, was the opposite of Laura. Laura could let a silence go on as long as possible if it meant the person in front of her would start talking. On the other hand, my mother was the kind of person who needed to fill the empty space with words.

"Are you hungry? Do you want me to make a *tortilla*?"

At least she had the decency of offering us the only dish she was good at making. I imagined her peeling the potatoes with her tiny knife, worn out, and dull. The only one her aichmophobia allowed her to utilize.

Suddenly, it registered where her fear of knives came from. Whenever I'd read about my mother's condition, experts mentioned that its cause was usually a traumatic event involving a sharp object.

I walked over to her and hugged her.

"Thank you, Mom," I whispered in her ear. "Thank you for saving my life."

CHAPTER 84

Julián

When I broke away from my mother's embrace and dried my tears, Laura was looking at me nervously.

"There's more," she said. "Alcántara revealed the identity of the three Chaltén bodies to his former colleagues."

"What's going to happen now?" I asked.

"Diplomats from both countries are going to reach an agreement to return the bodies to Spain. Once they're here, they'll ID them again and notify the families."

"They'll want answers," my father said. "It won't be long until they realize the hotel was called Montgrí and belonged to Fernando Cucurell."

"What are we going to do?" my mother asked.

"What do you *want* to do?" Laura asked back.

"I don't understand," I said.

"The Spanish police have no jurisdiction to investigate a murder in Argentina," Laura explained. "That's why, on the Spanish side, they're going to deal with this as if it were a diplomatic issue. They're going to focus their efforts on returning the bodies to Spain and give them a burial so that their families can mourn them. They'll probably get a copy of all the files the Santa Cruz police have, but the information doesn't add up to much. I saw it with my own eyes. They won't allocate many resources to a crime that happened thirty years ago. There are far more urgent matters."

"Sooner or later, someone will come around asking about Fernando," Consuelo said.

"Perhaps. Or perhaps not. If word gets out that you lived in Chaltén back then, yes. But it would be difficult for that to happen."

"Why?" my father asked. "We flew there and back on a plane that belongs to an airline that still exists. There are records."

"That doesn't mean they keep passenger lists from flights thirty years ago. Back then, digital information was just being established. And even if those files exist, perhaps no one will make the connection to look through them."

"What do you suggest, then?" my mother asked.

"Laws exist to impart justice, but it's not a perfect system. Ninety-nine percent of the time, laws work. But one percent of the time, applying them is unfair. Miguel was raped, something that marked him for the rest of his life. Years later, one of his rapists came back to provoke him and his family. He acted in self-defense. He ran, but they didn't leave him alone. They came looking for him to kill him, and he had to act in self-defense once again. The same as you, Consuelo."

"All of that would be considered by the justice system," my mother answered. "Self-defense."

"If a lawyer can prove that the wolves raped your husband, yes. But that'll be challenging after almost forty-five years."

"If we stay quiet, we'd be tarnishing my brother's memory."

"Fernando's memory is already tarnished," Laura answered. "Three people from his hometown dead on the other side of the world, one of them in his own hotel. All clues point to him. As sad as that might be, that benefits you because he's dead."

The four of us remained silent for a moment.

"What about your book?" my mother asked.

"That doesn't matter now."

"It might not right now, but what about in the future when this is just a distant memory for you? How can we be sure you won't reveal everything? What happens if a publisher or a TV producer shows up and offers you a lot of money?"

"Mom, I don't think that happens in real life."

"But it might."

"There are enough books in the world," Laura said. "Mine isn't essential. What I really cared about was answering the questions about what had happened, not publishing them. If it's worth anything, I give you my word that the book will never see the light of day."

"Have you answered all those questions?"

"Almost. I'm still missing some details."

"Like what?"

"For example, why did Fernando leave Arnau Junqué's body on the bed in room number seven? Didn't it make more sense to hide it, say, in the basement?"

"I guess we'll never know," my father said.

"I guess not," Laura answered.

CHAPTER 85

Many years earlier.

When he opens his eyes, Arnau Junqué sees the same thing he did when they were closed. Darkness.

Slowly, he starts to remember the fight with Miguel Cucurell and his wife. Did they really stab him? Sometimes he dreams that he loses a tooth and when he wakes up, he finds that luckily his tongue can't feel anything amiss. This time, however, when he presses his hand to his stomach, he feels a thick, warm liquid that sticks to his fingers.

He doesn't know where he is or how long he's been there, but if he wants to live another day, he has to find a doctor. He crawls around in the dark, feeling the floor around him. Each movement hurts like a rat eating at his insides.

His forearm rams into something hard. A wooden shelf? No, a stair.

He wants to stand up, but the pain forces him back down to the ground. He tries to scream but all he can manage is a muffled sound.

He pauses for a few seconds, then tries to stand up again. The pain is so intense it makes him clench his teeth as hard as he can. This time, like in his dreams, he hears a 'crack' in his mouth and feels a filling break. He spits it out and grabs onto the staircase.

He's dizzy. He tries to breathe deeply, but that also hurts. He can barely manage a few shallow breaths, like a woman about to give birth.

He goes up one step. He thinks he might faint from the pain but makes it up one more. At the third step, his head crashes into a wooden ceiling. He's in a basement.

He tries to open the trapdoor but can't raise his hands higher than his neck without feeling like something is stabbing his lungs. He pushes with his head, and the door opens to one side.

The light that streams in through the opening gives him the energy to keep climbing. The trap door opens a bit more. He's in one of the Montgrí Hotel rooms.

When he finally makes it out, the trap door closes behind him with a muted sound. He stays lying on the floor, breathing in the air that feels like it's burning him from the inside. He doesn't think about Miguel Cucurell or the woman who stabbed him. The only thing he can focus on is getting help. But he needs to catch his breath.

He drags himself across the floor with the little strength he has left, and sits on the bed. *Just for a second*, he tells himself.

When he closes his eyes, a darkness much deeper and infinite than the one in the basement, surrounds him. A sweet darkness, the kind you can't resist surrendering to.

CHAPTER 86

Published by the Spanish press.

THE THREE MEN WHO DISAPPEARED IN THE PYRENEES TWENTY-EIGHT YEARS AGO WERE MURDERED IN PATAGONIA

April 5th of 1991 was the last time Gerard Martí, Mario Santiago, and Arnau Junqué were seen at the information center of the Cadí-Moixeró Natural Park (Catalonia). Twenty-eight years later, their bodies have been identified on the other side of the world, in the tourist destination of El Chaltén, located in the Argentinian Patagonia. According to the autopsies, the three men were murdered.

Two years ago, almost by chance, a group of tourists discovered a body embedded in the wall of the Viedma glacier near El Chaltén. After an enormous effort by the diving team of the Argentinian Naval Guard, the body was recovered along with another one which was also found trapped in the ice. Autopsies revealed that they were two young men who had been in the ice for approximately thirty years. One of them had a gunshot wound to the stomach and the other had a head injury.

The Argentinian police failed to identify the bodies or make significant progress in the case until last March when a third body was discovered in an abandoned hotel in El Chaltén. The body was mummified due to the lack of humidity in the environment, and was estimated to have been there for approximately thirty years. This date coincides not only with the death of the other two but also with the period that the hotel has been closed for.

The twists and turns of the story do not end there, as the abandoned hotel was called Montgrí and the three victims were originally from Torroella de Montgrí. The establishment had belonged to Fernando Cucurell, a native of the same village and of a similar age to the deceased.

It was possible to identify the bodies thanks to the collaboration of retired policeman Gregorio Alcántara, who, following an independent investigation, managed to establish that the three men who disappeared in 1991 in the Cadí-Moixeró Natural Park, 120 kilometers from Barcelona, were the three bodies found on the other side of the world. How Martí, Santiago, and Junqué ended up in Patagonia is unknown.

Diplomatic personnel from both countries are already coordinating the return of the bodies to Spain. As for the investigation into the murders, the Spanish Foreign Affairs Office has stated that it will use every means at its disposal to urge Argentina to re-open the investigation. The Argentinian police, for their part, assure that the appearance of the third body in the Hotel Montgrí could constitute a solid basis for clarifying the three deaths.

Sources close to the investigation of this triple homicide have pointed to Fernando Cucurell, owner of the Montgrí Hotel, as the main person of interest. Cucurell died at the end of last year in Barcelona, where he had lived for at least 25 years.

It remains to be seen whether the homicides of Martí, Santiago, and Junqué will ever be solved after three decades, with the main suspect dead and both governments working together. If nothing else, their families will be able to say their final goodbyes.

CHAPTER 87

Laura

"This is our stop," Julián announced when the subway door opened at the Plaza España station.

After walking through a maze of hot, damp tunnels, they emerged into the daylight. Laura smiled at the feeling of the cool night breeze on her face. She would never have imagined that the air next to a large traffic circle full of cars, would feel so fresh to her.

Julián pointed at a cylindrical building with a shallow dome on top, which to her, looked like a combination of a birthday cake and a spaceship.

"It used to be a bullfighting ring. Now it's a shopping mall."

"It's... unique."

On the other side of the trafic circle, two immense brick towers flanked the wide avenue that ended half a kilometer further up, at the foot of a hill.

"That's Montjuic Mountain, another one of Barcelona's symbols."

Laura smiled to herself. Once again, what was in front of them didn't look anything like the mountains she was used to.

"You wouldn't be a bad tour guide. If you ever go back to Chaltén, there's another way you can make a living."

"Hotel owner and tour guide... sounds too much like Fernando, don't you think?"

"Well, if you put it that way..."

They walked in silence until the towers were far behind them. At the end of the avenue, an escalator rose between square trees and concrete esplanades, to a building that reminded her of the Congress building in Buenos Aires. From the building's cupola, seven beams of light projected out into the sky.

Even though they were walking down a wide promenade, there were so many people around them that Laura had to be careful not to bump into anyone. Walking around there was harder than in front of the Sagrada Familia.

"I know you're going to ask me any minute now," Julián said to her, "so I'll give you my answer: I still haven't thought about what I want to do. At times, I consider selling the hotel and never going back to El Chaltén. But on the other hand, I feel almost like it's my responsibility to restore it with my own hands and give it the life my uncle dreamt for it."

"It's normal to be confused. You have a lot to process."

"What about you? Are you seriously not going to finish the book?"

"Seriously. It doesn't make sense. It would destroy your parents, and the wolves' families. I bet it isn't easy to find out you've been mourning a monster for thirty years. Those families have suffered enough."

"So, what are you going to do?"

Laura had been wondering the same thing for the past twenty-four hours. She wasn't sure she wanted to stay in El Chaltén now that the glacier crimes were solved. She didn't plan to spend the rest of her life brushing horses and taking tourists out on hikes. She wanted to keep investigating murders.

"I'll find myself a new bone to gnaw on."

"You can stay at my apartment as long as you like. Look at this city. It doesn't deserve for you to leave without exploring it."

"I've had some time to walk around."

"Express tourism and getting to know a place are two very different things."

She knew that well. She was used to receiving tourists who wanted to do all the Chaltén hikes in three days because, after that, they had to go to Calafate, Ushuaia, or Bariloche. For many of them, the main goal was checking off destinations on their bucket list.

"Besides, you'd have an amazing guide," Julián said, pointing at himself.

She laughed and took his arm. They walked together in silence for a while until he stopped among the throng of people.

"Now, we have to wait for nine twenty-five," he said, looking at his watch.

Next to her, a family of Indian tourists vacated a bench that Julián was quick to take. They sat, looking at the avenue. Large pools of water separated the thousands of people walking, from the traffic.

"What happens at nine twenty-five?"

"You'll find out in three minutes."

Laura smiled and went back to observing the tourists who walked in front of them, speaking every language imaginable.

Three minutes later, the water in the pools filled with light. For a moment, the crowd went silent. Many pointed toward the end of the walkway, next to the mountain.

Laura noticed that the water in the last pool had come to life and now a jet of water taller than she shot was up into the air. A few seconds later, the next pool came alive, then the next, and the next. The water rose up in columns like a reversed set of dominoes. A minute later, the entire avenue was surrounded by vertical jets of water. The tourists went back to chatting, but the sound of the water drowned their voices out almost entirely.

She felt Julián's hand on her shoulder.

"Monjtuic's Magic Fountain," he said, pointing at the mountain.

When she turned, she realized that what she'd just witnessed was only the opening scene. Where there had only been stairs leading up to the palace, now hundreds of illuminated jets of water rose up forming a liquid cage the size of a church.

Julián took her arm and together they walked toward the fountain. However, before they got there, the lights went off and the water suddenly stopped. All that was left was a light dew and a subtle smell of chlorine floating in the night air.

"Is it over already?"

"It hasn't even started."

Fifteen seconds later, the water flow resumed, this time full of colorful light. It moved and changed shape to the rhythm of classical music that sounded across the esplanade. It went from red cylindrical streams that looked like crystal tubes, to a lavender mist of tiny droplets.

"Now I see why it's called the Magical Fountain."

"They say that whatever you wish for, this fountain will grant."

"That's original."

"You got me, I just made that up. But that's also the sign of a good tour guide, isn't it?"

Laura laughed and hugged him without thinking. She felt his arms surround her and it felt nice. It had been a long time since anyone had hugged her.

"You know," he said. "If the choice between staying in Barcelona and going back to El Chaltén depended on this moment, I'd choose to go back."

Laura stroked his cheek and looked him in the eyes. It was the perfect place and time for a kiss, but neither of them moved their face forward. She had read once, that hugs conjured up calm, and kisses caused whirlwinds.

She wasn't ready for a whirlwind. He needed to get over Anna, and she had to figure out what to do with her life. They were two sailors who'd just weathered a storm, and they needed to regain their bearings.

And while the calm lasted, Laura could use a tour guide.

CHAPTER 88

Julián. One year later.

I feel dirty. I'm not walking down the Ramblas at night to confirm that I'm being cheated on or rummaging through my father's things to uncover a secret. This time is different. I feel dirty because I *am* dirty. The sticky sweat of a long day's work makes the thin dust of the sandpaper stick to my skin. If I looked at myself in the mirror, I'd probably see that my face looked like a poorly painted clown's. But there's no mirror in the Montgrí Hotel reception area. I took down the only one there was, to paint.

I sit down on the newspaper that covers the floor and lean back on the wall I'll be painting tomorrow. In front of me, in the fireplace, I can see the ashes from yesterday's fire. If it weren't Friday, I'd sit there for a long while, until the Patagonian chill crept up and beat the heat built up during the day, forcing me to start another fire.

But Fridays are the days she comes. I turn off the lights, leave the hotel, and cross the lot to my house. In the distance, a group of tourists laugh in Mauricio and Roberto's brewery. I no longer refer to them as Beard One and Beard Two. I look up and see the Southern Cross in the sky. If it's sunny tomorrow, it'll be the tenth day in a row that the Fitz Roy is visible. Quite a record.

It's eight, and she usually arrives at nine on Fridays. I take a quick shower, hoping to greet her with dinner on the table, but she walks in the second I walk out of the bathroom.

"Hello, Julián," she says, leaving the keys on the small table by the door.

I like that even though we've been living together for two months, she still uses my full name. Wrapped in a towel, I walk up to her and wrap my arms around her waist.

"Hello, Inspector Badía."

I give her a long kiss, one that makes the five-day wait worth it.

I don't ask her about her day, because then she'll tell me about dead people, wounds, and blood. She loves it. She was born for it. Ever since she got her job back with the police, she spends the entire week investigating crimes around the province. And that makes her happy.

She tells me she's starving and I announce that I'm about to make her a dish worthy of a Michelin star. When she gets into the shower, I put some water on to boil for pasta. Luckily, neither of us was born with a very sophisticated palate.

I set the table and sit down on the sofa to wait for the water to boil. I look at my phone out of habit. People complaining about things and adorable animal videos never seem to get old on social media. I scroll down until one post catches my eye.

It's a photo Anna posted three hours ago. She's blonder than the last time I saw her a year back. She's smiling with her eyes closed, while a woman I don't know kisses her cheek. There's too much tenderness coming from both of them for it to be just a friend. If they weren't the same age, it could have been a kiss between a mother and her daughter.

In the photo description, there's only one word. A hashtag, to be precise: *#loveislove*.

I smile. The image, which would have bothered me then, now makes me twice as happy. Happy because Anna is doing well, and happy because I can be happy for her. But as I re-read the hashtag, that feeling bitters slightly. Anna lives in a world where she still needs to put a label on her love.

In a way, seeing Anna is like seeing my father. And most of all, it's like seeing myself trying to put a label on them. Lesbian? Gay? Bisexual? Slightly heterosexual? Someone able to fall in love with someone else, without caring about what's between their legs?

My father's life has been governed by labels. The ones he put on himself, but especially the ones others put on him. If instead of kissing Manel, he'd kissed a Manuela, his life would have been different.

I suspect that if John Lennon were alive, he'd change the verse of *Imagine* where he speaks about living in a world without religions, to one without labels. That would be a society where we could all live in peace, without feeling imprisoned by a sexual orientation, a skin color, an accent, or a disability.

But if Anna chose to apply that label it's because she thinks it's necessary to make her reality visible. We aren't ready for the new version of *Imagine*, just like fifty years ago we weren't ready for a world without religions.

I click the heart beneath the photo. I like it. I hope one day the only hashtag that makes sense is *#people*.

Because that's all we are: people. It's taken me a year to understand that. For others, it'll take more than a lifetime.

AUTHOR'S NOTE

Dear reader,

Thanks for reading this story! I hope you had fun with it. If you did, I'd love to hear what you think: cristian@cristianperfumo.com.

If this book left you wanting more, I'm sure you'll enjoy *The arrow collector*, another crime thriller set in Patagonia where you will find out all about Laura Badía's past.

Finally, please consider leaving a review on the website of the store where you purchased this book. It will only take you a few seconds and it will help me immensely.

Till next time!

THE ARROW COLLECTOR

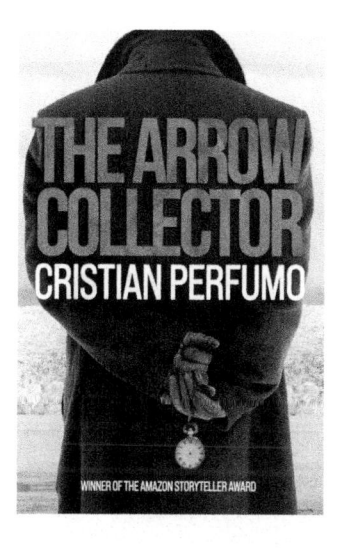

Find out what led Laura Badía to El Chaltén.

It takes murder to complete the collection.

The calm of a sleepy Patagonian fishing port has been broken by murder. It's the case of a lifetime for brilliant and headstrong forensic detective Laura Badía. The crime is brutal and baffling. The victim is Julio Ortega, a local heartthrob and an old flame of Laura's. The apparent motive is the theft of a collection of ancient and mysterious iridescent arrowheads that Ortega had recently acquired. Carved nearly six thousand years ago out of Amazon opal, they are now missing from Ortega's home, vanishing once again into legend.

With the help of a Buenos Aires archeologist, Laura begins to assemble the pieces of a deadly puzzle. It starts in Puerto Deseado with the secrets of Ortega's friends, enemies, and lovers. Where it leads is the panoramic reach of the Perito Moreno Glacier and far beyond, to the most remote corners of Patagonia. Can they uncover the dark history of the most infamous lithic art collection in the world? Generations have killed and died trying to solve its mystery, and now Laura will risk her career, her life—and her own secrets—to be the one to do it.

THE SUNKEN SECRET

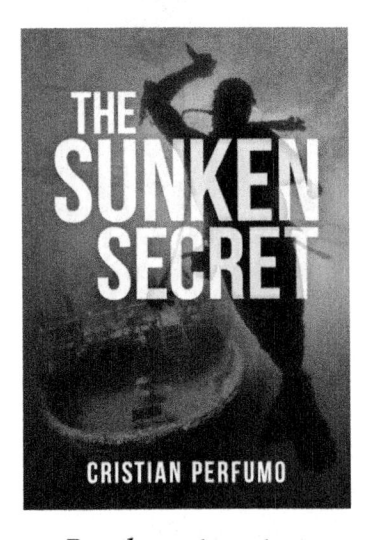

Based on a true story

When diver Marcelo learns of a sunken 18th-century warship located off the coast of his Patagonia hometown, he can hardly wait to explore the wreck himself — but a shocking murder and a dangerous secret will turn his dive into a race for survival.

"Read of the year" by *Diver*, UK's best-selling SCUBA-diving magazine.

ABOUT THE AUTHOR

Cristian Perfumo is a best-selling author read by hundreds of thousands of crime fiction fans around the world. His stories are mostly set in Patagonia, where he grew up. He won the 2017 Amazon Annual Literary Award for Independent Spanish-Language Authors with *El coleccionista de flechas* (available in English as *The arrow collector*). Cristian's books have also been translated into French, Polish and Italian. His novel *The glacier murders* is currently being adapted for television. Learn more about his work at www.cristianperfumo.com.

Printed in Dunstable, United Kingdom